PRAISE FOR *NEW YORK TIMES* BESTSELLING AUTHOR CHRISTIE CRAIG

"Hold on to your Stetsons...A thrill ride of hunky heroes, hilarious high jinks, and heartwarming romance."
—Lori Wilde, *New York Times* bestselling author, on *Only in Texas*

"A fabulously great read. I absolutely loved the characters...I can't wait for the next one in the series."
—NightOwlReviews.com on *Only in Texas*

"An entertaining tale with delightful, fully formed characters and an intriguing mystery, along with a nod to dog lovers with a likable pooch."
—*RT Book Reviews* on *Only in Texas*

"4 stars! Hot! Craig returns to Texas and the hunky boys of the Only in Texas PI agency in this sexy, lighthearted romp centered around a sassy heroine on a mission and the gorgeous hero who falls for her. Complete with genuine characters who have heart, this story will keep you laughing as you turn the pages. A truly fun read!"
—*RT Book Reviews* on *Blame It on Texas*

"An excellent contemporary romance that will make you swoon!"
—FreshFiction.com on *Blame It on Texas*

"Fans of fast-paced thrillers and Craig's other books will feel at home."

—*Publishers Weekly* on *Texas Hold 'Em*

DON'T CLOSE
YOUR EYES

ALSO BY CHRISTIE CRAIG

HOTTER IN TEXAS SERIES
Only in Texas
Blame It on Texas
Texas Hold'Em

DON'T CLOSE YOUR EYES

CHRISTIE CRAIG

FOREVER
New York Boston

Copyright © 2018 by Christie Craig
Preview of *Don't Breathe a Word* copyright © 2018 by Christie Craig
Cover design by Leason Beckford Jr.
Cover image by Julie McInnes
Cover image by Stephen Mulcahey Trevillion
Cover copyright © 2018 by Hachette Book Group, Inc.

Forever
Hachette Book Group
1290 Avenue of the Americas, New York, NY 10104
forever-romance.com
twitter.com/foreverromance

First Edition: August 2018

Forever is an imprint of Grand Central Publishing. The Forever name and logo are trademarks of Hachette Book Group, Inc.

The publisher is not responsible for websites (or their content) that are not owned by the publisher.

The Hachette Speakers Bureau provides a wide range of authors for speaking events. To find out more, go to www.hachettespeakersbureau.com or call (866) 376-6591.

ISBN: 978-1-5387-1159-0 (mass market), 978-1-5387-1160-6 (ebook)

Printed in the United States of America

OPM

10 9 8 7 6 5 4 3 2 1

Here's to my hubby, who does my laundry, makes me coffee, and brings me hot and sour soup when I have a cold. Thank you for making me laugh, for believing in me when sometimes I don't. Thank you for being my real-life hero. Thank you for being so brave, for not letting the health hurdles you've faced strip you of your sense of humor, and your sharp wit. I love you.

Acknowledgments

I've been extremely lucky to find editors who get me. Editors who connect with my characters, my voice, and whose advice resonates with me and my career goals. Thank you, Michele Bidelspach, for helping me climb upward in this career. I have loved working with you, but have faith we'll cross paths again soon. And Amy Pierpont, thank you for taking me on and helping me get this book in the hands of fans.

Thank you to my agent, Kim Lionetti, for taking the journey with me on this publishing path. Thank you for trusting me enough to follow my game plan, for pushing me when I need a push, for pulling me back when I start to take a step down the wrong way. I think we make a pretty good team.

And thank you to my parents, Virginia Curtis and Pete Hunt, from whom I got my work ethic, my sense of humor, and just enough zaniness needed to be a writer.

And thank you to my fans for leaving reviews, for the emails letting me know you liked my book, and for the word of mouth you send out in the world that helps my career.

Here's to getting lost in a book.

Christie Craig

PROLOGUE

Thu-thump. Thu-thump.

The sounds came to Annie Lakes first. The sound of her young heart thudding in her chest. The night sounds of insects, owls, and unknown creatures scuttling around the woods at night.

The sound of...fear.

Then a panic-laced young voice echoed in the dark distance. "Faster, Annie."

She couldn't run faster. She couldn't breathe.

She couldn't...wake up.

She felt trapped in the blackness. Then the dark curtain lifted and she saw it all. The thicket of trees, the thorny brushes encroaching the dirt trail. Her pink Cinderella tennis shoes slapping against the dirt. Her small feet racing, rushing, running to someone to save her. Running away from someone who wouldn't.

"Keep up!" The same voice, a young voice, echoed again. All Annie could see of this person was snippets of a pink nightgown appearing and disappearing between the trees ahead. Too far ahead.

Alone.

She didn't want to be alone.

She hugged the teddy bear, once white but now sticky and red-stained.

"Don't leave me!" Annie cried, unable to move faster. Her side pinched from running. Her leg muscles burned.

She wanted to scream.

Wanted to cry.

Wanted her daddy.

Thorns caught and snagged on the ruffle on her Smurf nightgown. The toe of her tennis shoe hit a stump.

She tripped. Went down. Hard. The bear hit the dirt before she did.

Small rocks ripped at the tender flesh on her palms. A jagged one sliced into her knee. The raw sting brought tears to her eyes. She could no longer hear the person in front of her, but the footfalls of the person chasing her grew closer. Louder.

She really wanted her daddy. Now.

Struggling to her feet, she let soft whimpers slip from her lips. She took one slow step, and someone grabbed her from behind. Grabbed her tight.

She screamed.

And screamed.

Annie's own bloodcurdling cry echoing through her bedroom yanked her awake. No longer the frightened child, she was now a frightened woman, but she still wanted her daddy.

Swallowing air that felt solid, hand clutching her chest, she felt her heart slamming against her rib cage.

Realizing what this meant, she rolled over and buried her face in the pillow. The dream, the recurring nightmare was back. And she knew why.

Brittany Talbot.

She really needed to stop watching the news.

CHAPTER ONE

Annie, sitting at her usual table, refocused on the stack of ungraded papers. The dark circles under her eyes were hidden behind darker sunglasses. Blond and fair skinned, she lacked sleep, which brought out raccoon eyes. Too bad she couldn't wear the shades while teaching.

"Happy hump day." Fred waved his cup of espresso with extra milk as he moved to his booth. For reasons unbeknownst to Annie, the elderly widower was always happier on Wednesdays. Sometimes, when the place was full, he'd even sit with her to chat.

Annie smiled. "Did you have a good night last night?"

"Sure did." A sparkle brightened his light blue eyes. He sat down and pulled out his newspaper. Was he seeing some lady on Tuesdays? Not that it mattered, Annie liked seeing happy people.

Glancing out the window, she took in the early-morning walkers trying to get their steps in. The quaint coffee shop nestled between high-rises in downtown Anniston, Texas, was conveniently located a block from the junior college where she'd taught for the last five months. Coming here had become part of her morning ritual. Being an only child, she liked feeling as if she was part of a community. She knew the regulars. They knew her. At least most of them did.

The door swished open. Pretty sure who it was, she glanced up, without lifting her head. He always arrived between seven and seven thirty. The coffee shop was conveniently located a block from the police precinct, too.

Detective Sutton liked the dark roast and drank it black. Sometimes, he added a skinny hazelnut latte to his order. Probably for some long-legged, lucky secretary at his office.

While Annie was certain he'd never noticed her—he was one who didn't speak or even nod—she'd noticed him.

Even before she'd seen him on television.

It wasn't just his big-gulp size, or his big-gulp good looks. Oh, she noticed those, too—hard not to—but it was the fact that, like her, he hid behind sunglasses. Considering most of his cases involved murder and some involved children—she wondered if he wasn't suffering from some bad nightmares, too.

He shot to the counter with his usual determined pace. Not so much rude as running late.

Today, he wore his navy Dockers and his light blue buttoned-down oxford. The shirt, creases down the sleeves, no doubt professionally cleaned, hugged his broad chest. His dark hair appeared freshly showered damp.

The customer ahead of him, an elderly grandmother—not a regular—looked antique and frail. "I know I've got some coins…" Her arm, lost in her big purse, fumbled for loose change.

Annie waited to see if he'd do it again. She'd seen it happen six times.

"I got her coffee," he spoke over the woman's gray hair to Mary, the barista.

The older woman looked back, and up. And up. "Why that's sweet, but I've got…"

My good deed for the day, Annie said in her head, right before he did.

A smile curled up in her gut and gave her good-guy butterflies. She'd even borrowed his act of kindness herself.

Shamelessly, she'd considered attempting to be his good deed for the day for an introduction—and maybe more. But she'd failed at her last attempts of "more." And considering the return of her nightmares, she needed to get her life fixed before she asked for company.

He eased up to the counter, paid for the elderly woman's coffee, then carefully—with more patience than he normally exuded—he handed it to her.

The good-guy flutters commenced again. Annie's phone chimed. She pulled her gaze away from the detective and glanced at the number. Her mom. She never called this early. Something had to be…

"Hello." The soft sounds of her mom's sobbing sent thick air rushing into Annie's lungs, and her heart filled with empathy before even understanding.

"Mom? What's wrong?"

* * *

Detective Mark Sutton skipped his Thursday-morning coffee run and went straight to the lake.

It was one of those perfect days for fishing. Hot, but not too damn hot. Windy, but not too damn windy. Cloudy, but not too damn cloudy.

White cotton-like clouds hung in the blue sky, appearing so picture-perfect they looked like a lie. The sunset sparkles danced on top of the water. The breeze, cooler than the air, flowed through the trees and offered relief from the Texas temperature.

But nothing ruined a good day at the lake more than when it wasn't a fishing line in the water, but a winch connected to a wrecker. When what was being reeled in wasn't a blue cat, or a bass, but a fifty-pound drum containing the body of a four-year-old girl.

Days like this caused a raw kind of hurt—the kind that chipped away at one's soul.

"I'd give my left ball to be wrong about this." Mark looked at Juan Acosta, another cold-case detective, standing beside him.

"No shit," Juan said.

Mark, Juan, and Connor Pierce, the three-man team that made up the Anniston Cold Case Unit, had spent hours of personal time the previous week scuba diving in the lake searching for barrels.

Forget asking the local volunteer divers. Homicide had them booked. Forget having a special dive team do it. Their division didn't have a budget.

If they needed something done, they had to do it

themselves. The fact that they'd gotten cases solved shocked the shit out of the big brass. And this particular case was going to be a real pisser for their sergeant.

That was why Connor and Juan had chosen the case. Well, that and because the kid had been related to the mayor. Mark would've preferred a different case. One that didn't feel so goddamn familiar. He had only so much soul left.

Exhaling a piece of that soul now, he watched Albert Stone, the medical examiner, use a crowbar to pry the top off of the drum they'd pulled from Sunshine Lake. Stone looked into the barrel, grimaced, then glanced at Mark and Juan. He didn't say anything, or even nod. The despair in his eyes said it all.

"Damn!" Mark's stomach muscles cramped like he'd just done fifty sit-ups.

Stone re-capped the drum and gave the motion for the forklift driver to load the evidence into the van. After taking a few seconds, he walked over.

"I won't be able to say it's her for a while. But there's long brown hair." Stone ran a hand over his face as if to wipe away the image. A move every cop who'd ever worked in homicide knew well. A damn shame it didn't work.

"The body is submerged in concrete." Stone's tone came out as heavy as the barrel looked. "Weren't they looking at the father for this?"

"Yeah, but they couldn't prove it," Juan said.

"Then prove it. Catch the bastard who did this." Stone exhaled.

We will. We have to. Mark gave him a tight-lipped nod.

Catching bastards was the way to get back a tiny piece of his soul that these cases robbed from him. He never got it all back, but a little was better than nothing.

"This would make...what? Three cases you've solved this year?" Stone asked.

Four. *But who's counting?*

Mark nodded. Juan did the same. They weren't doing this for the notoriety. Not that it didn't feel good every time they showed the department how wrong it'd been to discount them.

The forklift groaned as it picked up the rusty metal drum. Stone frowned. "It's been years. How the hell did you know where to find her?"

"Johnny Cash," Mark said.

Stone chuckled. "You been hitting the bottle early?"

"No." Mark resented the implication, even when he didn't resent Stone. "It was the only lead they had on the case," Mark explained. "A day after she went missing, a homeless man, Mr. Johnny Cash, reported he saw someone pushing a barrel into the lake. Reports says he was drunk and about as credible as a rock, but being the only lead, APD sent some divers out. They found nothing. One of the divers was on record stating that due to the weather conditions earlier, visibility wasn't really good. Between the lack of a budget and a drunk witness, they didn't do another search."

"Well, keep this up, and the department will be forced to move you off the shit list."

"I hope not," Mark said. "*Shit list* equals 'no expectations.'"

Stone offered a half-assed grin. "Where's Connor?"

"Searching for Cash." They watched the forklift loading the evidence.

"Is the poker game on for Saturday night?" Stone asked as if needing a mental U-turn.

"Not this Saturday, but next," Mark answered.

"Well, I should get back..." Stone looked over Mark's shoulder, and his expression soured. "You're gonna get a chance to secure your place on that list. The vultures are waiting." He waved toward the road and walked off.

Mark didn't have to look back. He knew what vultures Stone meant.

Proving him right, someone, a feminine someone, yelled out, "Detective Sutton? Can I have a word?"

Recognition of that voice struck like a painful thump to his balls. "Fuck."

Probably not the word the Channel 2 reporter wanted. But it was the one Judith Holt pulled out of him.

Glancing away from the police van, he looked at Juan. "Who called the press?"

"Why don't you ask your girlfriend?" Juan's tone said he hadn't forgiven Mark for almost screwing up the last case. Not that Mark blamed Juan. He hadn't forgiven himself, either.

Mark looked back. Judith stood in front of six other reporters from both newspapers and television stations. "Ex-girlfriend."

Not that she'd really been his girlfriend, just a warm body for about a month. One he hadn't missed. Oh, the sex had been great. But she'd been using him, and not just for fun in the sack. She wanted story leads, inside information, and she didn't care who it hurt.

When he refused to give her anything, she'd stolen it. The leaked information had almost cost them the arrest. If he could've proven she'd stolen the info from him, he'd have hauled her ass in. But he couldn't. So she became another life lesson for him to file away.

A lesson that had kept him celibate for five months.

Juan looked back. "I'm walking through the woods and will meet you by the car."

Juan hated the press more than Mark did. Well, not the press—it was the cameras and seeing his face on the six o'clock news or on the front page.

Mark didn't know a cop who'd served for more than ten years who didn't have a few scars. Most of them on the inside. Juan hadn't been that lucky.

"Keys?" Juan held out his hand.

Mark watched the detective take off. Swallowing a mouthful of hopeless air, he told himself to hold his temper. His bank account couldn't take another hit. Who knew film cameras cost that much? Thankfully, the city had picked up that first one. But when APD stuck him in the Cold Case Unit, they'd made it clear. Any further destruction of news-media property would come out of *his* pocket. So the tripod he'd used to dent the bumper of the Channel 6 van a few months back had been on him.

He started back to the street, away from the crowd, but

like hungry piranhas they followed. With Anniston's population encroaching on a hundred and thirty thousand, they had plenty of piranhas.

"Detective Sutton?" They pushed toward him.

"We don't know anything yet." He quickened his pace.

"But Detective—" one of the newspaper reporters started.

"No comment!" He got about two feet past them.

Someone snagged his arm. Unfortunately, he'd know the feel of Judith's nails anywhere. "Was Brittany Talbot's body in the drum? Isn't that what the Cold Case Unit is working on?"

She shoved her mic in his face. Damn it! Didn't she realize how hearing and seeing this on the local news would make the kid's mother feel? Sure it'd been four years, but hurting from losing someone you love didn't have time limits. He knew firsthand. It was the scar he carried with him.

"No comment!" he growled.

"Can you confirm that this is about the Talbot case?"

"Go chase another ambulance!" He started off. He heard her say something to the camera. Another reporter blocked his path and then Judith grabbed his arm again.

He stopped. Stared at her nails biting into his forearm. He'd never been into scratchers.

She cut off her mic, lowered it to her side. "Just because we didn't pan out—"

"This has nothing to do with us." He shot forward.

The *wish-wush* of her expensive heels sinking in and

out of the wet ground as she chased after him ratcheted up his frustration.

"You got that right!" she said to his back. "It's about my career. And if you think—"

He swung around so fast the heels of his shoes cut divots in the ground. Then, because he didn't care to air his dirty laundry—and fuck yeah, he considered their relationship to be dirty laundry—he pulled her away from the crowd of reporters. Scowling, he held out his hand in warning that no one should follow.

Once he got out of earshot, he swerved and faced her. "This may be a hell of a shock to you, Judith, but it's not always about you." The muscles in his neck knotted.

Her eyes glittered with determination. The kind that didn't let up. The kind he didn't admire. The kind that stemmed from selfish ambition.

"I'm just doing my job," she said with a jab.

"And it doesn't matter who you step on as long as you come out looking good. I'm still dusting off your footprints myself."

"Just because I don't have to drink myself into oblivion when bad things happen doesn't mean I don't care."

Okay, that poke was personal. Too personal.

"I don't *have* to drink myself into oblivion." He yanked off his sunglasses. "I *choose* to. But the difference between you and me is that I do my job to catch sorry sons of bitches. You do your job so you can prance your little ass up the career ladder."

He stormed off, not caring if his words struck a

nerve. Not even feeling better for delivering them because, like he'd told her, this wasn't about her. Or him.

He had to go see Bethany Talbot now, the kid's mom, hoping like hell she wouldn't see the news report before he got to her.

Mark hadn't made it to the road when another reporter and his cameraman blocked his path. It was Matthew Kelly from Channel 6, one of Judith's on-again, off-again lovers, who'd been pissed that Judith had taken a shine to Mark. So this approach was likely to be just as personal, but probably more fun. Call him a male chauvinist pig, but he couldn't completely unleash on a woman. Even when they deserved it.

"No comment." Mark gave it a good college try.

Matthew stuck his mic in Mark's face. "Is it true that the Cold Case Unit is the police department's dumping ground for cops who don't play well with others?"

Yup, personal! Mark hoped this was a live feed. "Is it true you still fuck Ju— a certain Channel Two reporter even though you got married last year?"

The cameraman let out a burst of laughter. But before Matthew could react, Mark yanked the microphone from the man's hand and chucked it. The splashing sound in the lake was as good as a big-mouth bass slapping against the water.

"That was a five-hundred-dollar piece of equipment," Matthew seethed.

"I know," Mark said. "But it was a lot cheaper than paying to have your nose fixed."

Mark took off to his car. Juan, in the driver's seat, had the engine running as if he expected the worst.

Climbing into the passenger seat of his racing-green Mustang, stepping into a week's worth of fast-food bags, he looked at Juan.

A touch of humor reflected in his partner's brown eyes. "I think you enjoy that."

"Yeah, but it's an expensive hobby."

Juan chuckled, but his smile faded fast. "I'll go help Connor look for Cash. You going to see Bethany Talbot?"

"Yeah." He'd have loved to push that job over to either Connor or Juan, but he'd drawn the short straw.

Mark snatched his file from the backseat to get the Talbots' address.

"Do you still like the dad for this?" Juan's fingers tightened on the steering wheel.

Mark reached back and squeezed his knotted right shoulder. He'd only spoken with Brian Talbot once. He didn't think he was behind this, but the guy's alibi had been shakier than a drug addict needing a fix.

"I don't know." Mark wanted to believe no father could do that to his child, but he knew better. Being a parent didn't stop someone from being a sick bastard. He let out a gulp of frustrated air. "When I'm done, I'll call you and hit any shelters you haven't."

"You know finding him is going to be almost impossible. It was four years ago, and Johnny Cash probably isn't even the guy's name."

"I know," Mark said. "But I'm hoping if he picked that name, it means he actually sings, and that might help us find him."

Juan turned into the precinct and parked. Mark set

the file on the dash. A picture of the dark-haired little girl slipped out. He saw the toothy, gotta-love-me grin and the sweet life in her freckled face. But mostly he saw the innocence.

There went another chunk of his soul.

* * *

"He's dead."

"I know, Mom. I'm sorry." Annie meant it. She wasn't heartless. She just . . .

"How could you *not* want to go?" Her mom's arms crossed over the front of her yellow tailored suit. Then Annie got the you-disappoint-me sigh.

Annie hated that sigh. Hated disappointing her mom.

"You've turned me down to go see them three times since you've lived here."

Yeah, her move to Anniston five months before—for a job—had put her only an hour drive from her mother's family. She'd worried her mom would use her location to push Annie closer to the Reeds. She'd been right.

She met her mom's woeful gaze and felt heartless, like she'd feared. Her mom's visit was a surprise, but after she'd called yesterday morning to inform Annie that her uncle had died, she should have expected it.

"I said I'd go."

Her mom popped up from the living room chair. "After you said you preferred not to."

Well, there was that. "I was thinking about work

when I said it." *Lie*. The truth—it was hard going to the funeral of someone you didn't know. Okay, maybe it was harder to go to the funeral of someone you did know. Someone you loved.

Like her dad's. And if he were still alive, he wouldn't let her mom put her through this. Annie stared at the papers she'd been grading in her lap.

"He was your uncle." The grief in her mom's voice drew Annie's gaze up.

The emotion echoed inside Annie. "I'm going."

"How could you be so uncaring?"

Uncaring? No! Annie had lost two jobs because she cared too much. She had to give up teaching elementary school because she cared too much. She couldn't watch the news because she cared too much.

"I didn't know him. He wasn't even at the reunion I went to. It makes it awkward."

"We lived in the same town until you were almost five."

"I don't remember him." Nada. Zip. She refocused on her papers. Her sketchy childhood memories had created interesting discussions in her therapy sessions. Sessions Annie no longer indulged in. After more than a year of getting nowhere, and doubting herself even more, she decided to keep her distance from shrinks and got herself a cat instead. And frankly, she was better. Or had been until...

"It's because of your dad, isn't it?"

Maybe. Not completely. "No." Annie ran a finger over the scar right below her kneecap.

Harsh streaks of sunlight slashed through the miniblinds and brought with them the ugly memory of hearing her parents in the kitchen having a blowout. Her mom's mother had died—a grandmother Annie hadn't known she had. Her mom had wanted to take Annie to the funeral. She'd never heard her soft-spoken, choir minister of a father so outraged.

The next day, worried about her mother, Annie confronted her dad. He didn't hold back. *They aren't nice people. They're angry and they're alcoholics and they've spent more time in prison than they have in church.*

Since her dad's death, Mom had reconnected with her family. Six months back, she'd begged Annie to go to a family reunion. Curious but leery, she went. And maybe her father's opinion had tainted her view, but the Reed clan gave her the heebie-jeebies.

Her mom's blue eyes teared even more. Guilt took a few laps around Annie's sore heart. No matter how she felt about the Reeds, her mother had lost someone she loved.

Setting her papers down, Annie stood. "I'm sorry. Drive here tomorrow, and we'll go together." Annie hugged her.

"Thank you." Her mom ended the embrace a second earlier than a normal person.

Funny how one second made a difference.

Her mom, three inches taller than Annie, frowned down at her. "You've got dark circles under your eyes. Are you...having sleeping issues again?"

Sleeping issues? Mom always called it that as if it would make it less than it was. "I'm fine." When twelve, she'd asked her mom about the recurring nightmare she'd been having. It had felt so real. Mom had blamed it on her watching *The Blair Witch Project* at a friend's house. That could've explained things. Well, everything but the scar. Her mom, however, insisted Annie had fallen off her bike.

Five minutes later, Annie stood by her apartment window, still longing for that extra second, and watched her mom drive off. Her dad had been the hug giver. Sometimes Annie missed him so much her toenails ached.

All grown up and still a daddy's girl. She'd have to discuss this with her cat.

Speaking of Pirate: The one-eyed, three-legged orange tabby sashayed into the room. It wasn't easy to sashay with a limp, but he pulled it off with charisma.

She scooped him up. "Looks like I'm going to a funeral in Heebie-Jeebie Land."

Pirate bumped her nose with his scarred face. Annie moved toward the sofa. "I know, going makes me a pushover. But don't rub it in. I brought you home, didn't I?"

Dropping into the soft leather cushions, Pirate in her lap, she clicked on the television.

The screen flashed with a breaking news story. A perky blond reporter was saying, "We believe there may be news on the Brittany Talbot disappearance."

Emotion crowded Annie's throat. *Turn it off!*

She couldn't. The image of the five-year-old ballerina shot straight to the heart.

The screen again showed the reporter standing in front of a lake. "We've—" She turned, and the camera did, too. "Detective Sutton, can you give us a word?"

Coffee-shop Sutton filled the screen. Once again, he wore Dockers and dark shades, but new to his apparel was a darker frown. Darker than usual.

"No comment!" The camera focused on his face. Annie leaned in closer. What was he hiding behind his glasses?

"Can you confirm that this is about the Talbot case?"

"Go chase another ambulance." He left the woman holding the microphone and a scowl.

"A man of few words." The reporter's perky mask reappeared. "Sources tell us that the body of a child fitting the description of..."

Eyes closed, Annie saw a little girl twirling in her tutu, clutching a white teddy bear.

Annie's eyes shot open. Brittany Talbot didn't have a teddy bear.

A shiver climbed her back. The news went to a commercial. She clicked off the TV.

Her phone rang. The number belonging to Isabella, Annie's neighbor and the one friend she had made in Anniston, showed on the screen.

"Come over for wine," Annie said in lieu of hello.

"Sure. I just saw your coffee-buddy cop on TV."

"He's not my buddy." The teddy bear image flashed again.

"Right. Was that your mom's car I saw?"

"Yes." Annie stared at the blank TV screen, wishing she could cut off her mind.

"You cratered, didn't you? You're going to the funeral."

Annie nipped on her lip. "You said I would."

"You didn't have to prove me right. It's not too late. The stomach virus is going around. Diarrhea works like a gem."

"I can't. She's hurting. Besides, it's only two days. What could possibly happen in two days that I can't survive?"

CHAPTER TWO

When Bethany Talbot opened the door, Mark knew he was too late. She brushed her tear-streaked cheeks and looked up with the kind of sorrow he still saw in his own eyes. Judith Holt needed to see this.

"Is it her?" Bethany asked.

"Looks like it."

A moan of pure sadness slipped off her lips.

"I'm sorry." Mark fucking hated his job right now.

"After all this time, I didn't think it would hurt this much. I mean, I only held out the slightest hope that..." She swallowed.

He heard the agony in that gulp. It was all too familiar to him.

"If only I'd made her come inside with me when the phone rang." Falling against him, her shoulders shook from heartfelt sobs.

Mark wasn't a touchy-feely kind of guy, but he wasn't an asshole, either. So with awkward not-sure-how-to-do-this pats, he tried to comfort her. Just like he'd tried to comfort his mom and failed.

"I'm sorry." His sincerity echoed in his tone. Her pain was too damn familiar. Her sobs too close to those of his mom's seventeen years before.

He offered more words. "You shouldn't blame yourself." While true, he knew firsthand those words wouldn't help. That kind of guilt couldn't be consoled. You had to live with it.

Obviously sensing his discomfort, she pulled back. "I'm sorry."

"It's okay."

She wiped her pale cheeks. "No. Nothing about this is okay. Do you think my ex-husband did this?"

"I don't know. We called requesting he come to the station for another interview, but he's not in town until Monday."

"You spoke with him, though. Did he sound guilty?"

"I'm not sure." He looked at the woman, early thirties, probably his age. Yet she looked older. The despair in her face told him life hadn't been kind to her. Men just carried the scars better.

"What do you believe?" he asked, turning from consoler to cop.

She pulled in another shaky breath. "I don't want to believe it, but I wouldn't swear on it." Her head fell back onto his shoulder, and Mark resumed the awkward patting.

* * *

"What the hell do you think you're doing?" Sgt. Tom Brown bellowed. He fell into pace with Mark as he made haste to his office.

"My job." It was five o'clock. Quitting time. He'd left Bethany Talbot to search for Johnny Cash and found nothing. But damn, he could use a stiff drink. More than one. The weekend couldn't come fast enough.

Brown's short legs worked double time to keep up. Mark didn't slow down. If the man was going to read him the riot act, let him do it in the privacy of Mark's office. Not that it'd be private. Connor and Juan were back.

"Do you have to be a dick doing that job? We got a call from Channel Six."

"Finding a murdered kid brings the dick out in me." Mark sped up.

"Damn it, Sutton! I'm going to get shit from the commissioner over this."

"And here I thought he'd be happy. We're a step closer to finding who killed the kid." Mark knew "the kid's" name, but using it made it feel more personal.

They arrived outside the opened door to the office, which was actually the file room where three on-probation cops had been assigned to do the department's grunt work. Sift through endless cold case reports.

APD didn't have enough ammo to fire their asses, so they stuck them there and waited for them to quit. The Cold Case Unit was known as the exit route. They'd decided not to accommodate them. Of course, after the day he had, he could change his mind.

Mark faced his sergeant. "Is that what's really chapping your ass? That we did what you and your partner, Gomez, couldn't do?"

Brown's nose grew red. A bad sign. Mark had watched too many older officers get pudgy, red nosed, and lost in a bottle. A heart attack always followed.

Was that what he had to look forward to?

"Watch it, Sutton," his sergeant warned.

"Or what?" Mark asked with jaded confidence.

Brown's jowls slapped shut, and he rushed off.

Mark walked into the room. Connor and Juan, at their desks, clapped, a slow one-beat-at-a-time applause. Both of them had bones to pick with Brown. Mark's bone wasn't so much with Brown as it was with the political bureaucracy of the system. They wanted them to go out and solve crimes, then put so many friggin' rules in place that they couldn't.

He knew they needed rules, but damn if every one of them hadn't been written more to protect the guilty than the innocent. And even when they followed the rules, if the public didn't like it, the big brass threw the officer under the bus.

He had a few tire tracks on his ass. Connor had more. They'd trained him on when to use his weapon and when not to. And when he'd been forced to protect himself they couldn't even argue that discharging his weapon hadn't been justified. But when the shooter turned out to be seventeen, the press and the precinct turned on Connor.

"Spill it," Connor said.

"Spill what?" Mark sat behind his messy desk. He liked it messy. Just like his life.

"What you've got on the sergeant's ass."

"Who said I've got anything?"

"Don't bullshit a bullshitter," Connor said. "If I or Juan here had said that to the old fart, we'd be cleaning out our desks."

"I'm just more likable." Mark leaned back in his chair.

The info he had wasn't anything he'd ever share. If the sergeant pulled his head out of his ass, he'd know that. Right now, Mark hoped the man's head never saw the light of day.

* * *

Saturday morning, dressed in funeral black, Annie found a row of creaky metal chairs, behind which was a door in case she needed to escape. Condensation dripped from her glass of watered-down lemonade.

The home, old, large, and rambling, would've made a perfect haunted house. It felt as if some wannabe contractor had added a couple more bedrooms every few years. Most of the rooms didn't have closets but held antique armoires. Not the nicer ones people bought at auctions, but worn pieces that looked as if they'd been used all these years. She had a creepy suspicion that secrets and skeletons lay hidden in those scarred wooden wardrobes.

People milled around in a proper funeral mood. Yet nothing felt proper.

Her gut said this eerie somberness hanging in the stuffy air wasn't brought here by a funeral, but lived here.

Growing up, she'd seen touches of it in her mom, but Annie's father's easy-to-smile persona had overridden her mom's brief slips into depression.

Her gaze caught on the casket in the front of the living room. The air in her lungs felt like liquid concrete. What kind of family held a funeral in their home?

"Annie."

At the sound of her name, she quashed the need to duck through her escape route. Aunt Doris, one of her mom's sisters, darted across the room toward her.

"Look what I found last night. I thought you'd like it." She held out a photograph.

Annie forced a smile and tried not to stare at her aunt's false eyelashes. The woman reminded Annie of a slightly drunk, downplayed version of Dolly Parton—a look completely opposite from her mom's Sunday-best style.

"Thanks."

The yellowed photograph showed two girls sitting in kitchen chairs. She recognized herself. She looked about five. Her gaze shifted to the untied Cinderella tennis shoes on her feet. Her heart took a time-out. The scar on her knee itched.

Trying not to react, she continued to gaze at the snapshot. The other girl, who appeared to be older, another blonde, wore a cast on her right arm. *Fran?*

Annie had heard Fran's name. The Reed gossip mill, which she'd already been privy to, said that the divorced Fran had drinking problems. That she'd left a kid with her ex-husband.

"You two were best friends." Doris's slurred voice had the hair on Annie's neck dancing.

Annie studied the picture harder, drawn to the expression on Fran's face—the sadness, a silent yearning begging for someone to save her. That look on a few of her students had haunted Annie when she'd been an elementary school teacher. That look had ultimately cost her the job. That look had resulted in a restraining order against her.

That look had gotten her arrested for breaking that restraining order.

She really didn't like that look.

"Fran should be here," Doris said. "I hope she behaves. She didn't grow up as *nice* as you did."

Little did Aunt Doris know. Annie's "nice" was running on fumes. She wanted to get out of there so bad the bottoms of her feet itched.

She glanced at the grandfather clock that ticked and chimed in the corner like a bomb about to blow.

"But she's my girl." Doris's words rode on her liquor-scented breath.

Annie's cousin obviously came by her drinking problem honestly.

"I'm sure she means well." Annie watched Doris bumping her way through the crowd.

The photograph found a spot in her purse, beside the panties that she'd almost left behind in her hotel room this morning. Cold drops of condensation from the glass of lemonade ran down the side of Annie's hand and spattered on the toes of her black heels. The tiny splats echoed in her ears as she thought about Cinderella shoes and Fran's expression in the photo.

Fidgeting, she looked up. Aunt Frieda, Uncle Harry's widow, draped in black, paced the room in a cloud of misery. A red-haired woman, an aunt by marriage, whom her mom had introduced earlier as Aunt Karen, stood talking to her mom. Sarah, her mom's youngest sister who'd never married, sat in a metal folding chair, staring at her hands in a not-really-there way. A vague but eerie feeling of déjà vu hit. She'd seen that woman sitting that way before. Not at the family reunion, but from some other time in the far reaches of her memory.

Right then Uncle George, her mom's brother, a short, pudgy, red-faced man who looked angrier than he had the previous day at the wake, walked in complaining about the pastor being late.

"Annie?" Her mom's voice rang out. "Come here."

Annie saw her mom had moved to stand beside the casket. *No.* But her mom called again. Heart thudding, Annie walked over. She'd managed to be in the house for over an hour without looking at the guest of honor.

"Do you think his tie works?" her mom asked.

Intent on offering only a glance, like swallowing a bitter pill fast, Annie cut her eyes downward. Her gaze stuck on the dead man. Her heart raced and yanked her back to the recurring dream. *Thump. Thump. Thump.* Run. Run. Run.

"The tie's fine." Annie's gaze shot to the door. "I . . . need air."

When she swung around, she accidentally ran into

her aunt Karen. Muttering an apology, Annie moved as fast as her liquid knees would take her. Feeling raw, feeling vulnerable, feeling chased.

Faster, Annie. Faster!!

* * *

"Let's bow our heads." The hour-late pastor began.

The *swish* of a door opening brought the pastor's words to a halt. Annie turned to see a blonde saunter into the room.

"Better late than never." Her voice didn't match the room's mood. Neither did her red dress. She stumbled to the closest available chair.

Murmurs echoed from the crowd. *Red. Drunk. Not again.* Annie glanced at her mom.

"Fran," her mom whispered.

Annie tilted her head to the side just enough to study her cousin. She saw similarities to the picture Aunt Doris had handed her. Fran's hair was darker, she wore the years on her face, but the lost look in her eyes hadn't changed.

Almost as if she could feel Annie's stare, her cousin turned. Their gazes locked. Recognition filled Fran's eyes. Memories that Annie couldn't quite reach clawed at her mind. She looked away.

The metal folding chair under Annie suddenly felt unstable. She fought the desire to reach for something to hold on to.

How soon could she get the hell out of here?

The service ended. The crowd thinned. Back to hugging the corner of the room, the one beside the door, she waited for her mom to say it was time to go.

Twice she watched Fran make trips to the kitchen to refill her glass with something stronger than lemonade. When Fran stumbled, spilling her drink, Annie moved in.

Fran, gripping the back of a chair, looked up. "So the little cousin finally comes out of hiding."

Annie took the glass from Fran's hand and knelt to collect the ice cubes. When she stood up, she met Fran's one-too-many gaze.

"It's not a big deal," Fran said. "I was on my way for a refill." She took the glass and started walking. Then she swung around. "You coming?"

Annie followed. The kitchen was empty except for herself and Fran, who rode her tiptoes as she pulled a bottle of vodka from the pantry's top shelf.

Freshly brewed caffeine flavored the air. "How about coffee, instead?" Annie asked.

Fran's brows rose with too much expression. "Still trying to be the good girl, huh?"

Had Annie been a good girl back then? "Just being helpful."

"Then pass the lemonade. It helps this cheap vodka go down."

Annie spied the coffee cups on the counter. "You take it black?"

Fran stared. Annie continued, "People are talking." Why she wanted to save Fran from the gossip was a mystery. She recalled her aunt's words: *You two were best friends.*

Fran's laugh bounced around the yellow kitchen, but there was nothing cheery about the sound. Or the room. "They always talk."

"One cup," Annie pleaded, her voice too small for the big space.

Fran leaned against the old refrigerator. The noisy icemaker clanked out ice. Annie took Fran's posture as a sign of resignation. As Annie poured hot coffee into the cups, steam rose in the air.

"Black?" Annie asked again.

The fridge spit out more ice.

Fran stared. It wasn't resignation shining in the watery pools of green. "I don't want any fucking coffee. And I don't fucking care what they say. Do you?" She grabbed the bottle again. "Because if you think by not coming back all these years that you saved yourself from their hypocritical judgment, well think again."

The bitterness in Fran's tone scraped across Annie's nerves.

"They say you lost two jobs 'cause you couldn't handle the pressure. That you had a nervous breakdown. Then you became a regular on some shrink's couch. Personally, I'd rather drink."

Anger burned in Annie's stomach. How dare her mother...

Fran raised her glass. "We all deal with it somehow, don't we?"

Annie took a backward step, her heart crashing against her chest like a trapped bird seeking freedom. She had to leave. She started for the door.

Fran blocked her path. "Do you ever think about her?"

"Move," Annie managed.

"Mom said you live there now. When you drive past the park, do you think about her?"

Annie shook her head, her blond hair scattering over her eyes. "I don't know what you're talking about."

"Don't tell me you don't remember Jenny." Fran slapped a hand over her lips. "Oops, not supposed to say her name, am I?"

A wave of nausea swelled in Annie's stomach. She had to get out of here. Away from these crazy people. She took off, bumping into several people standing right outside the door.

"What's wrong?" Fran's question chased her out.

But in Annie's head she heard Fran scream, *Run, Annie! Run!*

She snatched her purse. Outside she spotted her mother and met her halfway across the yard. "How could you tell them my problems?"

"What?" her mother asked.

"Me losing my jobs, my therapy. How—?"

"They're family," her mom said.

"They aren't *my* family. Daddy made that clear." Annie took one step then swung around. "I'm going home."

Her mom's eyes rounded. "Annie? You can't—"

"I can."

Don't tell me you don't remember Jenny.

Shaking, she dug through her purse and found her keys. Then Annie did just what Fran had told her to do all those years ago.

She ran.

She flung herself into her car. Gravel spit from beneath the tires as she put it into gear. *Faster, Annie, faster.*

As her wheels made tracks back to Anniston, her mind took her to the dream. The footsteps.

Getting closer.

Closer...

And just like that, she remembered Jenny. She knew the bloody teddy bear had belonged to Jenny. She knew Annie and Fran had gone into the woods looking for Jenny. Then another image flashed, of Jenny lying in a hole in the earth, dirt being tossed over her too-still body. Blood running down the side of Jenny's face.

Annie yanked her mom's car to the side of the road, opened the door, and puked.

CHAPTER THREE

Someone's here to see you."

Mark looked up from his messy desk to see Mildred, the front desk clerk, standing at his door. Round, pudgy, with dyed red hair. He frowned at his cell phone, noting it wasn't even eight o'clock yet.

Too early on Monday morning to have people popping in. It didn't matter that he'd been here since five, going back over the case files of the dead little girl. Coming in was better than staring at the damn ceiling all night, not wanting close his eyes. Because when he did, he saw things he wanted to forget. Images that stained his soul.

The concern of a mother bear puckered her lips. "You look like something my cat dragged in and then refused to eat."

"Good. That's the look I was going for." His tone hinted at sarcasm.

He pressed a finger to his temple, wishing he could rub away the headache. Friday night he'd lost himself in a bottle of scotch. Or—how was it that Judith had put it? He drank himself into oblivion. Something he hadn't done in about a month. It seemed the less he drank, the longer the hangovers lasted when he did. And there he had it: a reason not to slow down.

"Who is it?"

Mildred leaned in. "A Ms. Lakes. She said it's about a murder."

Mark stopped massaging his forehead. "The Talbot case?"

"I assumed. She asked for you."

He rolled his shoulders. "Is she one of the crazy ones? You know I don't do crazies on Monday."

"Do you do crazies on Tuesday?" The question came with tease. "She's pretty."

"Well, hell. Why didn't you start with that?"

The smile in her eyes faded. "Take something for your headache."

When Mildred left, the two plastic cups of cold coffee he'd poured and hadn't drunk caught his attention. He'd skipped his coffee run, but he still couldn't drink this shit.

He set them in the trash can, an attempt to come off like less of a slob.

The tapping of heels echoed down the hall.

He stacked up a few more papers. The tapping stopped at his door. He stood up, hoping to come off well-mannered, even though his present demeanor leaned more to don't-give-a-damn curt.

"Hell...o." The *o* of the greeting stuck to his tongue when his eyes lit on the package in pink. Pink sandals, a wispy skirt with pink flowers, and a fitted pink cotton shirt that looked as soft as what filled it.

Pink looked good on her, too.

Real good.

Add blond hair and blue eyes, and, hangover or not, old-fashioned lust washed over him.

Then recognition hit. He knew her. Didn't he?

He motioned her inside, trying to place her while trying to recover from his initial, completely normal male reaction. One he hadn't felt since a certain news reporter.

"Come in. Ms. Lakes, right?" She nodded. He continued. "I'm Detective Mark Sutton, but you know that."

She nodded again.

"Have a seat."

"Thanks." She fiddled with the sunglasses on top of her head as she inched closer.

Her hesitation told him she had doubts about being here.

When they'd each settled into their chairs, he watched her fidget with her purse strap. Patience had never been his strong point. *How the hell do I know you?*

An uncomfortable thought hit. He hadn't met her in a bar and gone home with her, had he? He'd done that a few times before Judith.

"You wanted to see me?" His tone was soft, but her reaction wasn't. She flinched as if he'd asked for her bra size.

Then she blinked and replied, "Yes."

That was when he noticed the purple rings under

her eyes. Blatant evidence that, like himself, she hadn't been sleeping that well. The fact that she hadn't taken the time to hide those purple smudges told him something, too. This problem was serious enough to keep her awake, and she wasn't the overly vain type.

He liked that. Not the seriousness of the situation, but the lack of vanity. His fling with Judith had taught him a few things. Mainly, stay away from women whose egos were larger than their breasts.

She crossed her legs, then uncrossed them. "I don't know where to start."

Her voice didn't ring any bells. He picked up a pen, and ignored his instinct to lean in and glance down at her legs. Not that he hadn't already noticed them. He had.

"How about starting at the beginning?" He offered her the police-regulated smile, hoping to put her at ease. She brushed a strand of hair off her cheek, and he got the feeling again that he'd watched her do that before.

Her gaze met his. The haunted look staring back at him seemed familiar in a different way than before. His faux smile slipped off his face. The woman looked as if she might pass out.

"Do you need something to drink?"

She played with the flap on her purse. "It was a long time ago." Her voice barely reached him.

He leaned in. The chair protested with a squeak. "What was a long time ago?"

"The beginning."

"Is this about the Brittany Talbot case?"

She frowned as if it was a trick question. "No."

"So what's it about?" he asked, growing more impatient. Her fidgeting must have been contagious, because he ran his finger over the lip of his messy desk.

"I think it's about a murder. Another girl. Not Brittany."

"You *think* it's about a murder? But you're not sure?"

"I'm pretty sure." She sat up taller, as if his question had put her on the defensive.

"Care to elaborate?" he asked, back to worrying about the crazy factor.

"I saw . . ." Her voice thinned. Her chest rose and fell as if the air was too thick. "I saw someone burying her."

Vertebra by vertebra, Mark's spine tightened. "Where? When?" He shook his head. "Who?"

"Jenny. Her name was Jenny."

"Last name?"

She sent him a blank look. "I'm not sure. Maybe Reed? Maybe not. She lived in Pearlsville." Another strand of wispy hair fell to Ms. Lake's cheek. "She was my cousin."

"Cousin?" *But you don't know her last name?* "What happened?"

"The family had gone camping. We were asleep in the tent, and—"

"Who's 'we'?" He edged his chair closer to the desk.

"My other cousin. Fran. Francyne Roberts." She pulled a photograph from her purse and handed it to him. "She's the one with the broken arm."

It was an aged image of two girls. His gaze stuck on the youngest. He looked up. Same round eyes. Same sweet face.

Why she'd brought the picture baffled him. He set the photograph on his desk. "So you woke up and..." He motioned for her to continue.

"Jenny was gone. Fran was supposed to watch us, so—"

"Watch?" He pushed a thumb to his throbbing temple. "When did this happen?"

She took another nip at her lip. "About twenty-four years ago."

He ran a hand through his hair. "And you're just now coming forward?"

"I would've, but..."

"What?" He tapped the end of his pen on his desk. The *click* bounced around the room, making the silence seem incredibly loud.

She hugged her purse. "I didn't remember...until now."

He rolled the pen between his palms. "It just came to you. Just like that?"

"No. I went to an uncle's funeral and..." Her words faded. "I guess I never really forgot. I've dreamed it, over and over again. Well, some of it. But when I was there, I remembered."

He leaned forward. "You dreamed that this happened?"

She nodded.

Yup, crazy. And it's Monday! "If you dreamed it, and then forgot it, how do you know it really happened?"

Her chin inched up, a tiny gesture that spoke of her guts.

"The shoes." She pointed to the photo. "I dreamed I

was wearing them. And the scar. I fell in the dream, and I have a scar."

His grip on the pen tightened. "Normally, it takes more than a dream to report a murder."

"I'm sorry," she said breathlessly, her tone hinting at a touch of anger. "It was a mistake coming here."

She stood.

Guilt tugged at his gut. "If it happened in Pearlsville, you should talk to someone there."

"I thought you'd..." She inhaled as if to pull the words back in. As if she decided he wasn't worth her words.

"You thought I would what?" He clicked the pen.

Instead of answering, she bolted out of his office with a hell of a lot more energy than she'd come in.

Frustrated, he finger-locked his hands behind his neck and closed his eyes. His mind flashed the image of the haunted look he'd seen on her face. And while he still didn't know why she looked familiar, he knew that look. He'd seen that same expression in the mirror every morning when he woke up, or when he crawled out of bed and hadn't slept, because the images robbed him of sleep and sanity.

Determined to focus on the Talbot case, a real case, he leaned forward. He saw her picture. Picking it up, he stared at the younger girl's image, the sweet face. He thought of his half sister. Sweet, innocent, and dead. Her body tossed in a dumpster.

"Well, shit!" He took off, hoping to catch Ms. Lakes. What he'd say to her when, or if, he caught her, was anyone's guess.

* * *

Insides trembling, hands sweating, she walked, weak-kneed, down the hall. Coming here had been a mistake.

She made it outside the precinct. Hot air and hotter sunshine hit her. Lowering her sunglasses, she fought the need to cry. Not in public, damn it. People would think she was crazy. Just what Detective Sutton believed—what most of her old coworkers, her friends, and Ted, her fiancé, believed. Hell, she could probably add her mother to that list.

Why had she told him about the dreams? She could've just said . . . what?

There was nothing she could say about any of this that didn't sound crazy. *If it happened in Pearlsville, you should talk to someone there.*

It might've helped if she'd told him she thought the murder had happened here. Or maybe not. He was right. She needed something besides dreams, and rants from her drunk cousin.

She needed Jenny's last name.

She needed to talk to her mom. The knot in her throat tightened. Tears threatened.

"Ms. Lakes?"

She turned. Detective Sutton sprinted across the parking lot. Feeling a tear slip from beneath her sunglasses, she brushed it from her cheek and nudged her frames up on her nose. Had he changed his mind?

His dark hair, a tad too long to be considered stylish, stirred in the wind. He carried his big frame like a man comfortable with his size. The type of man who always made Annie wish she had a few more inches.

As he got closer, she spotted the photograph in his hand.

He stopped beside her.

Yep. He made her feel small.

"You forgot this."

Not trusting her voice, she reached for the picture.

"The coffee shop," he blurted out. "That's where I know you from. I don't think I've ever seen you without your sunglasses on."

Great, now she was going to have to find a new place to drink coffee. She slipped the photograph into her purse. When her hands shook, she didn't bother zipping it, but swerved around and started to her car.

"Wait."

His one word gave her pause.

She stopped. She waited. But she didn't turn around. Then not wanting to come off like some meek, too small female, she squared her shoulders.

He stepped beside her. She didn't look at him. But she felt him. His scent, a spicy, male soap kind of aroma, filled her senses.

She gazed up at him, and a tingling awareness skittered down her spine. A male/female kind of tingle, the last emotion she expected to feel right now. The last thing she wanted to feel. But hadn't she felt it every time she'd watched him come into the coffee shop? Oh, Lord, why had she thought this was a good idea?

Nudging those thoughts aside, she glanced up but waited for him to speak. Waited to see what he'd say.

Then her patience snapped, she tossed words out. "I shouldn't have come here. Forget..." She started to leave, but he spoke up again.

"Wait." He looked down through his dark sunglasses. "You didn't answer my question. What is it that you thought I'd do?"

While she couldn't see his eyes, she felt them studying her. She suddenly wished she'd taken the time to notice his eyes earlier. What color were they? What was he hiding?

"I thought you'd care." An assumption she'd gotten from him buying coffee for strangers and the way he'd come across in the on-camera interviews. And the way he'd shielded himself with those glasses, as if hiding his pain.

Wasn't that the reason *she* wore sunglasses? To hide.

"You think I don't care?" His tone deepened.

"I think...it doesn't matter. Because you obviously believe I'm crazy." She shook her head. "Like I said, coming here was a mistake."

"That's my job." His comment felt like a jab, hitting her ribs, heart, and nerves.

Her shoulders squared. "Your job is to think I'm crazy?"

"My job is to mistrust everyone." He let the words hang in the air before continuing. "And your job is to convince me otherwise."

"What happened to innocent until proven guilty?"

"I never assumed you were guilty." His right eyebrow rose above his dark glasses. "Just crazy." A whisper of a smile pulled at his lips.

His honesty both disturbed and intrigued her. "And what do I need to do to convince you I'm sane?"

"You could start by buying me a cup of coffee."

"Bribery?" she asked.

He ran a palm over his mouth as if to hide a smile. "It's right around the block, as you know." He pulled a set of keys from his front pocket. "I'm parked right here." He started walking to a line of cars.

She hesitated. The idea of having coffee with him made her feel as if she'd already indulged in too much caffeine. And the reasons weren't about Jenny or about him believing she was crazy, but about the insane male/female thing again.

He glanced back. "Coming?"

CHAPTER FOUR

*W*as she?

She followed him to a green Mustang. He slid behind the wheel. Still leery, she climbed into the passenger seat. She didn't see the assortment of fast-food bags at her feet until she stepped on them and the smell of cold fries filled the air.

His gaze shifted down her legs to the floorboard. "Sorry." He reached toward her floor space.

Nervous, she shifted her legs the wrong way—and his hand brushed against her bare calf.

Her breath caught. Sweet sexual tingles—unwanted, but sweet nevertheless—ran up her leg to her stomach, and then swooped back down to places that hadn't tingled in years.

Note to self—panic must be an aphrodisiac.

"Sorry." His voice came out a little huskier than before. He snatched a handful of trash and tossed it into his backseat then went back for another handful.

"That's fine." Her pulse thundered.

To avoid looking at him, she started to place her purse on the floorboard, then realized more bags were in the way.

"Let me put it in the back." He reached for her purse.

Not wanting to chance touching him, she twisted and tossed it into the back with about as much care as he had the fast-food bags.

One silent minute later, they arrived at the coffee shop. As soon as her feet hit the pavement, he clicked the locks on the car.

"I need to grab my purse."

"I was joking about you paying," he said.

"A deal is a deal." Their locked gazes felt like a debate.

She won.

He hit the clicker. Opening the back door, she bent at the waist to grab her purse and her billfold that had spilled out. When she straightened and swung around, his guilty gaze flickered up. Great. She'd probably given him a nice rearview shot.

As they walked in, the smell of dark roast filled Annie's senses. The occasional brush of his arm against her shoulder sent jolts of emotional currents to play dodgeball in her stomach.

"Excuse me a second." He pulled out his phone and dialed. "Mildred, I'm picking up coffee. Mr. Talbot is supposed to be in at ten. If he shows up early call me." He paused. "Small or large?"

He cut his eyes toward Annie, almost in apology. "Yeah, skinny vanilla decaf."

He hung up. "Front desk clerk. Sorry."

"Hello, Detective." Mary the cashier offered him a smile. "Missed you this morning."

"I missed your coffee," he said.

While he ordered, Annie noted him close up. His light green Dockers were perfectly ironed, with a firm crease down the middle. His dark five o'clock shadow said he hadn't shaved.

"Annie?"

Annie jerked, realizing Mary was waiting on her order. "Just regular coffee." She pulled out money and paid.

They sat across from each other, their coffees sending up steam between them. Annie noticed he'd chosen a secluded table in the corner. Her table.

Sun flooded in through the glass walls. He hadn't removed his sunglasses. Looking at ease, he picked up his cup and sipped. "You have a first name, Ms. Lakes?"

Tearing open a pink packet, she added the sweetener to her coffee. "Annie."

"You know that stuff will kill you?" He motioned to the packet.

She nodded and sipped, aware his gaze followed the cup to her mouth.

"Is there a Mr. Annie?"

"No." She almost fired back the same question, but felt uncomfortable. His reason for asking could be legit, her reasons not so legit.

He settled back in the chair. "What do you do to keep the wolves from your front door?"

It took her a second to understand what he meant. "I'm a teacher."

"Not what I pegged you for. What grade?"

"College." No need to elaborate. Not when he questioned her mental status.

"A professor. I'm impressed." He shook out a coffee stirrer from the glass container on the table and chewed on the tip.

"Don't be. I teach junior college. A long way from professor status." Over his shoulder, she saw Fred, the regular patron, staring. She forced a smile. He smiled then ducked back behind his paper.

"What do you teach?"

"English mostly. And some continuing ed courses...if the wolves are closing in." Which was often.

Bringing his cup up, he sipped the hot brew. Steam touched his lips. "You grew up in Pearlsville?"

She figured this was his way of backtracking to the conversation they'd left at the precinct. "Until I was five. We moved to Houston. Which is probably part of the reason I can't remember...people's names. I moved to Anniston five months ago."

"Why Anniston?" he asked.

"A job."

"Reed your mother's maiden name?"

Wow, he'd remembered. She supposed cops were trained to do that.

"And you never visited the Reed family through the years?" Doubt flashed in his eyes.

"Not until recently. My mom visited. Dad and I didn't."

"Why?"

She stirred her coffee as his question stirred up something she'd never quite understood.

He eased in. "Why didn't you go with your mother?"

"Dad didn't like her family. He called them angry alcoholics." She tried to say it with confidence, yet her father's excuse had never sounded like enough. Now Annie suspected the truth, that her mom wasn't the only one keeping secrets from her. Had Dad known about Jenny?

"Is it true?" he asked.

"What?"

"That they're angry alcoholics?"

"Yes."

"Is your mom an angry alcoholic?"

"No. She never drinks." She had to give her mom credit for it.

He stared at his cup. "Have you spoken to your parents about your suspicions?"

The sound of grinding coffee beans buzzed in the air, sending a rejuvenating aroma of caffeine in the store. "I didn't...suspect anything until this weekend. My dad passed away last year. My mom's still in Pearlsville. Her brother just died."

"You said you went to the funeral, right?"

Moistening her dry lips, she answered. "My mom begged me to go."

He turned his cup one way, then the other, as if trying to figure out what to ask next. "What exactly do you think you saw twenty-four years ago?"

She didn't miss the *do you think* in his question. It rubbed her the wrong way, but it was better than the look he'd shot her back at the precinct. That look had been too close to the one she'd received when she'd been escorted out of the elementary school for making false accusations of child abuse. Too close to the look the judge had given her when she'd explained why she'd broken the restraining order.

"Someone was burying her." A chill ran down her back. Deep inside she heard Fran's voice screaming for her to run. Instantly, she realized she was tracing her finger over the scar. She stopped.

"You were camping, right? In Pearlsville."

She almost corrected him, but...

"Who was burying her?"

She'd questioned her sanity for accepting his coffee invitation. But it was too late to back out now. "I don't know. It was like a ravine. There was foliage. I couldn't see who was shoveling the dirt over her."

"Then what happened?"

"I saw Jenny's teddy bear at the edge of the ravine, and when I picked it up, dirt rolled down the edge. The shoveling stopped. Fran screamed at me to run. Someone chased us." A shiver ran through her, and she felt her heart, her pulse, felt herself running.

He scooted closer as if she spoke too low. "Who was chasing you?"

She grabbed her stirrer and gave it a few laps around her cup. "I don't know. I don't remember anything after that."

His expression changed, but she couldn't read it. Not with his dark glasses on.

She dropped her stirrer. "I swear I'm telling the truth."

His reply was another question. "You said you dreamed this, too, right?"

"Part of it. I started dreaming it when I was twelve—only the part about running and being chased. I'd wake up in cold sweats. Hearing footsteps behind me."

"Did you tell your parents about the dreams?"

"Yeah. Mom blamed the dreams on me watching *The Blair Witch Project*."

He rubbed his neck. "Had you watched the movie?"

"Yes, but—"

"Your parents never mentioned Jenny to you? Surely, if she was a cousin, your mom would have said something about her . . . sometime."

A strand of hair whispered across her cheek and she brushed it back. "No. We never talked about her family."

His glasses lowered a quarter of an inch. She tried to see what color his eyes were. But he nudged the glasses back up.

"You said you didn't know her last name. Is that because you don't know who her parents were?"

She pulled her napkin over and folded it. "All I remember is she was a cousin. My mother has six siblings."

"Did you see pictures of Jenny when you were back there?"

"No."

His brows rose from behind the glasses, telling her exactly what he kept hidden. Disbelief.

"Isn't it possible the stress of attending a funeral made you edgy, and the memory of the dream played tricks on your mind?"

She wadded the napkin up like emotions wadded in her stomach. Anger that he didn't believe her. Gratitude that he'd given her this much of his time. And the slightest bit of doubt that maybe he was right. Maybe she was crazy. Hadn't doubt driven her to a therapist years ago?

"I wasn't stressed about the funeral. It was uncomfortable, but it wasn't the funeral that made me remember."

"What was it?"

"My cousin, Fran. She asked me if I ever thought about Jenny."

"So Fran remembers you two seeing Jenny being buried?" His shoulders squared a bit.

"She didn't say that." It would have been so much easier to lie, but Annie had never been one to take the easy route. She sat straighter. "It was when Fran asked if I ever thought about Jenny that the pieces started coming together in my head, and I..."

"You what?"

"I felt like a kid again. I wanted out of there." A loud pause hung in the coffee-scented air. "Yesterday I called Fran's mother and got her phone number."

"Did you ask Fran's mother about Jenny?"

She shook her head. "I was..."

"...scared?" he asked.

She didn't deny it.

"You think one of them killed Jenny?"

"Yes."

He paused. "What did Fran say when you called her?"

"I never spoke to her. A recording said the line had

been cut off. I called my aunt back, she said that Fran has a bad habit of disappearing."

"Are you saying something happened to Fran?"

His question startled her. "I never thought that. Rumor is she has a drinking problem."

He brushed the side of his hand over his chin. The raspy, soft sound seemed too intimate. As if she was too close. She shifted back, claimed a few inches.

"You don't remember anything about Jenny being missing? An investigation? Talking to the police?"

"No. It's as if my life didn't exist until I lived in Houston. My..." She almost told him that her therapist had concerns about her sketchy childhood memories, but decided to keep that to herself.

He drummed his index finger on the table. *Tap tap tap.* "Have you asked your mom about this since you got back? Found out if your cousin really existed?"

"I need to talk to her. I will, but I'm waiting until she gets back into town. Her brother just died."

Leaning closer, he ran a finger between his lip and chin as if assessing, drawing conclusions. "You're scared of your mom, aren't you?"

"No." The answer left a bitter flavor like a lie. But it wasn't. "I'm not. I'm afraid of upsetting her. She's fragile. But I'll talk to her."

He sipped his coffee. "How long is she staying there?"

"I don't know." Her mom's gold Toyota Avalon was still parked at Annie's apartment.

With a pinched brow, he looked at his phone. The little action sent Annie flashing back to her therapist's office. She'd had her time and was being dismissed.

"I'm sure you need to get back to work." She made it easy for him. Why not? Unlike the therapist, she wasn't paying him.

He ordered a coffee to go, then they drove back to the precinct. Again, she was aware of his scent and how it occupied his car. The silence following them was almost deafening.

After parking, he looked at her. "I'll make some calls and see if there's a missing Jenny Reed. I don't know if I'll get anything, but—"

"Thank you." His offer wasn't much, but it was all she had.

"Don't thank me yet. I can't promise anything. With it being that old of a case the chances are slim." He reached inside the console and passed her a pen and tablet. "Write down your phone number. If I find anything, I'll call you. And write down all of Fran's info you have."

"Why?" she asked.

"To have another witness."

Because I'm not believable. She scribbled the information. When she passed him the pad, their hands brushed. Skin to skin. So innocent. So seductive.

The tingle happened again. Her throat tightened, holding in air that seemed to belong to him. Her gaze went to his mouth. She ached to feel her heart race with something besides fear.

He kept his thumb on her wrist. His right eyebrow lifted; she heard him inhale. He'd felt it, too.

Isabella had been right about them needing some male company. But why now? Why him?

"I should go." He pulled back.

They got out of the car and faced each other through protective, shaded lenses. Annie couldn't help wondering if Detective Sutton had as much to hide as she did.

"Do you still think I'm crazy?" She figured he'd lie for politeness's sake. But she needed to hear that someone believed her, even if it was a lie.

His chest expelled a gulp of air. "I wouldn't bet on you in a horse race."

His answer hit, hard, and hurt.

Before she thought, she spoke. "A lie would've made me feel better."

His jaw tightened. "My job isn't to make you feel better. Never was much at sugarcoating things." He turned to leave, then swung around. "I'll call if I find something."

"And if you don't find anything?" The question tumbled out. She blushed, realizing how that could be interpreted. Hell, maybe she'd even meant it that way. She wasn't sure. Then her gaze went to his mouth. Anticipation made her next breath sweeter. Yup, that was how she meant it.

He shrugged. "Then it was nice to have met you."

Embarrassed for being so brazen, she hotfooted it to her car.

When she pulled out, she saw him in her rearview mirror, watching.

Probably relieved to see her go. Why did that hurt a little too much? Because like it or not, she'd had a thing for the big, tough cop for a while. Because being lonely sucked.

* * *

Mark delivered Mildred her coffee and made his way to his office, rubbing his temple. His mind said Annie Lakes, with talk of dreams and funerals and a missing cousin, was loonier than a Saturday morning cartoon. His gut said she wasn't lying. His libido said it didn't matter. She was hot, and considering his reaction, he was done being celibate.

He entered the unit's file-room office. Juan and Connor sat at their desks.

"Who was the babe in pink?" Connor grinned. "I thought you weren't seeing anyone."

"I'm not. She was a concerned citizen." Mark dropped in his chair, not ready to talk about this until his gut, mind, and libido came to a consensus.

"Concerned about what?" Juan asked.

"It's not about any of our cases. Not even in our jurisdiction. I don't know what she thought I could do."

"Give me her number and I'll take care of her," Connor said with tease.

"How do you know I got her number?" Mark shot back.

Connor chuckled. "I'm taking your man card away if you didn't."

Mark picked up his pen and started clicking it.

Mildred walked in and set a glass of water and a bottle of Advil on his desk. How could she read him like that?

"Brian Talbot's here," she said. "Sergeant Brown said he and you were doing the interview."

"What?" Connor snapped. "This is our case, not his."

"He expected someone to say that. Told me to tell you because he worked the case before, he knows Talbot."

"Fuck that," Connor said.

"Language," Mildred scolded and left.

Mark downed the painkillers and stood up. "Maybe he has something to offer. It's one interview. Let's see what he can pull out of his hat."

"What he's pulling is coming out of his ass," Juan said. "And it stinks. He knows if we solve this case, it'll make him look bad."

"I think this might be more about our perp being the mayor's cousin. Let him do it? If things go bad, the mayor will come down on his ass and not ours."

Their silence meant they'd reached a consensus. They all stood.

"Herc." Connor handed him the manila envelope. "Stone dropped them by."

"Pictures?" Mark asked, his gut tightening.

Connor's expression hardened. "Kid's mostly covered in concrete, all you can see are parts of her face. They're ugly."

They always were.

Brown waited outside the interview room. Connor and Juan ignored him and went to the connecting observation room.

Nodding, Mark started for the door.

Brown stepped in front of him. "We do this right."

Mark grimaced. "I send one suspect to the hospital, and people never forget."

Brown's brows pinched. "I'm dead serious."

Hell, maybe Mark had been wrong about Brown being here. Mark didn't like Talbot for this, but he planned on finding out, and he wasn't going in soft. "No, it's the kid who's dead. I'm not tiptoeing around this guy."

"I'm not asking you to tiptoe. I want this guy more than you do. I just know how you get when...when a kid's involved. If we go at this wrong, the mayor will shut us down."

Mark walked inside the room. Brown's steps clipped on his heels.

Mark kept a tight grasp on the envelope, unsure if he'd use the photos. Sometimes the shock of seeing pictures offered a peek into the suspect's mind. Sometimes, it shut them down. Later, if Mark realized he'd put an innocent person through hell, he felt like shit. But catching a killer trumped worrying about someone's feelings.

"Mr. Talbot." Brown took the lead. "Thanks for coming."

Talbot's expression told Mark there was no love lost between these two. Obviously, Brown had only recently learned the fine art of tiptoeing.

"You got information on my daughter's killer?" Talbot asked.

"We were hoping *you* had some." Mark set the envelope on the table and pulled a chair across from Talbot, purposely letting the chair's legs screech across the floor. Nervous suspects had a tendency to let go of the truth, or at least it gave Mark a glimpse of the monster inside them.

Mark had danced with enough monsters to recognize them.

"I've told you what I know." Talbot palmed his hand over the edge of the table.

Mark studied the jittery moves. Watching. Waiting. Wanting his gut to tell him *yea* or *nay*.

"Yeah," Mark continued. "But we have a problem. You say you were driving around town at the time of your daughter's kidnapping, but—"

"It's a lie," Brown snapped. "We checked the cameras along the route you said you drove. Came up with zilch."

Talbot's jaw clenched. "You still suspect me? Haven't you ruined my life enough? Bethany left me. My family thinks I killed my own kid!"

Mark broke in. "All we're saying is we need—"

"Fuck you!" Talbot gripped the edge of the table.

Mark leaned closer. "Tell me exactly where you were that day."

"I'm not telling you shit!" Talbot's fist came down on the table. "I loved my daughter."

"Then why did you do this?" Brown snatched the envelope and slung the gruesome photos onto the table.

Talbot's attention shot to the pictures. His gaze locked. Raw emotion filled the man's eyes. Swinging around in his chair, he puked on the floor.

Silence filled the room while Talbot wiped his mouth with the back of his hand.

Mark studied the man and then slid the images back to his side of the table. He purposely didn't look at them. He had enough of them in his head.

"Take a polygraph test," Mark stated.

His sergeant made a gulping sound. Mark looked at him. His gaze was fixed on the photos. And he appeared to be a second away from puking himself.

Talbot glared at Brown. "Why would I have to take a test? I didn't do this."

Mark flattened his hand on the table. "That's why you take the test. We clear you, then we can look for the guilty party."

"You're wasting your time." Talbot's voice sharpened.

"No, you're wasting our time." Brown's tone took a deeper pitch. He shoved the photos back in front of Talbot again. "Look what you did to your little girl."

Talbot turned away. "I wouldn't hurt her. Ever!"

"Prove it by taking the polygraph," Mark said.

"No." The word slid through his teeth.

Before Mark could react, Brown had a fistful of Talbot's shirt and had yanked the man across the table.

CHAPTER FIVE

Y ou son of a bitch," Brown snapped.

Mark caught the sergeant's arm. Brown released the suspect and Mark realized he was playing good cop. Not his normal role.

An angered Talbot shot up from his chair. "Can I go now?"

"Yes." Mark eyed his sergeant as Talbot stormed out.

By the time Mark turned around, Brown was facing the wall. Silence filtered through the room as Mark collected the photos. Still not looking at them, he nudged them into the envelope.

"Thank you." Brown turned around. "I wanted to beat the shit out of him."

"Coming from someone who's done it once, I can tell you, it feels pretty good," Mark said. "But then your sergeant, or in your case your captain, might jump your ass."

"The thought of what he did..." Brown passed a hand over his face.

"The guy I hit had raped and beaten a sixteen-year-old girl. He told me he'd enjoyed it. It was worth going to prison for."

Brown exhaled. "I thought you'd lose it. You impressed me."

"And you impressed me by losing it. Funny how we measure people differently."

Brown motioned to the envelope. "How could he do that?"

"I don't think he did."

"What? He refuses to take the polygraph. Why—"

"He's hiding something. But I don't think it's murder. Who else did you look at for this?"

Brown shoved a chair under the table. "Just him. You basing this on gut instinct?"

"That and personal experience."

Brown was one of the few here who knew Mark's past.

"And your gut's never wrong?" Brown asked.

"I'd bet on it in a horse race." Mark's mind shot to Annie Lakes. His gut told him to believe her, even when her story sounded far-fetched enough to be a fucking movie of the week.

They walked out. Connor and Juan had left. As Mark and Brown walked down the hall, something about his sergeant tugged at Mark's memory. "Didn't you grow up south of here?"

"In Wilma. Why?"

"Isn't Pearlsville around there?"

"A rock's throw from Wilma. It's even smaller though. I'm surprised you've heard of it. Why?"

"I had someone come in today with a wild story about a cousin who may be missing. I told her I'd look into it."

"The woman in pink I saw walk into your office?" Brown asked.

"You spying on me?"

"Not you. Her." Brown grinned.

The sergeant stopped at Mildred's desk. "Get janitorial to clean interview room three."

"Got it," Mildred said.

Brown faced Mark. "A friend of mine is sheriff in Pearlsville. Adam Harper. Call him. Tell him it's to help someone who looks good in a skirt. He'll talk to you."

"Thanks." Mark started off.

"Sutton," Brown called.

Mark turned. "Yeah?"

"Watch your step with the press. I really don't want to fire your ass."

* * *

Juan and Connor were waiting when Mark walked into the office.

"You should have let Brown plow into him," Connor said.

Mark shrugged and grinned. "If they demoted him, he might end up in here with us."

They laughed. But not for long. Obviously, like him, their minds were on the case.

"What's your verdict?" Juan asked.

Mark sat on the edge of his desk. "What do y'all think?"

"I say guilty. Why else would he refuse to take a polygraph?" Connor leaned back.

"I disagree," Juan added. "The look on his face when he saw those pictures. It wasn't fake." A beat of silence lingered. "And your verdict?"

Mark squeezed his neck. "I think he's hiding something, but he didn't do this."

"So we have nothing," Connor seethed.

"No, we've got the body," Mark said. "And Cash, if we can find him." He released a breath of frustration. It didn't feel like enough. But it never did.

"Okay, let's say he's innocent." Connor stood. "What's he hiding? The logical thing would be an affair, but he and his wife are divorced. So what is it?"

"Good question," Mark said.

And this was why they were good at solving cases. They respected each other's opinions. Each of them came at a case from a different perspective, and together they found leads.

Connor sat back down. "What could he be hiding that's so bad he'd rather be accused of killing his daughter?"

"Don't know." Mark rubbed his shoulder. "But my gut says if Talbot knew who hurt his kid, he'd have taken care of them." When one was that hurt, they wanted to do it themselves. Mark knew.

"Perhaps that's why he won't take it. Maybe he killed the bastard," Connor offered.

"That's a theory," Mark said.

"Let me dig into the old files," Juan said. "Maybe Brown and Gomez missed something."

Connor stood again, pulled his Glock from his gun drawer, and slipped it into his shoulder holster. "I'll hit more shelters asking about Johnny Cash."

"I need to make a few calls." Mark's mind went to the sheriff in Pearlsville. "Then I'm going to hang out under a few bridges and ask about Johnny."

"What if we can't close this one?" Connor said.

"We will." Mark dared either one of them to argue. No way in hell could he walk away from a kid case.

* * *

Connor left. Juan went to lunch. Mark made the call.

"So how's my big-city friend doing? Giving you any shit?" Sheriff Adam Harper's voice boomed out of the phone.

Mark leaned back in his chair. Funny how small-town accents seemed to carry more of a Southern drawl. According to Brown—and Mark's quick Internet search—Pearlsville was about as small as they came.

"Just normal crap." Mark moved the conversation to Lakes. He kept it vague, saying she remembered something bad happening to her cousin and thought the girl had gone missing.

"She thinks the name is Jenny Reed. She was part of the Reed family." Mark's gaze caught on the manila envelope and reminded him he should be out trying to get another kid justice, but he couldn't forget the desperation in Annie's eyes.

Couldn't forget that it felt too damn close to the look that stared back at him when he shaved every morning.

He even skipped shaving some days so he didn't have to see it.

"Reed? Jennifer Reed?" Harper said.

The way Harper said it caught Mark's attention. "Yeah?"

"And this girl...how old would she be now?"

Mark leaned his elbows on his desk. "It happened twenty-four years ago. She was young—"

"So late twenties, right?" Harper asked.

Mark picked up a pen and started clicking the top. "Yeah."

Harper's laugh caught him off guard. "Well, you can put Ms. Lakes's fears to rest. Jennifer Reed's fine. In fact, if I lean my head to the left, I can guarantee you she's fine." He chuckled harder. "She's my desk clerk. I'd say she's twenty-eight. Pretty thing—blond, blue eyes. And she's got the kind of curves that make a man dizzy.

"Hold on a second," the sheriff said. "Jennifer," he called out. "Come here?" Pause. "Did you, or do you have a family member around your age who's also named Jenny?"

Mark pressed the phone closer.

"No, why?" The woman's weak reply reached Mark's ear.

"Did you go to school with any other Jenny Reed?"

"No," she answered.

Mark clenched his jaw. What was the chance of there being two Jenny Reeds in a town of three hundred? But...? "What about neighboring towns?" He wanted to believe Annie.

"Well, I'm over Jordan County. I can ask around,

but the other counties around here didn't even have their own schools until about ten years ago, so I'd think Jenny would have known her."

Mark stopped trying to believe. "Thanks."

When he hung up, he pulled out the paper with Annie's number. "Fuck." The lady was a few fries short of a Happy Meal. Why were the good-looking ones always crazy?

* * *

Ten minutes later, as Mark was still trying to forget Annie, Brown stormed in.

Mark stiffened. When his boss barged in, it was either bad news or an ass chewing. Or both. Mark tossed out words hoping to divert the shit storm. "Just hung up with Harper. He said hello."

Brown nodded. And when he didn't start ranting, Mark hoped . . .

"I went through my personal files on the Talbot case. I found the name of the shelter where Johnny Cash was staying."

Mark stood up. "That's the best news I've had all day."

Brown handed him a piece of paper. "Go find Brittany Talbot's killer."

* * *

It was almost eight that night when the jingle of her phone interrupted Annie's shower. She jumped out, grabbed her robe, and dashed into the living room. By the time her wet feet slid across the tile dining room floor to a quick stop, the phone quit ringing.

She checked missed calls.

She had two.

After her depressing and disastrous meeting with Detective Sutton, she'd forced herself to drive to Anniston State Park. She'd sat in her car. Breathing in. Breathing out. Feeling like a scared little girl.

She couldn't leave the car.

Feeling like a failure, she'd gone to Isabella and poured her heart out. Afterward, Annie did what she usually did. She'd reached down and snatched up her big-girl panties. Pulled them up so tight, she got mental camel toes.

Just because Detective Sutton didn't believe her, didn't mean she couldn't do it herself. She'd already started. She'd called Fran's ex-husband to ask where her cousin was. He wasn't home.

It had taken some verbal dancing to get Fran's mother to give Annie his number. But the conversation with her aunt hadn't been nearly as uncomfortable as the one she'd soon have with her mom.

You're scared of your mom, too, aren't you? Detective Sutton's words played in her head. He was right. But not in the way he thought.

All her life, her father had shielded her mom because she was emotionally fragile. Annie spent her life doing the same thing.

Now the thought of talking to her mom about all of this gave Annie stomach cramps. The thought of telling her her suspicions about Jenny Reed gave Annie's heart a workout.

But first, she needed some proof.

Staring at her phone, she hit the missed calls button. Her breath caught.

Mark Sutton's name flashed on the screen. She really hadn't expected to hear from him. She nipped at her lip. Just when she was about to listen to the message, a knock sounded at her door.

She jumped. Could it be him? She hadn't told him her address, but a cop could get it.

The knock sounded again. Her pulse knocked with it.

Pulling her nubby robe closer, her stomach plagued her with I'm-practically-naked-and-it-could-be-a-good-looking-man-at-the-door kind of flutters. Moving in, teetering on her tiptoes, she pressed her eye to the peephole.

Her breath released. From disappointment or relief, she wasn't sure.

She unlocked the door.

"Brought you a gift." Isabella raised the vase of flowers as she walked in.

Annie caught a whiff of the sweet floral scent as her friend rushed to the kitchen and set the flowers on the bar.

She met Isabella's faux smile. "You bought me red roses?"

Her friend studied her and bypassed her question. "What happened? Did Fran's ex call?"

"Not yet." Annie studied the flowers. "Explain?"

Isabella rolled her eyes. "Okay, I'm regifting them." Isabella's still-puffy eyes explained the rest.

"You should keep them," Annie said.

"Not happening. Take them, or the dumpster rats will enjoy them." Isabella's brown eyes picked up a new gleam. "Why the fuck is he doing this? It's over?"

Annie couldn't answer that. She'd come into Isabella's life post divorce, and her friend hadn't shared a lot of details. Annie still gave it a shot. "He obviously still loves you."

"Well, that's just pretty damn inconvenient." Isabella put up a front. One Annie saw right through. "So nothing from Fran's ex?" Isabella's conversational U-turn might as well have been a NO TRESPASS sign.

Annie's phone beeped again with the detective's message. "You want some wine?"

"Yeah." Isabella started to the kitchen then stopped. "I'm sorry. You've had a rotten day, and I'm tossing my problems at your feet."

"Are you kidding? You once listened to me whine for an hour." In fact, Annie had dumped all her life history on Isabella—too much wine one night—but Isabella hadn't opened up.

Her friend darted into the kitchen.

"Are you really over your ex?" All Annie knew was that the breakup had come right after Isabella's third miscarriage. Annie understood how that could've broken Isabella's heart, but should it have broken the marriage?

"Puh-lease, he's history." Her friend's tone said the conversation was over.

Annie didn't feel she had a right to push. "Give me a second. I just missed a call from the detective." She hit the receive message button, her chest tightening.

"What? Mr. Hot in Dark Shades called?" The wicked smile appearing on Isabella's lips had Annie regretting her honesty about the good-looking cop.

"I'm sure it's about the case." She placed the phone to her ear, unable to deny the anticipation fluttering in her stomach.

The recorded message came on. "Hi. This is Detective Sutton."

His husky, warm-chocolate voice brought on a visual of him sitting across from her at the coffee shop— wide shoulders and enough confidence to fill his brawny frame. Instantly, she became aware of her lack of clothes, of how the cotton robe rested against her nipples. Just the man's voice turned her on.

The message started, "Uh, Ann . . . Ms. Lakes. I made a call."

She stopped breathing. Pirate slinked over and rubbed his scarred face against her leg. She ignored the feline. Ignored everything. Even the warm flush in her body. Did Detective Sutton have answers? Was it going to be this easy?

"I found out that Jenny Reed did exist."

Her breath caught. Her heart raced. She'd been right. Validated. She wasn't . . . crazy.

"Actually," he continued, "she does exist. She

works for the sheriff's department in Pearlsville. I guess your dreams are...just dreams. Maybe you should go see someone about them. Get some professional help."

Annie closed her eyes. Why were the good-looking ones always jerks?

CHAPTER SIX

At eight the next morning, after a blessed two hours of sleep, Mark drove out to see Janet Rigley, who lived twenty miles outside Anniston. His visit yesterday to the St. Peter's Shelter had gotten him nothing...except Janet's name, address, and telephone number. Apparently she used to run the shelter where Johnny Cash had stayed four years back.

Janet Rigley might be their last hope of finding Cash.

But first he had to find her. After driving down three uneven dirt roads, coating his Mustang with dust not to mention having his teeth knocked loose by his car's violent bouncing—he spotted a mailbox with the right address on it.

He turned into the drive, and an old farmhouse with a wraparound porch appeared before him. Someone had put some TLC into it.

When he pulled to a stop, something moved on the front porch. A rocking chair. A woman sitting in it was staring at him.

As he reached for the door handle, his phone rang. Pulling his cell from his pocket, he eyed the number. The precinct.

He waved at the woman as he answered, hoping it wasn't an emergency.

"Hey, sweetheart," Mildred said over the line. "Sergeant Brown asked me to give you a jingle. Pearlsville's sheriff is trying to reach you. Something about a favor you asked of him for a friend."

A friend? Mark doubted Annie Lakes considered them friends. For the umpteenth time, he wished he'd been more diplomatic in the message he'd left. But he'd warned her that he wasn't good at sugarcoating things. He still felt bad. So bad that this morning he'd driven a mile to go to a different coffee shop.

The coffee wasn't worth a shit, either. "Did Brown say what the sheriff wanted?"

"Nope. Just that you should call him."

Curiosity bit. What did Adam Harper have? "You got the sheriff's number?"

"Have you ever known me to not be prepared?" Her tone brought on an honest chuckle. He'd never quite understood their uncommon bond. She looked after him. And since her husband died a year ago, he'd changed her oil and mowed her lawn when her son couldn't do it—and they traded off watching each other's dogs.

"Do I tell you enough how good you are?"

"Not enough," she responded.

He chuckled. "Well, you're great. Can you text the number?"

"Will do."

When he looked up to the porch, the woman now stood beside the rocker. She looked about sixty, wore jeans and a red T-shirt. A long gray ponytail rested on her shoulder. He got out and moved toward the porch.

"You lost?" the woman asked. Right then a man walked out onto the porch.

"Not if you're Janet Rigley."

A big dog stood up beside the man.

"Then I guess you aren't lost. What brings a good-looking guy like you out to see me?"

"Mama," the man scolded then turned to Mark. "She'd flirt with the devil."

"Only if he was good-looking," she said with humor.

Mark grinned and moved up the steps. The dog ambled over. Mark held out his hand for the canine to sniff, but it bypassed Mark's offering and jammed its nose deep into Mark's crotch. He flinched. The animal didn't have a soft nose.

"Pixie," Ms. Rigley scolded, then grinned. "She likes the good-looking ones, too."

"It's okay." Mark gave the dog a pat and a nudge away from his boys. Bacon, his own dog, had a crotch fixation.

Looking at the woman's son, Mark offered him his hand. "Detective Sutton with the Anniston Police Department."

Ms. Rigley spoke up, "You probably hear this all the time, but I swear I didn't do it."

Her jovial tone brought on his mandated smile. "I heard it once or twice, but I believe you. I'm looking for a homeless man who stayed in the shelter when you ran it. He called himself Johnny Cash. He was a witness to something several years back, and we can't locate him now."

Mark's phone dinged with a text, no doubt from Mildred. He pushed back his curiosity to deal with the problem at hand. Or two of them. Finding Johnny Cash and removing Pixie's nose from his crotch again.

Ms. Rigley set her rocker to creaking. "I remember Johnny. That wasn't his real name."

"I figured that. What can you tell me about him? You wouldn't know where he is, would you?"

"What I know is what he told me, and that's probably more of a pipe dream than reality. When you're down on your luck, you sometimes create a better past. But if there's one guy who could've climbed out of the gutter, it'd be him. He could play a guitar and sing like nobody's business."

"Anything you can tell me would be appreciated."

"Then pull up a rocker. We'll pick each other's brain and see if I can't help."

Since her dog had already checked out his privates, he supposed his brain was up next.

* * *

Mark left with a hell of a lot more information than he came with as well as a pair of slightly bruised balls. Pixie had gotten him four times. At least his dog was a gentle sniffer.

But it was worth it. He had the names of Cash's

homeless friends, and a church and bar where the man sometimes played. Finding Cash no longer felt impossible.

As soon as he got away from the house, he pulled over, found the text with Adam Harper's number, and called him. While it rang, Mark rolled down his windows to get a breeze. It was only April, but the Texas temperature had run off spring.

A second later, a dainty Southern voice answered the sheriff's phone. Jenny?

"Sheriff Harper, please."

"One minute." There was a pause and then, "Can I tell him who's calling?"

"Detective Sutton." Sweating, Mark ran a hand through his hair.

"From Anniston?" Her tone came out overly inquisitive.

Yup, this was Jenny Reed. And from her inquiring tone, it appeared the sheriff had explained the reason for Mark's inquiry. That annoyed him. One, because he came off like the village idiot, and two, if she told anyone in the family that a cop from Anniston was looking into the case, they'd suspect it came from Annie.

"Is he in?"

"One second."

Mark remembered Annie Lakes's voice carrying similar soft notes.

"Hey." Harper's voice came out boisterous after the lyrical voice.

Mark settled back in his seat. "You called."

"Yep. I went for a couple of beers last night with TJ

Gunter and Tom Patrick down to the Cowpoke Bar & Grill. Best little bar in a hundred miles."

Mark didn't know these men or why the sheriff felt the need to tell him about his night out, but he figured sooner or later the man would get to the point.

If the sheriff had one.

"Yeah?" Mark said.

"I was telling them about your call. Laughed our asses off."

Yup, the village idiot.

"Then, TJ, he's retired from the department. He gets confused sometimes, but he said something interesting. Something about a Reed girl gone missing years ago. That was before I got here."

Mark clenched the phone. So, he was no longer the village idiot. And Annie Lakes was no longer crazy. "Was there an investigation?"

"I'm assuming. But according to TJ, they were assisting you guys."

"What?" Mark asked.

"He said you guys asked us to look into the family."

"I'm lost," Mark said.

"It's hearsay," Harper continued. "To be honest, TJ's dealing with the beginning stages of can't-remember-shit disease, but he said the Reed girl went missing in Anniston."

"Here?" Mark sat up.

"That's what he remembers. He says it was suspected she drowned in the lake at Anniston State Park. But without a body they were suspicious, and they asked the sheriff to check it out. He doesn't remember what you guys ruled it, though."

He recalled Annie saying they were on a camping trip. Could her cousin have drowned, and she'd gotten it wrong? He didn't buy that. Did he? "Was her name Jenny Reed?" Regret for his call to Annie burned in the pit of his stomach.

"TJ's not good with names," the sheriff answered. "He just remembers she was from the Reed bunch. And like I said, his memory isn't what it used to be. I've got Rusty, my deputy, looking through the old files at the courthouse. But the courthouse flooded several years back and most of the old files were ruined. You might want to look into your own files."

"I will," Mark said.

"Oh," the sheriff added, "when I explained things to Jennifer, I found out she's only twenty-two. Her mom is on a cruise and won't be back until tomorrow. Her dad passed about ten years ago, so they can't tell us anything. So I made some phone calls to one of the Reed boys. George, I think. He hasn't returned the call yet. But I heard his brother passed last week."

At least Mark knew for sure it was the right family. "Will you touch base with me when you know something?"

"You bet your bottom dollar."

Mark sat there. Not liking it, but he'd bet his own bottom dollar he'd be making an apology to Annie.

"One more thing," Mark said.

"What's that?"

"Your receptionist. She knows not to repeat things, right?"

"You worried?"

"It's just Ms. Lakes lives in Anniston, and considering she might end up being a witness, I wouldn't want anyone there to know who she is."

"I see. I'll make sure Jenny knows not to say anything."

* * *

Mark texted Juan and Connor the information he'd gotten on Cash. They were heading out to check on the leads. Mark told them he'd meet up with them after lunch. He went right to the office and spent two hours going through old case files.

He'd gone through fifteen boxes, each one less organized than the one before. Anything dated earlier than 1995 appeared to have been shoved randomly in boxes.

Mildred walked in and stopped short when she saw him surrounded by boxes and files stacked on every flat surface of the room, including the floor. Frankly, until she'd walked in, he hadn't realized the mess he'd created.

"What the heck is this?"

He frowned. "Looking for an old case file. Nothing's organized. Not alphabetically or by date."

"I thought you had the Talbot files."

"Not that case. It's about Annie Lakes."

"Who?"

"The woman in pink."

"The one you thought was crazy?" Mildred frowned at the mess.

"Yeah," Mark admitted.

"Is she?"

"What?"

"Crazy?"

He exhaled. "I don't know yet."

"Well, she can't be worse than that reporter."

"True."

Mildred grinned. "I recall warning you about her."

"I know."

"Say it," she said.

"What?"

"That I was right."

He frowned. "You were right."

She put a hand over her heart. "That felt good."

He exhaled. "Why do I like you?"

"Because I dish out good advice."

He smiled. "So what advice do you have for me now, wise one?"

"Go eat something. That wrinkle between your eyes tells me you've got a headache on the way. I'm heading to lunch, too, when I come back, I'll help you look."

"That's why I like you." He watched Mildred leave. His stomach grumbled. A slight painful thump at his temple proved her right. Had he eaten breakfast? No.

Frustrated, he plopped down in his desk chair. He found the paper with Annie's numbers.

He dialed her cell phone. Got voice mail. He hung up. Her work number got him another recording. He didn't leave a message. After the last one he'd left, he owed her a real talk. Face-to-face.

Anniston Junior College was close. He had no idea

of her schedule. She might not even be working, but he could find out. Maybe he'd offer to buy her lunch along with his apology.

The thought of seeing her again made all sorts of ideas start forming. Ideas that took him to places he didn't need to go. Hell, being smack-dab in the middle of a murder investigation wasn't the time to get involved. But he owed the woman an apology and possibly a burger.

The vision in pink filled his head. He remembered the sheriff's description of the other Reed. *The kind of curves that make a man dizzy.* Definitely cousins.

He put on his mental brakes so fast his brain got whiplash. This was police business. *Nothing else.*

His libido and his empty stomach groaned. He had an hour for lunch to kill. Why not kill it with her in a complete uninvolved way?

He took off.

When he got into his car, he noticed last night's dinner mess on the passenger seat. He started to toss it in the back, but spotted the trash can beside his car.

Trash in hand, he got out and, opening the back door, started snatching up a week's worth of fast-food bags. With one of the crumpled-up handfuls, he caught a piece of flimsy material. Flimsy, sexy material.

His eyes widened.

A slinky pair of silk and lace black panties dangled from his thumb. *Talk about a Happy Meal toy for adults.*

The last woman he'd had in his car had been Mildred when he took her to pick up her car from the shop. The lacy, barely-there underwear did not belong to Mildred. Judith?

No. Couldn't be.

The Mustang had been detailed two weeks back.

Where...?

Annie Lakes?

He remembered her tossing her purse into his back-seat. The visual of her leaning over to collect something that had fallen out filled his head. It had been a nice view, too.

Being a man, and a suspicious man, he half-wondered if she'd left the panties on purpose. If so, it was a bold move. But what man didn't like bold moves?

Not the time to get involved. He repeated the mantra. But damn it, his little head wasn't listening. He tucked the panties into his pocket, tossed the trash in the garbage, and went to pay Annie Lakes a visit.

CHAPTER SEVEN

Does everyone understand the assignment?" On the blackboard Annie wrote the page numbers of the short story that appeared in the English Lit book. She looked over her shoulder at her class.

Heads nodded.

"Good." She refrained from nodding back. Last night's wine had done her in.

After hearing the detective basically tell her via voice mail to go find herself a shrink, Annie had welcomed the first, second, and third glasses of Merlot. It hadn't solved her problems, but the alcohol's numbing effect had felt pretty good, then.

This morning, she realized all she'd done was postpone the obvious. She had to talk to her mom. Especially when an Internet search on Jenny Reed had resulted in zilch.

Every time she considered how the conversation with her mom would go, she felt sick. Hell, maybe she should try to forget everything, follow the detective's advice and get herself professional help. *Again.* Maybe her cat wasn't enough after all.

And perhaps Annie needed to grow a pair and go back to the park. If it really happened there, she might remember...something.

The classroom door swished open. Annie looked up and...froze. Her head throbbed and her heart took a dive to hide behind her liver.

Detective Sutton loomed in the doorway. He hadn't even stepped inside, but his presence dominated the room. The first thing Annie noticed was...he didn't have his sunglasses on, and he had the most drop-dead gorgeous blue eyes she'd ever seen. She should have guessed. Great body, great voice, great features. Great eyes completed the package.

He pointed to an empty chair as if to say he'd wait.

Annie didn't want him waiting—or watching her. In spite of his appealing maleness, in spite of the fact that her core body temperature had probably risen five degrees due to his presence, she didn't care to listen to him tell her again that she needed to get her head examined.

"Why don't we break early?" Annie's gaze shifted around the class. "See you on Wednesday."

She heard the clatter of sounds—books shutting, feet scuffling, and her mind spitting out possibilities of how to deal with the detective.

Walking to her desk, she started straightening things that didn't need straightening. When the last student walked out, she glanced up.

Detective Sutton remained seated, staring at her with those killer blue eyes.

"Hello." His masculine voice that could melt ice cream faster than August heat.

Good thing she wasn't ice cream. Determined not to melt, she walked around her desk and leaned her hip on the edge.

"I'm surprised to see you." But she was more surprised by the relentless attraction she felt. The man considered her a nutcase. Did her hormones have no shame?

"You look surprised." He stood up.

As his big frame moved forward, Annie fought the desire to step back. To put the desk between them. But afraid he'd guess how affected she was by him, she didn't move.

He didn't stop until he stood a foot in front of her. Twelve small inches.

She could have used another six. Both of height and breathing room. She really didn't like the way his presence made her feel too small, too aware of her own body. Too aware of his.

Right then, she accepted that her hormones were hopelessly shameless.

Today he wore a pair of khakis and a white button-down shirt. She'd seen the outfit numerous times when he'd come into the coffee shop. The shop she'd avoided today, unwilling to risk seeing him.

His gaze whispered over her. "Pink's better."

"Excuse me?" she asked.

"It's the same outfit. Blue is good. But the pink is better."

She glanced down at her clothes. Well, yeah, the

outfits were similar but not identical. And who'd have guessed a man would notice?

"You're the fashion police?" She ran her fingers over the edge of her desk.

The corners of his eyes crinkled with confidence and humor. "It'd probably be a promotion from the Cold Case Unit." He studied her. Intently.

This close, there was no telling what he saw.

Perhaps her soul. Her mixed-up, mangled, mildly hungover soul. A soul that needed professional help. Or so he'd said.

"I wasn't being critical," he said as if noting her frown.

Maybe not. But last night's message had been.

She inhaled, unsure how she should play this. The woodsy scent of his skin filled her senses. Her hormones might have sold her out, but she had scruples. Weak scruples, but she relied on them.

"Is there a reason for this visit?"

The twitch of his brows told her he'd noted her less-than-welcoming tone. "A couple, actually." He moved closer.

"And they are?" In desperate need of space, no longer caring what he thought, she slipped to the side and put the desk between them.

He picked up the framed picture of her mom and dad as if it being out gave him the right. She supposed it did, but it still annoyed her.

After giving it a glance, he set it back down. "Adam Harper, the sheriff in Pearlsville, called me back."

A swallow of his spicy male-scented air caught in her throat. "And?"

"It seems there was a Reed girl who came up missing twenty-four years ago."

It took her a second to believe, another to respond. "And?"

"All we know now is that the missing girl is believed to be part of the Reed family. They're trying to locate the old files."

I'm not crazy. The three words happy danced around her head and her heart, bumping into too many memories that made her question herself.

"It's possible that whatever happened to her took place here. In Anniston."

"At the park," she said.

"You knew this?" He lifted a brow.

"My cousin...mentioned the park at the funeral."

"Why didn't you tell me?"

"Because...she was drunk, and you already didn't believe anything else I said."

He slipped his hand into his pocket. "Point taken. Have you been to the park to see if it jars your memory?"

"Not yet." She folded her hands together.

His eyes lowered, he studied her so intently her skin itched. "You're afraid to go there?"

"No." Her lie sharpened the edges of the word. And from his expression, he heard it, but the look in his eyes wasn't judgmental.

Their gaze held. Held to that point where it felt like too much, too intimate. She blinked. "So what do I need to do now?" All those years, all those doubts, all those lies her mom told. Annie felt a lump form in her chest.

"You could go grab a bite of lunch with me."

"I mean about what I saw."

He kept his right hand in his pocket. "Well, it de-pends."

"On what?"

"On what's in the files. We're looking for them here. The sheriff mentioned that she might have drowned, but her body was never found. If there's enough in the file to—"

"The fact that I saw her being buried isn't enough?"

"I'm not saying it won't be, but we need to look at the files."

She nodded. He stared.

She swallowed. He continued to stare.

With another wave of relief came the realization of how all of this could affect her emotionally fragile mom. But Annie deserved answers. "Thank you."

It was his turn to nod. "Have you found your other cousin yet?"

"No, I called her ex yesterday and left a message. I'm hoping he might know where I could reach her, but he hasn't returned my call."

"Give me his number and I'll call. He might be more likely to answer a police officer."

His willingness to help surprised her. Then again, hadn't she gone to him because he seemed the type to care?

She fought the need to chew on her lip. "I'll text it to you later."

"Okay." His gaze met hers. Silence danced between them. "You never answered me about lunch." He seemed to swallow her with his eyes.

"I can't. I . . . have a class in twenty-five minutes."

"Hmm." He tucked his right hand in his pocket again. His inquisitive expression told her he was trying to figure out if her refusal came because she really had a class or if she didn't want to have lunch with him.

To be honest, she was trying to figure that out, too. Oh, she did have a class, but even if she didn't she wasn't sure she'd go. See, she had some scruples.

"You didn't happen to lose something in my car, did you?"

"What?" She toyed with a paper clip on her desk.

"An article of clothing, perhaps?" His shoulders rose with the question and a certain gleam lit up his eyes.

"A what?" Was he moving closer on purpose?

He pulled something lacy from his pocket.

Annie stared at the black underwear and fought to get the air down her throat when her lungs refused to work. She grabbed her purse from her bottom drawer, praying she'd find her pair of black panties crumpled in the bottom. But honestly, she knew.

Knew the silk underwear he held in his hands was hers.

And just what do you say to a guy standing there holding your favorite pair of panties?

Lie. The voice screamed in her head. But she sucked at that.

"This is embarrassing," she managed to say. "They must've fallen out of my purse."

"Well, there went my fantasy." His smile was half tease and half temptation. "I thought, hoped you'd left them there . . ."

Her face flushed. "I would never—"

Another apology flashed in his eyes. "I was joking. Mostly." This time his smile was all temptation.

The door swished open behind them. Four of her students walked in. The panties got tucked back into his jean pocket. He looked back at the students. "I guess I'd better run."

"Yeah." The thought of ending this embarrassing moment suited her just fine. However, the man still had her panties in his pocket.

He offered her a smile, one invisible but for the crinkle at one corner of his lips. He paused and then took off for the door.

She watched him leave—with her underwear.

But he didn't get far. He stopped at the door—stood there, one second, two seconds, three.

Don't stop now. Don't stop now.

Turning around, he came right back to her. Each heavy-gaited step he took spoke of purpose—like he walked to the counter at the coffee shop—like a man who owned the room. Like he could own anything he wanted.

His heated expression said he wanted her.

And what woman wouldn't be thrilled at that thought? The memory of his hand on her calf flashed in her head, the memory of the sweet thrill that simple touch had caused. For one short, inappropriate second, she considered how his touch would feel other places. Her heart rate picked up speed. Okay, so there went her scruples.

He came all the way around the desk and stopped directly in front of her. "Have dinner with me tonight." The low rumble in his voice echoed in her chest.

He stood closer than before—not touching, but close enough that she could feel his words brush against her temple, feel his body heat. Feel her own body heat.

He leaned in a breath nearer. The want in his eyes had her holding her breath. "Say yes."

"Isn't that... against the rules?"

He brushed the back of his fingers over his jaw line. The tingle shot right to her breasts, beading her nipples. "I've never been much of a rule follower. Not even my own."

"So you don't think it would be a good idea, either?"

He paused. And that pause said something. She just wasn't reading what it was. A bad breakup? Or was it something worse?

The question tumbled out of her mouth before she knew she planned to ask it. "Do you still think I'm crazy?"

His hesitation vanished and his grin teased her better senses. "That depends on your answer."

She breathed in his scent again. Musky. Male. Too male. A little too self-confident. Ahh, but he wore the arrogance well. "So if I don't go out with you, I'm crazy?"

His right eyebrow arched ever so slightly. His blue eyes twinkled with something playful, something sweet, something she needed more of in her life.

"Actually, I was thinking you'd be crazy if you did." He hesitated as if gathering words. "My message last night, it came out wrong. I didn't mean... I'm sorry."

A slight forgive-me smile almost reached his eyes when he brushed a strand of hair off her cheek and behind her ear. His two fingers lingered there. Her pulse fluttered against his touch.

The apology—or maybe his touch—kicked her scruples to the other side of the room. Desire, want, and need washed over her. She wanted to feel his lips on hers—to have his arms around her. How would it feel to have someone that strong to lean on? Someone that strong to believe in her?

The students behind him started chatting.

Mark's blue eyes darkened with raw heat. "Can I call you later to set it up?"

A thousand reasons she should say no flashed neon in her mind. A thousand neon reasons she chose to ignore. "Okay."

* * *

Two o'clock that afternoon, Sheriff Adam Harper stopped his black-and-white in front of the white farmhouse about two miles outside of Pearlsville. He'd rather have taken the rest of the afternoon off and gone down to the local watering hole to call it the end of another boring day. But he'd given his word to Detective Sutton that he'd look into this. And while Adam might be the washed-up old sheriff of this Timbuktu county, he was a washed-up old sheriff of his word.

Plus, he'd heard TJ say he remembered all those Reed sisters he'd gone to school with being as pretty as their niece Jennifer, his receptionist. *Pretty as sweet apple pie*, TJ had said. And they were age appropriate. He found it odd that he didn't already know them. According to TJ, the Reed clan wasn't townspeople—sort of stuck to themselves.

Adam ran a hand through his thinning hair. He could use some apple pie in his life.

When Ella died five years before, he'd wanted to follow her to the hereafter. God knew he never dreamed of wanting another woman. Sure, he talked like a rounder, but he was a one-woman man. Losing Ella had sent him to a dark place that still haunted him sometimes.

He had one leg out the door when the voice of Rusty, his one and only deputy, echoed over the radio. "Sheriff? You still there?"

Dropping back into the seat, he picked up the mic. "What's up?"

"It's about the ol' Reed file you sent me to the pits of hell to find. Do you know they don't air-condition the basement of the courthouse? Do you know how hot it is?"

"You calling in a weather report, or did you find something?" His laugh evaporated in the hot car.

"Looks as if half the file is missing, but I got it."

"Anything interesting?" Adam stared out at the dogtrot-styled house. The home was probably a hundred years old but kept up. The flowerbeds were filled with color and care.

"Not much more than TJ told ya. It was Sheriff Carter who wrote the file. Girl came up missing on a camping trip at Anniston State Park. Supposedly, they'd been swimming in the lake earlier in the morning, and family thought she might have gone back there."

Rusty paused. "It says the lake was searched, but a body was never found. Since no one other than the family ever saw the girl at the park, Anniston PD asked Pearlsville PD to poke around."

Adam ran his hand over the steering wheel. "And what did Carter tell 'em?"

"That's the part that's missing. But considering there was actually a file on it, it seems something was suspected."

"Bring the file to the office. I'll look it over."

"Will do. Catch you in the morn, if I don't die of heat stroke first."

Adam set down his mic on the holder and crawled out of his car. As he stepped onto the dirt driveway, he saw a woman's face in the window. Before he could decide if TJ's description of the Reed women was right, the curtain fluttered back into place. Sucking in his gut, he continued to the porch.

His hand had been poised midair to knock when the door swung open. He'd been prepared for a slice of sweet apple pie. Instead, he came nose to nose with the barrel of what looked like a sawed-off shotgun.

CHAPTER EIGHT

N o!" A female's voice screamed from behind the woman holding Adam at gunpoint.

Taking advantage of the interruption, he snatched the weapon out of his assailant's hands.

Thankfully, it'd taken him only a second to realize the barrel shoved in his face wasn't a sawed-off shotgun but a sawed-off pellet gun. Not that he was altogether thrilled with the idea of having his face pumped with BBs. But it was a hell of a lot better than thinking his deputies would be sweeping pieces of his face off the front porch.

"What the hell are you doing?" he yelled at the gray-haired woman. If she didn't look frail, and if he hadn't been bred to be a gentleman, he'd have her eating the carpet right now.

"I'm sorry." The other woman, obviously the one he'd heard scream, rushed to the doorway. With one hand held over her heart, she put a protective arm around the older woman.

"Is she crazy?" he snapped. "I could have—"

"It's not a real gun," the sensible woman said in a sensible tone. "And yes...yes my sister suffers from mental illness. Please, I'm sorry."

Her sincere tone and sweet voice had his fury sobering. But the panic from seeing the gun pointed at his nose still fizzed in his head. He met the soft-spoken woman's blue eyes and took in her blond hair and attractive features. While the fine lines around her eyes put her in her fifties, her slender shape held a youthful appearance. And just like that, the thought that ran amok in his head was...*pretty as apple pie*. Taking a breath to chase away any remnants of his anger, he spoke. "I saw it wasn't a real gun. But—"

"I don't think it even has BBs in it." She patted the frail woman's shoulder, who stood there with an empty, permanently-out-to-lunch kind of look on her face. "Normally, Sarah wouldn't do this but our brother just died and—"

"JoAnne, if I'm going to get you back to Houston, you'd better get your things." A man, early sixties, medium height, walked into the room behind the two women. His gaze cut to Adam. "What's going on?"

The pretty woman turned. "Sarah met the officer at the door with Johnny's gun."

The man clenched his jaw. "Put her to bed." His tone sounded as if it might shatter. Inhaling, as if trying to control his emotions, he faced Adam. "Sorry, Sheriff. My sister's not...she's mentally challenged." His frown deepened. "My name's George Reed. I...I've been meaning to return your call, but we've had a death in the family."

Adam's leftover grief for his wife raised its head and left his chest feeling empty. "I understand about not returning the call. This"—he held up the gun—"is what I'm having trouble wrapping my head around."

"Would you like something to drink, Sheriff?" a singsong female voice interrupted.

Adam looked over George Reed's shoulder to see another woman in the doorway. She had the same blue eyes as the one who'd met him at the door, but she wore more makeup on her face than should have been legally allowed. Between the bright blue on her eyelids, the red on her lips, and the tight red dress—that should have been worn by someone half her age—she brought to mind the expression of "worn hard and put up wet."

"A glass of tea would be mighty nice," Adam said.

"Come into the kitchen." She turned and sashayed into the next room.

Adam saw George Reed's shoulders tense at the invitation, but he motioned Adam inside and took the gun from Adam's hand.

Adam followed the crowd into the large kitchen. Another woman, mid-fifties, brunette, sat at the table, her posture spoke of defeat. Of grief. He offered a polite nod.

Leaning against the counter was another middle-aged man who looked enough like George Reed to assume them to be brothers. A ceiling fan hung above the table, tossing around warm, bacon-scented air and filling the room with an electric hum of grief.

"This is Freida Reed." George pointed to the brunette. "My brother's widow. This is my younger brother, Sam. And my sister Doris Roberts." He pointed to the woman in red.

They nodded in a cordial but tense manner. Everyone but Doris. She shot him a smile as she moved—one hip at a time—carrying a glass of tea. The ice in the glass rattled as she moved. When she stopped in front of him, a smidgen too close, she held out the tea. Adam's next breath caught a whiff of liquor on her breath.

"Thank you." Another person walked into the room. It was the pretty woman. She had a small suitcase in her hands, and she propped it against the wall.

"My other sister," George added. "JoAnne Lakes."

A beat of silence filled the room and JoAnne asked, "Has anyone seen my phone?"

"Back porch," Sam answered. "I'll grab it for you."

"Did Sarah go down okay?" George asked.

"She's not asleep, but she's resting." Ms. Lakes turned her gaze on the sheriff. "I hope you won't hold my sister responsible for what happened."

Adam looked at the ice cubes floating in his glass. Everyone would laugh their asses off if he arrested anyone for holding him up with a BB gun. "Considering it's just a pellet gun, I can look the other way, but I recommend getting rid of it. Fake guns are supposed to have orange tips on them."

"It's my grandson's," Sam Reed spoke up, walking back into the room. "I'll take care of it."

"Good." Adam paused and awkwardness crowded the room. His mouth was dry. He sipped at the tea. The sound of the fan whirling grew louder in the beat of silence. "The reason I called and stopped by is because there's been some questions—"

"We know why you're here." Frieda Reed, the widow, lurched up from her chair. "Isn't it enough that we have to deal with my husband's death? Now you want to drag us down by reminding us of another tragedy?"

How did they know? Adam wondered.

George placed a hand on Frieda's shoulder and pushed her back in her chair. "What my sister-in-law is saying is that we're not certain why this is important. Why would the police want to bring this out now?"

Adam's gaze went from one face to the other. A mixture of emotions played across their expressions. Anger. Grief. Suspicion. The grief, he got. The anger? Yeah, he remembered the fury he'd carried around with him for months after the unexpected heart attack took his Ella. But the suspicion? That puzzled him.

The cold glass in his hands grew colder and so did the awkwardness in the room. "I'd think you'd want the case reopened if it brought the killer to justice."

"Jennifer said the detective who called was from Anniston," Doris Roberts snapped and scowled at her two brothers. "Is that true?"

By damn, Adam thought he'd made it clear when he spoke to Jenny. His department was just like Vegas— what happened there, stayed there. Now he'd need to call Sutton back and tell him his department had leaked info.

"We don't know anything," Ms. Lakes added, her tone no longer soft. "A lot of people live in Anniston."

"Stop it," George snapped, and took an angry step toward the two women.

Adam shot in front of him. "I think everyone needs to calm down," he said, not liking the way George Reed clenched and unclenched his fist.

Before he cemented his judgment in his mind, he recalled those weeks following Ella's death. Recalled the night he'd sat at the kitchen table staring at her picture. He could still feel the weight of the gun in his hand, the cold feel of his barrel pressed against his temple. If his daughter hadn't called... Grief made people crazy.

"Are you reopening this case?" Sam bit out.

"It depends what we learn. I was hoping you could fill me in about what happened."

Sam clenched the back of a kitchen chair so hard his knuckles turned white. "Either our niece was kidnapped by some lowlife motorcycle thug or she drowned in that lake. It was the cops' job to find out which. They never did their job then, and I can hardly believe that you'll do any better now."

Adam let the verbal dig roll off his back, but made a mental note of it. "We won't know until I've gotten all the facts in." He looked back at the door, which led to the bedroom where Sarah Reed slept. *Sarah?* Then he remembered Rusty said he thought the missing girl was the child of a mentally challenged woman. "Your sister Sarah, she's the mother of the child who came up missing?"

His question met dead silence. The fan's whirling became loud again.

"Did someone report something about the case?" the

pretty blonde asked in a tone that told him she wanted him to refute the fact.

"Sometimes they just reopen cases," Adam said and it was true. Sometimes they did. Just not this time.

"Well, we've already been through hell over this," George spoke again. "Is it necessary that we go through it again?"

Yeah it was. But the timing wasn't right. Adam sent JoAnne Lakes one last look. Of all of them in the room, she appeared the most normal. "I'll be back later."

Later, after he knew exactly what this friend of Detective Sutton's had to say, and after he'd read the file, then he'd return with his questions. But one thing was for sure. This family had secrets. He just didn't know if one of them was murder.

* * *

Annie arrived home that afternoon, bypassed her apartment, and went straight to Isabella's. Tiptoeing on this side of panic, Annie neglected to knock and just stormed in. Her friend, sitting on her sofa, bolted up.

"I'm an idiot!" Annie blurted out.

Isabella, hand over her heart, calmed immediately. "Why are you an idiot?"

"I agreed to go out with Mark Sutton. What the hell was I thinking?"

"Detective Sutton?" She squealed when Annie nodded. "Oh. Ahh. I think I know what you were thinking. I've seen him on TV." She smiled.

Annie plopped on her friend's sofa then covered her face with her hands. "He had my panties."

"What?"

Dropping her hands from her face, she looked at her friend. "I lost my panties in his car the day we went for coffee."

Isabella's eyes rounded. "I think you skipped that part when you told me the had-coffee-with-the-detective story."

"We didn't... The panties were in my purse when I tossed it in the backseat. They must have fallen out."

Isabella dropped onto the sofa and cracked up laughing again. "Seriously?"

Annie nodded. "I'm an idiot."

"Wait," Isabella said. "Is tonight a... I-found-your-panties kind of date, or is it a let's-talk-about-the-case date? Or is he even going to look into your missing cousin?"

"I think it's the panty kind of date." She exhaled. "But he did find out there was a missing Reed girl."

"Shit," Isabella said. "So it's true, you really saw your cousin being buried?"

Annie sat up, emotions taking laps around her heart. "All he knows is there is a missing girl. He's looking into it."

Isabella reached over and squeezed Annie's shoulder. "Are you okay?"

Her sinuses stung. "No. I'm an idiot, remember? What am I going to do? I'm not ready for this. Not for a relationship and not... My mom is going to kill me when she hears what I've done!"

"No. When she learns what you saw, she'll understand." Her friend got a worried look on her face. "You don't think that... that she's behind this, too, do you?"

"No," Annie said. Except why did the entire family pretend Jenny never existed? Was that why her dad moved them away? Why he wouldn't allow her to ever see the Reeds? Did both her mother and father look the other way and let someone get away with murder? Didn't that make them both as guilty as the one who did it?

Isabella appeared puzzled. "Have you talked to her since the funeral?"

"No. I'm afraid she's upset. I figure when she comes for the car, we'll talk."

"So she's still with her family?"

"Yeah. I'm sure she'll come home soon. She volunteers at the hospital every Friday."

A heavy silence filled the room. "Wait," Isabella said as if she could see Annie sliding into a dark place. "Let's stop thinking about the bad part and go back to the good part. The date."

Annie shook her head. "I told you that's not good, either. I'm not ready."

"Hey, you said yes. So there's a part of you that's ready."

"Or maybe I'm just horny." Annie hated saying it, but there it was. Since she'd laid eyes on the hot cop, she'd started missing things. She missed being touched. Missed feeling protected and pretty, wanted, and a little wild. Missed sleeping on a man's shoulder. Feeling him on top of her, inside her.

"Oh, God. That's it. I'm just horny."

"So. You're going to beat yourself up over that? You're human. Half the population is horny. I'm horny."

"I'm scared," Annie countered.

"Which is also part of being human," Isabella said. "You want a glass of wine?"

"Right. Get me drunk, then send me off on a date."

Her friend laughed. "What time is he showing up?"

"Seven."

Isabella grabbed her phone to check the time. "It's six. Go get ready."

"Yeah." Annie stood up.

"Wait. I have something for you." She took off down the hall. Returning, she placed an object in her hand.

Annie rolled her eyes when she saw it was a condom packet. "I'm not sleeping with him."

"Just in case." Isabella smiled.

"You're terrible."

"You deserve some fun."

"What about you. How long have you had this and haven't used it?"

Isabella pushed her toward the door. "Go get beautiful. And enjoy yourself. I'm going to my aunt's in Malcomb for the night, but I expect all the dirty little details tomorrow afternoon."

Isabella was still hanging on the doorjamb when Annie's phone rang.

"Maybe it's him canceling." She answered without checking the number. "Hello."

"Shut up bitch! Keep your mouth shut!" the voice said. Then the line went dead.

"Shit," Annie said.

"What?" Isabella asked.

"Someone knows."

"Knows what?"

"That I went to the police. How could they know?"

* * *

Mark pulled into a parking spot at Annie's apartment. He turned his engine off, cut his gaze to his car clock, and slowly slid his hands over the steering wheel. Seven on the dot.

When he'd spoken to Annie this afternoon, he'd told her he'd be here between seven and seven fifteen. Which meant arriving right at seven made him look eager.

But he *was* eager. And leery.

The Talbot case was gnawing at his sanity. And in spite of the fact that Annie's case would carry the same bite, and that now wasn't the time to jump into a relationship, Annie Lakes had turned into a welcome distraction.

Instead of wanting a shot of Jack Daniels, he wanted a shot with Annie.

He reached into his jeans pocket and pulled out the slinky pair of black panties. After the expression on Annie's face when she'd seen the underwear, he knew the panties hadn't been left on purpose.

Still, he kept the slip of silk in his pocket all afternoon. A dangling carrot. Only he wanted Annie in them. Then, he wanted Annie out of them. He ran his thumb over the silk, letting his mind go there.

Anticipation made his blood rush, and an extra supply pumped straight to his groin. Seriously, how long had it been since he'd wanted anything or anyone with this vigor? A long time.

And for a good reason, his conscience stabbed back. Between work and fighting his demons, a real relationship took energy he wasn't sure he had. But today, standing that close to her, he felt energetic enough to take the risk.

This afternoon, while Mildred searched for the missing file about Jenny Reed, unsuccessfully as of five o'clock, he'd chased Johnny Cash leads—leads that led him nowhere. Normally, he'd have been frustrated to the hilt, but instead he channeled that energy. He even indulged in a few Annie fantasies, her standing before him minus some clothes and with a smile. Oh, Mark was no fool. He knew first dates didn't usually end the way he'd like them to.

Not that the idea of just spending some time with her was a bad thing. Annie Lakes intrigued him. She had spunk and smarts. She came across as someone who could actually have a conversation about something other than herself. Unlike Judith Holt.

One deep breath later, he went to stick her panties back in his pocket, intending to return them. Suddenly, the idea of parting with his new touchstone didn't sit well. Leaning over, he tucked the underwear under a map in the glove compartment. If she asked for them, he'd hand them over, if she didn't . . . maybe just keeping them would give him patience until he got Annie to a place their clothes could come off.

He got out of his car. It took a second to find the number on the apartment buildings and then, with an anticipation he hadn't felt in too damn long, he headed that way.

Before he got out of the parking lot, his phone rang. He considered not answering, but he didn't want a missed call messing with his head tonight.

"Sutton," he said, none too friendly when he realized he hadn't checked the number.

"Detective Sutton?" a male voice asked.

"Yeah?"

"This is Don Blount. You left a message and asked me to call."

Blount? It took a second to connect the dots. Blount, Annie's missing cousin's ex. Mark stopped. "Yes. I'm...uh, trying to reach Fran Roberts, your ex-wife, and thought you might be able to tell me how I could find her."

"Is she in some kind of trouble?" the man asked.

"I just have a few questions."

The man paused. "I don't know where she is."

Mark tried to read the man's tone, not sure what emotion hinged on his words.

A sigh echoed across the line. "Fran isn't what you'd call dependable, but..."

"But what?" Mark looked around to find the stairs leading to the second floor, to Annie's apartment.

"The last time she called was Sunday. Kept saying something about someone wanting to shut her up. She sounded drunk. I was in a bad mood and yelled at her about what kind of mother she was. When she didn't call the next day, I thought...she was mad. I called her back but she wouldn't pick up. I started getting calls from everyone looking for her. And now you...the police."

Mark absorbed what the man said and got his questions lined up. "Does she call often?"

"Every day to talk to our daughter." Concern deepened his voice. "She's not really a terrible mother."

"Who's been calling for her?"

"Her mom, her aunt Karen, then another aunt, and some cousin I've never heard about. And let me tell you, look up *dysfunctional family* and you'll see Fran's family portrait there. Oh, and then some man who didn't leave his name. I even went to see the guy she's living with. He said he hasn't seen her in a week since she went to her uncle's funeral." Blount paused and so did Mark.

Standing at the bottom of the staircase, he got an itchy feeling he always got when a case went bad. "Can you text me those telephone numbers?"

"Yeah. What's really going on, Mr. Sutton?" The concern in his voice rose a notch. The man's question pulled at Mark's gut. "Has something happened to my ex-wife?"

CHAPTER NINE

I don't know," Mark said. "But don't think the worst until we know something." Thinking the worst was *his* job. Had something happened to Fran Roberts because she knew too much about their missing cousin? And if so, did that mean Annie could be next? "Has anyone made a Missing Persons report?"

"Not that I know of. Should I?"

"Yeah." He looked up and saw the door to Annie's apartment. "Do it ASAP. I'll call Austin PD tomorrow and back it up with my concerns. Look, I have other questions, but I'm in the middle of something."

"Sure. But if you find out anything..." His voice cracked. "I still love her. I shouldn't, but I do."

"I understand." His line beeped with another incoming call. Damn, he hadn't gotten a call all day. "Tomorrow, then." He clicked over to the other call. "Sutton."

"Bad time?" someone asked. A male someone.

It took a second to recognize Sheriff Harper's voice.

"I got a minute. But just one. What's up?"

"You're not going to like this," the sheriff said.

* * *

Annie dropped down on the sofa. Pirate jumped up in her lap. She gave him two good scrubs under his chin then popped up. Antsy. Nervous. Certain this was a bad idea.

"Sorry," she said to her cat, who meowed as if rejected.

Annie did two laps around her living room then looked at the clock. Seven fifteen. Maybe he wasn't going to show? That'd work.

Then again, she wanted him to come so she could tell him about the call. *Shut up bitch! Keep your mouth shut!* The words echoed in her head and settled in the pit of her stomach.

She'd checked the number. Didn't recognize it, but the prefix numbers were from Pearlsville.

A knock sounded at her door. She inhaled, stiffened her shoulders, and went to answer it.

For good measure, she pressed her eye against the peephole. All she really saw was a chest and a pair of arms. Wide chest. Strong arms that could hold her. She could use a holding right now. It was the detective for sure.

She opened the door. *Keep it casual.*

His expression went from his normal slightly tense look to something else. Something softer, sweeter, sexy. The pin-striped shirt fit him to a tee, ditto on the jeans.

She'd never seen him in jeans. He always wore dress pants. He did jeans justice.

"You wore pink for me." His voice held husky, sensual tones that sounded like bedroom talk.

Her gaze shot down to her pink blouse. Crap. She'd forgotten he told her he liked pink.

When she glanced up, he laughed. It was deep and refreshing like a soft rain on a hot day. The kind of rain kids liked to dance in. The kind she'd like to dance in. But there was something about the sound...it came out rusty, as if he hadn't laughed in a long time.

"I can tell by your expression you didn't wear it for me."

"No, I...just..." She stopped.

"Don't worry. I know I'm an acquired taste. I'll win you over."

Almost drunk on his woodsy, clean scent, she smiled and a feeling, a good feeling of anticipation, curled up inside her.

"And how do you plan on doing that?" No sooner than the almost-suggestive words slipped off her lips did she wish she could suck them back in. This was not keeping it casual.

"I'm still working on my plan," he said.

He looked at her as if she was a small, delectable appetizer he didn't want to share.

It had been a long time since she'd cared if a man noticed her. A long time since she'd noticed how a man smelled, and forever since a man's laugh had turned her insides to the consistency of grits. Warm, buttered grits.

"You ready?" His question had her realizing she was staring.

"I just need to . . . to grab my purse."

* * *

Mark's gaze had followed her down the hall. She looked good in that khaki skirt and sleeveless pink blouse. Not too dressed up. Not too dressed down. With a lot of smooth skin showing. He liked skin.

Slipping his hand into his pocket, he missed his silky touchstone. With thoughts of silk, his mind went to her hair that appeared soft, wispy, and touchable. Every inch of her looked touchable. He allowed himself the fantasy of following her into her bedroom. Taking off that pink blouse and khaki skirt and whatever pair of silky underwear she wore. Envisioned laying her back on her bed and tasting every soft inch of her.

He ran a hand over his face. "Slow down."

He gazed around the room, doing a rundown on Annie's place. Homey, comfortable, feminine but not the froufrou design that made a man feel out of place. Warm, womanly scents filled the air, a candle or flowers. Inhaling, he caught traces of freshly showered woman.

The living room was neat, not perfect. A couple magazines and some junk mail lay tossed on the chest-like coffee table. A pair of tennis shoes and socks sat beside the gold sofa. Two colorful throw pillows rested against the back of the sofa, but they weren't the frilly kind that made a man think he couldn't sit down for fear of messing them up. Things matched, but the decor didn't appear stark, stiff, too perfect to use, like Judith Holt's condo. This place looked as if a real person lived here.

Spotting the bookshelves lining one wall, he moved in to check out her reading material. Being a college English teacher, he figured her to be a classics reader. *Romeo and Juliet*. His gaze scanned the titles. There were classics, but not the ones he expected. *Charlotte's Web*, *The Secret Garden*, *A Wrinkle in Time*, and Dr. Seuss books.

He ran his fingers across the book spines. He loved to read, but he didn't get a lot of time to do it. Or maybe his mind was just too wound up on murder to enjoy it anymore.

On the second shelf, he found some contemporary material: a few romance novels, mysteries, and some self-help books. He read the title of one. *How to Leave the Past in the Past*. He recalled the haunted look he sometimes spotted in her eyes. So he'd been right. Like him, she was running from something.

There was also a framed photograph. A young Annie, nine or ten, with her parents.

Picking up the image, he studied it. The threesome sat on a park bench, with Annie between her two parents. She had her head resting on her father's arm. If proximity said anything, she was closer to her dad than her mom.

He remembered Annie telling him that her father had recently died. Had Annie suffered from the loss? Not that Mark would understand the relationship between a father and a child.

He didn't remember his dad. Even his relationship with his mom hadn't been flawless. When he was young, she worked too hard, too many hours, her free time divided between him and whatever man she had attached to her hip.

When she married his stepdad, things looked up. She became more of a mom. But then the bastard took it all away.

Pushing the past away, he studied Annie's mother in the picture. Had Annie spoken to her about what she remembered yet? How bad was Annie's relationship with the woman? The sheriff said the family came off odd, dysfunctional. He recalled Annie telling him his father had refused to let her have anything to do with the Reeds. Looked as if her father was a smart man.

As he replaced the image back on the shelf, his mind flipped to the phone call from Mr. Blount.

He needed to talk to Annie about the call, but selfishly, he didn't want this date to be all about the case. Probably best to get it out of the way. Maybe before they left, too.

He turned around and his gaze was drawn to the bar separating the living room and the kitchen. A wine rack held six bottles of wine. All reds. Good taste.

Opposite the kitchen was a breakfast area with a small round table, and centering that table was a vase of flowers. Not just flowers.

Roses. Red.

The kind a man sent a woman when he sought forgiveness, or attempted to make a statement about his feelings.

Damn. Even as a kid, Mark had never liked playing with some other guy's toys.

"You ready?"

Mark turned around. Annie stood by the sofa. Nope, he wasn't the sharing kind.

"Yeah." He moved closer itching to ask about the flowers, but a bigger itch was his desire to touch her. "Did I tell you how nice you look?"

She toyed with her purse strap. He remembered her doing that the first day. "Thank you."

Right then he saw an orange flash leap up on the arm of the sofa. A cat. The feline dipped its head and stretched toward him as if wanting Mark's attention. He didn't adore cats or hate them. He reached to give the cat what it wanted, but then he got a good look at the animal.

"Jeezus. What happened to him?" He took a step back.

Annie dropped her purse on the sofa and scooped the cat in her arms. "Sorry," she said and he thought she was talking to him, but no, she pulled the one-eyed, three-legged, scarred animal up to her breasts. "He didn't mean to react that way, Pirate," she cooed.

"I didn't. But it's just...Seriously, what happened to him?"

"He got into a tussle with a Bronco." She rubbed her fingers under the cat's face and cooed at her pet. "And you won, didn't you, Sweetie?"

"I'd hate to see the horse," Mark said.

Annie gazed up. "The four-wheeled kind. The lady at the shelter actually saw it happen."

"Why didn't she just have him put down?"

Annie pursed her lips. "Would you want to be put down just because you lost an eye and a foot?"

He ducked his head to one side and gave Pirate a quick glance below. "I would if on top of all that, you neutered me."

Annie laughed. The soft, bell-like sound filling his ears and chest should be heard in Disney movies. Sweet, pure. Yet alluring as hell. Damn if that wasn't better than any whiskey he'd ever had.

"I didn't have it done, they did," she said.

"How did you end up with him?"

"I volunteered at the vet sometimes. When they had a really sick animal, I'd come in on Sundays and give them some attention. Pirate took to me. And I to him."

So she was either a sucker or a lover of the underdog. And she volunteered to take care of sick animals. Her halo was showing. She might just be too good for him.

The cat stretched out his paw to Mark. He touched the cat's good side of his face.

"See, he likes you," she said.

"He just doesn't know me."

"And what are your deep, dark secrets?" Her tone held tease, but her expression seemed serious.

"That's not first-date material." He offered up a smile.

She set the cat down. "Should we go?"

He started to say yes, but his gaze moved to her mouth. If she had lipstick on, it was a natural color. "Uh, there are a couple of things I'd like to get out of the way."

"What?"

"One, I got some phone calls today."

"Me too," she said as if she'd just remembered. Fear flashed across her face and somehow landed in his gut.

"Who?"

"I don't know, but it had the prefix numbers from Pearlsville."

"What did they say?"

Her shoulders tightened. "'Shut up, bitch.'"

Shit. "Male? Female?" he asked.

"I don't know. It was muffled, as if someone had their hand over the phone."

He frowned. "Do you have the number?"

"It's in my phone. And I wrote it down." She moved past him into the kitchen, grabbed a Post-it note, and handed it to him.

"Give me one minute." He called David, a detective who worked the night shift and was good at running things down. He gave him the numbers that Annie and Donald Blount had texted him, and requested David look into it. "Oh, and put a trace on this cell phone," he added, giving him Fran's number. He felt Annie watching him and listening. When he hung up, he looked at her. "Done."

She nodded.

He hesitated, but needed to ask. "Have you spoken with your mom yet?"

She shook her head as if saying it aloud would somehow hurt. "I'm going to call her," she offered.

"Why do you think she hasn't called you?"

"I don't know." He saw it then. She wasn't just

frightened of her mom. She felt abandoned. Damn if Mark hadn't faced that demon himself.

Not good with words, he stood there hoping when this was done, her mom wasn't somehow responsible for the murder.

He recalled the awkward hug he'd given Bethany Talbot. The temptation to reach for Annie was strong. He didn't even think it'd be awkward.

She tilted her chin up as if trying to hide the vulnerability he saw in her eyes. "How would they know I'm talking?"

"The sheriff, Adam Harper, has gone out to ask a few questions," he said. "And ... your cousin works at the police station."

"So everything I told you they know."

"No, just that an Anniston detective is looking into the case."

She closed her eyes a minute. "What were your calls about?"

"One from Sheriff Harper and one from Donald Blount."

"Fran's ex?" she asked.

"Yeah."

"Does he know where Fran is?"

"No and he said she always calls her daughter every day, but hasn't since she went to the funeral."

Annie caught her breath. "Do you think something happened to her?"

"I don't know. Blount agreed to file a Missing Persons report in Austin. In the morning, I plan on calling to follow up. Tomorrow Sheriff Harper plans to go back to visit the Reeds and ask about Fran Roberts."

She hugged herself. "I don't like this."

"I know. But I'm looking into it."

She nodded. "I appreciate that."

"I know that, too." And he did.

The few beats of silence seemed to push that conversation away. "We should go," she said.

They started moving to the door when she stopped and faced him. She was so close her scent filled his air.

"Wait. You said you had a couple of things to get out of the way. What was the other?"

"This." He leaned down and kissed her.

He intended the kiss to be short and sweet. An appetizer for what he hoped to indulge in later, but the second his lips brushed hers, the short part of the equation got lost in the sweet part.

Then sweet turned into heat. She shifted closer. He turned slightly so his shoulder holster and gun wouldn't get in the way. Then the amazing softness of her breasts pressed against his chest. His right hand shifted up to her neck, where his fingers met up with the silk of her hair. His left hand went to her waist. Finding and easing into her soft curve.

Her tongue slipping between his lips was all the invite he needed to let his own explore. Sweet bypassed heat and shot straight to hot.

Want and desire tightened his southern regions and had his hands itching to explore some too. When the idea to lift her skirt and push her against the wall crossed his mind, he pulled back, caught his breath, and yanked his libido to this side of sanity.

He waited for her to open her eyes.

Her lashes fluttered open. She appeared dazed, then embarrassed. She inched back, breaking the feel of her body against his.

"The first kiss is usually awkward." He looked at her wet lips. "Getting it out the way is best. But that wasn't awkward."

"Yeah. No. I was...I mean...We should go." She motioned toward the door.

Her inability to string a sentence together told him a lot. So did the little voice in his head warning him that he might like her too much.

CHAPTER TEN

Smokey scents of grilled meat filled Buck's Place restaurant, and Annie breathed it all in as she dropped into the chair across from Mark.

The ride over here had been uncomfortable. She couldn't move past the kiss. Or rather her reaction to it. One kiss and she was practically his for the taking. Since when . . .

"They serve just about anything, lots of Cajun dishes, but their barbeque is the house specialty." He frowned over his menu at her. "Don't tell me you're vegetarian."

She forced a smile. "No. My mouth's watering."

"I've never been disappointed with the food," he added. Their gazes met across the table and held.

"Speaking of my food." A barrel-chested man who spoke with a slight Cajun accent stopped at their table, holding a bowl. "I was leaving when someone said you were here. I've been waiting for you to come in. This"—he set a small bowl on their table—"is my new barbeque sauce and I want your opinion."

Mark dropped his menu. "Buck Bradley, this is Annie Lakes. Buck's the owner and chef."

"Nice to meet you," Annie said.

Buck looked back at Mark. "You always do know how to pick the pretty ones. Now try my sauce."

"Why mess with perfection?" Mark said. "Your sauce is the best."

"This is better." Buck looked at Annie. "Mark's a sauce expert. Did he tell you him and couple of buddies took second place at this year's Rodeo cook-off?"

Annie glanced at Mark. "No, he didn't."

Buck reared back on his heels. "Not that he'd tell me their secret ingredient."

"I told you, give me your secret ingredient and I'd give you mine." Mark picked up a spoon and dipped it into the sauce and tasted it. He grinned. "Okay, you win. This is better. Is that whiskey I'm tasting?"

"I'll never tell, but I knew you'd like it." Buck grinned. "You two enjoy your dinner. Dessert's on the house. And we've got a band starting soon. Hang around and enjoy the music." He looked at Annie again. "Make this bum dance with you. He has enough Cajun in him he should know a few moves."

When Buck left, Annie looked at Mark. "You're Cajun?"

"Mom was." He glanced back at the menu.

"Your parents live here?" She realized how little she knew about the man she'd have gone to bed with if he hadn't stopped the kiss. Admitting that took a swing at her moral compass, but denying it wouldn't have helped.

"No." His focus cut back to the menu. "I recommend the sliced beef dinner."

"Hmm," she said, before she could stop it.

His gaze rose. "Hmm, what?"

"Hmm, you're trying to change the subject."

He hesitated, then dropped his menu down. "Both my parents are dead."

A flutter of empathy filled her chest. "I'm sorry."

"It was a long time ago." His words sounded indifferent, but she'd bet the pain wasn't.

"Yeah, but sometimes it doesn't feel that way. I miss my dad like he died last week." She almost ask how his parents had died, but instinct told her not to push. Since she had her own unapproachable issues, she had to respect his.

He looked up. "I saw the picture on your bookshelf. It looked like you were close to him even as a kid."

"Okay, I confess. I was a daddy's girl."

'That's not a bad thing," Mark settled back in his chair. "What did your father do for a living?"

"He was a teacher."

"College?" He sounded genuinely curious.

Annie reached for her napkin and stopped before she started fidgeting. "He taught English, elementary school. And he was also choir minister."

"Explains your book collections and your halo."

"What?"

He grinned. "I checked out your books. A lot of children's classics."

"And the halo?"

"Volunteering to take care of sick animals. Taking in a mangled cat."

"I don't wear a halo. And Pirate's beautiful."

He smiled. "I guess beauty really is in the eye of the beholder."

And the way he looked at her made her feel beautiful. How long had it been since she'd even entertained that thought? "You don't have any pets?"

"I do. His name is Bacon. Seventy-five pounds of yellow Lab."

She grinned. "You named your dog Bacon?"

"We're both fond of it?"

"Hmm, dog person," she said with tease.

"Cat person," he countered and pointed at her with his spoon.

They laughed. "Back to good deeds," she said. "You've got your own halo going on."

"Me? You got me mixed up with someone else." The way he said it hinted that he really didn't see himself as a good person. For some reason that bothered her.

"Really? How many coffees have you bought for people? Your 'good deed for the day.'"

"It's five bucks."

"It's an act of kindness."

He leaned back in his chair and his smile, a little crooked and a lot sexy, came on slow. "So you've been checking me out."

Luckily, the waitress sauntered over and his sexually charged expression faded. But she had a feeling it would bounce back. And she needed to figure out how to handle it.

They both ordered sliced beef dinners. Mark handed her the smaller menu left on the table. "Since we both like red wine, why don't you pick out a bottle?"

"How do you know..."

"I checked out your wine rack."

"Oh." She ordered the wine. When the waitress left, Annie said, "You learned a lot about me in the short time you were in my apartment."

"Part of being a cop. And"—his voice deepened and lowered—"part of being a man interested in a woman."

Yup, it was bouncing back.

His phone rang, and he checked the number. "Excuse me."

Annie tried not to listen, but she did. "Yeah? That's quick." Pause. "Wait. They still exist?" Pause. "What about the others?" Pause. "Okay, thanks."

He hung up. "The number that called you is a pay phone in Pearlsville."

"So, it doesn't help us?"

"It might. David said it's downtown. I'll call the sheriff tomorrow and see if there are any cameras in the area. I also had David run down some numbers of the people who'd called Fran's ex looking for her."

"And?"

"You, her mom, your mom, and your uncle Allen."

Annie let that sink in. "So if they are looking for her, then it means that they aren't responsible for her disappearance, right?"

He brushed a palm over his chin. "It'd seem that way."

She heard uncertainty in his voice. "But you don't believe it."

"It's not...I've just seen too many cases where the person responsible for a missing person pretends to be looking for them." He hesitated. "I also had them check on Fran's cell phone. It's been turned off since Sunday afternoon."

She got a bad feeling. "You think something has happened to her?"

"I don't know. Her ex was clear that she does behave erratically sometimes. I wouldn't start thinking the worst until we know more."

The wine and their food came quickly. While they ate, she asked about the barbeque cook-off contest.

He told her about him and his partners in the Cold Case Unit entering the contest almost as a joke. "It was something to do. We never really expected to win. I mean, I have a nice smoker and enjoy cooking, but I'm far from an expert. Actually, I'm a jack of a lot of trades and not an expert in any."

"Yet the news media sings your praises with your ability to close cases."

He shrugged.

"That's a talent," she said.

"Not unless you consider not trusting someone a talent."

His words hit hard and she recalled he hadn't trusted her at first. She wasn't altogether sure he did now.

He stared down at his wine as if he knew he'd said the wrong thing. "What do you do when you're not at the college or the coffee shop?"

She picked up her glass. "I like to read. I'm a regular patron at the local library. I'm going to start volunteering at an animal shelter here next month, and for the record that doesn't constitute halo status. Oh, I jog. Not because I love it, but because I love wine and have to offset my wine calorie intake."

He grinned. "It's working. You look great."

The compliment was warm and welcome. "And you?"

"I don't know. Do I look great?"

She chuckled. "I meant what do you do when you're not solving crimes or at the coffee shop?" When he didn't answer right away she lifted a brow. "You can't ask me questions you don't want to answer."

"I didn't know there were rules."

She lifted a brow.

"I'm answering," he said. "Just getting my ducks in a row. I like to read, but don't do it because I work too many hours. Don't volunteer for anything. I like music. Jazz. I know it's not trendy, but I like it. I play poker twice a month with some of the guys at the precinct. I also run, with Bacon. I don't love it, but Bacon does. I like to fish, but I don't do it often because—"

"—you work too many hours," she finished for him.

"See, you already have me figured out."

She recalled the dark shades he wore. "I think I've only scratched the surface."

"The best part is the surface." An undertone of seriousness laced his words.

And damn if she didn't know what he meant. She didn't like the idea of him discovering below the surface stuff, either. Especially since he already had a hard time believing her. And there it was: a good reason not to let this thing go anywhere. She needed to remember that.

"So why do you work so many hours?" she asked.

"It's the job."

"You're required to work too much."

"Not...Okay, maybe I like catching bad guys."

After eating less than half of her food, she stopped the waitress and asked for a takeout container.

"So tell me about the job." She sipped her water.

He hesitated. Was he dodging the question? No. He shared the story about the first case he'd worked as a homicide detective. A fisherman had spotted a body, panicked, and ran to call the police. After he and other cops spent two hours mucking through the muddy banks of the lake in hundred-degree weather, they found a mannequin.

He made it sound intense, interesting, and then funny. He was easy to listen to, easy to talk to. Easy to kiss.

The waitress cleaned their table, and he poured the rest of the wine in her glass. Wine she wasn't drinking. She needed her scruples intact.

"I'm going to have to run five times this week," she said.

"Make that six. The dessert is on the house, remember?"

"Oh, but I can't eat another bite."

The waitress walked up. "Can we have two Better Than Sex Cheesecakes to go?"

Annie nearly choked on her water when she heard him. The waitress chuckled and walked off.

Mark grinned. "You can eat it later, but you can't pass this up. It's worth jogging for." His smile deepened. His gaze heated. "Not that I agree with the name."

His gaze shifted to her mouth as if he was thinking of the kiss.

She was thinking about that kiss, too, and she was losing the war. Reaching for her purse hanging on the chair, she pulled out a credit card.

"No," he said. "I invited you to dinner."

"Thank you, then." She replaced her card, slung her purse over her shoulder, and looked around for the restrooms. "I'll be right back."

In the bathroom, she dug into her purse looking for her lipstick and her powder, but what she really needed to find was her willpower.

But nope. She obviously hadn't brought that with her.

* * *

Mark had watched the soft sway of her hips as she moved toward the restrooms. And while she'd disappeared behind the door, he kept seeing it. Feeling it stir up anticipation.

The sexy sound of a saxophone suddenly filled the air. The bluesy tune with Cajun influence added a new burn to his libido. This was the kind of music Mark liked to make love to. The kind of music he'd like to listen to tonight while feeding her cheesecake and taking off her clothes.

Turning to the right, trying to turn his thoughts off, he caught a glimpse of the three-man band. He watched the dark-skinned man on center stage sway as he practically made love to his instrument. Mark remembered that feeling from his early teens. His band teacher had sworn Mark had natural talent. The love of music was another thing he lost when he lost his sister.

His gaze caught on the saxophone. He had almost the same one at home. He'd bought it on a whim as a gift to himself when he graduated college. He'd never played it. At the time, he swore when his life got less complicated, he'd pick it up and see if he could still feel that magic.

But his life never got less complicated.

Yet tonight hadn't felt complicated at all. He could use more nights like this. More of Annie.

The music flowed and he felt it in his soul. His appreciation for all things Cajun sometimes made him wonder if he wasn't trying to hold on to roots that might be best dug up and left to die. But everyone needed something to hold on to, didn't they?

As long as they didn't count on it. He'd learned that the hard way.

The chair beside him scratched across the floor as someone pulled it out. He turned around to face Annie. "Hey..." The rest of his words sat on his tongue. Unspoken.

It wasn't Annie.

Judith Holt lowered her size three ass in Annie's chair, picked up Annie's wineglass, and downed the rest of the wine.

"What the hell are you doing?" Fury leaked from his tone.

"What are you doing bringing a date to our restaurant?"

"This isn't *our* restaurant. It's *my* restaurant. I brought you here twice."

"Forget that. Why don't you give me a scoop on the Talbot case, and I'll leave before I ruin your date."

He leaned forward. Ultimatums always did rub him the wrong way. "Read my lips, Judith. You'll never get another lead from me. And if you steal another one, I'll make it my life's work to put you behind bars for it."

She tilted her head to the side. "You know, you're a piece of work. What made you like this?"

"Women like you didn't help."

The waitress came over with the bagged desserts. He grabbed Annie's leftovers and stood, handed the waitress his card, and took the desserts.

Looking up, he saw Annie walking toward him. He met her halfway across the room.

"You ready?" he asked, unable to control the tone of his voice.

He saw her look over at Judith Holt sitting in what had been her chair.

"Yeah." She sounded unsure.

He walked her to the front of the restaurant then stopped. "Let me get my credit card."

She nodded. He turned but saw Judith walking toward them. He swung back around and put his hand on Annie's lower back and guided her out.

He'd get his card later.

When they got into his car, he looked at Annie. "I'm sorry. That was—"

"I know who she is. I've seen her on the news."

He started the car. A screwed-up silence filled the air,

and it took everything he had not to slam his palms on the steering wheel.

He felt Annie looking at him. "Are you and her—"

"No," he snapped. "She wants a lead on the story I'm working on."

It wasn't a lie. They weren't anything. Not anymore. But it wasn't exactly the truth. And the almost lie hung between them.

He stopped at a red light. "We used to date. Not anymore."

"And she doesn't want it to be over?" she asked cautiously.

"That's not it. She really just wants a lead. We haven't gone out in over five months." Their gazes met. Hers suspicious, his pleading. "All she wants is a lead."

"Okay."

But it wasn't okay. The feel-good mood they'd found seemed lost. Fuck Judith Holt! She'd done exactly what she'd threatened to do. Ruin his date.

He pulled up in Annie's parking lot and turned off the engine. The western sky still held a hint of color, the street lights buzzed overhead spitting out wattage.

She faced him. "It was a nice evening."

He exhaled. "It was until a few minutes ago. I don't want..." His gaze lifted past her out the window and he saw... "Shit!"

"Don't want what?" she asked.

"Isn't that your car?"

CHAPTER ELEVEN

Oh, God," Annie said when she saw *Shut up, bitch* spray-painted in bright red across her driver's door. Chills ran like tiny spiders down her spine.

She grabbed for the door handle, he grabbed her arm. "Stay here." He reached into his shirt and pulled out a gun.

Her breath caught. He'd had a gun on him the whole time.

"It's going to be alright," he said.

No, it wasn't! He had a gun. And someone had...

Pressing a hand above her left breast where her heart thudded against her chest bone, she watched Mark exit the car. He held the gun out, looking left then right. Looking like a cop ready to shoot someone. Someone who was part of her mother's family. Someone her mom loved.

Oh, God, don't shoot anyone!

He eased up to the car. She bolted out.

Swinging around, he frowned. "I said—"

"Don't shoot anyone."

"Get back in the car while I check out your apartment?"

Panic shot through her. "Pirate!" She took off running, her purse hanging off her shoulder bounced against her side.

"Annie, stop!" The thumping of his feet against the pavement sounded beside her.

She only ran faster. He shot forward and took the lead.

She took the steps up to her apartment two at a time. He was already at her door.

He caught her by the arm and pressed her against the wall. He leaned in, his cheek against hers. His breath, coming a little fast, feathered against her ear. "Your window is broken," he whispered. "Someone could still be in there. Give me your keys."

She gasped for air.

"Breathe," he said doing the same himself.

While she tried to feed her lungs oxygen, he slipped her purse off her shoulder, fumbling inside until he found her keys. "Now, go to the last door. There." He pointed down the balcony. "The last one. I'll tell you when it's safe."

"Pirate," she managed one word.

"I'll find him. Go stand where I told you. Understand?" His expression was firm, his words almost gentle, as if he knew she needed gentle. Her heart rocked against her rib cage. What would she have done had he not been here?

She nodded.

"Say it. Tell me you understand, Annie. I can't have you running inside the apartment."

"I understand."

"Go." He swiped his fingertips across her cheek, the touch soft and comforting, so opposite of the emotional storm happening inside her.

On weak knees, she moved down the landing to the last door.

"Police!" she heard him say and he disappeared inside her apartment.

* * *

Twenty minutes later Annie sat on her sofa holding a nervous Pirate, watching Mark walk in from checking her car with two uniformed officers. In his hand, he had the carryout containers from the restaurant.

The police arrived minutes after he'd gone into the apartment. Her next-door neighbor had spotted the broken glass and called the police.

Mark glanced at her and offered a reassuring smile. It didn't work.

Strangers buzzed around her apartment making her dizzy. Mark had either been on the phone or dealing with the police. A rock the size of a golf ball sat in the middle of her living room. According to Mark's assessment, it didn't appear as if anyone had come inside.

To his credit, nothing looked out of place, but it felt as if everything had been contaminated. Even if they hadn't come inside, they'd been here. They knew where she lived.

She thought of Fran missing, and the possibility that the person who'd thrown the rock was the same person responsible for Fran's disappearance. The same person who killed Jenny. Her stomach churned.

How did anyone even know where Annie lived?

An ugly answer surfaced. Her mom.

"No." The word slipped off her lips, and guilt for even considering it curled up in her chest. She recalled seeing the nasty words spray-painted on her car and realized what she hadn't seen. Her mom's car. Had her mom...?

She set Pirate on the sofa and moved outside to confirm.

Gripping the banister of the second-story landing, she stared out at the parking lot. The lights positioned on high poles offered her just enough clarity to see what wasn't there.

Her mom's Toyota Avalon was gone. Her mom had been here. Her mom's car had been parked next to Annie's. Had her mom not seen Annie's car? Why hadn't she called Annie?

What did this mean? Nothing, she told herself. Her mom wouldn't do this. And she wouldn't let anyone do it. But Annie would've never thought her mom would have lied all these years, either. That she'd let someone get away with murdering a child.

"You okay?" Mark's voice echoed behind her. His hand came to rest on her shoulder.

"Yeah." The lie slipped off her lips.

His touch hurt. Suspecting her mom hurt. Fran missing hurt.

She had to tell him. "My mom's car is gone."

Even though she'd expected it, the flash of suspicion on his face hurt. "Do you think—"

"She wouldn't have done this." And she believed it even more now.

"Did she call you?"

"No."

"Does anyone besides your mom know where you live?"

The question ran over her nerves before it hit against her heart. "She wouldn't do this."

He ran a hand over his face. "I'm not saying she did. I'm just trying to figure this out." He exhaled and shook his head. "It's apparent that her family is involved. And your mom appears to be on their side. I have to look at this from all angles."

Annie couldn't deny anything he said. She stood there, the night air too hot. "Mom probably mentioned where I lived. When I was at the funeral I learned that... she talked to them about me."

"Talked about you how? What do you mean?"

She almost told him, about her loss of jobs, about the students she'd been certain had been abused. Told him about seeing a shrink, about the restraining order.

But he didn't trust easily. And if he knew this... She needed him to believe in her. Besides, her past didn't have anything to do with Jenny's case.

"About me losing a job. I'm sure she told them I moved to Anniston."

He didn't say anything.

"I love her, Mark. She's my mom."

He glanced down. "You realize you're going to have to talk to her eventually, and I'm going to have to speak with her, too."

"But you'll be nice."

He frowned. "Nice doesn't come easy for me." His arm slipped around her as if to soften the blow of his words.

Only it didn't work. And she only thought her life was a mess before. "Did the police get anything?"

"No. And your apartment's security cameras aren't working."

"So we've got nothing," she said, her throat tight.

"Pretty much."

Annie closed her eyes as fear and despair took up residence in her chest. Mark pulled her a little closer and she let him.

* * *

"No," Annie said an hour later. "I'm fine." She continued to scratch Pirate under his chin. She just wished Isabella was here and she could go crash on her sofa.

She stared at the broken window. She'd swept up the glass. Mark had helped. Leaning on him out on the balcony had helped her even more. That made her feel slightly disloyal to her mom.

Pirate pawed at her to keep rubbing him. The Anniston police had gone, and her feline was calmer and demanding his nightly affection.

Mark dropped beside her on the sofa. "I don't mean . . . I'm talking about me sleeping on the sofa."

"I know, but I don't think it's necessary." Pirate reached his paw out and touched Mark's arm. Mark gave the cat a quick rub behind his ear. Pirate purred then ran off.

It was almost eleven on a weeknight. It felt as if everyone had gone to bed. It felt as if she should be in bed. Not that she'd sleep. Not a wink after what happened.

"Your place isn't secure," he said. "Let me stay. Just tonight until your window is replaced."

"But—"

"I don't want to scare you, but you're an eyewitness to a possible murder."

She caught the *possible* part. He still didn't believe her. But he was here. Helping. Holding. And investigating. That had to be enough. Didn't it?

He continued, "Your cousin, also a witness, is missing. Someone was here to do God only knows what."

He wasn't helping her sleeping issue. And with those facts, she couldn't see how he could still doubt her. "I'll be fine. Isn't it unlikely that this person would come back?"

A loud crash brought a yelp out of her, and she grabbed Mark's arm. When she looked down she saw Pirate had pushed a glass off the kitchen table. Great. More glass to sweep up.

She released her grip. Mark met her gaze dead-on. "You're not fine. Let me stay. A practically platonic sleep-on-the-sofa night. Practically because I'll demand a good night kiss." His smile came slow and sexy.

Knowing how afraid she was, and trying not to think about how good his kisses were, she patted the sofa. "It is comfortable."

"I know. I checked before I offered." He grinned.

"What about your dog?"

"I have a doggy door. I fed him before I came here."

"I'll get you some blankets and pillows."

"And I'll get out the cheesecake." He stood up. "You gotta try it."

* * *

When she brought in the bedding, two plates of cheesecake and two glasses of milk adorned the coffee table, and Mark was sweeping up the glass. "Do you dust and vacuum, too?" she asked.

Armed with an easy smile, he answered, "Nah. I mowed yards for years and had to learn to wield a broom to sweep off driveways. I've never learned the fine art of vacuuming or dusting."

She dropped the bedding in a chair and the lawn mowing info away in her mental what-I-know-about-him file, because she got the feeling the little slips of his past were probably all she'd get.

She grabbed the dustpan and held it for him as he swept up the glass. She emptied the dustpan into the trash, then they both sat on the sofa.

He held a plate and fork to her. "I'm waiting to see your face when you try this."

"And if I don't like it?"

His brows tightened. "Then we'll have to end the

relationship," he said. "I can't date anyone with poor taste."

She laughed. "Then let's see if I can get out of that good night kiss."

Forking a small bite, she closed her lips around the utensil. Flavors exploded on her tongue. Salted caramel, pecan, a hint of coffee, and smooth sweetness of cheesecake danced in her mouth. "Damn, I'm gonna have to kiss you."

Laughing, he took his fork and cut off a bite from her plate. She pulled the plate back. "I think you've got your own."

He pointed his fork at her. "Fine...but noted. The girl doesn't share."

"It's the only-child syndrome, and only when something is really good." She cut off another bite.

He picked up his plate. "I get it. I don't like to share, either. Actually, I split one piece. There's another slice in your fridge."

"So we're eating yours, huh?"

He laughed. He ate another bite of cheesecake, studying her as if he had something to say.

"What?" she asked.

"Back to the not-sharing thing. The red roses...?" He motioned toward the breakfast table. "Are you involved with someone?"

"No. My friend was, and...she was going to toss them, but brought them to me instead."

"Good to know," he said.

Since he'd asked a question, she decided it was fair he give her one. "Other than the Judith Holt thing, should I watch out for other disgruntled exes?" Then she tossed in a second question: "Have you been married?"

"No and no. You?"

She sliced another bite of cheesecake. "No. Came close. You?"

"Close."

She didn't ask him what happened, because she wasn't willing to reveal the answer about herself. It would expose her whole considered-crazy past. Because that was why Ted dumped her. How had he put it? *You need to get things straight in your head before you and I take the next step.*

She slid another bite into her mouth. Salted caramel dripped from the spoon, and she savored the taste and pushed away all thoughts of Ted. "This is better than sex."

He cut his eyes at her. "Then you haven't been having sex with the right person."

Okay, she really should learn to keep her mouth shut. He dished his last bite into his mouth.

Heavy footsteps sounded outside her door. She looked that way, and saw he did the same. But the steps kept going. Accepting his offer to stay felt right.

She put the fork down and pushed it toward him. "Now I'll share. I can't eat another bite."

"But the bite I want is right...here." He leaned forward, pressed his lips to the side of her mouth and kissed and licked the obvious caramel away.

His warm, now-sweet lips shifted ever so slightly and met hers. She closed her eyes and let it happen. His taste complemented the cheesecake.

She inched closer, wanting more. He obliged. The kiss deepened. Their tongues danced. His hand came around her neck, positioning her head so the kiss went even deeper.

She lost the ability to think and savored the happy place where her whole body tingled and left nerve endings sparking to life and begging for more. She reached up and wrapped her hand around his neck. He caught her and pulled her closer.

Before she knew it, she sat on his lap, straddling his pelvis. His hands moved over her. Her back, her shoulders, her waist. His thumbs inched up her rib cage and caressed the edges of her breasts. Her nipples tightened, wanting, needing, a more deliberate touch.

She let out a low moan. He matched it. His hips shifted and she felt a bulge in his jeans. Realizing where this was heading gave her a start.

He must have felt it because he ended the kiss. His blue eyes, with heat and want, met hers.

"We should...stop." He brushed a finger over her lips that felt wet and swollen. "I think we're coming close to crossing the line of 'practically platonic.'"

She breathed in air, seeking logic. "Yeah." She lifted off his lap. "It's late."

"Yeah." He tugged on the legs of his jeans as if things had gotten too tight. She fought the desire to glance down to see how tight.

She stood. "There's a sheet in there. Do you want me to put it on?"

"No. I got it." He stood. "I didn't mean for the kiss to..."

She nodded and started down the hall. One step. Two. She turned around. He stood there watching her. "There's clean towels hanging up in the bathroom."

"Thanks." He wiped a hand over his face.

"I'm going to...bed."

He nodded.

She nodded. *Damn. Damn. Damn.*

Then without thought, without the least bit of shame, she said, "Would you, by any chance, like to join me?"

His eyes widened and he started moving toward her. Slow. Steady. "I would but, uh...what about my promise to..."

"I'll take the fall for it," she said breathlessly.

"No one's falling." He smiled and swooped her up.

There was only one tiny part of her that said this was a mistake, but all her other parts, the ones aching to feel his touch, won over.

She put her hands around his neck and pulled him down for another kiss. He carried her to the bedroom.

He lowered her onto the bed and settled in beside her. His mouth found hers again, then devoured her lips, then trailed kisses down her neck. Licking, kissing, nipping.

His hand shifted under her pink blouse. He cupped her breasts, his thumbs found her tight nipples. She moaned.

His palm smoothed its way down her rib cage, past her waist to the hem of her skirt. With confidence, he slipped his hand up between her thighs. The sweet ache had her holding her breath, and damp heat pooled inches from his touch.

His mouth came back to hers. But the kiss ended too quickly. He stood up, slowly unbuttoned his shirt, and let it slip off his shoulders. She saw the gun holster.

"Do you always carry a gun?"

"Not now." He removed the holster and gun and sat it on her nightstand, then pulled his white T-shirt over his head. Muscles rippled as his arms went up.

Her breath caught at the need to touch the sculpted muscles, bare chest, and warm skin. He had a dusting of dark hair covering his chest and a thin line of hair trailed down from his navel into his jeans.

He dropped down beside her, then kissed the edge of her lips.

Kissed as if he had all night. She let her hands move over his bare back, savoring the smooth skin. His hand eased over her breast—bringing her nipple taut again. Somehow, without her even realizing it, he had her shirt unbuttoned.

He stared down at her breasts covered in the lacy pink bra. "Beautiful." Reaching behind her, he unhooked it with the ease of a man who'd done it numerous times.

He slipped the bra off her. Tracing her nipples with his index finger, he watched as they puckered. She was ready to beg for more.

Reaching down, she tried to unsnap his jeans. "Patience," he said teasingly. "I like to play."

"So do I," she said, feeling braver than normal.

Grinning, he unzipped her skirt, then pulled it off. His palms brushed against her bare outer thighs. Then with one knee on the mattress, and a bulge in his jeans, he stared at her pink lace panties. "Pretty," he said in a hoarse voice. He slipped one finger down her mound and didn't stop until it was at the V of her legs. "Someone's wet."

She reached down to remove her panties, but he caught her hand. "No. I'm doing it."

With a slow hand he slid the silk down her legs, then he sat up again and stared at what he'd uncovered.

"I'm feeling naked," she said.

"You are naked. And I like it that way." He moved his gaze up and down, making her feel less vulnerable and a lot turned on.

He unsnapped his jeans. Leaning over, he pushed his jeans and underwear down and stepped out of them. When he stood back up she saw him, hard, erect, ready.

He dropped back beside her. His sex rested against the side of her leg. The ache between her thighs increased. She reached down, eager to touch him, but he caught her hand before she caught him.

"Here's the rules—"

"I didn't agree to follow any rules." She freed her hand and wrapped her palm around him.

He hissed. "No." He pulled her hand up to his chest. "I get to touch. Play." His other hand moved down over her breasts and dipped between her thighs.

Already close to orgasm, a sound of pure pleasure whispered off her lips.

"To taste," he continued and slipped a finger inside her.

She tightened her thighs around his hand. "Sex is a team sport," she muttered.

He laughed. The sound came so fresh. "True, but I'm so hard if you touch me, I'll be out of the game."

"Then maybe we'd better move things along," she said, her voice low, part tease, part bravado.

CHAPTER TWELVE

I like a girl who knows what she wants." Mark ran his thumb over her clitoris before he pulled his hand away from the soft wet spot between her legs.

She let out another sweet moan, and he felt it all the way in his chest.

Damn, she was beautiful. The perfect blend of bashful and bold. He knew he was breaking the rules—the department's and his own—he never let himself want something this bad. But hell, he'd pay the consequences. It'd be worth it.

He rose up, grabbed his wallet, and snatched out the foil packet.

When he got back in the bed, she took the condom from him. "Let me."

He leaned back, locked his hands behind his head, and let her take charge. On her knees, her breast shifted ever so slightly. He devoured her with his eyes.

She used her teeth to open it. Her big blue eyes stayed on him.

Packet opened, she reached for him. He let out a slow hiss through his teeth as her soft hand surrounded his hardness. Instinctively, he lifted his hips and moved up and then down in her hand. He had to fight not to explode.

Smiling, she placed the cool rubber on his tip and rolled it down him. Her hand squeezed tighter. His patience snapped.

He reached for her. "Top or bottom?"

"Surprise me." She looked about as happy as he felt.

He lowered himself on his back and picked her up to straddle him.

She found the right spot and slowly lowered herself onto him. Tight pleasure hit.

Leaning her head back, a sigh escaped her. She pressed her hands on his chest, as if unsure she could take him all in.

He wanted to bolt up, roll her over, and bury himself all the way inside, but he gritted his teeth and let her do it.

She started rocking, and with each downward sweep she took more of him.

As the pleasure built, he closed his eyes and thought of baseball, taking out the garbage, cleaning up Bacon's messes, anything to stop himself from exploding.

Then, knowing he couldn't last too much longer, he unlocked his hands. With one hand, he fondled her breast. The other he slipped down where their bodies joined and rubbed his thumb over her nub. Up. Down. Up. Down.

She moved faster. Faster. "That's right. Enjoy it."

Her breath caught, then she made soft, happy noises. She dropped on top of him.

He let her have a few seconds. Then he rolled her over, and pumped inside her. The position gave him another half inch into pure ecstasy.

Using his elbows to hold his weight, he moved his hips up, down, deeper. Then he exploded. The pleasure tightened every muscle inside his body. He rolled on his side, taking her with him, not wanting to leave her body until every last drop of pleasure had seeped out of him.

When he finally got his breath and she got hers, feeling accomplished and a little powerful, he brushed her hair from her eyes.

Those big blue eyes blinked. When she opened them again, he saw her tears.

"Good tears?" he asked, his voice hoarse.

"Mostly," she said in a hiccupy voice.

He swallowed, his accomplished feeling fading. "Explain the not-mostly part."

She wiped a hand over her eyes. "I'm just a little worried that it might not have been the wisest thing."

He frowned. "Were you not in the same bed as me?"

She nodded.

"Then...was that not amazing?"

She nodded again.

"So how the hell could that not have been wise? That was...It doesn't always feel like that." Frankly, he couldn't remember the last time it had been that good—that emotionally cleansing.

"You're working on my case. We barely know each other."

"How can your mind go from awesome sex to worrying it's not right so fast?"

She didn't answer. So he continued, "I'll deal with the case issue. That's on me. And I'd say we know each other a hell of lot more now than we did an hour ago."

She laughed.

He pressed a kiss to her cheek. "No regrets allowed."

He pulled her against him. The feel of her skin against his was fucking amazing. She was fucking amazing.

"It was good, wasn't it?" Her words came against his chest, and he could hear and feel her smile.

"'Good'? That's all I get."

"How about 'great'?" she offered.

He exhaled. "For an English teacher who is well read, you need to work on your adjectives."

She laughed. He breathed in her scent, their scent, the scent of sex. He couldn't remember the last time he'd felt this happy, this satisfied. Never with Judith.

His fear of wanting too much, of wanting her too much, vanished, and he decided somehow, someway he had to keep Annie Lakes around.

* * *

Thu-thump. Thu-thump.

The sounds came to Annie first. The sound of her young heart thudding in her chest. The night sound of insects, owls, and unknown creatures.

The sound of . . . fear.

Then a panic-laced young voice echoed in the dark distance. "Faster, Annie."

She couldn't run faster. She couldn't breathe.

She couldn't . . . wake up.

She felt trapped in the blackness.

She screamed.

"Shit! You okay?"

Annie caught her breath, attempted to pull the scream back in as she jackknifed into a sitting position. For one second, the dream's panic turned into who-the-hell-is-in-my-bedroom panic.

Last night's details started falling into place. Her panic shot straight into embarrassment.

They'd made love twice. And she didn't even know the man's middle name, if he voted Republican or Democrat, or if he flossed regularly. "I'm sorry. Just a dream."

He sat up and touched her shoulder. The dream, the raw emotions were so fresh, she flinched.

"Sorry." He pulled his hand back.

"No, I'm sorry." She saw her clock on the bedside table. It was three a.m. "Go back to sleep." She dropped back on the bed, gave him her back, her heart still thudding, embarrassment swimming in her chest.

Time passed. One minute. Two. Three.

Ten.

"Annie?" His voice rang soft.

"Yes."

"Can you roll over and look at me?"

She closed her eyes. "Don't you want to go back to sleep?"

"Please?"

She rolled to her back, but stared at the ceiling.

"Can I touch you now?"

"Uh-huh."

He scooted close, so close she felt the bare skin of his chest against her arm. While she'd donned a silk night-shirt before they went to sleep, she was pretty sure he was naked beneath the sheet. She looked at him. He'd folded his pillow in half and placed it beneath his head so he could look at her.

"The dream, is it the one you told me about?"

She nodded.

"Can you tell me about it?"

"I already did."

"I know, but...it might be fresher in your mind."

Sitting up, she hugged her knees and told him the dream, the running, seeing the Cinderella shoes, the footsteps following her, clutching the bloody teddy bear. The voice she felt certain was Fran's, screaming for her to run faster.

"Then, I fell and cut my knee."

"Is this the scar from it?" He caught her hand that absently traced across the puckered flesh.

"Yes. But...my mom says I got it when I fell off my bike."

"Do you remember that?"

"No."

"After you fall in the dream, what happens?"

"I hear the footsteps. Someone grabs me. Picks me up." Her heart picked up speed just thinking about it. Even now, she wanted to squirm free. Free from the hold and free from the memory. Free. She wanted free from all of it.

"Who was it?"

"I don't know. The dream ends. I never see them."

"Do you see the person burying Jenny?"

"No, I don't dream that. I remembered that after I went to the funeral. The dream starts with me running. Ends with someone grabbing me."

He repositioned his pillow, pulling her onto her side so he could see her. "Do you remember anything else?"

"No."

"Are you sure?" he asked.

Was he doubting her again? Her chest tightened with hurt. "I told you."

"I know. I just need to know everything so I can find answers."

She closed her eyes, remembering that even though they'd slept together, this was still about the case. For some reason that hurt. "I've told you everything." The only thing she wasn't telling him was how that affected her life. "We should go back to sleep."

"Yeah." He kissed her forehead, tempering her frustration and confusing her heart.

She couldn't sleep. She lay there, curled up beside him, completely still, eyes closed, trying not to breathe too loudly. His breathing slowed, and she knew he'd managed to do what she couldn't.

With only silence around her, she thought about Fran. Was she being held against her will? Was she even alive?

From there, Annie's thoughts went to her mom. About talking to her tomorrow.

After that bit of torture, her subconscious offered her a reprieve, because she recalled with clarity how good it had been to make love to Mark. And how wonderful it felt now, to listen to someone else breathe, to not feel so alone.

Even if this was more about the case than them, it still felt wonderful.

* * *

"I'll call him and see when he can do it," Mark said.

"You don't have to do that." Annie refilled his cup. They'd both found themselves up around six. They'd made love again, and while he showered she made coffee.

"All I'm doing is calling someone and making sure he'll give you a good deal. And I know he will. He owes me."

"Why don't you save that favor for yourself?"

"I saved his ass from going to prison, so he owes me more than one favor. And I'm sure he needs the business, too." He sipped his coffee, his blue eyes staring determinedly over the rim. And there it was again. That twinkle that spoke of soft touches and seduction.

While caught, mesmerized by his charm, she felt the bubble of unease sitting in her gut. The morning-after feeling. The nagging little voice that said this could turn out to be a mistake.

But damn if her body wasn't ready for a replay. Had

sex always been this good, and she'd forgotten, or had her previous lovers sucked that bad? Was she fixating on the sex so she didn't have to fixate on other things?

"Okay," she agreed. "You sure you don't want some eggs?"

"No. Coffee is great. And so was what you cooked up in the bedroom this morning."

Her mouth dropped open. "I didn't—"

"I don't blame you. I'm hard to resist." He laughed.

She couldn't help smiling. Could he see right through her? Was his teasing a ploy to make her feel better? She'd give it to him, it almost worked.

"I'm lying." He brushed his thumb over her lips. "Not about me being irresistible." His grin deepened. "But about you starting it. You're addicting." He stood up, leaned down, and kissed her, a warm, remember-what-we-did kind of kiss. "I should go. You off today?"

"My first class doesn't begin until eleven on Wednesdays."

"You want to do lunch?"

A part of her had been worried he might be the get-laid-and-leave type. "I only have forty minutes."

"How about I bring us something and we can eat in your room? A hamburger? Salad?"

"Salad. I'll be free at eleven twenty-five."

"I'll be there." He kissed her again. Their eyes met. Something seemed to be left unsaid. Was he having doubts? Or was he as confident on the inside as he appeared on the outside?

"Will you call me if you find anything about Fran?" She palmed the warm coffee mug.

"Yeah. And I'll call you with Brad's Auto Paint shop info." He looked down at her. "You're going to talk to your mom, right?"

Bam. Dread skipped up and down her conscience. She nodded.

"Be careful," he said.

"You think someone might try something again?" she asked.

"I don't know. But if you get a call or see someone following you, or even *think* they are following you, call me."

His sharp tone had her inhaling. "Should I be afraid?"

"No, you should be careful."

Her thoughts tiptoed back to Fran.

But crap, her life was a mess. And she was sleeping with a guy she hardly knew. A guy who until recently thought she was crazy.

* * *

Trying not to become consumed in regrets, Annie dressed in jogging clothes and pulled down the kitty food. She recalled worrying someone had hurt the feline. How sad was it that besides her mom, Pirate was all she had?

Or was her mom even speaking to her? Annie felt justified in being angry, even in leaving her mom there, but being right wasn't everything. She looked at her phone. Then looked away.

As the Kibbles and Bits clattered into the ceramic

paw-printed bowl, she wondered if she'd ever meet Mark's dog. She recalled him mentioning he had a doggy door. So he lived in a house instead of an apartment. One more tidbit for her all-I-know-about-Mark-Sutton file. Yet she knew things she shouldn't. Like how it felt to have him move inside her. How it felt when his mouth found places on her body that hadn't been found in a long time.

As she put the cat food up, Pirate came around to paw at her. "I'll be back," she told him.

Slipping on her cell phone arm band, she was connecting her earplugs when her phone rang.

Did Mark have news on Fran? Freeing the phone, she checked the number. Not Mark.

"Tell me it was great." Isabella's voice hinted at laughter. At friendship. Something Annie needed right now.

"It was good."

"Just good?" Isabella asked.

Annie wanted to borrow her light mood. "No. It was..." Annie tried to decide how much to give.

"Oh, my gawd. You slept with him."

"I don't know what got into me." The confession leaked out, and she leaned against a wall.

"Obviously, he did," Isabella teased. "Are you sore?"

Annie felt the slightest discomfort between her legs. "I'm...not..."

"So you did it at least twice, huh?" Laughter exploded on the line.

"Does that make me a slut?" Annie asked.

"No. It makes me jealous. And I hope it makes you happy."

"Yeah." There was a part of her that knew Isabella was right. Last night had been good, but...

"Are you at the coffee shop with him?" Isabella asked.

"No. He left for work. I'm about to go for a run. What time are you getting back?"

"Around five. Come over then. We'll order Chinese food, drink wine, and you can give me all the sexy little details."

"I might have to take my car in. But that shouldn't take long."

"What's wrong with your car?"

"It got spray-painted." She fought the spidering fear crawling up her backbone.

"What?"

"How about we talk about it later? I'm going for that run."

Hanging up, Annie left her apartment and took off slow.

As her feet pounded the pavement, she headed toward the park and repeated the mantra she always did at the start of a jog, "Stay in the present."

Sometimes, on bad days, just the feel of running took her to the dream. Sometimes she knew she ran just to know she could, just to exercise that little bit of control she still had over her own life. The sound of her feet resounded in her head. She managed to push away the feel of being chased, and her mind went to something equally bad. Calling her mom.

She had two miles to figure out exactly what she planned to say to her mom.

* * *

Realizing the time, and knowing he had a shitload of work to do, Mark headed straight to the office. On the drive, he called his neighbor, Peter, whom he sometimes jogged with on the weekends. He asked him to run by and feed Bacon. "And if you're going for a run, can you take Bacon? His leash is in the laundry room."

Bacon was a good dog, but if he didn't get regular runs, he tended to eat Mark's shoes and socks as a form of punishment.

"Sure," Peter said. "What's her name?"

"Huh?" Mark played ignorant.

"Don't bullshit me," Peter said.

"Annie." Saying her name gave him a shot of pleasure.

"Is she hot?"

"Yeah. Later." He hung up, feeling good about hooking Bacon up with a run, and pulled up into the precinct's parking lot.

"No coffee?" Mildred asked as he passed her desk.

"Sorry, I'll grab you some in a bit." He stopped briefly. "Can you go through some more files today looking for the Reed case? I'll take you out for a steak dinner if you find it."

"I'll hold you to that, but I had..." She looked him up and down. "Hmm."

"Hmm, what?"

"Who is she?"

"What?" Peter guessing was one thing, Mildred puzzled him. "How...?"

"You didn't bring coffee. Your clothes weren't just pulled out of the cleaner's plastic sleeve. And your frown line is gone."

He grinned and took off but looked back. "You missed your calling to be a detective."

"Morning," he said to Juan, who already had his nose in his computer.

Juan gazed up. "I'm going over Gomez's electronic file on the case."

"Finding anything?"

"Mostly a shitload of useless info. Gomez noted everything."

"Nothing good?"

"Maybe. I think Talbot was running around on his wife back then. Not sure if that's important, but who knows. And I'm just getting started."

Connor walked into the office. His gaze zeroed in on Mark.

"Morning," Mark said, unsure what the look was about.

A slow smile spread over Connor's lips. "What's her name?"

Mark reared back in his chair. "What?"

"You know what."

"How do you know?" Was Mark wearing an I GOT LAID sign he didn't know about?

"You said 'morning' instead of grunting." He chuckled. "And I heard Mildred talking to you."

"Forget that." Mark found his list on his desk of the Cash leads he hadn't chased down yet. "We got tons to do." He needed to call Brad about painting Annie's car.

And call Austin PD about the Missing Persons report on Francyne Roberts.

Realizing he'd mentally lapsed into in his own to-do list, he looked up. "We've got about six more leads to chase down that I got from Janet Rigley."

"Who?" Connor asked.

"The lady who worked at the shelter where Cash stayed. The one I saw yesterday."

"Yeah," Connor said. "You need company?"

"Actually, I think we should divide and conquer." He didn't want Connor interfering with his lunch with Annie.

"Hand 'em over. I'll get started. I don't want to be cooped up in this cave all day."

The fact that they didn't have a window bothered Mark, too. While Juan seemed perfectly content to be here. Mark tore the list in two. Made a paper airplane with Connor's half and flew it to him. Connor unfolded the plane.

Mark drummed his fingers over his desk. He needed to tell them what he was up to. "I decided on a new case."

"What?" Connor asked. "Last week you said you wanted to give this case everything we had."

"I know, but give me this." Doubt stabbed at his conscience. Was he hurting their chances of solving the Talbot case by taking on Annie's? He recalled how scared Annie had been when they found her car and apartment vandalized. And even more frightened from the dream.

"Lady in pink? That's the case, right?" Juan asked.

Mark frowned. When had everyone gotten so good at reading his mind?

Juan must have read Mark's mind again because he chuckled. "I asked Mildred what she was looking for in the boxes you left out yesterday. She told me."

"Mystery solved." Connor leaned back in his chair until it squeaked beneath his weight. And Connor's six-four frame held a lot of weight. His partner looked as if he'd played pro football. And actually, he did play a year of college ball. But he said he decided chasing down badasses was better than being hit by an entire string of badasses.

"What mystery?" Mark asked.

"Your mood. You tapped that, didn't you? You lucky dog?"

Mark didn't deny it, although he didn't like Connor's tone. "She's nice."

"I bet," Connor said. "You going to give us the low-down on the case?"

"I'm still piecing it together. Tomorrow."

"Okay." Connor stood up. "I'm out to find Cash."

"Wait," Juan said. "We got a call from Stone. He said he'd have something for us around three. Wants us to meet him at the morgue."

Mark rotated his shoulders. "Can't he just write up a report?" The pictures were bad enough, but actually seeing the little girl's body was sure to chip out even a bigger chunk of his soul.

"You know him." Juan smirked. "He likes show and tell."

"Yeah," Mark said, begrudgingly. "So we'll all meet up at three at the morgue."

"Got it." Connor walked out.

Mark sat there grasping the threads of the good mood Annie had brought about. He let his mind go back to how it felt to have her on top of him, to be buried to the hilt inside her. To hearing those soft, happy sounds she made when she came. Then *bam*, he realized he had a ton of shit to do. He reached for the phone.

"Haven't seen you smile like that in a while," Juan said. "Must have been a hell of a night."

"It was." Mark looked at his phone and realized Brad wouldn't open his shop until nine. But he needed to give Austin PD a chance to finish their coffee before dropping the lost-cousin problem in their lap.

The temptation to call or text Annie tickled his mind.

He tapped her number and then tried to figure out what to say. But damn, how long had it been since he worried about what he should say to a girl?

"She's not a crazy bitch like the last woman you dated, is she?" Juan asked.

"No." Annie wasn't anything like Judith Holt. Then *bam*, the crazy part of Juan's question gave him the slightest concern.

But he believed her now, didn't he? The question bubbled up into his subconscious as if it'd been waiting to pounce. That thought scratched across his good mood. *But no.* He realized it wasn't Annie he thought was crazy, it was the case. And the evidence. A decades-old memory that wasn't even complete and nightmares that gave only part of the story.

Then, realizing where he might find answers, he stood, and glanced back at Juan. "I'll be right back."

CHAPTER THIRTEEN

Mark took the steps to the second floor. When he passed Brown's office, he realized he probably needed to update him on the case. But first things first. He continued three doors down.

"Is Murdock in?" he asked the woman sitting in the waiting room.

"Yeah, let me call him." She picked up her phone.

Afraid the man wouldn't see him, considering their last visit, he walked into the office.

"Wait," the receptionist called.

"It's okay." The forty-year-old man with red hair acknowledged Mark, but didn't stand up. Mark shut the door.

"Should I have brought my parka today?"

"What?" Mark asked, unsure if that was sarcasm in the man's voice.

Murdock leaned back in his chair. "You told me hell and Houston would be hit with a snowstorm before you darkened my door again."

Definitely sarcasm. "Don't take it personally." Mark dropped into a chair across from the doctor's desk.

"I don't. Ninety percent of all cops are like you. Although, I do think you come in at the top ranking of difficult." He straightened and appeared to mentally brush the chip off his shoulder. "What's up?"

"What's it called when someone can't remember something from a long time ago?"

Murdock leaned forward. "You mean a repressed memory?"

"Yeah. Tell me about them."

"You remembering something?"

"Not me. A friend." The second he said it he realized how that sounded. "She's a witness."

Murdock chuckled. "Don't worry, I believe you. You've only shown up on mandated visits. You'd never come on your own."

"Right. So?" Mark leaned forward and waited for the man to enlighten him.

"What do you want to know?"

Mark rubbed the back of his neck, feeling as if being here was somehow betraying Annie. But how could he believe in something he knew nothing about?

"Just tell me about them."

"Okay." Murdock drummed his fingers on the desk. *Tap, tap, tap.* The noise reminded him of the times he'd been forced into this office, sitting stoic and silent. There was no damn way he was giving this man a peek inside his head. Mark pushed his agitation aside and waited.

Tap, tap.

"Usually," Murdock said, "it stems from a dramatic event. Something the person can't emotionally handle, so the mind locks it into the subconscious."

"And what causes it to become unrepressed?"

"Something triggers it, or the person's subconscious thinks he or she is strong enough to deal with it. Our brains are a lot smarter than we think."

The dots started coming together. The funeral and seeing the Reed family could have been Annie's trigger.

Mark's mind continued to run. "Can a repressed memory give a person nightmares? Like recurring ones but only reveal part of the memory?"

Murdock leaned back and hesitated. "That's feasible."

"But not likely?" Mark picked up on the man's tone.

"Dreams are not that accurate. It's likely that there's only a kernel of the truth in the dreams."

"So . . . you can't believe the information from a dream?" And wasn't that what this whole case was based on?

"Only to a certain degree," the man said.

Mark recalled what the sheriff told him about the family saying Jenny probably drowned. Could Annie have witnessed Jenny drowning and the dreams were mixed up?

But why would anyone want to shut her up about that? And how would that explain the missing Fran Roberts?

Murdock's chair squeaked. "Do you think this person is being honest with you?"

"I believe she believes it." Saying that made this feel

less of a betrayal. It wasn't Annie he didn't trust. It was
the dreams and a decade-old memory.

"If it's a witness, I could talk to her. That's what I'm
here for."

"Yeah. Maybe." Mark stood up, unsure if he felt better with what he'd learned. But at least he wouldn't be
blindsided. "Thanks."

Mark hadn't turned around when Murdock continued, "Is this a cold case?"

"Yeah."

"Is it officially opened?"

"Not yet, why?"

"You should keep in mind. Investigating a case in
which most of the facts are based on a memory is difficult. But even harder is getting a DA on board. You'll
need solid evidence before you'll be able to take anyone
to court on this. Remember that before you dive too
deep."

"I plan on getting solid evidence," he said with a confidence that he didn't really feel. He'd already gone too
deep last night, but he couldn't find it in himself to be
sorry.

* * *

Almost home. Her playlist was almost done, and so was
she. She'd run three miles. But she'd gotten zilch on
what to say to her mom. Winging it felt wrong, Annie
had always been a planner. But this felt unplannable.

And unfortunately, unavoidable. Thinking about it
had her heart racing, even as Annie slowed down. Oh,

how she'd love to bury her head in the sand. Skip the call. She couldn't.

She deserved answers.

Plus Mark would ask at lunch if she'd spoken to her mom.

Not that she blamed him. She'd gone to him for help. He was doing his job.

She had to talk to her mom. *This morning.*

But to say what? Did asking her mom about Jenny somehow imply her mom was behind the murder? No? Yes? Maybe? She didn't believe her mom was involved. She didn't believe her mom had been the one who'd called her or wielded a spray can.

"So what do you believe?" The question slipped off her lips and went straight to her heart. Coming to her apartment stairs, she grabbed the railing and bent over to catch her breath.

While feeding her lungs oxygen, the answer to that question came back and was just as disconcerting as the question.

She believed her mom knew something. Believed her mom had lied to her about how Annie had gotten the scar on her knee. Believed her mom and father had known all along what her nightmare had been about. They knew. Yet they lied about it. Why?

Perhaps to protect Annie. But from what? Or was it from whom? Either way, did it mean they'd thought the truth was uglier than the nightmare?

She stood there for almost a minute, trying to believe it'd be okay. But would the truth set Annie free?

What would her daddy tell her to do? That thought

brought a thread of grief, and a question. She'd already lost her father. Was she going to lose her mom now?

Finally, squaring her shoulders, she moved up the steps.

Pulling her earbuds out, she put her key in the lock, only to realize it wasn't locked. She even turned the knob to confirm it. It turned.

Her mind raced.

Had she forgotten to lock it?

She'd been on the phone with Isabella. It wouldn't be the first time she'd forgotten.

Remembering Pirate gave her a jolt. She eased the door open but stood outside the threshold. Normally, all it took was the opening of the door for him to come running.

He didn't come.

"Kitty, kitty," she whispered, dread filling her stomach. Remembering her missing cousin. Remembering, *Shut up bitch!*

He didn't come.

"Pirate?" His name slipped off lips that somehow felt cold. "Kitty."

He didn't come.

Then Annie heard the footsteps coming down her hall.

* * *

"Okay. I'll have Annie drop her car in the morning," Mark said into the phone as he leaned back in his chair. When he'd finished with Murdock, he went to see

Brown, but the man had left. Mark came back to his office to take care of his calls before heading out to find Cash. But first, he'd called Doris Roberts and asked about her daughter. She informed him that she hadn't seen or heard from Fran since she'd left the funeral in a huff.

But there was something about her voice.

He refocused on his call to the garage mechanic. "And Brad, thanks for giving her a discount."

"Not an issue. I'd be locked away if you hadn't helped get me that deal. Plus, I need the work. When you decide to freshen up your Mustang, you know my number."

"I'll call you."

Hanging up, he was tempted to call Annie but stopped himself. It'd be best to call with news on the case and not look so damn eager. He found Austin PD's number and called. It took him five minutes to get transferred to the Missing Persons unit.

When he was finally connected, he mentioned Francyne Roberts's name. "Let me speak to the officer in charge of that case."

As he waited, his mind went to Murdock's info. Damn, he wanted good news to offer Annie at lunch.

"Detective Hash." The voice gave Mark an image of a mature officer.

"Hello. I'm Detective Sutton with the Anniston PD."

"Okay," Hash said. "Why's the Anniston police looking into the Roberts case?"

"I'm working a cold case and it seemed Ms. Roberts could've been a witness to a murder."

"A witness, not a suspect?" he asked.

"Right," Mark said, wondering where that question came from.

"We just got the case this morning, but this isn't the first time her name's fallen on my desk."

"She's got a record?" Mark asked.

"For public intoxication, and one DUI. But I meant her Missing Persons file. The woman's got a drinking problem, which leads to relationship problems, which leads to her dropping off the face of the earth for a few days."

"Oh," Mark said.

"A couple of domestic violence calls were made to her boyfriend's place, too, so I was going to drop by and see if I smelled trouble. My advice to you is, unless it's critical, to just cool your jets. She'll pop up in a week or so."

"Yeah," Mark said. "But I'm concerned someone might be trying to shut her up."

"If you think she could be missing permanently, we can look into this a little deeper."

"I can't say that for sure." Mark drummed the pencil. "It could be she's off on a bender. I have other feelers out, and if I find anything suspicious, I'll call. Meanwhile, just let me know what the boyfriend says."

"You got it," Hash said.

Hanging up, he muttered, "Shit!" Every question he sought answers to just created more questions. His good mood from being with Annie was wearing off.

And he wanted it back.

Realizing Juan had gone, he dialed Annie's number and curled back into his chair.

The phone rang once. Twice. Three times.

It went to voice mail.

"It's Mark. I spoke to the Austin PD. Call me."

* * *

Annie's phone rang as she got dressed. She cut it off. Finding her mom in her apartment had given her heart more of a workout than the run.

"Who did that to your car door?" her mom had asked, looking as frightened as Annie.

"I don't know," Annie had answered honestly.

Then her mom had taken a good look at Annie, sweat pouring out of her every pore, and insisted she take a shower before they talked.

Annie accepted the reprieve.

But now her reprieve was over. Clean, she walked out of her bedroom that still smelled like Mark, like sex, and into the hall.

She searched through her soul for courage and found none. Once in the kitchen, she picked up Mark's and her coffee cups from the table and set them in the sink.

"Did you have company earlier?"

"Isabella," Annie lied. She didn't need to explain Mark. Not to her mom.

Annie held on to the counter for one second, two, then turned around.

Their gazes met and somehow Annie knew this was just as hard on her mom as it was on her. Barely managing to stand on what felt like rag-doll legs, she sank into a chair. Pirate circled her feet, meowing.

Annie forced herself to speak. "What's going on, Mom?"

"They're family, Annie. People share things with family, things they worry about. I worried about you, so I told them. I'm sorry if that hurt you."

It took Annie a second to realize her mom was talking about the argument they'd had.

Was that all her mom had come here to talk about?

"It was wrong," Annie said, annoyed that her mom's apology included an excuse.

"I confided in my sister. I didn't know she'd tell...Fran."

"Your sister is a drunk, Mom. She probably told her gynecologist about me." Annie managed to keep tone level. Her mom hated raised voices.

"She's *not* a drunk. I admit she indulges too much, but..."

Unwilling to argue the obvious, Annie put her first question out there. "Where's Fran?" Needing something to do with her hands, Annie picked up a napkin and started rolling it.

"I don't...Why would you ask that?" Nervousness tightened her mom's tone. "I thought you didn't want anything to do with my family."

"She's missing."

"According to her mom, she regularly disappears. I'm sure she's fine."

The assurance dripping off her words, the same even-toned voice was what her mom used when she told Annie that her dreams meant nothing. She wadded up the napkin. "How about Jenny? Is she fine, too?"

Her mom's pupils shrunk, then enlarged. With trembling hands, she touched her mouth. "You are the one." Her weak voice trembled. "You talked to the police?"

"What happened to her?" Annie felt as if air were trapped in her throat.

Her mom stared at the wall. In the distance, Annie heard people leaving their apartments to go to work, to start a normal, ordinary day. Annie wished she could trade places, because nothing about this felt ordinary. Then the thought hit, that this, this talk, was going to change everything. Her relationship with her mom would never be normal or the same. But shit, what had her mother done?

Her mom looked at Annie. There was so much pain in her mom's eyes, Annie instinctively wanted to protect her. Protect her like her father had protected her all those years. But what was Annie really protecting her from? And who was protecting Annie?

"Don't do this. It happened a long time ago. It's best forgotten."

"What's best forgotten, Mom? Tell me."

Her mom closed her eyes, inhaled, and stayed frozen for a whole moment before lifting her lashes. "She drowned."

There was something so stilted in her tone, as if she pulled the lie from a dark place in her soul.

Her mom laced her fingers together, rested the tight two-handed fist on the table, and stared at her hands as if the truth lay locked between her palms.

"They never found her...body," her mom continued.

"That's not true. What are you hiding? Tell me so I can...I don't like thinking—"

"Stop! You shouldn't have gone to the police. You have to drop it. Call them, tell them it was all a mistake."

Annie tried to absorb what her mom was saying and what she wasn't saying. "I can't believe you've known, and...and you lied. Do you know what this did to me?" Her voice shook. "Do you?"

"Don't yell at me, Annie. And when did I lie to you?" For one second her mother met Annie's gaze, then she looked away as if it was painful.

But Annie had her own pain. "You're lying now. You lied about the scar. You said I got it falling off my bike. But I didn't. And the dreams? You knew what they were about. I lost jobs because of what this did to me. Lost friends. Lost Ted. I lost part of me. And you stood there and let my world fall apart." Years of hurt sounded in her voice.

With eyes filled with denial, her mom sobbed. "I need your daddy." She put her hands over her face as if to hide. Hide from Annie. And maybe hide from the truth.

"Damn it. Look at me!" When her mom did, Annie continued, "Did Dad know, too? Is that why he'd never let me go back to see your family?"

"Don't you dare talk badly of him!" Her mom's voice rose. "He was the kindest man I've ever known. Stop this, Annie."

"I can't. They're going to find out the truth, Mom. I just pray you aren't part of it. You need to talk to the police. Get ahead of this."

Her mom pounded the table. Anger. Fury. Desperation. It all swam together in her eyes, making them bright. Too bright.

"You don't know what you've done! Stop it."

"It can't be stopped."

"It has to be." Her mom snatched her purse from the table.

"Don't go! We aren't done."

But her mom obviously was done. Done listening. Done talking. She shot up from the chair so fast, she was out the door before Annie got to her feet.

And for one second, Annie felt certain that the truth was going to be worse than not knowing. Why did she feel as if she'd just opened Pandora's box?

CHAPTER FOURTEEN

Mark could have used some good news, but Sheriff Harper wasn't giving him any. "There are no cameras on the street at all," he said. "I'm about to head out to talk to Doris Roberts."

"Did she agree to speak to you?" Mark asked.

"In these parts of the woods, you don't need an invite. Besides, sometimes it's better to surprise 'em."

"True." Mark shared everything he'd gotten on Fran from Austin PD. "She drives a red 2016 Malibu." He gave him the license plate. "I spoke with Doris Roberts earlier about her daughter's disappearance. I swear she's hiding something."

"Doesn't surprise me," Harper said. "Oh, I spoke to my receptionist's mother. Karen Reed. Asked her about her in-laws. She pretty much told me what I knew, that they drank too much. When I asked if she remembered a Jenny Reed, she said her and her husband had just started dating then, and she couldn't remember her husband saying anything."

Adam continued talking about his visit to George's house earlier, which was something Mark needed to hear, just not now.

"Look, I was on my way out," Mark said. "Can we talk again this afternoon?"

"Yeah. I'll call you after I meet Ms. Roberts."

Mark hung up and muttered "Later" to Juan and the same to Mildred as he passed her desk. When he saw her combing through more boxes looking for the Reed file, he said, "It'll be a good steak. I promise."

He hurried to his car and took off chasing leads. His first stop was a place where he'd never felt comfortable. Almost worse than Murdock's office. Damn, why hadn't he made sure Connor had this one?

The office to the side of the church had been locked. But a car was parked out front. Opening the heavy doors, he stepped inside the sanctuary and rolled his shoulders, trying to knock off the chip he'd carried since he was a teen. When that didn't work, he squeezed his neck. He breathed in the dark, musty air. The place smelled of old hymnals, old people, and old sins. And a young boy's pain.

Blinking to get his eyes to adjust, he heard someone's shuffling, but he couldn't see them. He inched down the aisle toward the big cross, toward the shadowy figure, trying to move away from the anger that still burned in his belly.

Why did the past seem to live and breathe in this place? A slow burn crawled up into Mark's chest, and he clenched his fists.

He'd been fifteen. He'd lost his sister to murder, his

mom to suicide, and his stepdad to prison. The foster father Mark had been placed with had brought Mark to church to find comfort. Mark hadn't wanted to be comforted. He shouldn't have worried.

The priest explained that the Heavenly Father had forgiven his stepfather for killing his sister and suggested Mark do the same. Mark, young and angry, had said things he didn't mean. One of which was that his mom had been smart to kill herself. That led the priest to explain that killing oneself was a sin God couldn't forgive. Mark, not stupid, understood the implications. His stepfather could be forgiven but not his mom. Mark had reacted accordingly.

Even after all these years, he didn't regret breaking that priest's nose or being removed from that home.

"Can I help you?" The voice rang out, echoing up into the vaulted ceiling.

Mark continued down the aisle toward the man lingering around the pulpit.

"Depends," he replied curtly. "You Father Turley?"

"I am. What can I do for you, Detective?"

"Do we know each other?" Mark asked.

"No," the man said. "Thirty years of living on the wrong side of the tracks honed my skill for spotting a man carrying a badge. Especially nervous ones."

Uneasy at being read, Mark stopped in front of the older man, who he noticed still carried a few prison tattoos on his neck. "Who said I'm nervous?"

"Uncomfortable then. And in the house of peace."

Mark started to make some off-color remark but caught himself. "You wear different hats, huh?" Mark motioned to the broom.

"Have to. Tithing has fallen out of favor. But I don't mind. It keeps me humble and my doors open."

Mark dropped his clenched hands in his pockets. "Janet Rigley gave me your name."

"Janet? I haven't seen her in years. What's that woman up to?"

"Retired. Lives with her son."

"She deserves to retire. She spent years working for nearly nothing at jobs so she could help others."

Mark nodded. "That's what led me to her. She worked at a shelter where a homeless man who called himself Johnny Cash often stayed."

"There's someone else I haven't seen in a while," Father Turley said.

"And that's why I'm here. She said you might know where I could find the man."

"His name wasn't really Johnny Cash."

"Janet told me. Do you know his real name and where I could find him?"

"Can I ask why you're looking for him?"

"He witnessed something years back and we'd just like to talk to him."

"Good. I was going to say if you thought he'd done anything, you were wrong. The man's lifestyle almost killed his liver, but it never killed his heart."

"He's dead?"

"I said almost. He stopped drinking. Or had when he came by two years ago. Even left a hundred-dollar donation. Said he got himself a job changing oil and was playing in a band for extra money."

"Do you have contact information on him? His real name?"

"His real name is Johnny Harden. Don't have his number or address, but he was playing at the Barn Grill, off Cabot Road. I think he said the garage was at Sanders Avenue and Second Street."

"Thank you." Mark pulled out his wallet and handed the man two twenties.

"You don't have to do that," the priest said.

"My good deed for the day." Mark turned to leave.

"I'll pray for you."

Mark looked back over his shoulder. "I'm fine."

"Lord's house isn't supposed to make you nervous or upset."

And yet it did. Mark left, but wondered how many good priests it'd take to make him forget the bad one's harsh words that had stained his soul.

Starting his car, he looked at the time. He might have enough time to check out the garage before grabbing his and Annie's lunch.

He checked to see if he'd missed a text or a call from her.

He hadn't.

Was she regretting their night? He'd sensed she had been this morning.

He started to text her, but didn't. They'd talk at lunch.

* * *

Five minutes early, Mark walked into the building carrying a bag with two salads. He had an Altoid in his mouth and a sense of accomplishment in his gut. The man at the garage had said Johnny no longer worked there, but he gave him Johnny's cell number. Mark had called it and got his voice mail: *Johnny here, have a happy and sober day. And leave a message.*

Mark had found him. He'd found Johnny Cash!

The fact that right after his message came *Sorry, voice mail is full* didn't discourage Mark too much. Even though he was out of message space, the man could still see missed calls. To make sure Johnny wouldn't think it was a misdialed number, Mark had called him again.

Approaching Annie's classroom, he saw what looked like the last straggling students leaving her room. His chest expanded with anticipation.

Nearing the opened door, he heard voices. Peering in, he saw a female student walking toward the teacher's desk.

Annie wore black slacks and a light blue blouse. She had her hair up. He liked it better down. He recalled with visual and tactile detail how it felt to run his fingers through the strands as they'd made love. Annie spotted him and nodded as if asking for a minute.

He pulled back and leaned against the wall, but the voices in the room carried.

"Is there a problem?" the girl asked.

"No," Annie said. "I just... You haven't turned in some work, but I heard from some of the students that your mom's sick."

Annie's comment brought silence. Then finally, the girl answered. "It's cancer. She's in hospice." The young voice shook.

"I'm so sorry, Madison. I wanted you to know you can take your time handing in the makeup work. And if there's anything I can do ... Please, let me know."

"I appreciate that," the girl said. "You're an awesome teacher, by the way. I'm not saying just 'cause ... I've been meaning to tell you that."

"Thank you," Annie said.

Steps moved to the door, Mark moved back so it didn't look as if he was eavesdropping, never mind that was exactly what he'd been doing.

When she walked out, Mark walked in and shut the door. It hit him with one swift thought. Here, he felt peace, unlike at the church. There was still goodness in the world after all.

Annie looked up. "Sorry." She didn't devour him with her eyes like he'd wanted her to, but she smiled.

"No problem," Mark said, realizing again how different—*good* different—Annie was compared to Judith and even the women before her. She was the type a man could bring home to mom. If he had a mom.

As he got closer, he noted the worry line between her brows. "You okay?"

"Tough morning," she said.

"What happened?"

"My mom came by."

"And?" He felt slammed back into the case. He set the bag on her desk.

"She ... said that I should haven't said anything.

When I asked what happened, she said Jenny drowned."

"And...?" He didn't finish his question, but he figured she knew what he meant.

She bit down on her lip. "She was lying. I could tell. I'm scared. Maybe I was wrong to bring this up."

"Hey... You weren't wrong." He pulled her against him.

She buried her head on his chest. He held her for several long seconds. "I'm here for you," he said, his own words surprising him. Not that he didn't regularly want to help someone. He just didn't put his offer in words so often.

"I'm sorry." She pulled away.

"For what?" He brushed a strand of hair from her cheek.

"For being an emotional twit."

He caught her chin and lifted it so she could see his eyes and know he was serious. "This is emotional and I'm pretty damn certain you don't have an ounce of twit DNA in you." He used a thumb to swipe away a sole tear rolling down her cheek. "In fact, your halo was showing again."

"My halo?"

"I overheard the conversation between you and your student."

She looked confused. "Her mom's dying of cancer."

"Yeah, and when I went through college, not one of my teachers would've given a shit what was going on in their students' lives. You give a shit. That's rare."

He pressed a soft kiss to her lips.

She deepened it, even inched closer until her breasts met his chest.

When he pulled back, her eyes held a hint of leftover passion.

"Have you heard anything?" she asked. "I'm sorry about not returning your call; the morning got away from me. Then I had several students show up early."

"No problem." He suspected the conversation with her mom had done a number on her. He kissed her again, briefly, one meant to soothe, not seduce. "I got some info, but waiting on more." He told her what the Austin PD said about her cousin.

"Mom said about the same thing about Fran disappearing."

"You asked her about Fran?"

"Yeah."

Her tone told him how much that talk hurt her and he knew he'd pushed for it, but that was his job. It was why she'd come to him in the beginning. "Someone from Austin PD is going out to Fran's boyfriend's place to check things out there. They'll call me when they get back. Someone's combing through our old cases to find the Jenny Reed file. Sheriff Harper says there aren't any cameras near the pay phone that your call came from, so that might be a wash, but he was going to see Fran's mother. He's supposed to report back to me."

She nodded.

"Finding your cousin will get us halfway to solving this thing," he said, hoping Fran Roberts hadn't permanently disappeared.

Annie sat completely still as if to take it all in. Then

she took a deep breath. He recognized the haunted look in her eyes as the one he often saw in his own. Maybe they could help each other move past that—and if not past it, at least help each other forget for a while.

She blinked, and he saw her try to pull the curtain over her pain. "Thank you."

"No thanks needed." Studying her, he was hesitant to ask, but it had to be done. "Did you go to the park to . . . to see if it brings back any memories?"

The soft blue of her eyes darkened.

"I tried," she said. "I drove there but I couldn't get out of the car. I know it's silly, but—"

"Not silly," he assured her. "But it's something we should do sooner or later."

She nodded. "We should start eating or we'll run out of time." She grabbed a chair and pulled it around her desk for him, then pulled the salads out of the bag. "Are these the same?"

"Yeah." He took the salad she handed him. "I spoke with Brad, my friend with the garage. He said he can paint your car door for a hundred."

She looked up. "That's awfully cheap."

"He named his price. Said to drop the car off tomorrow morning. He'll try to have it for you by the afternoon."

"Thanks." She stabbed a piece of chicken. "I didn't like the attention I got driving it to work."

"Sorry, I didn't think about that. What time do you get off? I might be able to give you a lift."

"Don't be silly. I'm a big girl."

No, she wasn't. She was small, sweet, and even a little vulnerable. But he didn't think she wanted to hear that.

"I can take an Uber if I decide to. I'm fine."

He forked a bite of his salad. "I know. I've thought about just how fine all day."

She rolled her eyes. He laughed.

"Did your building superintendent send someone to fix the window?" He'd stopped by the office this morning, insisted they get it done today.

"Someone was working on it when I left."

They talked about her classes and college years. He tried to bring up Dr. Murdock. Maybe she'd be willing to see him. Perhaps Murdock could pull up more of her memories and try to figure out what parts of the dream were true. But he couldn't work it into the conversation.

Considering how he hated seeing a shrink, he worried she'd feel the same. Then again, she wanted to find the truth. He knew his own truth and was trying to forget it.

"You like cherry tomatoes?" He enjoyed watching her eat.

"Love 'em."

"Here." He held the tomato to her lips. She took the tomato into her mouth. Seeing her lips wrap around the fruit sent a jolt of need below his belt.

Moving from his chair, he sat on the edge of her desk and kissed her again.

It went from hot to hotter. When his jeans became crowded, he pulled back and ran a finger over her lips. "You wouldn't have a supply closet handy, would you?"

She slapped his chest playfully.

"I'm joking. Mostly."

"What do I owe you for lunch?"

"Nothing. It was seven bucks and well worth your company."

"I'm buying next time."

"How about you buy dinner tonight? I know this great hole-in-the-wall Chinese restaurant by my house. Afterward, you come over and meet Bacon."

"I...can't. I told Isabella I'd have dinner with her."

He had to work to hide his disappointment. "Okay."

"Rain check?" she asked.

"Yeah." How many times had he refused to see a woman the night after having slept with her? A back-to-back sleepover made it feel...serious. No matter how good the sex was, serious was scary. No matter how much he liked Annie, serious wasn't exactly what he was offering.

Was that her motivation for saying no?

A better question was why the hell he'd suggested it.

CHAPTER FIFTEEN

After lunch, Adam Harper pulled up at Doris Roberts's house. He'd gotten the address from Jennifer. Jennifer, whom he'd given a come-to-Jeezus talk about repeating anything she heard from his office. She'd apologized and explained that because he'd been laughing about it, she thought it was a joke.

He couldn't argue. He'd told a bunch of people, too, thinking it was funny. Maybe he owed himself a come-to-Jeezus talk.

It wasn't that he didn't take his job seriously, it was that his job was seldom serious. The biggest case he'd investigated lately was Pauline Patterson's stolen glider. Sure, they had a few arrests for weed, a couple DUIs, and too many domestic violence cases, but Pearlsville's aging population just didn't cause much trouble.

When he'd taken over as sheriff, he'd been a father of two teens and a husband to a gem of a gal. He'd had everything to live for, and lower crime meant a longer life expectancy. Now that his girls were grown and gone and his wife passed, he wouldn't mind a few good cases. He supposed he just didn't have that much to live for anymore.

He pushed that thought aside. He'd moved past the depression, but he needed to find something to fill his time with besides work.

His daughters, who lived in Dallas and Houston, suggested he find a hobby. But building a ship in a bottle or chasing a golf ball had never been his thing. His two sons-in-law suggested he get on the Internet and meet women.

He liked their suggestion better.

And he might do that just as soon as the idea of doing it stopped feeling like a betrayal to his wife. Then again, it had been five years. Maybe it would never stop.

He got out of his car. The house, a mile from George Reed's place, was just as secluded as her brother's, not nearly as old, but it could win yard-of-the-month. Colorful flowers and manicured beds.

As pretty as the house looked, his gut labeled it a façade. Dysfunction lived there.

He took one step when the garage door groaned open. A woman holding a ten-pound bag of mulch walked out.

She saw him, shrieked, dropped the mulch, and shot back in the garage.

He recognized her and her scream. The same woman who'd pointed a BB gun at his face. The garage door started lowering, but not before he spotted the car. A red 2016 Malibu.

He rushed to the door and knocked. Knocked again. "Open the door!"

"Leave or I'll get my gun again!" came the reply.

Well, shit!

* * *

By two thirty, Mark had chased down the last lead on Johnny. He'd hoped to get something, but he got shit. He'd called Johnny two more times. Johnny hadn't called back.

Remembering his morgue appointment, his mood nosedived.

With some time to spare, he went to the coffee shop, got a cup of coffee, and parked his ass at a table. He pulled out Annie's case notes, hoping to be ready for the case update with Connor and Juan.

But he ended up thinking about Annie. About her no-show vote for tonight. About how damn disappointed he was. At her for not accepting, and at himself for asking. Breaking his own rule.

After so long of not being that invested in a woman, being invested now shocked his system. What was it about Annie that sucked him in? Sure, she was beautiful. But he'd done beautiful before.

It was more. It was her halo. Her intelligence. The familiar, haunted look he sometimes saw in her eyes. It was the blend of spunk and vulnerability. Sweet yet sassy. It was the peace he felt when he was with her.

His phone rang. Hoping it was Johnny, he answered without checking the screen. "Detective Sutton."

"You ain't gonna believe this shit."

"What shit?" Mark recognized Sheriff Harper's voice.

"Guess what I spotted in Doris Roberts's garage?"

"What?" he asked, less than thrilled with the old man's way of dispensing information.

"A red Malibu."

"Fran's there?"

"Her car is. No one will open the door. I'm thinking Ms. Roberts isn't here. I did see the other sister. The one with mental issues. She saw me and ran inside. When I insisted she open the door, she threatened to get her gun."

"Damn."

"Yeah. I called Jenny and asked about her aunt Doris's whereabouts. She said her aunt worked part-time for a used car lot in the next town over. I called the brother, George, and he's not answering. Neither are any of the other Reeds. I suspect someone will be home by dinnertime. So I'm parking my ass in this car and sweating my balls off until someone shows."

Mark ran a hand through his hair, remembering what he'd told Annie. *Finding your cousin will get us halfway to solving this thing.*

He needed more info to present to Connor and Juan about this case. He needed to be there. Connor and Juan could attend the show-and-tell at the morgue. The only thing pressing was waiting for calls, he could do this.

Hell, by missing the trip to the morgue, he'd save himself a chip of his soul.

"I'm on my way."

* * *

Adam sat in the car wondering about the first sign of heat stroke.

Every five minutes, he'd turn his car on and point the air vents in his face. It took three minutes to cool off but two to get hot again after cutting the engine off. He'd have kept the car running, but the dang thing was on its last life.

He'd told the county he needed a new one, they'd told him they couldn't afford one.

He saw the curtain flutter in the window. Whether it was just Sarah Reed, or the missing cousin, was anyone's guess. But no way in hell was he leaving and let that red Malibu disappear and make him look like a fool.

Especially with Sutton headed this way.

Adam glared at his watch. Did the green-behind-the-ears cop drive like an ol' woman?

In all fairness, it'd only been forty-five minutes, but when miscrable, you wanted company.

He heard a car. Using some rescued napkins from the diner, he wiped off his forehead and prepared himself to meet Sutton. He got out of the car and saw the purple Cadillac, needing shocks, bouncing down the dirt driveway.

He didn't see Sutton driving a Cadi the color of a grape Tootsie Roll Pop.

The car pulled around his cruiser and parked in front of the garage.

Out of that car, wearing a dress two sizes too small,

came Doris Roberts. It wasn't that she didn't have a good figure, she did, but between the Texas hair, too-thick makeup, and tight clothes, she looked like she worked on a corner.

Her car door slamming filled the hot air. Smiling, she came strutting over. "I always was a sucker for a guy in a uniform."

"Ma'am." He made a mental note to wear street clothes next time.

"What can I do for you, Sheriff?"

If nervous, she was hiding it. Or good at lying. "I wanted to ask—"

"Not in the heat," she said. "Come on inside. I'll make you some iced tea. I'll even put a splash of some-thing in it."

"Can't drink while on the job."

"Don't tell me you're a rule follower."

"I try."

She moved to the door. Adam dagged her steps, noting, but not appreciating the exaggerated sway of her hips. It was nice knowing he wasn't desperate enough to go for it.

As she unlocked the door, he added, "Your sister saw me, so you might want to make sure she knows it's you. Wouldn't want her to accidentally shoot the wrong person."

She looked over her shoulder. "I like a man with a sense of humor, too."

"I wasn't joking."

"Sarah. I'm here." Ms. Roberts motioned Adam inside.

Sarah stood in the doorway. "He's been watching our house," she said, sounding like a ten-year-old tattling.

"It's fine. Why don't you read while the sheriff and I visit?"

"I wanna work in the flower beds."

"Then go." Ms. Roberts led him into the kitchen. A kitchen that looked cleaner than the local diner on health-inspection day. "Have a seat."

"I prefer to stand."

She pulled a pitcher from the fridge, set it on the counter, and turned around. "You're here about Jenny, aren't you?"

"In part."

"I wish I could tell you more, but there's nothing to tell. Jenny went missing. We called the police." She filled two glasses with ice and tea. She topped off one glass with whiskey.

"What did you tell the police?"

"I recall mentioning Fran had seen her playing in the river. Of course, there were those scary bikers camping there, too. Poor child. No telling what she endured."

The ice crackled and popped in the glasses. She handed him the virgin one.

She didn't know he'd seen the car and he decided to use it. "You have a child, right?" He sipped his tea. With his body's core temperature still right at a hundred, it felt good going down.

"Sure do. Tell me...Adam, right?"

"Sheriff Harper," he said.

She blinked away the flash of discontent. "How does

your wife stand it, a good-looking man like yourself going into lonely women's homes?"

Adam touched his gold band with his thumb. "I'm doing a job. Tell me about your daughter? Did—"

"Now why would you care about Fran?"

"A detective in Anniston is trying to reach her. Your daughter seems to be missing. Her ex-husband filed a police report."

"Don should know better. Fran gets in her moods and takes off somewhere to be by herself."

"She came to her uncle's funeral, right?"

"Of course. She's a good daughter, just still finding herself. She'll show up in a few days."

"Was she upset at the funeral?"

"No."

He frowned. "We heard she seemed—"

"Fine," she conceded. "She was upset and drunk. Her uncle had died."

"Did she say where she was going?"

"No. Just up and left."

"And you ... let her go?"

"Why would I stop her? She's an adult."

"Because you said she was drunk."

For the first time, Ms. Roberts appeared genuinely annoyed. "She's a big girl."

And drunk big girls die while driving drunk. "So she just drove off."

"How many times do I have to say it?"

Enough to catch you in a lie. A knock shattered the kitchen silence.

* * *

"Details, and don't gloss over the sexy parts!" Isabella pulled out glasses while Annie opened the wine.

Annie had finished her classes and gone home to dish out food and love to Pirate. The quietness of her apartment drove her thoughts to her conversation with her mom. The idea that her mother was in any way involved in Jenny's disappearance rocked Annie's already shaky foundation.

What if by reporting this, she got her mother sent to jail? Annie's lungs suddenly felt oxygen deprived. Telling herself her mom was innocent wasn't cutting it. So when she saw Isabella's car pull up, she snatched a bottle of wine and headed next door.

Annie pulled out the cork. It made a pop that echoed in her still-tight chest.

"Start talking." Isabella rubbed her hands together.

Annie offered a half-felt grin. "It was good."

"Wait. Good, or great?"

Bottle opened, she carried it to the table and poured. "Great."

"No first-date awkwardness?"

Annie sipped her wine. Flavors of cherry and chocolate danced on her tongue. But her mind danced on something else. "I slept with him. That was awkward."

"Stop beating yourself up. You're an adult. He's an adult. You didn't hurt anyone." She paused. "He didn't pressure you, did he?"

"No. It was me."

"Yes! I love a woman who goes for what she wants."

"I don't know what made me do it." She closed her eyes a second. "Oh, God, Isabella. I don't know if I'm ready for this."

"Quit worrying." Isabella sipped her wine. "Has he called?"

"He called this morning. We had lunch together."

She clinked her glass against Annie's. "Has he asked you out again?"

"He suggested we go out tonight."

"Then why the hell are you here?"

"I'd already agreed to meet you and . . ."

"And what?"

"I'm scared. It happened so fast, and he's investigating what happened to Jenny. That first time I went to see him, he thought I was crazy. What if he finds out about me being fired for reporting those kids? Or about my arrest for breaking the restraining order?"

"You haven't told him about that?" Isabella asked.

"No, it wasn't anything to do with Jenny. And it's not something you tell some guy on the first date. Not even the tenth date. I'm done with guys thinking I'm crazy."

"It was only your ex," Isabella said.

No, it wasn't. It was my friends, my boss. It was that little voice of doubt inside me. Annie dropped into a kitchen chair. "I finally find a guy who tempts me to dip my toe back into the whole dating scene, and it happens to be the one who can, and probably will, learn all my ugly secrets."

"Hey, they're not ugly. You were concerned about some kids. And the reason you did it was because of all this shit."

Isabella was right, but... "It still makes me look crazy. I got this bad feeling."

"Then tell him."

"What if he stops looking into the case. Or—"

"Then don't tell him. But don't let it destroy what might be something good. Which reminds me, you haven't really told me how good." A tell-me smile passed on her lips.

Annie sipped her wine. "It was awesome."

Isabella squealed. "That good, huh?"

"Yeah," Annie said. *But good doesn't mean it was right.*

The fried rice arrived, and they ate and talked.

"Have you spoken with your mom?" Isabella asked.

Annie swallowed and spilled. "I'm worried, Isabella. I don't believe my mom could have done anything, but..."

"You did the right thing," Isabella said. "You have to remember that while the right thing might suck, the wrong thing would suck more. I know."

Emotion flashed across her friend's face. Maybe it was the wine, or maybe it was the spill-your-guts mood, but Isabella appeared willing to talk. "You're talking about your divorce?"

"Yeah." She refilled her glass.

"How did you know the divorce was the right thing?"

Isabella stared at her wine. "Because I couldn't look at him without knowing how much I let him down. How much I let myself down."

"You had a miscarriage. It's not your fault."

Regret and what looked like shame filled Isabella's eyes. "Yes it is. I had an abortion when I was seventeen. I was young, scared, and ignorant. I asked the doctor if that could have been the reason I lost my babies, he said it was possible. I never told Jose about the abortion. I was ashamed, then to learn it could have caused... This is my punishment, not his." Tears slipped down her cheeks.

Annie stood and hugged her. "It's still not your fault."

They held each other tightly, like good friends do when life hurts.

CHAPTER SIXTEEN

Adam had finished his tea when the knock sounded. "That's probably the detective from Anniston. He'll probably need to talk to you as well."

Ms. Roberts downed the tea but made no move to go open her door.

"Mind if I get that?"

"Finc." She grabbed the bottle of whiskey. "I hope it won't take too long."

Adam set his glass in the sink and went to answer the knock.

Door opened and he locked gazes with the tall, dark-haired man.

"Sutton, I suppose," Adam said.

"Sheriff," the man said.

Adam motioned Sutton to follow him outside. They moved toward the car to make sure no one was eavesdropping. But Adam still gave the sister working in the flower garden a glance.

"Is Fran here?" Sutton asked.

"That's where it gets interesting," Adam said.

"Just tell me," Sutton insisted.

So impatient. "The mom doesn't know I spotted the car in her garage. I asked about her daughter and she told me her daughter drove off after the funeral."

"That's what she told me, too."

A ring sounded. Sutton pulled his phone out and eyed the number. "Sorry. It's about another case, I've got to take this. Give me a minute."

Adam started to the porch when he heard another car. A gold Toyota pulled down the drive and parked beside his cruiser.

The blonde stepped out of the car, JoAnne Lakes, if he recalled her name correctly. Adam found himself sucking in his gut, and wishing he wasn't so sweaty. *Lakes?* So this was the mother to Sutton's witness.

If the daughter looked half as good as her mother, Adam didn't blame Sutton for being interested in the case.

"Sheriff." Her lips pursed. "Is something wrong?"

"No, ma'am. Just here to talk to Ms. Roberts." He stepped closer.

Ms. Lakes glanced at Sutton.

"That's the detective from Anniston," Adam said.

A frown pulled at her eyes.

"Do you mind if I ask you a few questions, since you're here?" Adam asked.

Her posture tightened. "I guess." Locking her car, she started toward the house.

"In my car. I'll turn the air on."

She flinched. "Are you arresting me?"

"No ma'am. Just to talk."

"Stop!" The sister working in the yard came running over. "Leave her alone."

"It's okay, Sarah," Ms. Lakes said. "Why don't you go inside?"

"Doris said I could work in the flower beds."

"Okay," Ms. Lakes said. The sister went back to pulling weeds.

Opening the passenger door, Ms. Lakes hesitantly got in.

Adam crawled behind the wheel and started the engine and air. He saw Sutton shoot him a what-the-hell look but ignored it.

Ms. Lakes glanced around. "I've never been in a police car."

"It's not exciting," he said, still holding in his gut.

He studied her as she studied the dashboard. The similarities between her and Ms. Roberts were there, but the differences were more noticeable. One appeared hard, one soft. One appeared worn out, one fresh. One guilty. One...innocent.

Yup, his gut said JoAnne Lakes wasn't guilty of any wrongdoing. But gut instinct wasn't enough. "The main reason I'm here is that your niece, your sister's daughter, Francyne Roberts, is missing."

"Yes, but my sister told me Fran often goes off to be by herself."

He nodded. "Were you at the funeral?"

"Of course. He was my brother." Her quick intake of air sounded emotional.

His chest tightened in response. "I heard your niece was drinking and upset when she left."

Ms. Lakes folded her hands in her lap. "Unfortunately, she does that sometimes."

"And no one had a problem with her driving while under the influence?"

"We'd never let her do that," Ms. Lakes insisted. "My brother George drove her home."

And there it was. The truth. Confirmation his gut was right about JoAnne Lakes. But why would Ms. Roberts lie?

* * *

"Thank you for returning my call," Mark told Johnny Harden again, feeling successful at finding a man no one thought could be found. His sense of accomplishment peaked when Johnny claimed he could identify the man he'd seen pushing a barrel into the lake where his victim had been found. Yeah, Johnny had been drunk, but considering the barrel had been found, it might hold up in court.

"Yes. Two o'clock tomorrow would be fine. I'll see you then."

Mark hung up, trying to hang on to the feeling of success. His conversation with Juan about the morgue visit on the ride up here had darkened his mood. The kid had died from a head injury. Worse yet, the results hadn't offered any leads. And while Mark might have skipped the meeting, saving himself from seeing it, hearing about it had still taken its toll on him.

No way in hell was he letting the killer get away with this.

Pocketing his phone, his pain, and the desire for whiskey, he switched gears and cases. He spotted the woman working the flower beds looking at him. When he'd pulled up, she'd refused to speak to him. He'd figured this was the mentally challenged sister, Jenny Reed's mother, who'd taken a gun to the sheriff.

Unsure why he did it, he walked over to where she worked. "You enjoy gardening?"

She looked up. "I like making things pretty."

"I'll bet your daughter was pretty. Her name was Jenny, right?"

She didn't say anything. Her hands stopped moving in the soil. He almost walked away when she spoke. "She was pretty. But I'm not supposed to talk about her. George gets mad."

"Why can't you talk about her? Why does he get mad?" He held his breath.

Looking up from the ground, she put a dirty finger to her lips. "Shh."

Focusing back on the mulch, she started spreading it, and commenced humming as if the conversation was over.

He took one step when she spoke again. "Sometimes I can almost hear them singing." She went back to gardening.

"Who?"

"The flowers."

"Right." He walked toward the police cruiser, now occupied by the sheriff and the woman who'd shown up. A woman who'd looked almost familiar. Almost.

When the sheriff saw Mark approaching the car, he got out of his car.

"Who's that?" Mark asked, following the sheriff a few steps away.

Adam reared back on his heels. "That's JoAnne Lakes. Isn't she the mom of your witness?"

Shit. Mark dipped his head down to see Ms. Lakes. She looked up. Their gazes met. Held. She had blue eyes and a pretty face. But she frowned. Mark barely held his back. Face it, he was sleeping with her daughter, and getting on her bad side wasn't smart. Neither was dating a witness. So he wasn't smart, but he still had a job to do.

But keeping his relationship with Annie low-key would serve him and the case well. "What did she say?"

"It's interesting."

"Then tell me." Mark's impatience punctuated the sentence.

The sheriff stiffened.

Remembering his manners, and kicking himself for the lack of respect for a man who was helping him, Mark said, "Sorry. What do we have?"

"When I asked Ms. Lakes about her niece leaving the funeral while drinking, she told me that her brother George drove Francyne home."

"That's not what Ms. Roberts told me." Mark mentally rehashed the short conversation they'd had. She hadn't claimed her daughter had driven her car home, but she'd insinuated it when she'd said she didn't know where she'd gone.

"Yeah," the sheriff said. "When I spoke with her, I asked about letting her daughter drive drunk and she responded, 'She's a big girl.'"

"Okay." Mark's mind wrapped around that info. "Now we have to figure out why Doris would lie about her brother taking her daughter home."

"Yup." The sheriff glanced back at his car. "I don't think Ms. Lakes is behind this."

"She might not be behind her niece's disappearance, but her daughter believes she's lying about some things. Did you ask Ms. Lakes about Jenny?"

"No."

Mark glanced at the house. "Did you ask Ms. Roberts about Jenny?"

"Just briefly. She gave me the same answer as before. Drowned or some motorcycle gangster grabbed her."

"Why don't we each take one and question them again. See if their stories match. Ask for specific details."

"I've got Ms. Lakes," the sheriff said.

That had been Mark's plan, but…"What's wrong with Ms. Roberts?"

Adam spoke in a low voice. "She's got the hots for my body."

Mark chuckled. "Fine." He started toward the porch and saw Jenny Reed's mother watching him.

* * *

"Let's go over it one more time." Mark jotted down notes in the pad he carried in his pocket. "What do you remember about the day Jenny disappeared?"

"This is ridiculous!" Ms. Roberts looked out the window where she'd been keeping an eye on the police cruiser.

Turning, she glared at Mark. He actually preferred this look to the one of lust she'd had when he first walked in. But damn, he understood the sheriff's issues. Not a good feeling.

"Why is the sheriff keeping my sister in his car?"

"He's simply asking her questions."

She lifted up her chin. "How many times do we have to tell the story?"

"Until we get to the truth." Mark's voice remained even, but this woman raked across every nerve he had. He supposed he raked across a few of hers, too. And he hadn't even approached the fact that she lied to him about how her daughter left the funeral.

"We were about to leave when we realized Jenny wasn't around." She lifted her drink that looked like iced tea, but Mark smelled whiskey. He was tempted to ask her to pour him one. "So we called the police," she said, her tone a decibel too high.

"Wasn't Jenny with her two cousins?"

"Yes. Earlier."

"What did they say about Jenny's disappearance?"

"They were young. They didn't know what to say."

"Did the police talk to them?" Mark prayed Mildred found those files. Without them, the case wouldn't make.

"It was a long time ago."

"But considering your niece went missing, I'd presume you'd be able to recall if the police spoke with your daughter."

"Well, I can't!"

Her attitude only fueled him. "What time did you report her missing?"

"Enough already. I told you, it was eight in the morning. I can't remember more."

Mark rubbed his hand over his chin. "But your mind is fine, right? You're not suffering from any kind of ailment? Dementia?"

Her eyes became two slits, her left palm found her hip, and her right hand shook her glass, rattling the ice. "My mind is a steel trap. I'm not elderly."

"I didn't mean to insinuate that," he lied. Sometimes rattling a witness would shake something loose. "Maybe Jenny's mom would remember. Would you mind if I—"

"No. Leave Sarah alone. She's mentally disabled."

"So let me ask you about your missing daughter."

"I told you everything over the phone!"

He held out one hand. "Just so I'm straight. You told me your daughter left in a huff and didn't let you know where she was going. Correct?"

"Congratulations!" the woman snapped. "You don't have dementia, either."

"So the statement is correct?"

"Yes! Now leave. And tell the sheriff to let my sister go."

"Not so fast," Mark said. "You see, my problem is that I know your daughter's car is parked in your garage. And I'm having a hard time figuring out why you'd lie about that."

Her face reddened, her eyes tightened, her hand landed back on her hip. He could see her wheels spinning, trying to find a way out of the corner she'd backed herself into.

The front door opened. He looked back as the sheriff and Ms. Lakes walked inside. They entered the kitchen. Ms. Lakes looked a little pale, the sheriff a little pissed. Mark couldn't help but wonder if Harper still thought the woman was innocent.

"Don't say another word," Ms. Roberts snapped. "We need a lawyer."

* * *

Mark didn't get home until seven. He'd called Juan and Connor to inform them about Johnny. He wanted to call Annie. Was her window fixed? Was she still afraid? Mark kept backing-and-forthing on the amount of danger she was really in. Without anything else happening, a broken window and spray-painted car didn't set off too many alarm bells, but her missing cousin was another story.

He picked up his phone, then dropped it. She was probably still out with her friend. And how would he tell her he'd seen her mother? While Sheriff Harper wanted to believe Lakes was innocent, he'd admitted she'd behaved differently when questioned about Jenny's disappearance.

Was the whole family behind the murder?

How was Annie going to take hearing his suspicions?

How was he going to feel delivering them?

Yeah, Annie admitted her mom appeared to be hiding something, but that didn't mean she wouldn't want to shoot the messenger. He pushed thoughts of Annie to the back burner. He'd call her tomorrow, and maybe they'd do lunch again. Maybe by then, he'd figure out how to present the mother news.

Unfortunately, with Annie off the front burner, the Talbot case got upgraded. He paced through his house—something he regularly did when digesting a case. His fast, moving-to-move pace landed him in his game room. In one corner was the pool table, in the other was the big special laminated table he used for both Ping-Pong and poker. Saturday was his day to host it, too.

The saxophone in the corner of the room caught his eye. He remembered seeing the musician lose himself in the music at Buck's Place.

Every time he saw his own instrument, it called to him. Every time he walked away. He wasn't even sure why.

He did another walk through his house, concentrating on the Talbot case. Remembering the image he'd seen of the child on the news. Dressed in a ballerina outfit, twirling with a huge smile on her face. Looking so...alive.

But damn, he needed a drink. He started to the kitchen, but stopped. Instead of reaching for the bottle, he reached for his tennis shoes and jogging clothes and took Bacon for a run. As his feet pounded against the concrete, he hoped the exertion would pound out the images.

It worked. At least some.

Forty-five minutes later, sweat dripping off of him

and Bacon barely panting, he arrived back at his house. He went in the backyard, turned the hose on himself, and felt the cool water stream down his chest and abs.

When his phone, on the patio table, dinged with a text, he set the hose down and grabbed it. From Annie. His heart took a jolt.

A good one.

A picture of a slice of Better than Sex Cheesecake appeared on his screen. He laughed, then read the text.

I don't know if I can eat all of this.

Hope making his lungs expand, he texted back. Is that an invitation?

He waited for what felt like forever for her answer.

Yes.

He pumped his fist in the air then texted back. Showering and leaving. Don't take a bite until I get there.

It better be a quick shower.

Her reply brought on another laugh. The excitement, the sensation of being part of something with someone, the anticipation of spending another night with Annie, felt as refreshing as the hose water. He felt more alive than he had in years.

Recalling the conversation they needed to have about her mom gave him pause, but it didn't shadow his mood.

He hurried inside, stripping down as he went, hopping on one foot to remove his shoes and shorts as he made his way into the bathroom. Bacon, thinking it was a game, snatched up his socks and followed him.

Mark retrieved his socks out of the dog's mouth,

dropped them in the dirty clothes hamper, and made a mental note to pick up his shoes before he left so Bacon wouldn't eat them. When he turned on the shower, the dog plopped down on the tiled floor and glanced up at Mark with sad, you're-leaving-me eyes.

"Hey. We made this deal when I brought you home from the shelter. I give you two squares a day, a run—and today you had two—and a big backyard to shit in that's accessible to you twenty-four-seven, but I might be gone long hours."

The dog whimpered. "Tomorrow I don't work until two, so I'll come home early and take you for a run and take you to the dog park. And I promise no overnight stay tomorrow. Unless... How do you feel about cats?"

The dog whimpered. Mark reached into the dirty clothes and gave the dog one of his socks.

Bacon barked and his tail thumped from side to side. Mark grinned, only slightly embarrassed that he'd become such a sap when it came to his dog.

CHAPTER SEVENTEEN

Annie started stripping as soon as he'd texted back. She bolted toward her bathroom. Pirate hobbled excitedly beside her, certain they were playing a game of cat and mouse.

She got to the bathroom, turned on the shower, dropped her clothes in the hamper, and stepped under the spray of water before it was warm.

Squealing, she grabbed the soap and started washing. Yup, this made it official. She was definitely a slut. Not that she cared. Since she'd come home from Isabella's a little wine buzzed, she'd been trapped in a doom and gloom mood. Thinking about her mom, about Fran, about Isabella's problems with her ex. About Jenny. About her washed-up career as an elementary teacher.

And about someone wanting to shut her up.

Her life was a smorgasbord of pick & choose depressing topics. Each hurt in a different way.

Yet, when she thought about Mark, she felt lighter.

Yes, there was the I-might-be-screwing-up vibe low in her belly. But then a wiggle of happiness caused butterflies in the same general region. She wanted more of that. More butterflies. More of him. More time not thinking about the smorgasbord.

It wasn't just the sex. There was the teasing. The banter. The brand-new feeling he gave her. As if a better chapter of her life awaited her.

And then there was the sex.

Yup. She was buzzed but didn't care.

Showering in record speed, she jumped out, dried off, and debated her wardrobe. She could put on something slinky, something barely there, but...No. She could put on something nice, with heels, but...no.

She found a pair of folded cutoff jeans and snagged a yellow tank top. Spotting the pink one, she traded for it.

Dashing to her dresser, she found her only sexy matching bra and panty set. In pink.

She dressed, then found her pink socks and her pink canvas tennis shoes. For one second, she debated if it was too much pink. But nope. The man liked pink.

Putting on minimum makeup and blow-drying her hair, she studied her smiling face in the mirror.

"There are worse things to be than a happy slut."

Pirate jumped up on the counter begging for attention. He got it.

Realizing she hadn't changed her sheets from the night before, she hurried out of the bathroom, stripped the bed, and put on her nicest sheets—Egyptian eight hundred thread count.

Before she tossed the sheets and pillowcases in the

hamper, she put them to her nose. They smelled like him. Anticipation slid over her like a warm blanket.

She darted back into the bedroom, and had just finished fluffing the pillows when her doorbell rang.

Running to the door, she barely remembered to look through the peephole to confirm it was him.

It was.

She opened the door. He stood there staring and smiling and looking totally hot in worn jeans and a navy T-shirt. His hair appeared wet and a bit mussed. Then it hit what else he wore. Happiness.

"Hi," he said.

"Hi," she repeated his word and his smile.

"Don't you look . . . damn cute."

"Cute?" she asked. "Choose another adjective."

"What's wrong with cute?" He stepped inside, shut the door, and pulled her against him.

"Adorable is good." She looked up at him. He smelled like toothpaste and something musky, spicy, probably male deodorant. She wanted to bury her face in his chest and get drunk on that scent.

He laughed. "What's wrong with cute?"

"My mama said puppies are cute. Women are supposed to be glamorous, sexy, beautiful."

"You're that too." His lips met hers and the kiss was perfection.

When he pulled away, he looked around her. "Where's my cheesecake?"

They ate cheesecake. Talked. Laughed. Laughed a lot. The mood was playful. Everything she needed to push her problems back.

Somehow, she ended up straddling his lap and kissing him. His hands moved all over her. In her hair, under her shirt, and... between her thighs.

She became lost in his kisses, touches, the sound of her own breath. The sound of his.

When he tugged off her tank top, a smile tightened his eyes. "Pink. You wore it for me, didn't you?"

"Maybe," she said feeling both bashful and bold.

He ran a finger over the pink satin, circling her tightened nipple beneath. She dropped her head back, letting his touch be the only thing she felt. Let it take her to the only place where she felt free of that damn smorgasbord.

The next thing she knew he had her standing and was unzipping her shorts. As the material slid down her hips, he kissed her abdomen. The butterfly touch of his lips on her skin had her knees weakening and her pulse soaring.

"And they match."

He slipped one finger under the elastic of her panties and touched every nerve she had there. Damp heat pooled between her legs. Tugging her a little closer, he pressed another moist kiss to her stomach, then his tongue dipped into her belly button.

She flinched, never expecting it to be that sensitive.

He began easing her back on his lap, but she stopped. Reaching down, she caught the hem of his T-shirt and slipped it over his head.

The sight of his skin, his beautiful bare, muscle-ripped skin, filled her gaze. His chest, abs and arms were so damn perfect they looked photoshopped.

"Nice," she said.

He smiled. "Choose another adjective."

"Which one would you like?" she asked with humor.

"Irresistible would work."

"You got it." Then she noted, "No gun."

"Ankle holster."

"Oh."

He must have heard her lack of approval. "It's coming off."

He removed the gun, set it on the end table, then looked up. His gaze swept over her, standing in front of him donned in nothing but her pink panties, her pink bra, and, no doubt, desire shining in her eyes.

"Wow." He inhaled, then motioned to himself. "Anything else you want me to take off?"

"Perhaps." She motioned to his jeans.

"You want me naked?" His tone was teasing, tempting, and totally refreshing. The man had his own special brew of seduction and wit down to an art.

Standing, he picked her up. Her legs automatically wrapped around his hips. His forehead came against hers. "I want you in bed," he said.

The short walk to her bedroom went fast. He gently placed her on the mattress then started stripping, his shoes, his socks, his jeans, his underwear. He stood at the edge of her bed completely naked. His sex hard, erect.

She scooted the bedspread off, and when the satin of her underwear met up with Egyptian cotton she felt surrounded by softness.

But it was his hardness she wanted. Placing one knee

on the bed, he curled up beside her. So drunk on his seduction, she almost forgot, but managed to whisper, "Condom."

"Not yet. Relax. I've got a plan." He swiped his tongue over his lips. If that wasn't enough of a hint of his intent, he slipped his hand into her panties, into her damp readiness, then pulled it out and pressed it to his lips.

He kissed her, then started inching down, nipping, licking, tasting. Devouring.

Annie had never ever been so turned on.

* * *

Mark woke up when Annie crawled out of bed. His first thought was that he'd slept. Actually slept. How long had it been since...

He watched her wobble to the bathroom with a sheet wrapped around her. He watched the tent in the blanket covering his waist rise. Desire, even after a night of exhausting and satisfying sex, had him waking up a little more.

"Where are you going?" he asked, his voice morning hoarse.

Turning, she adjusted the sheet to hide her breasts. "Shower. I have to work at nine. Isabella is going to go with me to drop my car at the garage."

"I could do it. I don't go in until two."

"I got it covered."

She had lots of things covered he wished she didn't.

"You know, I'm pretty sure there's not an inch of you that I didn't see or taste last night."

Her cute look made his heart dip. "That was last night."

"I know. Which is why I'd like to see it again."

She rolled her eyes. "No time."

He continued to study her, loving that she looked as free from stress as he did. "You didn't have a dream last night, did you?"

"No. I think I was too tired to dream."

"I'd say I'm sorry, but I'm not."

Grinning, she turned and continued into the bathroom.

He looked down at his tent. "I tried."

Dropping back down on the pillow, he mentally gathered his to-do list for the day. His promises he'd made Bacon rose to the surface. Then, when his mind hit on checking in with the Austin police about Fran, he remembered he hadn't broached the subject with Annie about seeing her mom. Neither had he brought up the possibility of her talking to the police shrink.

Did he really need to do that this morning?

Another smell tickled his senses. Coffee. Annie must have her pot set on automatic. As he sat up, Pirate, lying on the end of the bed, hissed at him.

"We need to get along. And while I'm thinking about it, how do you feel about dogs?"

The cat hissed again.

"We'll work on it." Getting up, he found his boxers. Still sporting a stiffy, he went to collect some caffeine.

He cut the corner into the kitchen and stopped dead in his tracks when he and his stiffy found themselves face-to-face with Annie's mom. Annie's mom, who at this moment held his gun.

"Drop that!"

"Oh." She gasped.

"Shit," he muttered.

She set the gun down. He picked it up. She swung around as if his near nakedness bothered her, and he raced back into Annie's bedroom. Shutting the door, he went into the bathroom and set his gun on the counter.

"Annie?"

"Oh," she yelped, sounding just like her mom. The shower curtain shifted, and she looked out. "You scared me."

Your mom scared me. "Your mom's here."

"Here? Now?" Her eyes rounded.

"Yeah? I smelled coffee and ... she's in the kitchen."

"You didn't tell her who you were, did you?"

The odd question sparked a nerve. "No. But she knows."

"How?"

"I met her yesterday in Pearlsville. I went there to interview Fran's mother."

Annie stood frozen, water running down her face, eyes still rounded. "You didn't tell me."

"I was going to, but ... it didn't come up."

"Shit," she muttered.

"I said the same thing."

A door slammed. "I think she left." He ran a palm over his face. How messy was this going to become? The little impropriety of dating a witness just got a whole lot bigger.

Annie snatched a robe hanging beside the shower. She tied it around her waist, knotted it twice, then picked up her phone. "Should I text her?" She looked at him as if for advice.

He had nothing.

She hugged herself and frowned. "What did my mom tell you yesterday?"

He hesitated. "Sheriff Harper discovered Fran's car in her mother's garage. Her mother said Fran left in the car. When asked, your mother said your uncle drove Fran back."

"So Fran's okay?"

"She's still missing."

Annie stood there as if trying to soak it all in. "So my mom told the truth. She's not involved?" She looked relieved.

He didn't answer.

"What?" she asked, as if seeing everything he wasn't saying in his expression.

He ran a hand over his face. "She was up front about Fran, but when asked about Jenny, she was evasive. Then your aunt asked for a lawyer. Your mother did the same."

Annie pulled tighter at her robe's sash. "And that makes her guilty?"

"I'm not saying...It doesn't look good."

"You don't know her. She'd never—"

His frustration shot up. "You even told me you felt she was lying."

"She wouldn't hurt a kid."

Mark's frustration continued to peak. "Her finding me here isn't good."

Annie's small frame tightened. "I asked you if that was going to be a problem. You said no."

"It's one thing to date a witness, but another if that witness is the daughter of a suspect."

"You're saying my mom is a suspect?"

Fuck. He was saying the wrong thing, but he couldn't stop. "How did she get in here?"

"She has a key."

He shook his head. "Why?"

Annie took a step back and tightened the robe's sash. "I need to call my mom. You...you should go."

* * *

He screwed up. Blaming Annie was wrong. He came to that conclusion halfway home.

He pulled over and called her.

It rang once. Twice. Three times.

It went to voice mail.

"I'm sorry. I was wrong. I...I was caught off guard. Call me?"

He started to go back, but decided to let his apology settle in, then he'd call her later with a second.

Did trying not to worry about being an ass make him more of an ass? Fuck! He didn't know. At home, he got dressed in running clothes, and took off. While he drove to the park, he called Austin PD. The cop in charge of the case wasn't there. Mark left a message. After he arrived at the park, he and Bacon jogged three miles.

As he was running, his phone dinged with a text. Annie?

He stopped, breathing hard, and got his phone. Not her.

Mildred's name flashed across the screen. I'm ordering prime rib!

She'd found the old Reed file.

He didn't need to be at work until two. But the precinct was on the way home. His mind made up, he called off Bacon's sniffing adventure and they took off.

When he got out of his car at the precinct, he remembered Bacon. "Come on, it's too hot to leave you here."

Bacon jumped out. They made their way in, Bacon's tail wagging, Mark's mood much darker. Mildred looked up from her desk and smiled. "Is it bring-your-dog-to-work day?"

"Where's the file?"

She studied him. "Nice legs."

"Where's the file?"

She pulled it out of the drawer and handed it over. "Keep frowning like that and you're gonna get another headache."

He inhaled. "Tough morning. Anything we can use in there?"

"Not sure. It's sad, though."

"Yeah," he said, realizing Annie's case was getting to the ugly stage. Where it became more than just about a crime, it became about a victim. About another child. Another one he couldn't save.

His phone rang. *Annie?* He pulled it out and checked the number. He frowned.

"Hey," Mark answered.

"Where are you?" Juan asked.

"At the precinct, picking up the Reed file Mildred found. Why?"

"Come to the office. I just discovered something in Gomez's file about the Talbot case. You're gonna want to hear this."

"Coming." He handed Mildred back the case file. "Make two more copies of this, one for Juan and one for Connor? I'll pick mine up on the way out."

CHAPTER EIGHTEEN

Mark and Bacon walked into the small room that housed the Cold Case Unit.

"Bacon," Connor said.

His dog bolted to collect some attention.

Juan chuckled. The good mood of his two partners reminded Mark of his bad one. "I'd give a hundred bucks if Sergeant Brown could walk in right now."

"He wouldn't care," Connor said. "Remember Mark here has the old man by the balls. He just won't tell us why."

Mark dropped into his chair and swung around. "We were at the dog park when Mildred texted that she found the file. What you got?" He looked at Juan.

Bacon left Connor and ran to Juan. "Remember I told you that Stone said the concrete in the barrel appeared to be high-grade stuff? That he was testing it to confirm it?"

"Yeah." The information took Mark into a dark

place where he had to think about what else was in that barrel. But holy hell, he hated that dark place.

"The test came back. It's definitely high grade. Used in construction and stuff. And guess who worked at Colman Concrete Company who does mostly construction jobs that use high-grade concrete?"

"Who?" Mark asked.

"Brian Talbot."

Bam! Mark felt sucker punched. He'd already crossed Talbot off as a suspect. How could his gut be so damn wrong? Even after what Mark's stepfather did to his own sister, he didn't want to believe a father could do that. *When the fuck am I going to learn to never think the best?* "You sure?"

"That's in Gomez's file. I haven't confirmed it. Yet."

"Shit," Mark said. "Confirm it. I'm bringing that son of a bitch in for another interview." He stood there, his neck muscles tightening, clenching his fists. "Do we have a picture of that asshole?"

"There's one in the paper file," Connor said.

"Cash is due here at two to be interviewed. Let's do a photo lineup. He swore he could recognize the man he saw push the barrel into the lake."

"Done," Connor said.

Feeling duped, and wanting to put that monster behind bars, Mark stood up. "I'll see you later."

"While you're here, why don't you give us the lowdown on the other case?" Juan said.

"Mildred's making copies of the file now. I'll tell her to bring them to you. After Johnny leaves, we can discuss it." Mark got almost to the door. Bacon followed.

"Hey," Connor called out.

"What?" Mark swung around. He sounded annoyed, because he was annoyed. No, he was downright pissed at himself. For being wrong about Brian Talbot. For taking his anger out on Annie.

Pissed that another father had killed his own kid. Pissed that those kinds of monsters existed out in this world.

Fucking pissed that he'd let his sister down.

"You okay?" Juan asked.

"He fucking killed his own daughter! No, I'm not okay!"

* * *

Mark got home, fed Bacon, texted Annie another apology, and showered. The hot, sudsy water washed away his sweat but not his frustration. It wasn't like they'd really had an argument. No one had raised their voice. She'd been upset. He'd been upset. She'd asked him to leave.

He'd left.

Oh, hell, he'd screwed up. Or had the real screw-up been getting involved to start with? He wasn't cut out for relationships. Was that why he'd done it? Had he subconsciously sabotaged what Annie and he were building? Hadn't he been afraid of wanting her too much?

But fuck! He was beginning to sound like Murdock.

The temptation to pour himself a glass of whiskey bit hard. He even went in the kitchen and stared at the cabinet where he kept the stuff that got him through tough times.

He didn't open that cabinet. He opened the fridge, poured himself a glass of milk, parked his ass and his laptop at the kitchen table, and decided to do something constructive—combing through the Jenny Reed file and preparing his notes to present to Juan and Connor.

The information in the file had him taking notes every few minutes. Several different family members were interviewed. It appeared the whole damn family had gone on the camping trip. The notes, taken by an Officer Raffin, stated there were sixteen Reed family members there. He started his file by noting all of those whom he'd interviewed. It even listed Francyne Roberts. But Mark noted right away who wasn't listed as being interviewed—JoAnne or Annie Lakes. Why?

He started reading. There were discrepancies in the different family members' statements. One said they realized five-year-old Jenny was missing around six. One said eight. One said the kids had been playing in the woods, another said they were playing by the lake.

Which was it?

Officer Raffin noted the discrepancies and even wrote SDFR, which was standard for "Something doesn't feel right."

He also had names and addresses and notes on his interviews with a few bikers who'd camped at the park. Ruffin stated all the bikers willingly cooperated. That clearly meant the officer's suspicions were not aimed at them.

Mark continued to read the Reed interviews. Again, there were discrepancies. Raffin even circled those passages.

A few pages in, Mark read about the interview with the young Francyne Roberts: *Child, age six, not helpful. Child appeared traumatized. When asked where her cousin went missing, she claimed she didn't remember. When asked if Jenny went into the lake, she claimed she might have. The second child, Annie Lakes, who had also been with the missing cousin, is not present. I was told she fell and had to go to the hospital to get stitches in her knee. Will follow up on interview with her and her mother later.*

"Fuck!" And there it was. Another piece of the puzzle. Another piece of the truth. Annie *had* gotten that scar at the lake and not from a bicycle fall. Maybe Murdock was wrong about how accurate dreams were. Why had her mother lied to Annie?

Mark turned to the page in the file, but there wasn't one. All he found was an envelope resting inside the back of the manila folder.

Where were the notes on the interview with Annie and her mom?

He opened the envelope. A photograph fell out. A photograph of a little blond girl with big blue eyes. A photograph of innocence.

Jenny Reed smiled and looked right into the camera. A knot formed in Mark's throat. Normally, it was the pictures of the dead ones that gnarled his chest. Then again, she was another dead girl. A girl that from now on, he would refer to as the victim, because saying the name hurt too much.

It didn't even matter that it had happened twenty years ago.

It didn't matter that he'd been eleven at the time.

He stared at the image. The fact that she looked like Annie made it hurt that much more.

"Who hurt you?" he said aloud. "Who let you down? Who...didn't protect you?"

And there it was, the voice from his past. *Don't go, Mark. Please. I'm scared. What if Daddy comes home yelling again? Who will keep me safe from Daddy, if you go?*

It had been a fucking party. He'd traded his sister's life, hadn't been there to protect her, for a few fucking beers and a chance to get laid.

Milk wasn't cutting it. He went to the cabinet where he kept his whiskey.

* * *

"How many classes did you agree to teach in the fall?" Isabella asked as she pulled up in the college parking lot.

"Seven." Annie stared at her phone, at Mark's text, unsure what to text back. She'd been so upset, she hadn't even heard it come in.

He'd been wrong. But so had she.

The whole thing was wrong. They should have never gone out. Now, wouldn't it be best to...Oh, heck, she probably shouldn't have taken her car to Mark's friend and taken advantage of his offer.

Isabella said something, but Annie hadn't heard it. Instead, she offered, "Thanks."

"You're welcome." Isabella parked.

Annie reached to the floorboard for her purse and briefcase holding the papers she needed to grade. She should've done them last night, but she'd been too busy having sex.

Could something that had felt so right have been a mistake?

And speaking of mistakes, why had Annie thought dredging all this up would help? It was making things worse. Fran was missing. Annie's mother might not ever speak to her again.

Annie reached for the door handle as Isabella touched her arm. "You okay?"

She hadn't told Isabella about the mess, because she hadn't come to grips with it. "My mom let herself in my apartment this morning."

"Did you talk again?"

"Mark was there."

"Ohh..." Isabella said it like it was a good thing. Followed by, "Ohh," like it wasn't. "What happened?" A smile lit up her eyes. "She didn't see him naked or anything."

"He had on his boxers, but the thing is, she knows he's the cop investigating Jenny's disappearance."

"How?"

"Yesterday he went to interview my aunt about my cousin Fran being missing." Annie slumped back in the car seat. "He thinks my mother is behind Jenny's murder. And he didn't tell me any of that until this morning."

"He told you that?"

"He called her a suspect." She swallowed back tears. "How am I going to live with myself if my mom goes to jail? I was nuts to start this relationship."

Isabella took her hand. "Hey, in all this time, all these years you've had that dream, you never suspected your mom to be the bad guy, did you?"

"No. Recently I've started to suspect she's hiding things but not—"

"Then believe it. Hold on to that. I've met your mom. She's not a murderer, Annie."

* * *

Mark walked into his office at noon. He had two hours before the Harden interview. Both Juan and Connor were gone. Probably out to lunch.

He dropped into his chair, almost missing it. Putting his gun in the drawer and his phone on the desktop, he snatched a pencil. He rolled it between his palms as he stared at his phone. Annie still hadn't called or texted.

That was fucked up. He was fucked up. Fucked up for starting this. And even more for being an ass.

He tossed the pencil across the room, wishing it had made a bigger crash to fit his mood. But hell, he had work to do. And getting to the bottom of what happened to Annie's cousin was his work. He hadn't wanted this case. Annie had brought it to him.

His mind went to the Reed report. He had questions. He rushed out of his office, hitting the edge of his desk in his haste, and went to seek answers.

The obvious place to find them wasn't the wisest lead to follow right now, but he didn't care.

He walked into his sergeant's office. Brown sat at his desk, a Big Mac in his hands, French fries on a napkin, and ketchup on his tie.

"What's up?" Brown asked.

Mark dropped his ass in the chair. "Did you read the morgue report on the Talbot victim?"

"Not yet. Why?"

"It's pointing us to the father again."

Brown dropped his burger and it fell apart. "I told you I liked that bastard for this."

"I know. I was wrong." Mark hated admitting that. "Anyway, we found Johnny Cash. His real name is Johnny Harden and he's coming here. I talked with him yesterday. He swore he could still identify the guy who rolled the barrel into the lake."

"He can swear all he wants. But he admitted to being drunk, so his testimony won't impress a DA."

"Why? His testimony was what led to us finding the body."

"I see your point, but they'll question it."

Mark leaned into the desk. "I don't give a shit what they question. He's a good witness."

Brown lifted his chin up and sniffed. "You've been drinking?"

"A couple at lunch," Mark lied. "I'm not due in until two."

"Then leave. Get some coffee, I can't have you here like this." Brown put his hamburger back together. "Out! Come see me after the interview. And be sober, damn it!"

Mark ignored the order. "Did you know an Officer Raffin?"

Brown frowned. "Yeah. He worked here when I hired on. Why?"

"Remember our case I called Sheriff Harper about?"

"Yeah, but I didn't know it was *our* case. Is it?" He took a bite of his lunch. Another glob of ketchup landed on his tie.

"It turned out the kid went missing here. Raffin is the one who looked into it. I read the report and I have questions. Is he here?"

Brown swallowed. "Retired. I saw him last year at a little coffee shop down the street. He'd lost his wife and was moving into an assisted living home. He has to be eighty, but he sounded good."

"You have his number?"

"No, but I remember where he said he'd moved to. My mother-in-law used to live there. It's called Retreat Living. By the old library on Macon Street." Brown frowned. "Now, get your ass out of here and don't come back until you're stone sober. Being drunk on the job is what landed you in the Cold Case Unit!"

"And I've been happier ever since," Mark said.

Brown's scowl was enough for Mark to realize he'd pushed it.

"I'm leaving."

* * *

Mark snagged the old Talbot case file Juan had been working on and walked to the coffee shop, now sober enough to realize he'd been stupid to have driven to work. He'd never done that before. Nothing about today was normal. Somehow, he needed to train Bacon to hide his keys when he drank.

He ordered a Venti espresso then sat down at Annie's table.

An old man sitting at a nearby table lowered his newspaper and nodded at him. Mark nodded back.

He opened the case files, swallowed two aspirins with his first sip of coffee, then started reading. As he read, something kept bugging him. As if his mind was about to connect some dots that hadn't been connected.

He continued poring over the files. What was bothering him?

The bell over the door rang, Mark looked up.

Annie walked in. Their gazes met. Seeing her sobered him quicker than the coffee he'd consumed. He smiled. The fact that she didn't smile back almost made him frown. He popped up and motioned for her to join him.

She lowered in the chair, he eased down in the chair beside her.

"Hey," he said.

"I can't stay. I have a class."

"I called, left a message, and texted. I'm—"

"I know."

"You're angry," he said.

"I'm not...I'm worried."

"About?"

"This." She waved a hand between them. "It's messy."

"I'll admit it's messy." He leaned in, remembering thinking he might have subconsciously sabotaged this himself, but right now he hated himself for it. "But can I say it's also friggin' great?"

She lifted her chin. "Have you been...drinking?"

He emotionally flinched. "I had a few at lunch. Annie, I don't want to lose this."

"I don't either. But there's the case and then there's us. I'm not sure we can keep them separate."

He chose his words carefully. "You're right. We can't. But we can accept that I'm doing what you wanted me to do. My job is to find answers. And yes, some of those answers might be difficult for you to accept. I don't like that, don't like hurting you, but I'd like to be there for you whatever happens. And this morning...I should have handled it differently."

Her frown said she didn't like his chosen words. "You really think my mom did this?"

He had to be honest. "I think she's lying about something."

"Have you found anything else out?"

He hesitated. "We found the Missing Persons file on Jenny."

"And you didn't tell me about that either?"

"It was found this morning." He decided not to add that there might be some stuff he couldn't tell her. Thankfully, he hadn't found anything that crucial, yet.

"And?" she asked.

"A cop interviewed everyone at the camp. There were discrepancies in their stories."

"What did my mom say?" The pain flashing in

her eyes sent guilt lapping around his sore hung over soul.

"Your mom wasn't interviewed." He should stop there, he wanted to stop there, but she'd hear this later. "It stated that she'd been there, but had left because she'd taken her daughter to the hospital to get stitches."

Annie's eyes grew moist. She reached down and touch the scar on her knee. All his pent-up anger suddenly found a target. Annie's mom. *How dare she hurt Annie like this!*

Annie buried her teeth into her lip before she spoke. "But it doesn't mean...she's responsible for what happened to Jenny."

"You're right. But I think she knows who is."

Annie blinked as if to hold back tears. One collected in the corner of her lashes. "Could she...go to jail for that?"

He wished he could offer her the answer she wanted. "I can't say without knowing the details."

She looked away. "I have to get my coffee. My class starts in ten minutes."

"Let me get it." He popped up, ordered her coffee, dropped a five-dollar bill, then sat down while they made it. He put his hand on hers. "Don't push me away. I'm not a dick, even though I behaved like one this morning."

He saw hesitation in her eyes. "I was upset, too," she said.

A weight lifted off his chest. "I work late tonight, but tomorrow, how about you come to my place?" He smiled. "Bacon's been dying to meet you."

His attempt at humor fell flat.

She nodded.

He leaned in and kissed her, not thinking about his whiskey breath or about being in public, until it was too late.

They called his name for her coffee. He popped up and delivered it to her. The up and down made his head pound, but he didn't care. He deserved the pain.

She stood up. "Thanks."

"You're welcome." He touched her cheek, wanting to pull her against him. Wanting to take the hurt away, the hurt he was partly responsible for.

She turned to go, and he caught her arm and moved in to whisper. "Don't forget to be careful. Whoever is responsible for Fran Roberts's disappearance could just as easily try to make you disappear." Saying it made his gut clench. "Do you want to stay at my place?"

"No. I'm staying with Isabella for a few nights."

"Okay. I'll call you later."

He watched her walk away and, right or wrong, he realized how much he wanted her to stay in his life.

CHAPTER NINETEEN

Annie had finished her class and had an hour to kill before her next one started. Feeling drained emotionally and physically, she'd decided to grab another coffee and a pastry.

She'd just gotten seated when Fred walked to her table.

"Mind some company?" he asked.

"No." She waved at the chair, determined to not let her mood rub off on the sweet old man.

He eased down. She noticed he seemed to be moving slower. "You okay?"

"Hunky-dory," he said.

"You finish the crossword puzzle today?" she asked.

"Yup." He frowned. "You don't look okay. You didn't look okay when you met with the famous detective."

"Oh." She didn't have words to explain, so she just said, "It's fine."

"You seeing him?"

She hesitated and decided not to lie. "Yeah, kind of."

"Can I kind of give you a little advice?"

"Yes."

"Be careful."

"Why?" she asked.

"He's a cop."

"You...don't like cops?"

He looked at his mug and turned it, before lifting his gaze. "I used to be one. Cops make lousy boyfriends. And husbands."

"I don't believe that. I've heard you talk about your wife Gertrude."

"She was my fifth wife."

"Wow. Seriously?"

"Yup. Finally wised up. It's mostly the job's fault. It damages you. But then you have to look at the reason why most of us become cops. Some join the force because they like playing God. Some because they feel like they owe God something. Point is, cops come with baggage."

"Don't we all?" Annie asked.

"Not as much as cops. They can be hard on women. You deserve someone who'll treat you right."

She couldn't help but wonder why Mark became a cop. She didn't see him wanting to play God. Was he carrying baggage? Was that what he hid behind his glasses?

"Of course, you don't have to listen to some old man, but it needed to be said."

She nodded. "I'll keep that in mind."

* * *

Sergeant Brown showed up at the interview room the same time as Johnny Harden. Mark wasn't sure if he was here to check up on him or to hear the interview.

Maybe both.

Either way, Brown had a right to do it. Mark deserved to be checked up on. He also deserved the whopper of a headache he had. Not that it stopped him from wishing it would go away.

Johnny looked around fifty, but considering his past lifestyle he could be younger. Mark introduced himself and then Juan and Connor. Connor held the envelope of pictures for the photo lineup.

When Mark introduced Brown, Johnny spoke up. "I know you. You interviewed me the first time."

The sergeant nodded. "You've got a good memory."

"Yup, I do."

Mark didn't really pick up any animosity on Johnny's part, but he wasn't sure if he'd blame Johnny if he did. The man had come in on his own to report something that he thought was connected to a murder. From the file, it appeared Brown and Gomez had blown him off.

Mark motioned for everyone to sit down. "We have your other statement, but could you tell us again what you saw that day?"

Johnny told how he gotten a bottle of whiskey and gone down by the lake to enjoy it. He'd hidden himself in some bushes to drink it because he'd been afraid a couple of other homeless guys would steal it.

"The truck pulling up to the dock woke me up. It was late, I didn't want to startle the guy, so I just watched as he climbed back in the bed of his truck. He rolled the barrel out of his truck and into the water."

"How late was it?" Brown asked. "Wasn't it dark?"

"Yeah. But there was a light right over the dock."

"And you think you could identify him?" Connor asked, opening the envelope and lining the photos up on the table.

"I do," Johnny said.

"Is the man you saw any of these men?"

Johnny leaned forward. His eyes skimmed from one picture to the next, taking time to review the information jotted down below.

"He's not there."

"That was fast," Brown said. "Are you sure?"

"Positive. The man I saw was a big man—no neck, like a linebacker. Looked like one, too. Big fellow. And he had red hair, carrot top."

Brown frowned. "I don't recall you telling us he had red hair."

"I tried. You weren't interested in what I had to say then. Not that I blame you. I wasn't what anyone would consider a reliable witness."

"I apologize for that," Brown said, surprising Mark. "Can you give us a detailed description now? I promise, we're interested. We need your help."

* * *

Annie finished up her last class. Dropping in her chair, she just sat there and tried to make sense of her crazy day. Crazy life.

Was she insane to keep seeing Mark? Her mind said yes; her heart said no. She thought about Fred's warning then looked at the time.

Isabella had agreed to take her to pick up her car, but she had another class. Deciding to make use of her time, she reached down for her briefcase to start grading papers.

She heard the sound of heels clipping down the hall, moving with purpose. The gait, the cadence of those heels, hit a familiar chord.

She stared at the door to her office, not sure if she wanted to be right or wrong.

Her mother appeared on the threshold. A wave of hurt washed over Annie. Since when had seeing her mother caused her pain?

Since she knew the woman had lied to her all her life.

Her mom shut the classroom door. Annie swallowed the need-to-cry knot down her throat as her mother moved to stand in front of Annie's desk.

"So this is how it is, huh?"

"How what is?" she managed to ask.

"You are more loyal to the guy you're sleeping with than me."

Annie shook her head. "I'm not more loyal to him. And you're a fine one to mention loyalty. You're more loyal to your family than your own daughter."

She shook her head. "That's not true."

"Yes it is. The Anniston police found the files from

when Jenny went missing. In it was a note about how you had taken your daughter to the hospital to get stitches."

Then a flash of memory hit. She was in the hospital bed crying as her mom tried to console her. She felt the sting in her knee, she felt the sting in her heart. Blinking the past away, she said, "You've lied to me my whole life."

Her mom flinched. "You don't understand."

"You're right. I don't." Annie's voice shook. "I can't see why you'd lie to me. Or why you'd protect someone who'd do something so horrible to a child."

"It's not what you think. I was trying to protect *you*!" Anger gave her mom's words a cutting edge.

"From what? Help me understand. Because right now I don't feel that I know you."

Her mom shook her head. "I'm here one last time to beg you to stop it."

"You stop it." Annie stood up, but her knees felt jelly filled. "Tell me, or better yet, tell the police. Tell them before things get worse."

"Baby, if you don't stop it...it could get ugly. I don't want...I tried to tell them—"

"Ugly?" Annie lurched back. "What are you saying?" Her voice rose, her heart hammered against her chest. "That someone's going to hurt me? Like they did Fran and Jenny?"

"I'd never let anyone hurt you. Why do you think we moved—"

"Moved? To Houston? Tell me! Tell me the secret that you and Daddy kept from me my entire life."

Defeat flashed in her mom's eyes. "No one has hurt Fran. But..."

"If Fran's okay, why did Aunt Doris lie about her car being there?"

"She was embarrassed about her daughter being a drunk."

"Why would that bother her? She's a drunk, too."

Her mom inhaled, her breathing as shaky as Annie's. "George took Fran home. I told the police."

Annie's hands clenched, and her heart tightened with the knowledge that her mom really had a part in this. "I can't even believe you anymore."

Her mom turned to leave. She got to the door, stopped, then turned back. "I'm sorry." Tears rolled down her mother's pale cheeks.

"For what, Mom? What are you sorry for? What did you mean by 'get ugly'?"

Her mother didn't answer. The *tap-tapping* of her mom's heels leaving gave Annie chills and felt like the end of a love that was supposed to last forever.

* * *

At five o'clock, Mark, alone in the office, still sported a headache. It wasn't only from the booze. It was that kind of a day. Convincing his partners that the Reed case was solvable was like selling rainbow sherbet to Satan.

They agreed to work it, begrudgingly, but priority went to the Talbot case.

They'd thought the case was about to be closed. Now

they were back to nothing. Well, not nothing. It felt convenient that Brian worked at a concrete place. But every attempt to follow that lead left them stonewalled.

Mark's call to Brian Talbot went unanswered. He left messages. But got shit back. His call to the Austin police had him leaving another message.

Connor's calls to character witnesses for Brian also landed him on everyone's voice mails.

Ditto with Juan's luck contacting Colman Concrete Company. No one answered the damn phone. Frustrated, he left to drive over there.

For Juan, that was big. He'd practically become a shut-in cop. Leaving the office only when he couldn't find a reason to stay. Juan claimed he wasn't worried about facing people, it was seeing people face him.

Mark supposed Juan's scars caused a reaction in some, and if Mark had them, perhaps he'd feel the same way. But Mark wondered if Juan used the scars to punish himself. Put himself in solitary. Mark supposed that was logical, too. The newest member of the Cold Case Unit blamed himself for being alive when his pregnant wife had died. Grief and guilt did a number on people. Mark knew.

"Hey," a voice boomed. Sergeant Brown, perched in his door, had a briefcase in his hands, as if he were leaving.

"Yeah?"

"You get anything from the concrete company?"

"No. Juan called and said there's a sign on the door saying they are temporarily closed for a death in the family. We'll try tomorrow."

"You trust Mr. Harden?"

"Yeah. Don't you?" Mark asked.

"Yeah, I just wanted this case solved."

"Me too."

Brown started to walk off and Mark remembered. "Hold up."

His sergeant turned.

Mark motioned to a chair. "Can we talk?"

Leery, the man squeezed into the chair. "Why am I certain I'm going to need a pack of Tums after this?"

Because you obviously can read me too damn well! Mark picked up a pencil and rolled it. "I want to get ahead of something that might be a problem."

Brown's brows pinched together. "Don't tell me it involves the media."

"It's the Reed case. The witness is . . . she and I are—"

"Oh, hell no! Just because some fine piece of ass steps into your office to report something doesn't give you the right to bang it!"

"It's not like that." Mark searched for a defense, one that didn't include throwing out the fact that the woman the sergeant had been married to for ten years had been a witness to one of the biggest cases Anniston had known.

"We've been seeing each other before the case." It wasn't a lie.

"Bullshit! Where did you meet her? Don't stop and think about it."

"At the coffee shop down the block. She teaches at the college and goes there every morning. I go there for coffee. And like you said, she's noticeable."

"How likely is this to be made public?"

He remembered the look on Annie's mom's face. *A guarantee*. "Likely."

"You're off the case," Brown bellowed.

"No. The case is twenty-five years old. Us seeing each other isn't going to affect what happened. The evidence will speak for itself."

The man's face reddened. "Just because a case is cold doesn't change the damned rules."

"The rules can go fuck themselves." Mark rolled the pencil.

"What's going to get fucked is you. You can't keep disregarding protocol. I can't keep going to bat for you. I don't care what the hell you're holding over my head."

Mark broke the pencil. "I've never held anything over your head!"

Silence followed and then Brown spoke. "You saw us there."

"Yeah, I knew you and Gomez planted the hair evidence. But have you ever stopped to wonder what I was doing there that day? I had the same damn evidence in my pocket. There was no way I was letting that guy get away with raping that kid because of protocol. We had him. We knew he was guilty. He confessed."

Brown shouldered back in the chair as if trying to take it all in.

Mark continued, "So there. You don't have to put up with my ass. Fire me. My life would be better."

The two of them stared at each other and Mark knew the answer. "You aren't going to do that, are you?

Because you're a cop who gives a rat's ass and solves cases because he does care."

His sergeant breathed in, breathed out. Mark feared he'd given the man a heart attack. But Brown stood up. "Connor or Juan can take the lead. If it's made public I'll pull you off the case."

"I'm fine handing the lead off," Mark said, leaving unsaid that he didn't intend to be pulled from the case.

Brown frowned. "You're a pain in my ass."

Mark leaned back. "I kind of remind you of yourself, don't I?"

"Yeah." Brown took off.

* * *

"I was about to call you," the officer from Austin said.

"Right." Mark didn't hide his sarcasm. He'd called the officer before calling it a day.

"Yesterday, I paid Francyne Roberts's boyfriend a call."

"He was there?"

"Half drunk, but there."

"And?"

"He swears Roberts never came home from the funeral. Told me I could search the place."

"Did you?"

"I walked around. Didn't see anything."

"You believe him?"

"I arrested his ass six months ago for busting Roberts's lip. So could he be guilty of doing something worse? Yeah. But I'd swear he was telling the truth. He claimed if something happened to her, we should look at her family. Said they were a fucked-up bunch."

Mark gave the boyfriend credit on that one. "We found Fran Roberts's car at her mother's."

"So she's not missing?"

"Found her car. Not her. First her mom lied about Fran leaving in the car. Then the aunt tells us that Fran's uncle drove her home. Is there any way Fran could have gotten home, grabbed her things, and left?"

"I didn't ask him."

Mark glanced at his phone for the time. He could be in Austin before eight. "I don't want to step on toes, but would it be okay if I spoke to this guy directly?"

There was hesitation. Cops were territorial about their cases.

"Just to ask some questions," Mark added.

"Honestly," the officer said, "I think Roberts is off on a bender, but if you don't want to wait it out, help yourself. If you need anything, call us."

"Thanks." Mark reached for his gun and was ready to leave when his office phone rang. He saw the number flash across the screen. "About time." He picked it up. "Mr. Talbot."

"You caught the bastard who killed my girl?"

"Sorry." Mark felt the effects of flip-flopping on this guy's guilt or innocence. "Quick question. Where did you work when your daughter went missing?"

"Why?"

"Just answer."

Silence echoed. "I was between jobs."

Mark moved to the file cabinet where Juan stored

his case notes. "That's not what"—he pulled the report out—"we have on record." He flipped pages to find the info. "You said you worked at Coleman Concrete Company, but were off that day."

Did Brian know they were on to him, was that why he was distancing himself from Coleman Concrete?

"I never said that. My wife did. I hadn't told her I'd lost the job. She thought it was my day off."

That was *almost* believable. "Why would you keep that from her?"

"To stop her from worrying."

Mark dropped in Juan's chair, not knowing what to believe. "Why did you get let go?"

"Either arrest me or leave me the fuck alone." Talbot's tone gave Mark's suspicions credibility.

"Look, I lost my daughter, my wife. My brother won't let me around his kids because he thinks I ... I'm done." The line went dead.

Mark sat there feeling as if he was missing something. He'd had the same feeling this morning when he'd read the case file. He stared at Juan's notes. Bingo.

The name Coleman. He'd seen it in the file and it wasn't connected to Talbot's employment.

He flipped through the pages until he found it. Michele Coleman was the victim's aunt. The mother's sister.

He turned back to the front of the file where phone numbers were listed. He dialed Bethany Talbot's number. He rolled his shoulders, uncomfortable, remembering how she'd leaned on him and cried.

"Hello." One word and he heard her depression.

"This is Detective Sutton."

"You caught him? Tell me. Please."

Mark's gut knotted. "No. I have a question. Your sister, Michele Coleman, is she connected to Coleman Concrete?"

"Yes. Her ex-husband Gary Coleman owns it. Why?"

"Your husband worked there, right?"

"Yes."

"He just informed me he was fired from the position."

"Fired? No. Brian and Gary were friends. All of us were. We used to hang out. Have barbeques, pizza night. Gary had a daughter the same age as Brittany by his first wife."

Why would Talbot lie about that? One possibility stuck out. Working there would connect him to the evidence. But that didn't explain Harden not recognizing Talbot. There was still a missing piece to this puzzle.

Or maybe Johnny got it wrong.

"So you're still looking at Brian for this?" she asked.

"We're looking at all the angles. Do you have a number for Gary Coleman?"

"No. I haven't... My sister and him don't even talk anymore." She paused. "I think she blames what happened to Brittany for her marriage failure as well."

Why? "Sorry."

"I can give you the company's address."

"We have that. Thank you."

Mark hung up and stayed sitting on the fence of what to believe. If Brian had lied, and it appeared he had, there had to be a reason. Tomorrow he was paying Coleman Concrete Company a visit.

But right now, he needed to head to Austin. The sooner he got the Reed case put to bed, the sooner he could relax about himself and Annie.

CHAPTER TWENTY

Annie sat on Isabella's black sofa, hugging a red throw pillow as she spilled her guts about her mom's visit.

Pirate, still unhappy about being there, paced on his three legs around the room and meowed his discontent. Annie related to his anxiety. Not that she wasn't comfortable at Isabella's. It just...it felt as if the whole foundation of her life had cracked. The only thing that felt half right was her involvement with Mark. Yet the truth was they didn't even have a foundation.

"Pirate," Annie called, but the cat jumped on the window seat as if trying to find a way home.

"I don't know what to say, or what to think," Isabella said.

"Me either." Annie refocused on her friend, sitting in the chair across from her. "I feel as if I've fallen into a movie of the week."

"Real life can be as fucked up as fiction," Isabella said.

"Tell me about it." Annie thought about what Fred had told her and almost told her friend. Then didn't. She'd whined long enough.

"Hand me your glass and I'll refill it," Isabella said.

"No, I'm fine."

Isabella sighed. "You're telling Mark what your mom said, right?"

"I have to, don't I? I went to him to help me get to the bottom of this. But... how did I get myself in this mess?"

"You didn't get yourself in it. It happened to you. And don't get mad, but what she said to you sounded like... a threat."

Annie hugged the pillow tighter. "My mom never raised her hand to me. Neither did my dad, even though he did all the grounding and stuff. She was always so gentle, almost fragile."

"But that doesn't change what she said to you."

"I know." Annie inhaled. "But she said she'd never hurt me. I believe that."

"I get it, but your cousin's missing. God only knows what happened to her. And your mom said it could get ugly. I don't know about you, but I don't like ugly."

Annie closed her eyes to keep the well of tears she felt from filling them. When she did, the memory, the one that had hit her during her conversation with her mom, came back. She popped her eyes open.

"I remembered something today." She rubbed her thumb over the scar on her knee.

"What?"

Annie let the memory pull her in. She could almost

taste the astringent and bitter smell of the hospital. She could feel her chest going up and down, trying to breathe while sobbing. She could feel her young heart flapping against her chest like a bird trying to find a way out.

"Being at the hospital for the stitches. Mama tried to console me, but I wouldn't stop crying."

The memory kept coming, Annie was there on her friend's sofa, but she wasn't. She existed in the snapshot memories, feeling the snapshot fear. The room was white and cold. Something terrible had happened.

"Dad showed up," she said. "He was angry. Yelling at Mom. I'd never heard him yell before. The nurse made them leave the room. I was so scared."

"Afraid of getting stitches?"

Annie shook her head. "Something to do with what happened in the woods. But I don't remember...what?" Annie blinked away the threat of tears. "I want to peel the fog away. I want to know what happened. To remember and get it over with! Why can't I just remember? Why is it coming to me in tiny bits?"

"I don't know," Isabella said.

Annie's phone rang. Thinking it was Mark, dreading telling him, she let it ring. Then she snatched up the phone from the coffee table.

It wasn't Mark.

"Shit!" She gazed up at Isabella. "It's the same number that called before, the person who called me a bitch."

"Don't answer it." Concern tightened her friend's tone.

"I have to." She hit the accept button. "What do you want? Where's Fran?"

"Keep it up and you'll die, too."

Fear, old, new, like shards of glass sliced into her chest, but the words still slipped past her chilled lips. "Like you killed Jenny! Who is this? Tell me!"

* * *

Mark parked in front of the run-down trailer in the run-down trailer park. Light leaked out of the windows. He walked up the porch and knocked. Four times.

He heard a television blaring and moved to the window. A man lay facedown on the sofa, dead to the world.

Not dead, Mark hoped.

His knock on the window caused a sharp, cracking sound. The man jerked up. Mark pressed his badge to the glass. The guy stumbled to open the door.

Mark had hoped the Austin PD was wrong about Fran's boyfriend being innocent. If he could pin Fran Roberts's disappearance on him, it'd mean Annie might not be in danger.

Yeah, someone had spray-painted her car and broken her window, but that action paled in comparison to someone being kidnapped or killed.

Unfortunately, the man, who went by Bubba, had a big *L* on his forehead for loser, but he wasn't nervous about Fran's disappearance or being questioned about it. That meant his ass was probably clean.

"Where were you on Sunday?"

"Out with the boys. We went to the bar. Closed the place down. I stayed at a friend's house."

"I'll need the address of the bar and the phone numbers of your friends."

Unflinching, the guy gave Mark the information.

He hadn't done it.

"Fran hasn't called?" Mark asked.

"No. Pisses me off, too. She's supposed to help with the rent."

"Have you checked·if she might've been here and taken some clothes?"

"No, but she's got more clothes than God."

And how many clothes did God have? Mark's concern for Fran and for Annie rose. "Has anyone called looking for her?"

"Hell yeah." He inched closer. Close enough that Mark noticed the soured-whiskey breath and the sozzled way he spoke. Was that how he'd appeared to Annie and Brown this morning? Brown thinking less of him didn't bother him. But Annie? *Damn.*

"Who called?" Mark stepped back, claiming his personal space.

"Her drunk-ass mom? Her aunt? And I think one of her uncles—the voice was muffled and it was from an anonymous number."

"Do you have those numbers?"

"Yeah."

As Mark wrote down the numbers, one stood out. The pay phone. What the hell? A guilty party calling and pretending to be worried about a victim they'd made disappear wasn't uncommon. But calling and not identifying yourself...? Did this mean the person threatening Annie wasn't the person behind Fran Roberts's disappearance?

Shit! He'd come to get answers and was leaving with more questions.

* * *

Mark made the drive back to Anniston in record time. After learning Annie had gotten another threatening phone call, he contacted Sheriff Harper. The man was all too eager to drive to the pay phone and even dust it for prints.

Obviously, he didn't have anything better to do on a Thursday night.

Mark called Annie back and asked if he could drop by her friend's apartment. She agreed.

A hour later, when he knocked on the door, Annie answered it.

One look at her vulnerable expression and he pulled her against him. The way she clung to him for those twenty seconds brought out every serve-and-protect instinct he had. He would've given anything for another twenty, but she stepped back.

"It's okay," he said.

"No, it's not. My mom came to see me."

"When?" he asked.

"This afternoon."

"And?" He followed her inside. Annie's friend sat at the kitchen table.

Annie looked around. "Mark, this is Isabella."

Mark nodded, but his thoughts stayed on what Annie had said, or what she needed to finish saying. "Thanks for letting me swing by."

"No problem. We've got a bottle of wine open. You want a glass?"

"Yes. But I'm on the clock."

"In that case," Isabella said, "I'm taking the bottle and my book and going into my bedroom."

"You don't have to do that," Annie said.

"Actually, I'm at a good part in the book. The heroine just returned from a vacation and she's about to find her ex-husband, naked, dead, and missing a certain organ, on her kitchen floor."

"Sounds delightful," Mark said, horrified.

"It is. He cheated on her." Smiling, the pretty brunette walked down the hall.

When the bedroom door closed, Mark moved closer to Annie. "She seems...fun."

"She is."

They sat at the kitchen table. "What happened?"

She told him about her meeting with her mom. When he saw the hurt in her eyes, he had to fight to keep his remarks to himself.

"I don't think she'd ever hurt me. She even said that."

"Yeah." He ground his teeth. He wanted to hunt down JoAnne Lakes and tell her what a piece of shit she was.

True, his mom hadn't won the mother-of-the-year award. Considering she killed herself, it could be viewed as the ultimate form of abandonment. But guilt that she'd allowed her husband to kill his own kid had made her do that.

What the hell was Ms. Lakes's excuse?

He listened to Annie as she told him about the memory of the hospital visit. That didn't up his opinion of the woman.

"She said George took Fran home," Annie said.

"Yeah." But did George really take her home? Or was the Austin officer right? Could Francyne Roberts be somewhere drunk on her ass?

If so, where would she be? He realized he'd failed to ask Bubba about any of Francyne's friends. He'd checked with the names her ex-husband had offered. No one had seen or heard from her. Which meant calling Bubba again got added to tonight's to-do list.

"Have you heard back from the sheriff to see if he spotted anyone at the pay phone?" Annie asked.

"Not yet. He'll call." But his finding something would be too easy, and nothing so far turned out to be easy about this case.

He told Annie about meeting Bubba and the phone calls he'd received.

"Are you saying you don't think my mom's family is behind her disappearance?"

"I'm saying it's possible. I plan on getting answers. I'm good at it."

"I know," she said. "That's why I came to you."

"And not because you have the hots for me?" he teased, knowing they both needed it.

When she didn't respond, he brushed a few strands of her hair off her cheek. "I get off in a couple of hours. Would you feel safer at my place?" He let himself hope.

"No, I'm fine here."

He couldn't help but worry if his behavior this morning hadn't played a part in her answer. "Tomorrow night?" If she said no, he'd know what it meant.

She hesitated, then nodded.

He kissed her. "I'm going to have a hard time sleeping tonight without you."

"You'll survive." She shot him a forced smile.

"Yeah, but surviving isn't nearly as much fun."

* * *

Sometime after one a.m. Annie, curled up on Isabella's sofa, must have drifted off to sleep. Because shortly after, it started.

The running, seeing the Cinderella shoes, the footsteps following her, clutching the bloody teddy bear. Fran's screams to run faster.

But this time, the dream didn't end where it had before. After those footfalls got close, then closer, two big male hands grabbed her up. She started kicking, screaming. She yelled for her daddy, even when she knew he wasn't there.

The words came spoken in her ear: *Stop it, Annie!*

The deep male voice playing in her head had no face. She couldn't put a name to it, but her five-year-old self had known the voice. For some reason that terrified her more.

She had to get away!

She clawed at the arms of the person who held her, while fear clawed at her young mind. Then another voice rose from the dark. A young voice. *Let her go! Let her go right now!*

Annie jerked awake, heart hammering, pulse pumping, fear smothering her. She kept hearing that last voice in her head. Tears filled her eyes.

Fran. She'd come back for Annie. She'd tried to protect Annie.

Now Fran was missing. And it was Annie's fault. Her fault for running out that day of the funeral. For going to Mark.

Annie pulled her knees close and hugged them like a frightened child, and silently sobbed. She had to find Fran. She had to.

Annie grabbed her phone and dialed Mark's number, but remembering the time, she didn't hit the call button.

* * *

At five thirty Annie, dressed, stood at her friend's front window, steaming coffee in hand, staring out at the still-dark sky and waiting for the first sign of the sun.

Anger curled up inside her. Anger at her mom. Anger at herself. Anger at her inability to remember more, to remember everything. Surely not knowing was worse than knowing. Why was her mind playing peek-a-boo with her past? Flashing a tiny memory here and then there, but disappearing before she had the answers.

She hated the feeling the dreams brought on. Scared,

vulnerable—like a helpless five-year-old girl needing her daddy.

She wasn't five.

Maybe it was time she stopped acting like it.

Moving to the kitchen, she set the cup down, found a notepad, and wrote Isabella a note. *Gone on an early run. Be back soon.*

As she moved to her car, she swore she heard footsteps. Stopping in the middle of the parking lot, her heart in her throat, the air too thick to breathe, she considered running back to the apartment, but then she remembered Fran. Her cousin had been afraid that night years ago, but she'd come back for Annie. Determined, Annie rushed to her car and drove to the one place she might find answers. The park.

When she pulled up into the parking lot, the eastern sky was welcoming the sun. She gripped the steering wheel, her lungs feeling as if they'd shrunk. She fed them short, shallow bursts of air.

She searched the lot, hoping she'd see someone safe looking, but the parking lot stood empty. It seemed abandoned.

And she felt the same way. Ted, her ex-fiancé, her friends, her coworkers, they'd all abandoned her. Even her father's death felt like an abandonment. Now her mom.

Determined not to crater, she squared her shoulders and got out of the car.

Automatically, she locked her car, and the beep startled her. Putting one foot in front of the other, she walked down a wooded path. The damp smell of earth and verdant scents of nature filled her nose.

She tried to remember being here before. But no memory rose from the fear swelling inside her.

Palms sweaty, she stopped at a sign that showed a map of the park. She used the flashlight on her phone to see.

Shaking inside, she studied it, but didn't have a clue which way to go. She recalled her mom saying Jenny had drowned. By the water? She needed to go to the lake.

Finding the location on the faded map, she started walking. The sound of her heart slamming into her breastbone was louder than the crunch of dead brush beneath her tennis shoes.

CHAPTER TWENTY-ONE

The smothering alcove of trees made it night again. Crickets and insects screamed in the darkness. Though warm and muggy, a chill tiptoed up and down Annie's spine.

No one was here, she told herself. No one had followed her. No one but the past, a voice said in her head. And perhaps that scared her more than anything.

Her phone's light barely touched the ground. Fear scented her breath, but she refused to turn back. She wanted the truth more than she wanted safety.

She moved slow, waiting for the recesses of her mind to hand something over. They were her memories. She wanted them.

In the distance she heard voices. Young voices.

Or was that...? With her next breath, she felt it. A sense of being pulled back, of the past closing in. The sound of water played in her head.

Fran, Jenny, and she were laughing, catching tadpoles. Behind them were voices, familiar, angry voices. Mom's family, always arguing.

As quickly as the memory came, it left. One snippet of data.

"No." She stopped walking.

She leaned against a tree. The bark scratched at her skin. The memory scratched at her mind. When nothing more came, she followed the path deeper into the woods. Each step, each footfall, brought dread curling up inside her belly.

What was the chance that she, Fran, and Jenny had taken the same path? What was the chance that Jenny's bones were still buried here in the earth?

She stared into woods. The *whoosh* of water whispered like a secret in her ear. Then she saw it. Jenny walking deeper into the water's edge. Saw Fran motioning her to come back. Saw Jenny going under. Saw the tip of her blond hair floating on the water's surface.

Air got trapped in her throat like a liquid. Gasping, she bent at the waist to breathe.

Had Jenny drowned?

* * *

Mark was up before the sun, and he hadn't fallen asleep until after two. Sheriff Harper had called when he'd left Annie's friend's apartment. The street was empty when he got to the phone booth. And it'd been wiped clean of fingerprints.

Mark knew it was too much to hope they'd actually get anything, but he'd hoped. Now all he knew was he wasn't dealing with a sloppy perp. And if they'd taken the time to wipe their prints away, they had to be guilty of something. Something worse than wielding a spray-paint can.

That made him worry for Annie's safety.

In spite of needing a few more hours of sleep, he got up. He'd showered, shaved, and shot out the door with Bacon by six. During his run, he'd made his to-do list: Find the old cop who'd written the report on the Reed case. Call Fran's friends, whose names he'd gotten from Bubba the previous night. Go to the Coleman Concrete Company.

The company didn't open until eight, so he went to the coffee shop, hoping he'd run into Annie.

She wasn't there. With twenty minutes to kill, he parked himself at her table and read the Talbot file. The old man he'd spotted yesterday waved at him and smiled.

Mark smiled back.

The man, apparently interpreting it as an invitation, got up and joined Mark.

That will teach me to smile at strangers, Mark thought. "Can I help you?" he said, pushing his sunglasses up a notch.

"You bought me a cup of coffee a few months ago."

"Oh." Mark didn't know what else to say.

"I thought I'd repay the favor."

Mark picked up his cup. "I got my coffee, but thank you."

"I'm not offering coffee. A piece of advice. Actually a warning. Probably not a great way to repay a favor."

"Okay." Curious, Mark shouldered back in his chair.

"That girl who always sits here. Annie Lakes."

"Yes."

"We've become coffee buddies. She lost her father not long ago. I'm kinda standing in for him."

"Okay," Mark said.

"I've been coming here every day since it opened. Since I lost my wife, I spend more hours here than at home. I sit there." He pointed to the booth. "I read, think about how I can fix my old mistakes, and I people-watch. Actually, I do more than watch—I figure out who's going to heaven and who's going to hell."

"That's quite a job." Mark wondered if the guy wasn't a few freeways short of a map.

"For five months, I've watched Annie. She's heaven bound, by the way. After she saw you buying others coffee, she started doing it. I've seen her smile and say hello to the grumpiest sour-faced strangers for no reason but to be kind. Once she held a woman's crying baby so she could order and pay for her coffee. She made paper airplanes for one little guy who was bored because his mom was too busy staring at her phone to pay attention to him. Annie's got a big heart. I'd hate to see someone break it."

Mark's grip on his cup tightened. "I don't plan on breaking it."

"Don't get me wrong. I'm not saying you don't have a heart. You bought coffee for a lot of people. But I know you. I know your type."

"Do you?" Mark asked, not quite offended, but working up an attitude.

"I used to be you. Carried a badge for forty-five years. I was pissed at the world, pissed that some of them got away, pissed at the system for letting it happen. I took it out on anyone close to me—women mostly. I was married five times. Divorced four. It took Gertrude before I realized it hadn't been my exes' faults. To be honest, it wasn't even all *my* fault—not completely. It's the job. Most guys I worked with were just like me. Unhappy fuckers needing a dog to kick. Gertrude taught me to stop kicking."

Somewhere in the talk, Mark had stopped being annoyed.

The old man looked down at his gnarled hands. Then his faded blue eyes met Mark's head on. "Maybe you aren't like me. Maybe it's not going to take you so long to learn how to stop letting the ugliness affect how you treat people. Perhaps you're ready to see and appreciate the slice of heaven Annie is. But if you're not, walk away before you hurt her."

The man stood, his stance shaky. He steadied himself with the back of the chair. As he shuffled away, Mark recalled thinking Annie was too good for him. In one quick swoop, he recalled his list of failed relationships and an uncomfortable feeling lodged in his chest. The same feeling he'd gotten last night seeing Bubba drunk and worried Annie had seen him that way.

Well, shit, this was no way to start a day.

* * *

Mark arrived at Coleman Concrete early. But a car was parked at the side of the building.

The CLOSED sign still faced the door, so he sat gripping the steering wheel, fighting the feeling the old man's words had brought on. No way in hell was he walking away from Annie. And yet...

Finally, someone flipped the sign.

Ready to tackle something less personal, Mark exited his car and walked through the door.

"Can I help you?" the feminine voice asked at the same time laughter—kids' laughter—spilled out of the back room.

He recalled what the old man said about Annie holding a screaming baby and making paper airplanes for a boy. Did Annie want that? The whole white picket fence and 2.3 kids? That certainly wasn't in Mark's cards.

But Jeezus! Why was he thinking about that? They were just getting to know each other.

He spotted the woman sitting at a desk in the corner. She looked like she belonged in the kitchen baking cookies and not in the dusty concrete office. "I'm Detective Sutton with Anniston PD." He moved his coat to show his badge.

Concern tightened her round face. "What can I do for you?"

He let his coat flutter shut. "Is Mr. Coleman here?"

"No, he's in Florida burying his mother and dad. They were killed in a car accident. I'm taking care of his kids."

"Sorry to hear about that," Mark said. "Is the office manager here?"

"That would be me. Babysitter, manager, sucker who can't say no to her boss because he's a decent guy."

The laughter in the back turned to bickering.

"Excuse me." She went to the door. "No fighting!"

Mark waited for her to return. "Brian Talbot worked for Mr. Coleman four years ago. Do you have any employee records telling how long he worked here, when and why he left?"

"That was before I was hired. But we keep the employee records"—she shifted her chair and faced a metal file cabinet—"right here." She glanced up. "What was that name?"

"Brian Talbot," Mark said.

"Here." She pulled a file out and opened it. "He worked here for a year."

"When was his last day?"

She turned a page. "On April nineteenth."

Talbot's daughter didn't go missing until the twenty-first. Brian hadn't been lying. Mark was surprised, yet he really wasn't. He'd believed Brian in the beginning. But why had the man acted put off when Mark asked about the job? Something didn't add up. "Was he fired?"

"Afraid so."

"Does it say why?"

She glanced down at the file. "No. There's a space to list the reason, but it wasn't filled out. Is this man in trouble?"

She obviously didn't follow the news. "Not really." He rubbed the palm of his hand against his chin. "When is Mr. Coleman due back?"

"Today," she said.

Mark got Coleman's number, but since he was at his parents' funeral he didn't plan to call now. "Thank you."

Mark was almost to his car when the two noise-makers ran out.

They yelled out hello. He waved. They had to be siblings with that matching bright red hair. He opened his car door then . . . stopped.

He looked at the kids. That would be too damn easy. But damn if he wouldn't welcome a little easy.

* * *

Annie, hiding behind her sunglasses, walked into the coffee shop. Fred, sitting at his booth, smiled, then commenced reading. She glanced around, realized she was searching for Mark, then stopped. Did she want Mark to be here? Would telling him about the memory of Jenny drowning make him doubt her story?

How could it not when it gave her doubts? What if the dream was wrong? What if she was destroying her relationship with her mom over nothing? But why would her mom lie about her cutting her knee? Why all the secrets? Why was someone threatening her?

Shit. She needed to stop obsessing over things and believe she'd done the right thing. But believing in one-self was hard when others didn't.

She recalled with clarity the time she'd put a pen on the dotted line to sign the form to commit herself. She'd lost her job, her friends, and her fiancé, and the dream had been happening every night. At the last minute, she chickened out.

It was one thing to watch people you love walk away, but when you questioned your own sanity, that was worse. Before her trip to the park, she'd felt validated. Now?

Stop. Stop. Stop.

Inhaling the coffee scent, pushing away from the negative, her thoughts went to Mark. She'd missed him the previous night. Missed sleeping with him. Missed waking up in the darkness and hearing someone else breathing. Missed knowing she could reach out and touch someone. Someone who believed her.

Two nights sleeping with him and she didn't want to sleep without him. Mentally, she reached down and pulled up her big-girl panties. Who wanted to be a woman who needed a man to believe in her before she could believe in herself?

She fake-smiled at James behind the counter and ordered her coffee.

As she reached in her purse for her wallet, a voice behind her said, "I got hers."

In spite of her concerns, Mark's voice washed her with warm relief. She turned around and grinned up at the six-foot man with dark hair who, like her, wore shades.

Fred's words echoed in her head. She knew what she was hiding, but what was he hiding? Still, she soaked up his smile. "I've always wanted to be your good deed for the day."

A sexy grin pulled at the creases of his mouth. He

leaned down and under his breath whispered, "Wait until tonight."

She smiled her most genuine smile of the day, and when she breathed in and caught his spicy male aroma, her senses devoured it. Anticipation purred low in her abdomen.

They ordered and moved away from the counter and both looked around at the filled tables. Annie saw Fred staring at her over the paper, but he quickly returned to reading.

"There's one outside." He placed his hand on the small of her back. His touch was soft against her skin. Sweet tingles climbed her backbone. It took everything she had to not turn around and fall against his chest. Beg him to hold her. To believe her.

Yup, she was investing in some elastic for those big-girl panties. They stepped outside. The warm air, probably already in the eighties, brushed over her. Before they sat down, he shifted his chair close to hers. Once seated, he lifted her glasses and frowned. "Bad night?"

"Yeah."

She lifted his glasses. His eyes looked tired, almost haunted. "You?"

He bypassed her question. "Another nightmare?" He was so good at bypassing, she wondered how many times he'd done it without her noticing.

"What was it about?" he asked.

Dread tightened her gut. "I went to the park this morning."

His blue eyes rounded. "By yourself?"

She nodded.

He frowned. "And?"

"I had...It was so fast and I'm not sure..."

He put his hand over hers, his thumb slowly brushed across the top of her hand. "What happened?"

"I remembered playing in the lake, catching tadpoles. Fran told Jenny not to go out too deep. Then she screamed and went under."

Shock filled his expression. "Now you think she drowned?"

"No. I mean, I don't...I even...The dream last night lasted longer. A man grabbed me. Fran ran back for me. She protected me."

His expression didn't change. "I've heard dreams are seldom accurate."

His words ran laps around her heart. "You don't believe me?"

"I believe you dreamed it. I'm not sure how much of it is real." He squeezed her hand. "There's a guy—"

"What about the cut on my knee?"

He let out a tight breath. "I'm not saying everything you dreamed is wrong. I have to look at this, at...all angles."

She swallowed disappointment. "One angle being that I'm wrong."

"Maybe, but that wouldn't explain the calls, your place being vandalized, or your missing cousin. So—"

"But you still think—"

"I don't think anything, Annie. I'm looking for the truth. Isn't that what you want?"

"Yeah," she admitted. "I'm sorry, I just don't like thinking my mind's feeding me lies." She looked at his hand over hers. The touch no longer offered comfort.

"Hey. Look at me."

She did.

"It's going to be okay. We're getting to the bottom of this."

She nodded.

"I'm serious. And I'm here for you."

Was he? Would there not be a point when he turned his back on her like everyone else?

He leaned in and peered into the coffee shop, probably checking to see if their coffees were up. "I can't stay long."

She noticed the tension in his shoulders. Had he learned something else? "What's going on?"

"What do you mean?"

"You look upset."

"Just the case. You want me to pick you up tonight?"

"No, I'll drive. Text me your address."

"Sure. It might be six before I get home."

"Do you want to cancel?" she asked, feeling uncertain about everything.

"No. Why—"

"Fine, I'll see you around six."

He placed his palm over hers and studied her. "Any more phone calls?"

"No."

"Good." He glanced at the crowd. "You still need to keep your guard up."

"I know."

"I'm serious. When you park anywhere, look around

and make sure there are several people around. If not, find a different parking spot."

"You're scaring me," she said.

"If scaring you keeps you safe, it's worth it." He leaned in to see through the glass door again to check on their order. "They're up."

He left and came out balancing three cups. "I'll see you tonight. I'm looking forward to it." There was the sexy smile again. He looked as if he wanted to kiss her. But he didn't.

She understood why he wouldn't. He was a detective. She was a witness. But she could have really used a kiss.

"I want to kiss you right now, but I shouldn't," he said, as if reading her thoughts.

She recalled her mom seeing him. Her mom knowing Annie was sleeping with him. "Will you get in a lot of trouble if it gets out we're dating?"

"It'll be okay. I'm planning on giving Connor the lead on the case."

"But you'll still—"

"I'll work it, but he'll be the face of the case. See you tonight."

She watched him drive away. Seeing several people leaving the shop, she went inside where it was cool.

She barely got settled when she sensed someone standing beside her.

Thinking it was Fred, hoping he wasn't going to say anything negative about Mark, she faced him.

It wasn't Fred.

Annie's heart stopped, dropped, and rolled. Her mother's brother, Sam Reed, stood there, a solid, angry mass. His blond hair was cut short. His blue eyes were just like her mom's, but never had her mom's looked at her with such contempt.

Annie's breath caught. He looked like every little girl's nightmare.

But had he been in hers?

She couldn't tell.

"We need to talk." Was it the same voice in her dream?

Mark's words rang in her head. *I'm not sure how much of what you dreamed is real.* Could she be sure the dreams were right?

Wasn't Sam showing up here proof that something had happened? Gathering her shredded self-confidence, she tilted her chin up. "Where's Fran?"

Sam looked around as if feeling crowded. "Let's go for a drive."

"No!"

He reached for her arm. His touch sent panic through her.

She jerked back.

"I just want to go somewhere that's private to talk."

She swallowed. "I want to stay where it's public to talk."

His mouth tightened. His thin lips turned white. "I can't believe you're hurting your mom like this."

She held her shoulders tight. "I can't believe she lied to me all those years."

"You're imagining things. I've heard you do that a lot."

Suddenly, angrier than scared, her backbone stiffened. "What happened to Jenny?"

"We don't know."

"You're lying." And right then she believed it with everything she had. She wasn't imagining things. She wasn't crazy. Someone had killed Jenny and she'd been a witness to at least some of it.

"Come on!" He stood and caught her arm again.

"Let me go!" she seethed, her mind yanking her back to the dream, to someone holding her against her will.

"Let her go or you're going to be sorry."

Annie glanced up. Fred's stance was rigid. For the first time, she saw the police officer in him.

"Mind your own business!" Sam said, but he let her go. "We're family."

Fred's shoulders hardened. "I know I'm just an old man, but—"

"—but he's not alone." The woman who always sat in the booth beside Fred stood up.

"Me too," said James, the young tattooed cashier. "And I can jump over this counter and whip yo' ass."

Emotion rose in Annie's throat. Her pretend family was more of a family than she knew.

Sam lit out the door.

"You okay?" Fred asked. "Do we need to call the cops?"

"No." She didn't know how to explain so she didn't. "It's fine. But thank you." She grabbed her phone, hit the camera icon, and rushed outside.

* * *

Mark, trying to make heads and tails of Annie's new memory, approached the office. Had this whole case been for naught?

Juan and Connor looked up as he entered.

"What?" he asked, reading something in their looks.

"Brown just left."

"And?"

Connor readjusted in his seat. "He made me lead in the Reed case."

"I know."

Connor and Juan looked surprised. "You're not pissed?" Connor asked.

"I'm still on the case." *If there is one.* He lowered himself into his chair.

"What happened? You don't think he knows you're dating a witness, do you?" Juan asked.

"Yeah. I told him."

"Damn, you got balls." Connor laughed. "And he didn't toss your ass off the case?"

Mark set his coffee on his desk. "No." He pushed that topic aside. "I solved the Reed case." Nothing helped a bad mood like cracking a case. So why wasn't he feeling it? Oh, yeah, Annie. The old man and his warning.

"What?" Juan asked.

"Maybe not the case, but I know who dumped the body."

"Who?" Connor and Juan asked in unison.

"Gary Coleman, concrete entrepreneur and Brian Talbot's brother-in-law." Mark glanced at Juan. "Check if he's on a sex offender list." But Mark's gut said he wasn't.

Juan's fingers went to work. The *tap-tap-tap* of the keyboard filled the small room.

"Doesn't look like it," Juan said.

"How do you know he's our guy?" Connor asked.

"Because I'm that good." Mark forced a grin. "I saw his kids at his business—bright red hair. And Johnny said our guy—"

"Then he has to be guilty," Juan said with sarcasm. "But hey, Murdock has red hair, too."

Mark shot him a frown. "I also asked how big their dad was. They said he's taller than me and looks like a football player."

Connor held his hands up. "Okay, I'm biting."

"Did you bring him in?" Juan asked.

"No. He's in Florida. Flying home this afternoon."

"What about motive?" Juan asked.

"I have a hunch. I called both Brian and Bethany Talbot and Bethany's sister to come in to confirm it. They should start arriving in a couple of hours." He looked at Juan. "Can you pull a picture of Coleman off the Internet and put together a lineup with several redheads? Johnny should be here to make the official identification shortly."

"Why bring in Mrs. Talbot's sister? What's this hunch?" Connor asked.

"I think someone was fucking around. Either Mrs. Talbot was screwing Mr. Coleman or Mr. Talbot was screwing Mrs. Coleman. And since Gary Coleman is the one who fired Brian and is now suspected to have dumped the body, I'm inclined to believe he was the scorned lover."

"Love and murder, just like peanut butter and jelly," Connor said.

Mark wasn't quite that cynical, but neither did he buy into the happily-ever-after thing. Not for him anyway. Another reason to heed the old man's warning.

"None of them know the others are coming. I'll play musical interview rooms. I'm going to see if we can't catch someone in a lie."

"We're likely to end up with a catfight," Connor said. "Then one or both of them might go after Mr. Talbot."

"I wish there was another way." Mark turned his cup.

"Yeah, sometimes after the claws come out, so does the truth," Connor said.

Mark exhaled frustration. Normally this was the part of the job he enjoyed. But the memory of Bethany Talbot appearing so devastated, leaning up against him, ate at his conscience.

"You okay?" Connor's tone and question pulled Mark from his thoughts.

"Yeah, why?"

"I don't know. This case seems to have gotten to you more than others."

"I'm fine," Mark lied.

"I think this case has gotten to all of us more than the others," Juan said.

No one disagreed. And for one second, Mark didn't feel so alone in his misery. He'd always resisted working with partners, but this...was good.

"And yet it's what we do for a living." Mark pulled out the numbers he'd gotten for Fran's friends. He punched in the number, hoping his earlier luck would hold and he'd find Fran Roberts. Waiting for an answer, his mind went back to the possibility of Jenny Reed having been just a victim of a drowning.

Was he chasing leads that didn't matter? Could Jenny's death have been an accident?

* * *

His luck didn't hold. He spoke with two of the three women. Both said they hadn't heard from Fran in weeks. The third didn't answer, so he left a message.

His phone dinged with a text just as Johnny Harden walked in. Mark gave it a quick glance. It was Annie. Call me when you can.

He would, but not now.

Connor had set up the photo lineup in an interview room. The three of them and the sergeant all walked into the room. Johnny kept fidgeting with his keys. Mark worried he was wrong. But Johnny only took seconds to point to Coleman. "That's him."

Connor and Juan shot Mark a smile. Everyone but Mark and Johnny walked out.

"You did good," Mark said.

"I hope you catch the bastard."

"Me too."

"Will I have to testify?" Johnny asked.

"You have a problem with that?"

"I don't look forward to having my past thrown in my face. But it's for the kid, right?"

"Right," Mark said.

Johnny walked out. Mark stood there and breathed. In. Out. For the kids, he thought. He just wished like hell he'd been there for his sister.

When he turned to collect the images, he saw Harden's keys on the table. Picking them up, he saw the leather keychain. In a slotted pocket in the middle was a bronze token. An AA token. A sobriety symbol.

Johnny returned. "Hey."

"Here." Mark held out the keys.

"Been sober for three years."

"That's quite an accomplishment." Mark remembered Murdock, the department shrink, asking if he was an alcoholic. He also remembered what he'd told him: *I don't have a drinking problem, I have a dead kid problem.*

After Johnny left, Mark went back to the office. Connor saw him and piped up, "We did it. Solved a case the sergeant couldn't."

"Yeah," Mark said without enthusiasm.

He knew getting to the bottom of this wasn't going to be pretty. Sometimes breaking a case meant breaking hearts. Normally, he still celebrated a win. But not this time. And it wasn't fair.

"So why the hell doesn't it feel good?" Connor echoed Mark's thought.

No one answered.

Connor left to grab lunch. Juan left to look for a Missing Persons file for another case that had been brought to their attention.

Mark started writing the interview report, then he remembered Annie's text. He dialed her number with anticipation. It went to voice mail. "Hey. I'm going to be tied up until later. Looking forward to tonight."

He was almost finished with the report when his office phone rang. The morgue's number flashed on the screen. Knowing it was his friend Stone, he picked it up. "Yes, the poker game is still on for tomorrow. Bring plenty of money."

"Right." Stone chuckled. "That's not why I called. I finished the Talbot autopsy."

"I thought you'd already finished it."

"No, I still had some tests to do. I told Juan and Connor that."

"They didn't mention it." An image flashed in his head. "So you found something else?"

"Yes. Something I wasn't expecting."

* * *

"Where are you going?"

Annie looked over her shoulder at Isabella down the hall. "Just to my car. I think I left some papers in there."

"When your class is over, drop in."

"Sure." Annie left the building. The parking lot was quiet, not a lot of foot traffic during the classes.

She heard her footsteps on the pavement. She recalled her time at the park. She recalled Sam's visit at the coffee shop.

The feeling of being watched hit. Fear bit. She slowed down, swallowed, and recalled Mark's warning to be careful.

This was crazy. It was daytime. She looked around. Saw nothing.

Her heart drummed in her ears as the hairs on the back of her neck stood up. Was she worrying about nothing? Or was she crazy not to worry?

CHAPTER
TWENTY-TWO

Connor and Juan returned at the same time Bethany Talbot showed up. Mark didn't have a chance to inform them about the call from Stone. Then again, it didn't change anything. The kid was dead. How she died didn't matter.

Mark walked Bethany Talbot into interview room one.

"What is it?" She went limp as she dropped into a chair. The grayness of the room seemed to soak her up and set the mood.

Sitting across from her, he had a front row seat to the anguish in her eyes. Regret drop-kicked his conscience. But he had to do this.

"We've made some headway."

"Did Brian kill our daughter?"

"No."

"Then who? Do I know them?" Her voice shook with soul-deep pain.

He felt the rattle all the way in his chest. "I'm not at liberty to—"

"'Not at liberty'? There is no liberty or justice in this world." Now her voice was laced with rage. He knew how quick pain could morph into fury.

He spoke before thinking. "Believe me when I say I know exactly how you feel."

"Really? You had a kid who was murdered?"

"My sister." The confession slipped off his lips and opened his own vein of pain and fury. Why the fuck had he . . . ? Ms. Talbot stared at him and he knew why. People needed to know they weren't alone.

Anger drained from her expression and with it faded a bit of his own. "I'm sorry," she said.

"I know this is hard, but I need to ask." He tapped his pen on the folder. "Were you having an affair when your daughter went missing?"

She tensed. "No. I taught school. I worked all day and took care of my daughter in the evenings and at night. When would I have had time to have an affair?"

Was her defensiveness a cover-up or honest indignation? "Other teachers manage it."

Her posture hardened, then softened. "Okay, you're right. But that's not me. I loved Brian."

Mark heard the honesty in her voice. "What about Brian?"

Her hesitation spoke loudly. "Right before Brittany went missing, I recall worrying that he was. But I told myself I was being ridiculous. My brother-in-law and sister were with him every day. When would he have had the time?"

Mark clinked his pen. "Your sister worked at Coleman Concrete, too?"

"She was the office manager." A frown wrinkled Bethany Talbot's brow. "Are you thinking Brian and...? No. Michele wouldn't do that to me. Brian either."

Mark wished he could save her this pain. For his mother, finding out someone she loved was responsible had been too much.

A knock sounded. Mark knew what that meant. "Give me a minute."

He left and walked into interview room two, another gray room with a flimsy table, identical to the room he'd just left. But in here, the air reeked of guilt and tension. Michele Coleman sat fidgeting with her hair. She lifted her gaze, suspicious. Were her nerves about more than the affair? Had she been a part of the kidnapping?

"I don't understand why you think I have information on Brian Talbot."

He'd given her that piece of info when he called, wanting to give her time to stew.

He dropped into a chair. "You want to come clean on this?"

"On what?" Her chin lifted to a stubborn angle.

"Tell me!"

She didn't answer. He slapped the table. She jumped.

"Did you have something to do with your niece's kidnapping?"

Something akin to relief filled her eyes. "God no! I loved Brittany."

He believed her. He leaned closer. "How long had the affair been going on?"

Her gulp sounded raw. Guilt brightened her eyes. "Please don't tell Bethany. She'll hate me."

Unfortunately, Mark didn't think there was a way to spare her sister. "You and Brian were together when the kidnapping happened."

She nodded. "We were ending it. It was our last time."

"Your husband found out?"

Her defiant chin dropped. "He caught us kissing."

"Did you know he kidnapped your niece?"

The answer flashed in her expression. "Gary wouldn't... You're wrong."

Mark wasn't wrong.

"He's not a monster."

"When people feel betrayed, they do things." A knock sounded on the door, and Mark stood up. "Excuse me."

He walked out and toward room four, hesitating a second before turning the knob. Solving a case was supposed to feel good. Nothing about this felt good. He now knew why. They hadn't caught anyone evil. Just people who'd made bad mistakes. It brought home the grave mistake he'd made.

He walked into the room. Brian, hands clenched, stood waiting. "Why are my ex-wife's and her sister's cars here?"

Mark dropped in a chair and motioned for Brian to sit. Only when he did, did Mark speak. "We know the truth."

Brian banged his fist on the table. "If you're saying I killed—"

"I'm not saying that. I'm saying I know where you were the day your daughter was taken."

His face paled.

"I was a fucking idiot. But putting that out there would hurt Bethany. She loves her sister. She's been hurt enough. And it won't catch my daughter's killer. So why are you doing this?"

"I wouldn't if I didn't think it was connected."

"So you still suspect me? Look, I was a piece of shit for cheating, but I loved my daughter and Bethany. It was a mistake. I'd never—"

"I believe you," Mark said.

Mark could see Brian's mind searching for answers. "You think...Michele? She was with me." Then his face lost its color. "Gary?" He shot to his feet and slung his chair across the room.

"Calm down," Mark said.

Talbot hit the wall with his fist. A loud, bone-crushing *clunk*.

"Stop," Mark insisted.

Talbot swung around. "I'll kill him." He breathed in. Out. His nostrils flared, then Mark watched as his fury faded into self-loathing. Talbot realized the truth.

His affair had been the catalyst for his daughter's death.

Mark recognized that pain. "You have a chance to be the one who tells your wife about the affair. Or her sister can tell her. Unfortunately, this will come out. The media feeds on this stuff."

"Should I talk to her now?" Talbot asked, sounding lost, hopeless, guilty.

"No, not now. Not here. But hopefully before any of this comes out." He took one step then turned back. "Go have your hand x-rayed."

Mark walked away, feeling raw and swollen inside. He wanted a drink. No, he wanted several. He wanted to forget that he knew exactly what Brian Talbot felt.

He couldn't.

He had to go pick up a murderer.

Then he remembered his plans for that night. Hell, he didn't need whiskey. He needed Annie. What had the old man called her, a slice of heaven? Yeah, he needed an extra-large slice.

Brown arranged for other officers to release the interviewees, one at a time. Reports would need to be written up later.

* * *

"Has he not called you back?" Isabella asked, as they hurried across the rubber-sole-melting parking lot and into the store.

Precious air conditioning welcomed them inside. "He called during class." Annie snagged a buggy. They'd finished their classes and decided to go shopping. On the ride over she'd told her about her uncle showing up at the coffee shop. About swearing someone was watching her.

"Why haven't you called him back? He should know your uncle threatened you, not to mention that thing in the parking lot."

"My uncle didn't threaten me. He just tried to get me

to go with him. And I didn't see anyone in the parking lot." Annie had been trying to put things into perspective. To not overreact. Yet overreacting seemed to be in her DNA.

"Yeah, it appeared so unthreatening that the entire coffee shop came to your rescue. You need to tell Mark."

Isabella wasn't helping Annie's perspective.

"I'm going to." Annie glanced around to get her bearings in the store. "In his message, he said he was busy today."

"Then you should've called the cops. Your uncle should've been arrested."

"I took a picture of his car driving away. Got the license plate. For proof that he was really there. And I'll give it to Mark tonight."

"You still think Mark won't believe you?"

"I don't know." She hesitated. "But I don't want to think about that tonight."

Hence the reason she headed to the lingerie department.

"What about this?" Isabella held up a sexy pajamas set and made them dance. "They're pink."

Annie rolled her eyes. "I should've never told you that."

"Please. Let me live vicariously through you. It's the most fun I've had in years." She gave the hanger another shake. "Yea or nay?"

"I like it." Annie took the hanger. The tight-fitting tank top had a little lace and came with matching boy shorts. Sexy, but not do-me-now sexy. Annie didn't go for the do-me-now style—at least not in the beginning. She'd gone there when she noticed the spice running low in her and Ted's relationship.

Perhaps Ted's leaving wasn't all about her being crazy. Maybe he'd just been bored with her. Oddly, she didn't know which was worse. Him thinking she was crazy. Or thinking she was a dud in bed.

She checked the price of the dancing pajamas. Seeing it was affordable, she dropped the set in her basket.

"Score one for me," Isabella said. "Let's pick him out a sexy pair of silk boxers."

"Not happening." But Annie's mind took her to how he'd looked in his fitted cotton boxers. She moved to the next rack.

It had been a while since she'd invested in underwear. She found her size and bought two bra-and-panty sets.

She'd be eating beans and rice for a few weeks so she could afford it. A smile warmed her chest. It'd be worth it.

Isabella pulled out a red bra-and-panty set and eyed it.

"Buy it," Annie said.

"Nope." Her friend rehung the bra.

"Why aren't you having fun? You're divorced. You claim it's over. And yet... you go to bed with a book."

"They're good books." She wiggled her brows.

"Seriously?"

"Don't worry. I put 'get laid' on my to-do list."

Annie cut her friend a stern look.

Isabella cut her one back. "When you've had the best, it's hard to accept less."

"Jose was that good?" Annie asked.

"One smile, and I melted into my panties. We were married for four years and we still had sex five times a week. I miss that."

"Then do something about it?"

"I've considered hiring a gigolo."

Annie laughed, but she wasn't fooled. Hum`or was Isabella's defense mechanism. In truth, Annie had been known to use it herself. "I think you should buy something sexy and call him."

Isabella sighed. "He'd never see it. All he wants to do is try to fix things."

"Then answer the door just wearing that."

"And then what?" Isabella said.

"Let the panty melting begin. Talk later."

Her friend drew in a sharp breath that held no humor. "He'd never forgive me."

"Maybe or maybe not. Maybe the person having a hard time forgiving is you."

"Jose didn't do anything for me to forgive."

"I don't mean forgive him. I mean forgive yourself. You were seventeen, scared. It's time to let it go."

* * *

"So she died from a fall?" Juan asked Mark.

"Yeah." While waiting at the airport Mark remembered the call from Stone.

"That's odd," Connor said. "Death by fall is a murder of opportunity."

"I know," Mark said. "It feels off. But no matter what, there's still the matter of the kidnapping."

They stood at Gate C23 waiting for the flight from Florida to arrive. They called the airlines and confirmed Gary Coleman had boarded. Since he'd gone through security check, chances were he wasn't armed. At least they hoped not.

"Why does this case feel different?" Connor asked.

"It's a kid," Juan answered.

"The Kemp case was a kid," Connor said. "This feels like more."

Mark didn't answer. He knew why it was more for him.

"Maybe because we found her," Juan said. "We had fun dragging that lake and then we found her and felt almost guilty for having fun."

Neither Mark nor Connor added anything. But Juan had a point.

Mark's phone rang. He looked at the screen. The frown stirred all the way from his gut to his lips. Judith Holt's number flashed across his screen. What the hell did she want? He hit decline.

"Girlfriend?" Connor asked.

"No," Mark snapped then saw a mother and two kids waiting to board the plane Coleman was supposed to arrive on. "Let's not take this guy here."

Juan nodded. "I was thinking the same thing."

Within a few minutes, the passengers started unloading. The three of them separated so as not to call attention to themselves. The rate of departing passengers slowed down to a crawl.

Had the airlines gotten it wrong? Had Coleman not boarded the plane?

Just then a big redheaded man walked out with his carry-on luggage. He looked unhappy. Considering he'd come from his parents' funeral, it was understandable. Unfortunately, it wasn't going to get any better.

Mark followed about eight feet behind Coleman. Both Connor and Juan moved to the other side of the walkway. Dogging the man's steps, Mark remembered Coleman's kids. Now, those kids would grow up without a dad.

When Coleman went into the elevator, Mark got on with him. Connor and Juan followed.

When the doors closed, Mark gave Juan and Connor the nod. He turned to face the murder suspect. "Mr. Coleman?"

The man appeared shocked. "Do I know you?"

Mark braced himself as he opened his coat to show his badge. "Detective Mark Sutton. I'm with the Anniston PD."

The man's shoulders tightened and Mark swore it was going to end ugly. "You might take on one or even two of us, but not three. Why don't you come down to the precinct with us willingly?"

The man closed his eyes, opened them, then raked a hand over his face. "What the fuck took you so long?"

CHAPTER
TWENTY-THREE

Annie pulled up to the white, one-story brick house in a nice neighborhood. She was twenty minutes late.

All the houses had acre lots. She wondered if the house had belonged to Mark's parents. Or maybe detectives made more than teachers.

Mark had called her about an hour ago to apologize for not calling, and added he'd been tied up with a case. She assured him it was okay. She planned on telling him later about Sam Reed's visit in person.

She searched for an address on the mailbox but didn't see one. Her GPS said she'd arrived. But how many times had her GPS lied to her? And not just the car's GPS, but the one guiding her life.

For one second, she worried that was what this relationship was—a bad turn.

Nudging her doubt aside, she snagged her phone and dialed his number.

"You lost?" he answered.

"Depends. Is your house a white brick one-story?" The curtain in the window pulled back.

"Come in." A smile rode his words.

The door opened as she moved toward the porch.

She'd no sooner crossed the threshold when he took her bag and then her. The kiss wasn't let's-go-to-bed as much as I-missed-you. Even with her doubts, she knew how he felt.

When the kiss ended, he smiled. "You. This. Is the best part of my day."

"Really?"

He ran a finger over her lips. "So you didn't miss me?"

"I did." She heard a big dog barking. "I'm guessing that's Bacon."

"Yup, I put him out until you're ready to meet him."

The barking increased in tempo and volume. "Is he friendly?"

"Too much. Unfortunately, he has one bad habit. I've tried to break him of it, but nothing worked."

"What bad habit?" she asked, a little leery.

"He's a crotch smeller. Until he gets into your business, he won't be happy."

Laughter bubbled out of her. "I thought you were going to tell me he was a humper. I can handle my crotch being sniffed more than I can my leg being screwed."

His laugh came out as free as hers. "This...this is why I like you." He pulled her against him. "I needed this." His tone told her he wasn't exaggerating.

"Bad day?" She saw a touch of frustration in his eyes.

"Not anymore."

"What happened?" She ran her palms up his torso, stopping to press them on his warm and wide chest.

"We solved a case but—"

"The Talbot case?" The visual of Brittany twirling in her tutu filled her mind.

"Yeah." The tenor in his voice deepened.

"How can that make for a bad day? I'd think you'd want—"

"I do. It's just . . . it's a mixed bag of ugly." He paused. "The guy we arrested, he didn't mean to kill her. He admitted to kidnapping her. But he just . . . wanted to make someone listen to him. He hadn't intended to hurt her. He took her to a construction site and she fell. It was an accident."

"Was it her father?" She noted his surprise at her question. "I followed the case in the news."

"No, but . . . the father's going to blame himself. And the mom is going to learn she was betrayed by two people she loves. A bunch of bad mistakes that ended in a kid's death. Like I said, a bag of ugly."

"I'm sorry."

His dog continued barking. "Don't be." His shoulders tightened as if he wished he hadn't spoken his mind. "It's my job."

Her gut said it was more than a job. She recalled Fred saying cops had baggage.

"You ready to meet Bacon?" Mark asked.

"Yeah. Not sure my crotch is, though."

He laughed, chasing away the sad shadows that had played in his expression. He brushed his lips against hers. Soft and sweet, and loaded with anticipation. Pulling away, he opened the back door.

A big yellow Lab barreled through the door. Mark tried to catch it, but the canine was faster. "I swear he won't hurt you," Mark called out. "Bacon, sit!"

Bacon didn't sit.

He bounced toward her, and his big black nose went right to her crotch.

Mark repeated, "Bacon, sit!"

The dog obeyed, gazing up at her with a look of approval while his tail *swish-swish*ed across the hardwood floors in happy mode.

Mark chuckled. "You aced the sniff test."

"Good to know." She petted the dog as his whole body wagged.

Mark picked up her bag. "I'll put this in the bedroom."

She followed Mark, and Bacon followed her down the all-white hall, which had no wall art. They passed four other doors, two on each side, until they reached the door at the end.

"This is big," she said.

"It's just twenty-nine hundred square feet, but it's well laid out. It's a four-bedroom, but I use one as a weight room and one as a computer room."

She walked into his bedroom, also with white, unadorned walls. Up against the back wall was a king-sized bed. A black bedspread covered the mattress. Lining the opposite wall was a dresser with a fifty-two-inch TV sitting on top. A chest of drawers was stationed on the wall with the door to the bathroom. Like the other rooms, it was neat, but somehow sterile, stark, like an apartment before someone moved in and made it their own. Had Mark just moved here?

It hit her again, how little she knew about Mark. She made it her mission to remedy that.

"All the bedrooms besides the master are small." He set her bag on his bed.

"Compared to my apartment, it's huge."

"Yeah, but you're so small. It fits you."

"Don't remind me."

"I like your size."

While she glanced around searching for clues and hints of the big man living here, he came up behind her, wrapped his arms around her, and kissed her neck. She tilted her head to the side and savored the moist feel of his lips sliding across sensitive skin.

Yup, melting into my panties.

She turned on tiptoes and pressed her lips to his. The kiss went hot really fast.

He pulled away. "We should leave the room before I throw you on the bed."

The sweet tingle whispering up and down her spine had her wanting just that. Sobering her was the realization she had no willpower when it came to him. What was wrong with her?

Or maybe it wasn't what was wrong with *her*, but with her past lovers.

He took her hand. "Come on. I'll show you the rest of the house."

He opened doors as they walked down the hall. Each room was void of personality. Was it a man thing? She visualized her ex-fiancé Ted's apartment, and remembered the personal items there. Family pictures. His degree hanging on the wall. A few old trophies, football paraphernalia. It wasn't just a Mars-Venus issue.

"Wine?" he offered, as they stopped at the kitchen.

"Sure." While he uncorked the wine, she looked around at the granite countertops and an island. "Do you cook?"

"I'm better on the grill or a smoker."

"Yeah, I remember." It was one of the few things she knew about him. She noted again the bare walls. "How long have you lived here?"

"Six years." He handed her a glass of red wine.

"Oh," she said, not meaning to say it aloud.

"'Oh,' what?"

"Nothing, I just... You don't have personal stuff around."

"Personal stuff?"

"Photos or keepsakes like old trophies or shot glasses you got from vacation." Worried it sounded like an insult, she focused on the wine. "This is good."

"Yeah." He looked around. "I have some photos." He walked into the living room, grabbed a stack of coasters off the coffee table, and handed them to her.

She looked at the images behind the glass on the coasters, four different shots of Bacon. "Okay, it's something." Smiling, she set them back on the coffee table.

"And there's more." He slid his arm behind her, curled his hand around the curve of her waist, and led her into a game room at the back of the house.

The huge room had more personality. On the back wall was a large picture of dogs playing poker. On one side of the room was a pool table, on the other was a Ping-Pong table.

"My knickknacks." He motioned to the two tables.

She grinned, her eyes going back to the picture. "You play poker?"

"Me and some guys play twice a month. Tomorrow afternoon. But not until four, so you don't have to rush off tomorrow."

She spotted something in the corner of the room. A saxophone on a stand. She recalled him saying he liked jazz. "You play?"

"Used to." His light tone changed somehow and made her even more curious.

"Play me something."

"No. I can't."

"Just something short."

Emotion flashed in his eyes. "I'll play you a game of pool." He grabbed two cue sticks off the wooden rack on the wall. "You know how to play?"

"I played before, but it's been years. I'm sure I suck at it."

"I don't see you sucking at anything." He chalked the cues.

She remembered. "Oh, I...meant to tell you that my uncle, Sam Reed, stopped by today."

"What?" He set the cues on the table. "When?"

"After you left the coffee shop."

"What did he say?"

"He wanted me to go with him somewhere else to

talk. I wouldn't. He got upset and tried to grab my arm. Fred and the others in the shop saw it and told him to leave."

The wrinkle between Mark's brows appeared. "Why didn't you call me?"

"I texted you."

"Sorry. Next time let me know it's important. Tell me everything he said."

She did, and added, "I got proof. I took a picture of his car driving off." She pulled her phone out.

He stared at the picture, then lifted his gaze. "Your mom knows you hang out at the coffee shop, right?"

"Yeah." Annie knew what he was insinuating. It hurt. "She's trying to stop me from talking, but she wouldn't send someone to hurt me."

His blue eyes met hers. "I'm sorry."

Was he sorry because he thought Annie was wrong, or sorry because of her situation?

"Give me just a minute, I want to call someone about this."

He grabbed his phone and dialed.

While he talked, Annie went back to worrying. About the case. About them. But why? The obvious answer bubbled to the surface. Fred's advice. Was she giving the sweet ol' man's advice too much merit?

* * *

Adam Harper leaned back in his office chair and cupped his hands behind his head. It was Friday evening. He should be out having fun, drinking beer with the guys. Maybe taking some sweet woman to dinner. His mind immediately conjured up an image of JoAnne Lakes.

Pushing that thought away, he straightened and went back to going through another box of moldy files he'd had Rusty get out of the basement of the courthouse.

Something JT recalled last night had Adam going on a fishing expedition. *If I remember correctly, Sheriff Carter said that this wasn't the first time the Reed name had come up in an investigation. That's why he even agreed to look into the Jenny Reed case for the Anniston PD.*

JT didn't recall what kind of an investigation it'd been. Probably didn't have anything to do with the Jenny Reed case, but Adam's mind kept wanting to play connect the dots. Instinct maybe, or perhaps just boredom. He'd needed something to fill his empty life. The Reed case fit the bill.

Not that he wasn't frustrated. He'd been out to talk to George Reed three times. George still was either out of town or avoiding him.

Adam had called the man's cell, and he had yet to get him. He'd dropped by and spoken with Sam Reed, but the man offered nothing new. Except Adam picked up on the man's rage, which he kept hidden right under his skin.

This whole thing smelled fishy. Hence, his fishing expedition.

Adam's cell phone rang. Seeing it was Detective Sutton, he took the call. "I was thinking about calling you."

"You got something?"

"Just a shitload more of questions. And a missing George Reed. He won't even take my calls."

"You think he's just avoiding you?"

"Hell, yeah. But I don't have enough reason to go drag his ass back."

"Yeah. Look, the other uncle, Sam Reed, paid Annie a visit. He tried to get her to go with him, grabbed her to get her to leave with him. I'm thinking it's time I come down and we interview everyone separately. Don't give them warning. Let's just show up at the doors."

"Good idea." Adam leaned back in his chair. "What about Tuesday?"

"Perfect."

"You got anything on the missing cousin?" Adam asked.

"No." Sutton's voice tightened. "Frustrating as hell."

"Tell me about it." Adam leaned forward. "I might just pay a Friday night call to Doris Roberts again. See if she's heard from her daughter yet."

CHAPTER
TWENTY-FOUR

An hour later, Annie pushed her plate back. "That was good."

Mark had suggested ordering in instead of going out.

After helping put the leftovers in the fridge, he pulled her back in the game room to finish their game of pool—which she sucked at!

Standing on the other side of the table, she watched him. "Why did you become a cop?"

"Just seemed to fit." He never looked up. "Right corner," he said, as if the ball knew to obey. One tap and it dropped in with a *clunk*.

With that game done, he tried to give her a few lessons. Standing behind her, his pelvis against her backside, he helped her guide a ball into a hole. He didn't pull away right away, but kissed her neck.

"Now you do it." He set the ball out.

Feeling tingly from his closeness, she chalked her cue, took a deep breath, then leaned over and tapped the ball. It darted across the table, bouncing here, bouncing there, but never fell in a hole. "See," she told him. "I suck."

He laughed. "You're hitting it too hard."

"How about let's move to Ping-Pong?" she said.

"You play that?"

"A little," she lied. As a teen, she'd worked at a camp for kids. They'd had a game room, and she'd found out she had a knack for Ping-Pong.

He kissed her. "I have to warn you, I'm good at that, too."

"Don't brag," she said.

"You know what else I'm good at?" The heat in his eyes answered his question. A flashback of just how good he was at it played in her mind.

When that kiss ended, she put a hand on his chest. "Come on, I'm going to teach you how to play Ping-Pong."

"Ah, earlier you said you played a little. Now you're going to teach me. How about we make it interesting?"

"Interesting?"

"Every game you lose, you lose a piece of clothing."

She laughed. "Strip Ping-Pong."

"Hey, if you are as good as you say, you'll keep the shirt on your back. And get to see me take mine off."

She grinned. "Get ready to get naked."

He brought the wine and glasses in. As they started playing, she realized he was better than she thought. It wouldn't hurt to have a slight advantage. She purposely lost the first set and took off her shirt, playfully and slow.

His eyes widened when he saw the bra, the new one she'd bought, of black and pink lace.

"Nice," he said.

He started to walk over and she held up her hand. "No. Let's play."

He chuckled. "But I'm warning you, either way you're losing those clothes."

"Is that a threat?"

"A promise." His smile was so sexy, she nearly missed his serve ball.

Nearly. He didn't even win a point.

He lost his shirt. And made a show of taking it off, like she did. "You know what I think?" he asked, picking up the paddle. "I think you purposely lost the first game knowing I'd be distracted."

"Please. Do I look sneaky like that?"

"Hell, yes. Standing there in your sexy lacy bra. You're evil."

She served.

He lost his shoes.

"You out-and-out lied to me. Were you a champion Ping-Pong player?"

He lost his socks.

Bacon collected them and Mark, barefoot and shirtless, chased him down to collect them.

He lost his pants.

"Don't you worry about hurting my ego?" he asked as he unzipped.

"No. Your ego's so big I think it can take a few hits."

He lost his underwear.

She laughed so hard when he dropped his boxers.

"Are you happy? I'm naked."

Yup, she was. And he was extraordinary.

Grinning so hard her jaw hurt, she said, "Really happy." And she was. How long had it been since she'd felt like this? As crazy as her life was, he made her happy.

Then the six feet plus of naked man came sauntering toward her. She couldn't stop laughing. With slow hands, he took her clothes off. And they made each other exceptionally happy.

* * *

Adam pulled into the dirt driveway. There were four cars parked out front. Getting out, he hitched up his pants and headed to the porch. The light was on, but it wasn't bright. When he was almost at the door, he heard yelling. As a sheriff, he'd visited dysfunction at its best, and this one wasn't disappointing.

He paused.

The front door swung open and a woman ran out and right into his arms.

He caught her. A soft, sweet smell rose from her hair. She lifted her face. But before he even focused on her he knew who it was, JoAnne Lakes.

"Sorry." She went to pull back, then didn't. Not for that extra few seconds. Her soft breasts came against his chest. How long had it been since he'd held a woman?

"Sorry." Her lips trembled and her eyes filled with tears. She pulled away.

He nodded and gave himself a mental kick in the pants for enjoying it so much. "It's okay."

"Do you have news on Fran?"

Her question came out full of honesty and concern, and again, his gut said this woman wasn't behind everything. The fact she couldn't answer anything about the missing Jenny Reed with the same honesty confused the hell out of him, though.

"No, nothing on Fran. Her mother hasn't heard from her?"

"No."

He nodded. "Is George Reed here?"

Her eyes tightened and went to the door. "Now isn't a good time. He's been drinking. Could you come back tomorrow?"

Adam noted the absence of alcohol on her breath. He considered doing as she asked, but he had a job to do. "I need to speak with him."

"But tomorrow—"

"He's been avoiding me for days."

She remained silent.

"Maybe you could clear it up for me and tell me the truth."

"I have," she said with confidence. "We don't know where Fran is."

"I believe you when you tell me that. It's Jenny I'm talking about."

He heard her inhale. "We . . . we've told you."

He stared into her still-damp eyes. "Anyone ever tell you you're too damn pretty to lie?"

She took another gulp of air and he mentally gave

himself another foot in his ass. He shouldn't go soft with her. "Do you know what this is doing to your daughter? Doesn't she deserve for you to be on her side of this?"

She looked slapped. "You don't... It's not—"

The front door swung open again. "JoAnne," a deep voice called. "Get in here. Fuck it!"

Fuck it, was right. Adam believed the woman was about to spill the truth. He glanced away from her to Sam Reed's cold, bloodshot eyes. "That's no way to talk to a lady."

Sam glared at him and then at his sister. JoAnne offered him a brief look of thanks then, like a whipped puppy, hurried back inside.

"What do you need?" The man's whiskey-laced breath crossed over into Adam's personal space.

"To see George."

"He isn't here."

"Your sister said otherwise."

The man's scowl deepened. "Why can't you leave us alone? We stay away from people, why can't everyone stay away from us?"

"I'm told you paid Annie Lakes a visit."

"She's family. I went to see her. Is that against the law?"

"I wouldn't plan another visit."

"You talk tough." Sam swayed on his feet.

"I'm tougher than I sound. Get George out here." Adam stood to his full height.

"God damn it! I'm here." George Reed stepped onto the porch. "Since when do people not respect a grieving family?"

"Since your niece is missing. And you were the last person to see her."

"My sister told you I took her home. What's the big deal?" Spittle sprayed out of the man's mouth as he spoke.

"She only told me that after I spotted her daughter's car in her garage. Why would she lie?"

"She was probably drunk. Reed women can't handle their drink."

Neither can the men. "And what home did you take her to?"

"To her boyfriend's place in Austin."

"Her boyfriend says she never returned."

"Well, the boyfriend's lying. I watched her sashay her drunk ass up to the trailer." George collapsed against the door. "I don't get why you guys are getting all wrapped up in what my niece Annie told you. You haven't checked on her, have you?" He whistled and twirled a finger beside his temple.

* * *

Mark could feel the light tickle of Annie's hair fanned across his chest. He glanced down at her, sleeping, looking so... peaceful, so innocent. A little of that feeling leaked into him.

He picked up a strand of hair. It glided across his fingers.

A slice of heaven. The old man's warning about not hurting her echoed. The last thing he wanted to do was to cause her pain. This wasn't pain. This was good.

Good for him. Good for her. That sad look he'd initially spotted in her eyes, the one he recognized from his own reflection, had lessened since they'd been seeing each other. They laughed. Had fun.

But for how long? The question tightened the muscles in his neck. Was he capable of having a long-term relationship? The longest he'd had was eight months almost two years ago with Shane, a nurse. He hadn't been the one to walk, but she blamed him. He'd been working the Evans case, the second dead-kid case he'd worked. A ten-year-old boy gone forever. It hadn't been the kid's father, but his uncle.

The case had brought it all back. The rage, the guilt, the pain. Unlike what the old man at the coffee shop had said, he'd never taken it out on Shane. Not physically. Yeah, he'd snapped at her a few times when she tried to figure him out, tried to fix him.

You do that when you're dying inside.

Was that how he and Annie were going to end?

Damn it. Why was he going there?

Annie stirred on his chest. Her eyes opened and with lids half masked, she looked at him. "Tell me a secret."

Was she even awake? "A secret?"

"Yeah, something that lets me inside you."

He stared at her pleading expression. "What kind of secret?"

"Something you've never told anyone else."

For some insane reason, he wanted to give her what she asked for. Perhaps he wanted to prove that this would work. That he could change. He sifted through his life to find a shareable secret. A safe one.

"My real dad walked out on my mom. I don't even remember him."

She offered him a sleepy frown and a warm hand to his chest. "I'm sorry," she whispered.

"Me too," he said. She continued to stare at him with those big, sleepy, caring eyes. He wasn't completely sure she was fully awake.

"I want you to play the saxophone for me."

"Maybe someday," he said, not sure that day would come. He realized something right then, something he hadn't completely put together until now. He didn't play the saxophone because making music made him happy, and he didn't think he deserved to be happy. Not when he'd left his sister alone and she died because of it.

But Annie made him happy, too. Did he deserve her?

Was that why he seemed to sabotage it at times? Her soft weight sank deeper into him. It felt as if the dip in his shoulder was created for her. She fit against him. Fit him. An hour passed. He was still sifting through his emotions when she jerked awake.

"You okay?" he asked.

"Yeah." Said with zero confidence.

"A dream?" He ran his hand over her back—to soothe, to comfort.

"No, I just remembered."

"What?"

"That Fran came back for me. And I'm not doing a thing to help her."

He pulled up closer. "We're looking for her."

"But we aren't finding her."

"We're doing everything we can."

"That doesn't feel like enough." She sighed. "And the fact that I'm happy and she could be dead, it doesn't feel right."

Her words made a direct hit. He offered her what he could. A piece of wisdom he rejected himself. "Would being miserable help her?"

"No, but happy feels wrong."

He couldn't argue with that.

* * *

Still wearing her tank-top-and-boy-shorts night set, Annie made the coffee while Mark made the eggs and toast. Waking up in his arms had been like a hug to her lonely soul. Yet once awake that hug stopped feeling right. She wasn't sure if it was just her, or him, too. He seemed...distant.

She felt out of her element. As if she'd stepped into someone else's safe life, in the arms of a man she knew so little about, in a bed that felt comfortable but was not her own, in a room void of personality, in a house that felt as if it had no owner.

This wasn't the first time she'd slept with him, so why all the insecurities now? Was it being in his place? Was it...

"Grab some more butter out of the fridge." He smiled, but even that didn't appear real.

She recalled the late-night pillow talk. "Do you have any pictures of your father?"

He stopped whipping the eggs. "No."

"Did your mom ever talk about him?"

"No."

"Have you ever thought about—"

"No." He didn't look at her. "Can we not talk about that?"

She emotionally flinched. His tone wasn't angry, just short. "Sorry. I just . . . I want to get to know you."

He continued to look down. "You do know me."

"No. I don't. Not really. Maybe it's because we slept with each other too soon."

He faced her, he looked apologetic. He looked nervous. "It doesn't feel too soon to me. I like this, Annie. I really like it. I don't want to try to analyze it anymore."

"You've tried to analyze it?"

"I just want to enjoy it. Is that wrong?"

"I guess not. I just . . . Everything feels crazy. Jenny, Fran . . ." *Us.*

He moved in and put his hands on her shoulders. His palms were warm. "You're in the middle of a murder investigation. It is crazy." When she didn't respond, he continued, "I'm going to make some more phone calls today about Fran Roberts."

She nodded. "I thought you had a poker game."

"Not until this afternoon. Juan, Connor, and I are all going into the office to finish up the paperwork on the Talbot case. I figured I can work in a few calls. And I'm going to go see the retired officer who worked the Reed case years ago."

"Do you think he'll remember anything?" She watched him cook the eggs.

"It's a long shot, but who knows." He dished the

eggs into a bowl and set them on the table. She heard the toast pop up, put it on a plate, and set it on the table. They sat down across from each other.

"Did you dream last night?" he asked as she dished some eggs onto her plate.

"No, not that I remember. You must be good for me." She put on her best smile and grabbed the butter. His dog, Bacon, curled up at her feet.

"The APD has a psychiatrist who talks to victims. He could possibly help you...remember things."

The eggs she'd just swallowed lodged in her tonsils. She coughed. "I...I tried that. It didn't work."

"Tried what?"

"Talking to therapists."

"When?"

"Several years ago." She picked up her coffee, wanting to shield herself from his questions.

"Oh, I thought it just started bothering you when you went to the funeral."

"I've had the dreams for a long time." She chased the eggs around her plate, feeling his gaze on her, feeling his doubt, and feeling her own dishonesty.

He leaned back in his chair. "Maybe now it'd be different."

"Perhaps." And just like that all the insecurities of having lost her job, her friends, her fiancé, and her life because people thought she was insane swirled inside her. And now here she was, on the outs with her own mom. Her life was a freaking mess.

What was she doing starting a relationship? She needed to end it.

"Do you want me to set it up?" he asked.

Panic clawed at her rib cage. She pushed out words, praying they sounded calm. Sane. "Can I think about it?"

"Sure." He studied her.

Guilt spread through her body like a virus. She'd gone to him with this and then kept secrets. And she'd done it to protect herself from his opinion. Another reason she shouldn't have let this happen.

Tell him the truth. Tell him. Tell him. "There was a time when the dreams were bad. I kind of got obsessed about them."

"When you were young?"

"No, not—" The sound of Mark's front door opening and shutting silenced her.

Bacon, warming her feet, pounced up and began barking.

Mark shot up from the table. He barely got two feet before stopping cold.

"What the hell are you doing here?" His voice rose.

CHAPTER
TWENTY-FIVE

I thought about knocking, then remembered you gave me your key."

Annie couldn't see the woman, but she recognized the six-o'clock-news voice. She set her fork down, unsure of the proper behavior in this instance.

"Get out!" Mark growled.

"Slow down," Judith Holt said, her voice drawing nearer. The woman moved in where Annie could see her. And she could see Annie.

Judith offered Annie her camera-ready smile. "Didn't mean to intrude. If he'd taken my calls, this wouldn't have happened."

Annie sat there, wishing she had on more clothes.

The woman faced Mark. "I wanted to ask you a few questions about the Talbot case. Word is you've solved it. Congratulations. Again."

"I said get the fuck out!" Mark's voice rose.

Judith looked back at Annie. "He needs to learn

a few manners, doesn't he?" She refocused on Mark. "Come on, give me something."

"I swear I'm going to throw you out!"

"No you won't. You're smarter than that. You know how easily I bruise, and it wouldn't look good on the news. But you know, I was afraid you'd act this way. So now my problem is which story to run."

Mark shot to the table and grabbed his phone. Probably to call the police. Never mind that he was one. Judith, completely calm, kept talking.

"The story about you dating your star witness in a new case." She motioned to Annie. "Or the one about some pathetic cold-case detective who's still trying to save his murdered sister all these years later."

Annie took in a sharp breath at the coldness of her statement. Was this his baggage? "Stop!" she said, glaring at the woman.

Mark's shoulders swelled with anger. "Leave or I'm picking you up and carrying you out."

"Which story?" Her tone was set to purposely annoy. Annie shot up, hoping to stop Mark from acting on his promise.

"You're psychotic!" Mark seethed then spoke into the phone. "Send a car to my house now!"

"I'm going." She turned on her spiked heels and sashayed toward the door. Looking back, she said, "Here's my key." She put it on the TV console.

The door shutting crackled in the tense air.

Annie put her hand on Mark's arm. He jerked away.

"Never mind," Mark ground out into the phone then threw it at the sofa.

"Mark?" Annie said.

He swung around. "What?"

"I . . . I'm sorry."

"You didn't do anything! Fuck! I can't believe that woman!"

His anger crowded the room. Not that she blamed him. She wanted to comfort him, but he'd already rejected her touch.

"Should I go?" she asked.

He ran a hand over his face. "I have to leave, but you . . . can stay a while."

"No, I'll go."

He stared at her, his eyes orbs of pain, emotional pain he didn't want to share, but . . . "Mark?"

He held up his hand. "Not now, Annie."

She left to gather her things. Within ten minutes, dressed and packed, she walked back into the living room.

He stood right where she'd left him. His face still masked with frustration. She wanted so bad to offer him something, but he didn't want it. She could tell that in his expression. He followed her to the door. She looked back. He closed his eyes, opened them, then clenched his fist. "Sorry about this."

"It's not on you," she said.

"Yes it is. Annie, I'm not sure . . . I don't think . . . " He pressed his palm against his forehead, squeezed his temples, and mumbled, "Shit."

"Not sure about what?"

"If she broadcasts the story . . . It's against the rules. We should take a break."

A break? What happened to you liking this?

"Yeah." Her heart went from being a normal beating organ to a heavy, swollen, and sore piece of meat. She walked out without another word. Why did it hurt so much? Hadn't she thought this was a mistake?

* * *

"I freaking can't believe him!" Isabella stood in the middle of her living room, fuming, watching Annie pack her things. "Bastard!"

"It was a mistake. I knew it from the beginning." Annie held back the knot of hurt behind her chest bone. If it climbed up her throat, she'd start crying.

But damn, that knot was large. It kept knocking against her ribs, bruising her heart.

She needed her own bed. Her own pillow. She needed privacy. She needed to stop comparing this to what happened with Ted.

"Why did he start this if he was worried about the rules?"

She'd wondered the same thing. One answer appeared obvious. Sex. Did she believe that? Her gut said it was more. Her gut said it was the baggage Fred claimed came with most cops. His murdered sister. And that had her hurting. Hurting for him.

But she couldn't help him. He didn't want her help.

Damn that hurt!

Annie went to Isabella's hall closet and pulled out Pirate's crate, which she'd stored there.

"Are you sure it's safe to go back to your place?" Isabella asked.

"Yeah." The truth was, she wasn't sure of anything. But she wanted to go home. To be alone. To hug a pillow and cry. To mourn for someone else she'd lost.

Since Sam Reed had visited her at the coffee shop, it meant he and the rest of the family knew where she hung out, where she worked. If they were the ones calling in threats—and who else could it be?—they could find her. If not at home, at work. She couldn't completely disappear. And a few days at Isabella's wasn't going to help.

* * *

Mark sat in the diner, a solid mass of knotted muscle, waiting to see if she'd show. He'd left a message on her phone. His gut said she'd be here.

The bell over the door chirped. He looked up. Score one for his gut.

Judith Holt walked in.

The blood running hot in his veins got hotter. He took a deep breath, told himself to hold his shit together. Stopping her from running with her stories was his goal. But damn if killing her right now wasn't tempting.

Her gaze met his. She smiled. He didn't smile back.

She power-strutted toward him as if his arranging this meeting was her win. If only she knew.

She eased into the chair across from him. "See, I knew you were a smart man."

No, he'd been stupid enough to date her. "What do you want?"

She smiled seductively and rested her hand on his. "What do you think I want?" She dampened her top lip with her tongue.

"Besides sex," he bit out. "That's not happening."

"Don't pretend you didn't enjoy fucking me. But you're screwing your witness now, right?"

Fury had his muscles cramping.

"She doesn't seem like your type. Too girl-next-door."

Acid from his clenched stomach rose to his throat. She was right, Annie wasn't his type. She was too damn good for him. The old man at the coffee shop had been right.

He sucked in another breath. "Just tell me what you want to not publish those stories about me."

"Who said I wanted anything?"

"Fine." He started to get up.

"Slow down, cowboy."

Mark's shoulders tightened until he thought they'd crack, his spine locked. "This is blackmail."

"Now that's harsh." She picked up Mark's water and took a sip. "It's news, Mark. You're a celebrity. People are curious. I feed curious minds."

"So you don't want anything in exchange for not publishing them?"

Again he started to rise.

"Sit down!" she growled.

"Then what the fuck do you want? I'm not playing games."

"What I've always wanted. Story leads. Exclusive leads."

He clenched his fist. "You don't care that putting a story out early might hurt a case? Or the victim's families?"

"I can't help that. It's not like I committed the crime. I'm just reporting it."

"If I start giving you leads, you won't broadcast those stories? So instead of stealing from me this time, you're blackmailing me."

She lifted a brow. "I didn't steal. You left the files in your car."

This was going better than he thought.

"They have to be good leads," she said as if she held so much damn power. "And I don't see why we can't . . . see each other occasionally."

"What happened to your affair with Matthew Kelly, the reporter?" He was pushing it, but why not?

"It's not an affair. We just meet up sometimes."

Mark figured it out. "He gives you his leads for sex, doesn't he?"

She grinned. "Personally, I think he's got the better deal. Let's just say he's not as skilled as you." She pinched her fingers together. "Little dick."

"You'll really fuck anyone for your job. Did you do your boss, too?"

She smirked. "I use whatever I have to be successful."

"But you've already slept your way to the top at Channel Two."

She smiled as if it was a compliment. "I have some

interviews coming up. We're talking my own New York–based TV show. Which is why I need leads."

"You didn't have to blackmail me, I'd have given them to you to get you out of town."

"You're not nice," she said.

"I never said I was nice."

"You're right. You never did. You didn't say much at all. You just fucked me. Used me for sex. And now you act as if you're better than me. You're more damaged than I am. You're on this crusade of finding murderers. But you do it to make yourself feel better. Why? What are you trying to make up for? It's about your sister, isn't it? What did you do? Did you cause it?"

Her words echoed in his head and shot darts at his heart.

She frowned. "All you have to do is drop some leads."

He leaned in. "Fine. Here's a lead for you. Hell, let me show you." He unbuttoned his shirt and exposed the wire taped to his chest that he and Connor had borrowed from the precinct.

Her eyes rounded.

"I got everything. You blackmailing me. Stealing from me. Screwing your boss. Prostituting yourself for leads."

Her eyes tightened into angry slits. "You... wouldn't do that."

"Wouldn't I? And in case the media wants something to go along with the audio..." He pointed to another table, where Connor sat holding up his smartphone, then Mark leaned back. "Don't ever fuck with me again. Don't ever stick another mic in my face."

He shot up, and he and Connor walked out together. "Thanks," Mark said, unable to unclench his jaw.

"Hey, you'd do it for me." Connor laughed. "That had to feel good."

"Yeah." But it really didn't. He kept seeing Annie's face when he'd ended things.

But damn it to hell and back. The old man had been right. Annie was a slice of heaven and he was a screwup. He recalled her questions about his father. She wanted to know his story. No, what she wanted was to fix his life. Fix him. He wasn't fixable.

Judith was right. He was damaged. If he hadn't been a goddamned selfish prick, his sister would be alive.

* * *

With stress riding his shoulders, and Connor riding shotgun, Mark pulled up at the precinct. The thought of finishing up the paperwork for the kid's murder had Mark's mood taking a deeper nosedive. He kept seeing the image of the girl half submersed in concrete. He kept remembering Bethany Talbot sobbing. He kept wishing he deserved someone like Annie.

But fuck, he needed a drink. He held on to the steering wheel and stared out. His gut knotted like a noose.

Connor got out of the car. "You coming in?"

"Yeah." And then, "No. I'm going to try to find Officer Ruffin." Mark reached into his shirt and removed the wire.

"Who?"

"The cop who first worked the Reed case."

"You want company?" Connor asked.

"No."

Mark drove to the old man's place. Someone was in the front office. He asked for the apartment of a Mr. Ruffin, and his badge got him the number.

Five minutes later, his knuckles aching from knocking on the unanswered door, he sat his ass back in his car.

He started the engine, started driving, not sure if he was headed to the bar, or to... Annie's. He wanted to see her. Wanted to tell her how sorry he was. Wanted to pull her against him and lose himself in the feel-good vibe her closeness brought on.

He parked his car in front of a bar. Before he got out, an older man exited the building. He couldn't walk a straight line. When he got to some bushes, he leaned forward and puked.

Rising up, he wiped his mouth with the sleeve of his shirt then just stood there—almost as if having some debate with himself. What debate was it? *Change his life. Face the demon that made him drink. Keep drinking.*

The man swerved around and headed back into the bar. So "keep drinking" it was.

Was that where Mark was headed? Would whiskey move from being a crutch to an addiction?

Fuck!

He left, drove to Annie's apartment, and parked by her car. He didn't get out. Closing his eyes, he leaned back, hoping that just being in the same block with her would calm his demons.

Ten minutes later, he and his demons drove back to the office.

Mark spent two hours finalizing his paperwork and telling himself he'd done the right thing by pushing Annie away. She deserved better than him. She also deserved the truth about Jenny. He was going to get that for her.

Stacking his papers, he looked back at Connor, who was staring at his computer. "You find something?"

"Yeah." Connor shifted in his seat. "I'm looking at one of the motorcycle gang witnesses on the Reed case. One of them is in jail for raping a minor."

"Shit!" Mark hadn't gone there because the old case file hadn't led him there.

"A couple of them live here. I think I'll try to find them."

"Do that." Mark soured on the thought he'd missed something that obvious, but he'd take that chip out of his pride to solve this case.

"When are you interviewing the Reeds?" Juan asked while tapping his keyboard.

"Tuesday." Mark answered feeling antsy to escape. "But I'm not holding my breath. The whole pack of them are strange." He stood. "I'm heading out."

"Wait." Juan's *tap-tap*ping on the keyboard stopped. He looked up.

"What?" Mark asked.

There was the slightest pause. "Did you run a background check on Annie Lakes?"

No. He didn't have to. "Why?"

Juan offered an apologetic shrug. "You better read this."

CHAPTER
TWENTY-SIX

Annie had gone home. Remembering Mark's warning, she double-checked the locks and took her dad's baseball bat with her to bed. She tried to imagine using it on someone.

She couldn't. Great. Was she such a wuss that she wouldn't defend herself?

The memory of kicking and screaming in the dream landed with a thud on her mind. Then she wondered if Fran was even alive.

At two in the afternoon, she crawled out of bed and washed her puffy been-crying face. While she'd had her meltdown for the day, Pirate hadn't had his midday snack. She'd left his food at Isabella's.

"I'm going to get it," she told the hungry cat circling her legs. In case her friend wasn't home, she took Isabella's key. Running her hands through her barely brushed hair, she took off. The moment she stepped outside she felt it again. As if someone was watching her. She walked fast, looking around as she went.

Her knock on her friend's door went unanswered, so she let herself in. She went to the kitchen, found a bag, and collected Pirate's food and kitty snacks from the pantry.

The doorbell rang and caused her to start. *What if someone had followed her?*

Lifting up on her tiptoes, she peered through the peephole.

A good-looking Hispanic guy filled her view. Jose? Her already beaten-up heart took a punch. Not for herself, but for Isabella.

Annie opened the door. "Sorry, Isabella isn't here."

Disappointment filled his expression. "Can you tell her Jose came by?"

"Sure." Empathy tiptoed out with the word.

He studied her as if he'd heard it. "Can you tell her I still love her?"

Her heart took another blow.

"Has she told you about me?" he asked.

"She mentioned you," Annie said in a mere whisper, her heart aching for her friend and for herself.

"In a good or a bad way?" He inched a little closer.

"Sort of in the middle." *Shut up. Shut up.*

He closed his eyes a second. "Is she seeing anyone?"

Annie didn't answer.

"Is she?" Pain laced his voice. One second passed. Two. "So she is?" Hurt deepened his tone.

"No," Annie blurted out.

"Because of me?" he asked.

Crap. She needed to shut the door. "Look, I shouldn't—"

"Do you know a way I could convince her to talk to me?"

"No."

He ran a palm over his face, exhaled, and met her eyes again. "Have you ever loved someone so much that...I'm dying inside." His eyes grew moist. His pain swelled inside her, and she thought of Mark again. But it wasn't love she felt. It was too soon.

"Should I give up?"

Her heart dropped. When she didn't answer, he nodded, as if reading more into her silence. He turned to go.

Words fell out of her. "Do you want to give up?"

He swung around. "Hell no. I'd do anything. Anything to get her back."

"Then...that's your answer. Don't give up."

"Does she still love me?"

Annie didn't answer. But she knew. Her friend loved Jose as much as he loved her. Yet secrets, mistakes in the past, stood in their way. Was that why Mark ended it? Too many mistakes in his past? In hers?

"She still loves me, right? Thank you," he said, obviously seeing the answer in her eyes.

He started to back away and Annie said, "She's lonely. You might try...not talking to her about your problems, but just...just, you know...flirt. Woo her."

His brow tightened. "Woo her?"

She nodded.

A smile flashed in his eyes. "I can do that."

Annie shut the door and leaned her head against the wood. And just like that, the feeling she'd done something good evaporated. She had no right to try to fix

Isabella's love life. Isabella was her only friend, or was. When she learned what Annie had done...

She went and collapsed on the sofa, calling herself a fool, and giving Jose time to leave before she did. After several minutes, panic still knocking against her conscience, she grabbed the cat supplies and almost got to the door, but the dang doorbell rang again.

She dropped everything back in the chair and returned to the door. Determined not to give Jose anything else.

Prone on her tiptoes, she pushed her eye to the peephole again. Her hurting heart swelled with hope, with promise. Since when had Mark become her touchstone? When did his presence instill a sense of safety, of wholeness? Remembering what she had learned about his sister brought pain to her chest. She hurt for him. She wanted to offer him the same comfort he offered her.

Maybe it was too soon to call it love, but she didn't want to analyze it; she wanted to breathe it in, to embrace it. She couldn't unlock the door fast enough. She wanted to hold and be held. Perhaps not love, but damn close.

The door swished open, and she faced him. Right before she fell against him, she saw his expression. The hope and happiness inside her wilted like a tired rose, once beautiful, once a sign of affection, now just a sad symbol of death. He stared at her, no warmth, no compassion. It was the same look he'd given Judith Holt.

"What's wrong?" she asked.

"Everything." He shot inside. She closed the door. Emotions bubbled inside her.

"I can't believe you didn't tell me you'd been arrested for stalking a kid's parents. That you got fired for making false accusations to CPS! Do you know what that looks like? They are going to think you made this shit up. They're going to think the only reason I believed you is because I'm sleeping with you."

Each vertebra in her spine tightened until she stood ramrod straight. "I didn't make it up. And...it doesn't change anything about Jenny."

"Are you kidding? There's no way I can make this case with you as a witness. The DA would laugh me out of his office. And do you know how long it takes for a cop to win back that trust? I work cold cases where evidence is sometimes in short supply. The main thing I bring to the table is the DA's trust in my work."

Golf-ball-sized marbles of hurt rolled around her chest. Another meltdown was imminent. "I didn't mean—"

"They got a restraining order against you. You broke it. Do you know how that makes you look?"

"I thought they were abusing her. I didn't care how it made me look. I cared." Desperation rose inside her. She swallowed tears.

"How could you not tell me this?"

Her knees weakened. "I was afraid you'd act like this!"

"You had every chance to tell me!"

She lifted her chin. "How could you be mad at me for not telling you things? You never shared anything.

I asked if you had siblings. You even lied and said no."

"I don't have any. She's dead! But this is about the case, not"—he waved a hand between them—"this."

She repeated his gesture. "What is this, Mark? Or I should say, what *was* it? You just needed a fuck buddy?" Tears filled her eyes.

He stared as if seeing her for the first time. "It's not—"

"Not what?" she demanded.

"You were wrong not to tell me and—"

"I was wrong to have agreed to go out with you."

"That, too." He left, slamming the door in his wake.

She dropped down on the floor, hugged her knees, and had herself a second meltdown.

The sound of the door lock turning caused her to look up. Isabella walked in with her hands full of grocery bags.

"Shit." Her friend dropped the bags on the floor. "I thought that was him I saw in the parking lot. Those are I-hate-men tears, right?" Isabella knelt down beside her. And then it came. The friend empathy brought more emotion rising in her chest, knotting in her throat.

Annie nodded. "I don't know if I'm angry or hurt!"

"Go for angry! It stings less," Isabella said. "He's an ass."

Isabella's unconditional support reminded Annie that she had encouraged Jose.

"What happened?"

"I hate love. I hate falling in love. I hate thinking you're in love but aren't. I hate thinking it's love when it's only you thinking it's love. I hate seeing people lose love."

"That cop has his head so far up his own butt that the only thing he sees is his gizzard and not what's he losing."

"I'm a terrible friend," Annie said in a hiccupy voice.

"No, you're not."

"I am. There was so much love in his eyes—"

Isabella frowned. "You think Mark loves you?"

"No, Jose."

Isabella's mouth dropped open. "You think Jose loves you?"

"No. He doesn't love me."

"Who doesn't love you?"

No one loves me. "He found out about the restraining order. He thinks I'm crazy."

"He said that?"

She nodded.

Isabella looked baffled. Annie felt completely baffled. "He loves you."

"Mark loves me?" Isabella said.

Emotion made Annie's chest ache. "I told Jose things I shouldn't."

Isabella plopped down on her butt. "Are we talking about Mark or Jose?"

"Jose, now." She wiped her eyes. "He came here and asked me if you'd mentioned him."

"And you told him I never even said his name, right?" Isabella stared at her.

Annie bit down on her lip. "I told him that you had. He asked if it was in a good way or a bad way."

"And you told him bad, right?" The words rushed out.

"I said in the middle. Then he asked if you were seeing anyone."

She frowned. "And you told him I was fucking a different guy every week, right? Because that's what a good friend would do."

"Told you I was a terrible friend." Annie put a hand over her mouth, then dropped it. "I didn't want to answer."

"So you didn't answer?" Isabella sighed with relief.

"I wasn't going to." Annie shrugged. "Then..."

"You did?"

"He asked if he should give up."

"And you told him hell yeah!" She gripped her hand. "Please tell me you said that!"

"He looked so... sad. I asked him if *he* wanted to give up."

Isabella dropped her head on her knees and stayed like that for several seconds, then she looked up. "What did he say?"

"He loves you, Isabella. I know I shouldn't have said... I'm sorry."

Tears collected in Isabella's eyes. "You're right. You are a terrible friend." She got up and walked into her kitchen and dropped down in a chair.

Annie got up. "I'm sorry," she said again.

Isabella just nodded.

"I'll go now."

Isabella nodded again.

Annie picked up Pirate's supplies and walked out, pretty sure she'd lost her one and only friend. She was alone. No one believed in her. No unconditional love. No one to wrap her in a soft embrace and tell her things would get better. Just like that, Annie wished her daddy was still alive. He'd been her champion. Her hero. Life was too hard to be without a hero.

* * *

"Stop!" Mark's phone was screeching. It was Sunday morning. His head hurt as if someone had split it in two and taken out parts. The pain reminded him this was what he deserved for drinking too much. Reminded him that the reason he drank was to forget about how good he was at disappointing people.

As the shrill ring continued, he rolled over and forced his eyes open. Light scratched his eyeballs. He grabbed the phone, hit decline, and tossed it on the end of the bed.

There wasn't anyone he wanted to talk to. Oh, hell, yes there was. Annie?

Had that been her? Had something happened?

He sat up. The damn jackhammer in his head jacked harder. He found the phone, hit missed call, saw it was Stone, his morgue buddy. Mark had a vague memory of Stone, Connor, and Juan pulling the whiskey bottle away from him last night. He hadn't argued. He'd just waited until they left to start again.

He threw the phone back down. But now he was awake, and his head hurt too damn much for him to go back to sleep.

He lay there, arm over his eyes, trying not to breathe, because it made his head pound harder.

Fifteen minutes later, unable to stop breathing, he rolled out of bed. Pain. Pain. Pain.

He made it to the bathroom, found some aspirin, and chewed up five.

Sitting on the edge of the tub, his head in his hands, he waited for relief. Something had to give.

His phone rang again. "Screw it."

Annie? For her, the pain would be worth it. Each step brought another explosion in his head. Finally there, he picked up the phone.

Stone again.

Pissed, he hit accept. "I'm sleeping, damn it!"

"It's after ten."

"So." He cradled his forehead in his palm, hoping to ease the pain that talking caused.

"Okay. But I heard you were looking for a blonde, mid-thirties. One just showed up at the morgue."

"Fuck!" he said, as Bacon plopped down beside his feet. "Any identification?"

"None."

"Where did they find her?" He petted the dog, because it wasn't his fault he was stuck with Mark.

"In some woods off FM 260."

"By the park?" he asked.

"A little south of the park."

"Cause of death?" He swallowed the balls of cotton in his mouth.

"It's a toss-up. Strangulation or the beating she took. Won't know until I open her up."

Mark breathed out. "Any tattoos, jewelry?"

"Nothing."

He recalled the description of what Fran had worn to the funeral. "What she was wearing?"

"Just the suit she was born with."

"Fuck," Mark said.

"And her face is pretty messed up. And here's the kicker...Brown heard about it. He called, said he pulled up your file and got Annie Lakes's number."

"Why?"

"He said he tried to reach Connor, didn't want you here with the witness. But Connor didn't answer, so he said he was calling her himself to come and identify the body."

"How long ago?"

"We spoke fifteen minutes ago. I don't know if he's called yet."

"Gotta go." Poised to hang up, he said, "Sorry I was an asshole."

Stone chuckled. "That's a first. You've been an asshole since I've known you and haven't apologized. Is it that Lakes girl?"

"Maybe I'm just getting old." He hung up and called Annie.

The phone rang once.

His chest ached with his next heartbeat, knowing he was going to hear her voice.

Or not. Because it rang twice.

He'd been present when at least twenty family members identified their dead relatives. Most walked out leaving a trail of tears. He needed to be there for Annie.

It rang three times.

Where was she? The coffee shop? Home? Ignoring

his calls? He'd find her. Standing up, pain shot from his base of his neck to his temples.

The line went to her voice mail.

"Annie, it's me. Please call me." The apology sat on the tip of his tongue. But should he offer it? He needed to let her go. Hadn't yesterday been proof enough that she deserved better? "It's about the case."

He threw on some clothes. Hopefully, she'd open the door to him. Bacon came in with the socks Mark had worn yesterday hanging from his mouth. "Go for it. One of us deserves to be happy."

He grabbed his keys, his sunglasses, and what was left of his heart, and walked out. His headache followed.

* * *

Annie set the coffee at her feet then knocked on Isabella's door. She'd accepted she'd lost Mark, but she couldn't accept she'd lost her friend. Sunglasses in place, a practiced apology in pocket, she knocked again, while clutching the bakery bag. She'd seen Isabella's car, so she knew she was home. Whether she'd opened the door was another matter.

She leaned in, praying she'd hear Isabella's "come in" request. There was no request.

Deciding to leave a text telling her she'd left coffee and a pastry at her door, she reached for her phone. No phone. Crap! Had she left it in her car? Her apartment? Or had she left it at the bakery?

Looking back at the unanswered door, she swallowed a lump of regret and started to leave. The turn of a lock had Annie turning back.

The door opened just a crack.

Afraid Isabella would shut her out, she started talking. "I'm sorry. I brought us coffee and croissants."

Isabella stuck her head out. "It's okay. But I can't—"

"Isabella?"

Annie heard the deep voice call her friend's name. Then she noticed her friend wore a man's shirt.

Isabella leaned in and whispered. "Did you tell him to text me near-naked pictures?"

Annie laughed.

"*Quien es?*" the male voice called.

"The breakfast fairy." Isabella reached for the bag. "You're forgiven."

The door started to close. "Wait. Coffee." Annie collected the tray and passed it to Isabella.

Smiling, fighting back her own problems, Annie went to find her phone.

She hotfooted up her apartment stairs to check there before heading to the bakery.

Before she unlocked her door, she heard her phone ringing.

It stopped ringing before she got to it. She had two voice messages. One was from Mark.

CHAPTER
TWENTY-SEVEN

Mark drove past the coffee shop. She wasn't there. He headed to her apartment. As he drove into the lot, she pulled out. He caught a glimpse of her sitting ramrod straight, sunglasses on, her hands gripping the wheel.

Sergeant Brown must have spoken to her.

He turned around and followed her. His phone rang. Snatching it up, he hoped it was her, that she instinctively knew she could depend on him, but Connor's name flashed on the screen. He ignored the call, got the ding from a voice message, and ignored that, too.

Annie turned down West Calvin Street, which led to the morgue. His chest ached, knowing this would hurt her. Knowing he'd already hurt her. Sure, she should've told him, but like the day her mom showed up, he'd come off like an ass.

When she parked at the morgue, he pulled in beside her.

Mark hadn't cut his engine off when he saw her bolting toward the door. Was she running from him?

"Annie." He took off.

She stopped, turned, and pushed her glasses up higher on her nose. Probably hiding the rings under her eyes.

"Hey." He stepped in front of her, fighting the desire to reach for her. She looked like she needed someone and he ached to be that someone.

"What?" she asked.

"I'm coming with you."

"You don't have to." Her voice sounded raspy, emotional, angry. "You don't have to pretend to—"

Hearing her pain hurt like shit. "I'm not pretending. I want to."

"Fine." She started hotfooting it inside.

He beat her to the door and opened it. When she passed, he caught her scent. Soft woman, shampoo, and sadness.

He hadn't known you could smell sadness, but he got a whiff of it.

He followed her inside. Her scent vanished with the sterile odors of the morgue.

Connor, who appeared to be waiting, nodded at Mark, then to Annie, as he walked over.

"I'm Detective Pierce. Thank you for coming."

Annie looked puzzled. "I spoke with a Sergeant Brown."

"Yes, he called you. But he had to leave."

Annie nodded.

Connor shifted. "It'll be five or ten minutes before we can go in."

She bit down on her lip. "Bathroom?"

"Through the door, on the left," Mark answered.

She barreled through the door without even looking at him.

Connor lifted a brow as if picking up on the tension. "You got my message?"

"Didn't listen to it. Stone called me."

"Brown called me. He didn't want you here."

"Since when do you give a rat's ass what he wants?" Mark snapped.

"I don't. But he seemed adamant. Just passing that along."

"Sorry." Mark released stale air he'd been holding since he spoke with Stone. "How bad is the body? I don't want her seeing it if—"

"Haven't seen it. Just got here. I only stuck my head in and Stone told me to wait for her."

Mark headed to the back to find Stone.

The cold silver door whooshed open announcing him. Stone looked up. "Hey."

Mark inched in. His gut turned when he saw the bloody mess that used to be a face. "She can't identify her like that."

"I plan on covering her face."

"Then why's she here?" His rib cage gripped as he imagined Annie losing a piece of her soul like he lost every goddamned time he had to come here. But this would be worse. Annie already felt guilty about her cousin.

Stone frowned. "Body shape, hair color, tattoos. People recognize more than the face."

"Wouldn't her ex be the best one to identify her? Or her mother? She only lives—"

"Brown called the ex. He's out of town. The mom didn't answer."

"Right." Mark dropped his shoulders and his attitude. He knew getting a vic's identification ASAP was vital to a case. The emotional price of a family member identifying a body was the first step to getting the victim justice. But the person paying that price had never been someone Mark cared about.

"I'm about ready," Stone said.

Mark walked out. Annie stepped out of the bathroom right then, too. He moved close and clenched his hands to keep from touching her.

"You okay?" he asked.

"Fine."

"No, you're not. You're wearing sunglasses."

"So are you." She darted off into the waiting room.

He followed her. Connor started to walk over. Mark shook his head.

Annie sat down and hugged herself. What he wouldn't give to be able to do that for her. To put his arms around her, hold her close, comfort her. He sat beside her.

She frowned. "I don't need you—"

"I'm trying to help. Call someone who knows Fran well enough and ask if she had a birthmark or a tattoo."

She touched her lips. Beneath the rim of the glasses, a tear crawled down her cheek.

Before he could stop himself, words spilled off his lips. "I'm sorry for being an ass and sorry you have to do this."

She brushed the tear off her cheek then pulled her phone from her purse.

He leaned his guilt-weighted shoulders back in the hard chair while she made a call.

"Mom, I need...Does Fran have any tattoos or birthmarks? It's important. Call me."

She scrolled through her phone and called someone else. She held her phone to her ear for at least a minute before hanging up.

"No one is answering." Her voice shook.

The *whoosh* of a door opening brought his eyes up. Stone walked out. "I'm Doctor Stone."

* * *

Bile rose in Annie's throat. She slapped a hand over her mouth and ran for the bathroom.

She barely made it to the toilet before she puked. The thought that she was about to see her cousin dead, cold, gone. It was too much. She'd seen only two dead people: her uncle and her father. But a voice deep inside argued with her math. A memory filled her head. The memory of Jenny lying in the hole, dirt falling like unclean snow over her pale face. Falling into her opened eyes that were void of life.

The image had the half gallon of chocolate ice cream—her unreliable broken-heart cure—refusing to stay down. She took off her glasses, dropped her purse, bent at the waist and puked again.

She heard the bathroom door open.

"Go away," she muttered.

She heard running water. The stall door swung open. Still clutching her middle, she straightened. Mark, looking through dark sunglasses, held out some wet paper towels. "Here."

She took his offering. "Go, please." She wiped her mouth. Feeling zapped of energy, she leaned against the stall wall and closed her eyes. A small shuffling sound brought her eyes open. Mark had moved into the stall. He pulled her against him.

She needed to push him away—stay angry, not hurt—but she needed someone to hold her. She leaned her forehead onto his shoulder and cried. "I don't know if I can do this."

"You don't have to." His strong arms drew her closer. Her cheek rested against his warm chest. His heartbeat sounded in her ear. Her own heart slowed to follow his. His soft breath brushed her temple.

Safe. He made her feel safe.

Annie stayed there for several seconds, would've stayed longer if her phone hadn't rung. If the voice in her head hadn't reminded her that he'd told her it was over. That he'd all but said they were a mistake. The voice that said he was here because he was a cop.

She pulled away, dug into her purse for her phone and into her soul for enough strength not to cling to a guy who didn't want her in his life.

She found her phone and prayed it was her aunt. Then prayed it wasn't. Isabella's name flashed on the screen. She walked out of the stall. Mark followed and stood in the middle of the women's bathroom as if he belonged, as if helping her had been a natural instinct. Why was he putting out mixed messages?

She took Isabella's call. "Hey."

"Are you home?" Isabella's tone spoke of smiles and happiness.

"No. Can I call you later?"

"Is something wrong?" Isabella asked.

"I'm at the...morgue." Her voice shook.

"The morgue?" Concern spilled into Isabella's voice. It had Annie's chest tightening again. "They think it's Fran."

"What morgue?"

"County Morgue. But you don't—"

"I'm on my way." The line went silent.

Tears filled Annie's eyes. She started to put her phone away when it rang again. One glimpse at the screen and her heart did a somersault.

"What's happening?" her mom asked. "Why would you need—"

"Give me the fucking phone," Annie heard a voice in the background say.

"Why do you need to know if Fran has tattoos?" Doris Roberts yelled. "Don't you dare tell me they think she's dead."

Annie swallowed her own pain. "They aren't certain. But they found someone who matches her description."

"No! She's just off somewhere drunk."

Annie breathed. "Does she have a tattoo or a birthmark?"

The cries on the other end of the line told Annie that Doris loved Fran. Her aunt might be a drunk, even a lousy mother, but she loved her daughter. And *bam*, Annie wished her mom was here for her now.

"Annie?" Her mom's voice came back on the line.

"Fran has a birthmark on her right shoulder, toward the front. Looks like a heart."

And just like that she saw Fran in a pink polka-dotted bathing suit. *I'm special, see. I have a heart birthmark. Mama says it makes me special.*

She recalled Doris telling her that she and Fran had been best friends. Annie had not only lost her cousin but a friend whose memories lived deep inside her. Had Annie ever told Fran *thank you* for coming back for her that night? Would Annie have ended up in a shallow grave had Fran not come back?

"Call us as soon as you know." Her mom's voice brought Annie to the present and with it came guilt. Had Annie's investigation led to Fran's death?

"I love you, Mom." Annie hung up afraid her mom wouldn't say it back.

Mark stepped closer. "I'll explain that you can't do this."

"No. I will."

"You don't—"

"I do." Her lips trembled again. "We'd just seen our cousin dead and being buried, but she came back for me that night. I can go in there for her."

She bolted out the bathroom door. In the hall, she looked at the man wearing dull blue scrubs. "I'm ready."

He led. She followed. The white, stainless-steel room felt sterile, no color, no emotion. Yet she carried enough of both in her chest to fill the space. A storm of colors called pain, regret, fear, and grief.

On a stainless-steel table, a body lay covered with a

white sheet. The oxygen filling her lungs felt thick. Black fireworks popped off in her vision. Annie hugged herself.

"Breathe," said a deep, soothing voice. Mark's voice. Breathing took energy she didn't have, her knees weakened. Then Mark's warmth came against her.

The doctor walked over to the table. Annie's lungs refused the next gulp of air. Mark's hand tightened on her shoulder.

"I'm here," he whispered.

But he wasn't, her mind said. Not really. He thought she was crazy.

"I'll keep her face covered due to her injuries." Dr. Stone's words came with empathy.

She felt herself trembling. The kind of trembling that came from your core, the kind you couldn't stop.

Mark drew closer, and she let some of her weight go there.

"It's okay," he whispered again.

The doctor moved around the table and pulled the sheet down to the body's shoulders. Another small cloth covered the face. Blond hair a shade darker than Annie's fanned out around the woman's head. Dark purple and blue stains circled the woman's neck.

Someone had choked her? Someone had put their hands around her neck and squeezed the life out of her?

Annie's own throat suddenly felt constricted.

Breathe. Breathe. Breathe.

She gulped air and forced herself to look. The woman's skin was grayish blue and looked almost plastic. Annie's gaze shifted to the right shoulder. The smell suddenly crawled up her nose.

Bile rose up her throat so fast, all she could do was bend at the waist and lose the rest of her breakup ice cream all over the shoes of the guy who'd broken her heart.

"Here." More wet paper towels were pushed in her hand. Mark wrapped an arm around her waist and led her out of the room and into the waiting room.

She collapsed in a chair, unable to stop shaking. Mark sat down. She wanted to lean against him. To feel safe. But it wasn't safe. He didn't believe her. He'd said it was over. She found her voice and pushed out the information he needed. "It's not her. It's not Fran."

He looked surprised. "Are you sure?"

She nodded. "Fran has a birthmark on her"—she reached up—"her right shoulder."

Mark took her hand and squeezed. "You did good. Let me tell them and I'll be right back."

Closing her eyes, she tried to chase away the ball of panic bouncing around her empty stomach. Then she remembered she needed to call her mom. That ball wasn't going away.

CHAPTER TWENTY-EIGHT

Are you sure?" Connor asked. "She seemed really upset."

"She's sure. Fran Roberts has a birthmark on her right shoulder." He glanced down at the body now covered.

Stone picked up the sheet. "Not her."

Connor stepped closer. "Why did she lose it when she saw the body?"

"Seriously?" Stone asked. "*You* puked the first time."

Mark walked out.

Annie was on the phone. He inched closer to listen.

"I'm sorry I scared you," Annie said. "I needed—" She bit down on her lip. "I can't do that." Pause. "I'm not trying to hurt anyone." Her voice trembled as she white-knuckled her phone. "I'm hanging up now."

The raw pain he heard in her voice made Mark want to hurt the person on the other line. And yet, he'd hurt Annie.

He sat down. "Your mom?"

"Fran's mom." She took in a deep breath. "Can I go?"

She didn't need to be alone. He wanted to be the one to hold her, help her. To feel her soft weight against him. What he wouldn't give to be her hero.

"I'll take you."

"I can drive." Hurt leaked out with those words and her pain shot right to his gut.

"You're shaking. You shouldn't drive. In fact, if you want to come to my place, I—"

"No."

"Just until—"

"I don't need to be around anyone who thinks I'm crazy." Pain and anger laced her words.

He deserved it, but... "I never said you were crazy."

The front door opened. Isabella rushed in.

Annie ran into her friend's open arms. The embrace spoke of friendship and trust. Everything Mark wanted and had a few days ago, but had lost.

* * *

Monday morning, low on sleep, high on frustration, Mark went to the coffee shop. Annie hadn't been here— or so said James, the guy working the counter. While waiting for his coffee, he saw Fred lower his newspaper and frown. The look he shot Mark came with accusations. He'd warned Mark not to hurt Annie, and Mark had done it anyway. Regret and guilt swelled up in his gut. He left without his coffee.

He drove by the college, looking for her car. He

found it. Since she was working, she must be okay. The fact that he was miserable was unimportant.

Arriving at work, he'd pushed away his Annie frustration and focused on his job. A job that involved solving the Reed case.

As he approached the door, he heard their voices. When he walked into the room, it went completely silent.

He read their expressions. "We are not dropping the case."

Connor spoke up. "There's no body, no weapon, and our only witness is someone a DA won't trust. And the sergeant wants you off the case."

Mark's empty gut churned up acid. "We have a missing kid. A missing witness. And a lying family. And someone spray-painted Annie Lakes's car, broke her apartment window, and has made threatening phone calls." He hesitated. "I'll deal with Brown. We're solving this case."

Doubt still played on their faces. "She's not making this up," Mark said. He turned to face Connor. "You saw her at the morgue. Did she look crazy?"

"It doesn't matter what I think. Or what you believe," Connor answered. "It's what a DA will believe."

"I'll make them believe it."

"How?" Juan asked.

"I don't know, but I will."

They nodded. Connor agreed to go to the park and see if they had files about the kid's disappearance. Juan was doing background checks on all the Reeds. If someone had sneezed wrong, they would find out.

Mark's to-do list included finding Officer Ruffin and dealing with Brown. And finding a way to make Annie's past inconsequential.

Before he'd thought finding a second witness would be enough; now he wasn't sure. But by God, he wasn't giving up.

Fifteen minutes later, he discovered Ruffin wasn't at home.

Back in his car, sweating and frustrated, he contemplated how to make Annie's story more believable. He was coming up with nothing, when an idea hit. It was a long shot, but he'd take it. He pointed his car toward Houston.

* * *

Mark knocked on the door. Officer Banks, the man who'd arrested Annie for breaking the restraining order, answered. Mark had sweet-talked the man's sergeant into calling Banks to see if he'd speak with Mark on his day off.

"Detective Sutton, I'm guessing?" Banks asked.

"That's me," Mark answered. "I appreciate you giving me a few minutes."

He nodded as he let Mark inside his small home in a well-kept older neighborhood.

"I'm here about the arrest—"

"Sergeant told me," Banks said.

"You remember the case?"

"Hard not to since you're the second person this month who's called me about it."

His words ran around Mark's head. "Someone else is looking into this?"

"Yeah. CPS. Children's Protective Services."

"Why?"

"CPS learned of the restraining order and wanted the facts."

"Wait? Why is CPS looking into it?"

"Recently someone else reported abuse. Sounds like they're removing the kid from the parents."

Annie had been right. Mark had come here hoping to find a crumble of hope and instead found the whole damn pie. "Can you give me the name of the person who spoke with you?"

"I can do better. I still have her number."

* * *

It was close to five when Mark got back to Anniston. Still reveling in what he'd gotten, he parked at the precinct. His phone dinged with a text. He hoped it was Annie. He'd texted her earlier, but she hadn't answered.

He stared at the screen. Not Annie. Mildred.

Where are you. Sergeant's having a cow. Needs to see you immediately.

Mark walked in.

Mildred frowned when she saw him.

"I'm going there now."

Stepping off the elevator, he headed straight into Brown's office.

"Where the hell have you been?" Brown's chair squeaked. "If you're drunk—"

"I'm not. I was following a lead."

"You left hours ago. Why didn't you report in?"

"It slipped my mind." Mark dropped into a chair. "What's up?"

"You're off the Reed case."

Mark sat back so fast his chair creaked. "No."

Brown's chubby cheeks reddened. "George Reed's lawyer called to tell me one of my officers is screwing the witness on his case."

Mark's neck muscles locked. So Annie's mom had spilled the beans. "George is a suspect in the case. You can't listen to him."

"We shouldn't even be looking at it."

Mark's shoulder muscles cranked up his spine. His posture now was as tense as a plastic soldier. "Since when have murdered-kid cases become insignificant?"

"Did you know Annie Lakes was fired from her job as an elementary school teacher for making false accusations? One parent had to get a restraining order against her!"

"I know." Mark pulled the folded paper from his front pocket and slapped it on Brown's desk.

"What's this?"

"It's the names of those four kids. And three CPS case numbers of when they eventually had to remove three of them from their homes. Annie Lakes isn't crazy. She's these kids' hero."

Brown glanced down at the paper. "Are you sure about this?"

"Yes. That's where I was. At Houston's CPS office.

Before we use it, we'll have to get a subpoena, because this was given to me off the record."

Brown leaned back in his chair, his expression unreadable. "Fine. Let's move with the case, but you're not working it anymore."

"I am."

He banged his desk. "No!"

"I'm this close to finding the truth!"

Brown's frown, creasing his fat cheeks, didn't waver. "Let Juan and Connor wrap it up. I got another case I want you to work."

"After I finish this one."

"No!" Brown's ears turned red. "It's an active case. The body of a nine-year-old girl, Candace Kelly, was found over the weekend. Homicide is asking for your help."

Mark's stomach responded by sending acid up his throat. He couldn't do it. "I don't work homicide."

"I know it's hard because..." Brown was the only one who knew. "But you're good at these cases."

"No." Mark white-knuckled the arms of the chair. His soul couldn't take it.

"So you're willing to let a murderer go free?" Brown's frustration appeared to soften. "Just look at it. Sergeant Edmond brought this by. They're stumped. Give them some advice." He pushed the file to Mark. "Do it for the kid."

Get justice for another kid, because he failed his own sister. Wasn't that why he'd become a cop? "When do they need it?"

"ASAP."

Mark snatched the file, his soul already flinching. He stood.

Brown leaned in. "Connor's going to Pearlsville to help with the interviews, not you."

"But—"

"Don't argue," Brown said. "Officially, you're off the case." His grimace softened. "If you work it behind the scenes, don't let me find out."

* * *

At ten o'clock Annie stared at a frozen meal. She'd barely eaten since yesterday's morgue visit. Three bites in, she pushed it away, and stared at her phone. She hadn't texted Mark back. It was best. Being angry stopped it from hurting so much. And she had a right to be angry. So why did she keep worrying about how much it must have hurt to have lost his sister? About how working cases with murdered kids must bring it all back?

No matter how tempted, she shouldn't text or call him. When Sergeant Brown called yesterday, he'd told her she was only to contact Detective Pierce now.

Obviously, Brown hadn't informed Mark.

Why did her heart feel like a pit bull's chew toy? It might not be love. But maybe it was the beginning. Or just old wounds being opened up. But if this was only about the past, why did her pain take her straight to Mark, not Ted?

Lying back on her sofa, her dad's baseball bat on the coffee table, she closed her eyes. Would she sleep tonight? How many times would the same nightmare put terror in her heart and wake her up?

Sometime later sleep claimed her. Then the dream claimed her. She felt herself running. Felt herself falling. Her heart pounded.

A noise jarred her awake, and she jackknifed up to a sitting position. It took her several breaths to realize the pounding she heard wasn't her heart. Wasn't her dream.

Fresh fear took another lap around her chest. She looked at the door. The knock hit again. It was midnight. Who'd be here now? She dialed 911 but didn't hit call. With her phone in one hand and the bat in the other, she inched to the door.

Her heart banged on her ribs as she pressed her eye to the peephole.

CHAPTER
TWENTY-NINE

Annie recognized the wide, warm chest through the tiny peephole. She stepped back.

Her phone rang. Thinking it was him, she answered. "What do you want?" Her words rang half leery, half longing. She had to stop hoping.

"Annie?" Isabella asked.

"Oh, I thought—"

"Mark just left here. He's drunk. I thought Jose was going to belt him. He kept insisting you were here."

"Sorry," Annie said. "He's at my door now."

"You aren't going to answer it, are you?"

Was she? "Yeah." He shouldn't be driving.

"Do you want Jose to come over?"

"No. I'm fine." She hung up and opened the door.

Mark stood there. Or not actually stood, he half leaned against her doorjamb.

"You're supposed to be staying at your friend's." He didn't slur his words, but there a slow drag that said Isabella was right. Mark was drunk.

"Did you drive here?" she asked.

"No. I took a taxi. I needed...to see you." He pushed off the door and came inside. His steps faltered as he passed her. He looked down at her. "God, you smell good."

"Why are you here?"

He dropped on her sofa beside Pirate. The cat jumped up and left. Mark looked up at her. At her bat. She set it against the wall.

"I needed to...tell you, that you aren't...aren't crazy."

"I know that." She tilted up her chin.

"Good," he said. "You needed to know."

And she needed to tell him to leave. If only he didn't look so sad. If only her heart wasn't breaking right now.

"You're beautiful." He blinked. "You make my soul feel better."

His words rang so honest. "What's wrong with your soul?"

"I keep losing pieces of it. But you give me a little of it back."

He wasn't making sense. "Do you have a drinking problem?"

"No. I got a dead-kid problem." His voice deepened and the words came out sad. "This time someone beat her with something. I shouldn't have looked at the picture." He paused. "They say I'm good at this."

Parts and pieces of what he said almost made sense and that broke her heart. Her throat tightened. "I'll make coffee."

She went into the kitchen and leaned against the

counter for several long seconds. Then she started the coffee but stayed there trying to get her head straight and her heart centered.

"Did you leave me?" he called out.

"Making coffee," she called back.

"Okay, I'll be patient. I'm not always a piece of shit."

"Good," she said, leaning against the counter while her chest swelled with even more emotion. Her sinuses stung, and she swallowed the need-to-cry lump.

Coffee done, she walked out with a cup. She was determined to sober him up and call him a taxi.

He sat up straighter when he saw her. "Did I tell you how beautiful you are?"

"Yeah."

"Did I tell you how sorry I am?"

"No." She handed him the cup. "Careful, it's hot."

"Well, I am." He studied the coffee but didn't drink it. Seconds later, he looked up. "She held you the way I wanted to."

"What?" she asked.

"Your friend at the morgue. She comforted you. I wanted to do that."

"You're jealous of my friend?"

"Noooo." He shook his head then nodded. "Yeah. Stupid, isn't it?"

"Yes," she said.

"I understand it. You trust her. Not me."

Annie stood straighter. "She didn't tell me I was crazy."

He nodded. "But I told you you weren't. And I proved it. I told you that, right?"

"You can't unsay some things."

"I know. Can't undo things, either. But damn, I wish I could." He put one hand on his chest. "It sits right here."

"What sits there?"

"Guilt. She asked me not to go. But I wanted to drink beer and get laid. If I hadn't been a sorry son of a bitch she wouldn't be dead."

Annie's breath caught. He was talking about his sister. She wanted to tell him it wasn't his fault, but now wasn't the time to tell him anything.

Two words still slipped out. "I'm sorry." She sat down beside him.

He leaned over and put his head on her shoulder. "Me too." After a second, he said, "Did I tell you that you smelled good?" He nuzzled her neck.

She inched over. "I'm not having sex with you."

He lifted his head. "I don't want sex." He made a face. "Well, I didn't until you mentioned it."

He shifted again and sloshed coffee in his lap. "Shiiit!" He held the coffee out with one hand and grabbed the crotch of his jeans and pulled them outward with the other. He met her eyes. "You're right. It's hot."

She stood and took the coffee from him.

"What are you doing?" he asked.

"I'm putting the coffee away before you scald yourself."

He chuckled and she carried the cup in the kitchen.

When she came back, he was sitting there, chin against his chest, eyes closed.

What would it hurt if he slept here? On the sofa? Alone?

Giving in, she went to collect a pillow and blanket.

She walked back in. "Mark, lay down. I got a blanket and pillow." When he didn't move, she gave his shoulder a nudge. He complied, and she barely got the pillow in place before he fell back.

He opened his eyes slightly. "You're a slice of heaven."

She took off his shoes and stretched the blanket out over him. When the back of her hands came against his chin, she got zapped by emotional pain.

She didn't love him, she told herself. But her heart begged to differ.

His eyes opened. He reached up and touched the back of her hand. Just one slow, soft touch.

"I wish I deserved you."

She swallowed a lump of emotion. "You don't think you deserve me?"

"Nope," he said. "Not you *or* music."

Annie remembered the saxophone in his game room. His eyes closed, but he kept talking.

"You want the white picket fence, the house, the kids."

"What do you want?" she asked before she could stop herself.

"I want... to keep my soul."

She recalled all the cases he'd solved, the justice he'd brought to others. How hard must it be solving cases like Jenny's and the Talbot case when he was haunted by his sister's death?

He let out a soft snore.

"I could do without the fence," she whispered.

Still hurting, Annie walked back to her bedroom.

* * *

"I wrote a list for you." Mark handed Connor the notebook with questions for the Reed interview. It pissed Mark off that he couldn't go himself, but he knew Brown was right.

Connor took the notebook but eyed Mark. "You look like shit again!"

"Thanks." Mark had woken up at four on Annie's sofa with only vague memories of the night before. Before he left her place, he found a piece of paper and wrote a one-word note. *Sorry.*

"Where were you yesterday?" Connor asked.

"Working. Can you look at the questions and make sure you understand everything?"

"Yeah." Connor parked his ass at his desk. Mark sat down, too.

He had to tell him what he found out from the CPS, but he wanted to wait until... "Where's Juan?"

"Right here." Juan stepped in. His gaze found Mark. "Something wrong?"

"No."

"He was trying to look like shit today," Connor said, laughing.

Juan claimed his desk. "I stayed up last night doing the background checks."

"And?" Mark turned his chair around and sat in it.

"DUIs all over the place. The whole family has a drinking problem. Well, everyone but JoAnne Lakes. And they're mean drunks. The old sheriff went out on six domestic violence calls. And that's not including Patrick Reed."

"Who?" Mark hadn't heard that name.

"He's another Reed," Juan answered. "Died eight years ago."

"How many Reeds were there?" Mark asked.

Juan turned a page in his file. "Seven. Four boys and three girls. Harold and Patrick are deceased. But Patrick's record was a tad more interesting. Child and spousal abuse. One time, the wife almost died, but she swore hubby didn't push her out of the car."

"Shit." Mark started putting the pieces together. "Patrick must be the sheriff's secretary's father. You know, Jennifer Reed."

"Yeah, but the abuse wasn't with Jennifer or her mother, but his first wife and kid. Supposedly he got his wife pregnant when she was thirteen. He was nineteen. He likes them young. She left him to keep CPS from taking her kid. He married Jennifer's mother a year later."

"Was there any sexual abuse charges?" Mark asked. It could have been the reason he killed Jenny. His chest hurt from just asking the question. Why did the world have to be so fucked up?

"No sexual abuse charges listed. But I've got a number for the ex-wife. She lives in Alabama. I'm calling her. Do you want to try to contact Karen Reed, Jennifer's mother, and see if she had anything on Patrick?"

"Since it's the mother of his receptionist, let's let the sheriff handle that one." Mark looked at Connor. "Did you get anything at the park yesterday?"

"They had a file. But it offered nothing new except the location of where the Reeds were camping." Connor picked up a file. "Here it is if you need it."

"Did you get anything?" Juan asked Mark.

"Yeah. The DA won't question Annie's credibility."

"What?" Connor asked.

"Three of the four kids she reported to CPS have since been removed from their homes. Annie was right."

"Shit. She needs to work for CPS," Juan said.

Mark looked at his watch. "Can you read over those questions? I gotta head out." Mark collected the file Connor had started on the park.

"Where you going?" Connor asked.

"To see if I can find Officer Ruffin again. And I'm contacting Roger Duncan to see if he can meet me at Anniston State Park with his cadaver dogs." He also had to meet the two homicide detectives working the Kelly murder case to hand over his thoughts and the piece of soul. But he didn't want to talk about that.

After that, Homicide was on its own. His soul was getting smaller and smaller. If he kept this up, he wouldn't have one.

After going over the questions, Mark got up to leave.

"Hey," Connor said.

Mark turned around. "Yeah?"

"You really okay?"

The question sat on his nerves. "Yes. Why?"

Connor rolled his shoulders.

"You seem to be drinking more," Juan said.

Mark looked from Connor to Juan. "What is this? An intervention?"

"No," Connor said. "It's friends letting you know we care."

"Well, stop worrying. I'm fucking fine."

"Don't get pissed," Connor said. "If the shoe was on the other foot, you'd be speaking up."

He bit back his anger. "You're right. I would. And I'm not pissed. But I'm fine."

He stepped out and then turned and walked back into the room. "Sorry I can be an ass. We make a good team. And I normally don't like teams."

"Ditto," Juan said.

Connor nodded and looked at Mark, who was standing a few feet from his desk. "But if you're waiting for a hug, you're going to be disappointed."

They all laughed. Mark left. And somehow, in spite of knowing he screwed up with Annie, the weight on his chest was a little lighter. He was going to solve her case. It was the least he could do.

* * *

"He left a note. 'Sorry,'" Annie said.

"What all did he say last night?" Isabella asked.

Annie stabbed a piece of lettuce in her salad. "He was so drunk most of it didn't make sense." She took a sip of her diet soda. The watered-down drink, slightly sweet and low on fizz, slid down her throat.

"Is he an alcoholic?" Isabella asked.

Annie looked up. "I asked. He said he wasn't, that he just had a dead-kid problem." Annie moved her salad around her plate. "His sister was murdered."

"What? When?"

"When he was young. I don't know the whole story, but..." She told Isabella about what Judith Holt had said the day she showed up at Mark's. "Last night he said his sister had asked him not to leave her to go to a party. But he went anyway. She was killed." She exhaled. "He blames himself."

"That's sad."

"I know." Annie inhaled. "He told me he wished he deserved me."

"What did you say?"

"Nothing. He fell asleep."

Isabella stared at her as if seeing through skin and bone. "You love him, don't you?"

"I barely know him." Annie gave her friend the same argument she'd given herself.

"I think I fell in love with Jose the first time I saw him. He was a cousin of a friend of mine. It was her *quinceañera*. He asked me to dance. We walked back onto her patio and he kissed me. Kissed me like I'd never been kissed before. Then he found out I was only fifteen."

"How old was he?"

"Nineteen. He told me to look him up in three years."

"Did you?"

"Yeah."

"And?" Annie needed to hear something positive.

"Two weeks after my eighteenth birthday, I got his phone number and where he worked from my friend. I showed up at his work right before noon and asked him to lunch."

"He remembered you?"

"He asked me what took me so long. Said he knew my birthday had been two weeks ago."

"That's romantic."

"Yeah." A touch of sadness echoed in her tone.

"Have you told him yet?" Annie asked.

"We agreed to talk tonight. I'm scared I'm going to lose him."

"Hey." Annie put her hand over Isabella's. "He loves you. It's going to be okay."

* * *

Adam Harper sat across from Mr. Erving, the Reeds' lawyer, who had insisted on doing the interviews at the office. They were on their first witness, Doris Roberts. Adam just sat and listened. Detective Pierce had taken the lead.

"I think we're finished here," Erving said. No doubt afraid the woman was too drunk to hold her tongue.

"I just have a few more questions," Pierce said.

"We'll reschedule," Erving said.

"Oh, honey." Doris Roberts leaned forward, letting her shirt drop open. "If you want to swing by my house later, I'll be there with bells on."

"No," Erving snapped, then looked at Roberts. "Call your brother to pick you up."

Ms. Roberts ignored her lawyer and ran her tongue over her lips while giving Detective Pierce a hungry look. The shock on the young detective's face had Adam coughing to disguise his laugh.

When Ms. Roberts walked out, Adam spoke up. "You'd better drive her home."

The lawyer frowned. "She's calling her brother."

"She won't do it. She's going to drive herself, and I think I'll follow her and arrest her ass."

Scowling, the lawyer walked out with his client.

Detective Pierce, one of Sutton's partners, looked at him. "Was she really—"

"Don't let it go to your head. She offered me the same thing." Adam stood. "I'm going to grab a cold water. Want one?"

"Yeah, but after that I think I need a stiff drink."

Adam chuckled. "You're only getting started. Wait until you meet the Reed brothers."

Pierce flipped through his paperwork and looked up. "I don't see Karen Reed, Patrick Reed's wife, on the list?"

"She's not," Adam said. "She wasn't married to Patrick when Jenny died. I talked to her, but I can call her in."

"Did she say much about her husband?" Pierce asked.

"She told me he was an alcoholic, but he was sober when they married."

"You know he had a record? We were even thinking he might be the one who killed Jenny."

"Yeah, Sutton told me. I asked his wife about her

husband's past. She said he wasn't nearly the man people accused him of being. She even accused the whole family of judging him when they were as bad as he was. Considering his daughter seems so well adjusted, I kind of believe her. But I'll call her if you want."

Pierce shook his head. "Nah. Who do you like for this?"

"I'm betting George. Though Sam is right up there."

Adam went to grab the waters from the breakroom. He pulled the last two out of the fridge. Heading back, Adam overheard Jennifer telling someone it'd be a few minutes before her lawyer returned.

When he got to his door, he saw JoAnne Lakes sitting in a chair. She had on a pretty light blue sundress, not too short. Not too tight. But it looked damn good.

He pulled in his gut. But damn, it was hard to believe she was kin to the woman who'd just left.

Jennifer looked back at him and her aunt. "I'm going to step out for lunch."

"Sure."

Jennifer left in a hurry as if she'd skipped breakfast. Ms. Lakes looked up. Emotion flashed in her eyes.

"How are you today?" he asked.

"I don't think we're supposed to be talking without the lawyer."

He frowned. "We just can't talk about the case. Water?" He held out a bottle.

"Thank you." She took it and glanced down.

It got awkward really fast. He was about to leave when she spoke up.

"I love my daughter." She still didn't meet his gaze.

"You could show it better." He recalled insinuating she wasn't a good mom.

"You haven't walked in my shoes." Hurt echoed in her voice.

His gaze lowered to her shapely calves, down to her sandaled feet. Her pale pink painted toenails. "I'm afraid my big feet wouldn't fit in those."

She glanced at his feet.

"They aren't that big."

"They get in my way all the time," he said.

They glanced up at the same time. Their gazes met and held. He wanted to help her. Because his gut said she was worth helping.

"Maybe you should tell me how it feels to walk in your shoes."

"If I did, would you..." She looked down.

"I would do everything I could to—"

The lawyer walked back in and glared at Adam and then JoAnne. "I told you not to speak to him without me!"

* * *

At noon, Mark's headache was still hanging on. He'd given the homicide detectives a few leads to follow.

He'd spoken to Connor twice. The Reeds' lawyer had attended the interviews and stepped all over his questions. Doris Roberts showed up drunk and hit on Connor. And JoAnne Lakes appeared willing to talk before the lawyer intervened.

Mark wondered if he should try to speak to her on Annie's behalf, but Brown would flip.

He had stopped by Officer Ruffin's place twice. The man still wasn't there. He left his number and a message for Ruffin to call him.

Roger Duncan and two cadaver dogs were waiting when he got to the parking lot.

"You're early." Mark approached the forty-year-old lab tech.

"It's a bad habit of mine," Roger said. His two dogs, one a mixed-breed German shepherd and the other a Lab-and-poodle mix, sat perfectly still, bracketing him. His passion was working his dogs. Mark thought he probably should see if Roger couldn't help him train Bacon.

He'd used Roger's dogs twice. The last time had been a wash, but the time before hadn't. Considering it'd been twenty-four years since Jenny went missing, Mark wasn't holding his breath. But Roger swore the dogs smelled bones, not just decomp.

"Are we doing just a few grids or are we doing the whole park?" Roger wiped a cloth over his forehead.

"I have a grid." The muggy heat dampened Mark's brow. This wasn't going to be fun.

An hour later, drenched in sweat, they'd walked Mark's grid and the dogs hadn't found anything. The thick trees seemed to hold in the heat and humidity, making it feel like a sauna.

"Let's call it a day," Mark said.

"Why don't we head north of your parameter for a few minutes?"

Mark had forgotten how obsessed Roger was to make a find. "Sure," he said.

Ten minutes later both dogs barked and marked the same spot.

Had they really found Jenny?

CHAPTER THIRTY

Mark called in the cavalry. Within an hour, Stone and his team were there digging.

Only a few feet into the dig, Mark, sipping the cold water Stone had brought, heard footsteps. Connor walked down the trail.

"We got anything?"

"Not yet," Mark said.

"How did the last interviews go?"

"Each one worse than the other. Sam and George Reed are bastards."

"The sheriff pretty much told me that," Mark said.

"They are all hiding something," Connor said. "But they'd practiced their stories. Not one word differed between them."

"Did you talk to them all?"

"All but Karen Reed and Jenny's mother, Sarah. The lawyer insisted she was disabled and it'd upset her too much." Connor frowned. "What makes a whole family like that so messed up? The most normal one is Annie's mom."

Mark ran a hand through his hair, soaked with sweat. "I don't know."

A *clunk* echoed from the hole. Stone called for the shoveling to stop. He got on his knees, took what looked like a small broom and swished at the dirt.

Roger, beaming with pride, came to stand by Mark. "My dogs are good."

Stone kept brushing. The low *swish swish* filled an unnatural silence. Even the wind stopped, as if in reverence for what was about to be unearthed.

The air in Mark's lungs grew heavy. It would just be bones after all these years, but he didn't want to see it.

Stone leaned down to see what he'd uncovered. Shaking his head, he got to his feet and met Mark's gaze. "It's an alligator snapping turtle."

"Damn," Roger said. "Turtle and human bones smell alike."

* * *

Annie, book in hand, sat down at her favorite Tex-Mex place. She was thrilled Isabella had reconnected with Jose, but she missed their dinners together. She missed her mom. Missed her father.

She missed Mark.

But she had a book. A good book. She loved this author.

Opening it, she read one page then set it down. She couldn't read. Couldn't concentrate. She'd barely eaten in three days. She was a mess.

She'd come so close to calling Mark. Wanting to be

held by him, comforted by him. Wanting to hold him, to comfort him. She no longer felt anger. She felt hurt and lonely. And her gut said he was feeling the same thing. She also remembered something he'd said about proving she wasn't crazy. Had that been the booze talking?

Reaching for a chip, she scooped up a big dollop of guacamole and put it in her mouth. It actually tasted good. As she was working on her second chip, her phone rang.

Hoping it was Mark, she snagged her phone.

It wasn't Mark's number on the screen. She didn't recognize it.

Her heart skipped a beat. "Hello," she answered.

"Annie..." The line kept going in and out. "You..." The voice was female, but Annie hadn't gotten enough of it to recognize it.

"Hello?" Static filled the line and her head. "Who is this?"

The call went silent. Dead silent.

Her heart fluttered in her chest. Fear curled up in the pit of her stomach. She looked at the number again. She didn't recognize it. But the caller had used her name. Who was it?

She started to call Mark, but to say what? She'd gotten a call with static. It could be nothing.

Or it could be a murderer.

Chills pooled at the base of her neck, then scattered down her spine and across her shoulders.

Setting her phone down, staring at the device, she waited for it to ring again. But why wait?

She hit redial. The phone rang. No one answered.

What the hell?

The hair on the back of her neck stood up, and she looked around, feeling watched.

* * *

Disappointed, frustrated and hungry, Mark headed home around eight, planning on picking up a burger. But when he saw the turnoff to the senior community, he drove in.

He parked in front of Ruffin's unit. Light spilled out the windows. Maybe today wouldn't be a complete wash.

Walking to the door, he recalled the questions he wanted to ask. He knocked. A television echoed from inside. No one came to the door.

He knocked again.

Still nothing.

He knocked harder.

"Not taking visitors," a voice called out.

"Yes, you are!" Mark called back.

The door swung open. Two things hit Mark at once. One: Marijuana. Two: The old man wasn't a stranger.

His eyes widened with recognition. "What the hell do you want?"

Mark tried to grasp the situation. "You're Officer Ruffin?"

"Yeah. Why?"

"You've been at the coffee shop all this time?" He moved inside.

Fred frowned. "I didn't ask you in."

Mark took another sniff. "You're smoking weed?"

"I suggest you don't hurt that sweet woman, and now you're going to come harass my ass?"

"No. I'm not here about Annie. Well, I am, but..." He shook his head. "You're really smoking weed." Mark's gaze hit on all the pill bottles on the coffee table. He looked back at the man's bloodshot eyes. "Cancer?"

The old man stiffened. "Maybe I just like weed."

"Sorry," Mark said.

Ruffin frowned. "Arrest me if you want to, but keep your pity, boy."

Mark exhaled. "The reason I'm here is because of an old case."

"Which one?"

"The Reed case. I know it's been a long time, but..."

The old man held up a finger. "Give me a minute." He scratched his head. "This stuff does affect your brain cells."

Mark almost chuckled.

"Reed?" Fred repeated. "Let me look at my files." He started into a small dining room that held a table and metal file cabinets.

"You kept all your files?"

"It was a part of my life for so long." He moved in front of the cases. "What year was it?"

"Ninety-three."

"What kind of case?"

"A missing kid."

Fred held up a finger. "At the park, right. It's coming back. That one bugged the shit out of me."

"How so?"

He opened a middle drawer.

"I have a copy of the file," Mark said.

"Yeah, but after I retired I went through every un-solved case and made more notes. Looked for things I missed." He rummaged through the files. "I helped solve three of those cases by doing it, too. When Gertrude died, I went through them again. It kept my mind off the grief."

"You think you missed something on the Reed case?"

He pulled out a file and opened it. "Yeah, here it is. The mother of the missing child. She was hand-icapped. I spoke with her briefly and she said some strange things. The brother insisted she didn't know what she was saying, that she wasn't all there. I spoke with my sergeant before I wrote up the file, I suggested we look into it. He said it sounded like nonsense."

Mark recalled his brief conversation with Sarah Reed. "What did she say?"

"She said it was her fault. That she'd shot him."

"'Him'? Shot *him*?"

"Yeah. I asked her, 'You mean you shot *her*.' She didn't answer. But when we spoke to the neighboring campers, none of them heard a gunshot. I ended up not putting it in my report, but I noted it in my files later."

Mark recalled Connor saying the lawyer refused to let Sarah Reed be interviewed.

Fred's brow wrinkled. "Wait, you said this had to do with Annie."

Mark nodded. "Annie was the kid who'd been taken

CHRISTIE CRAIG

to the hospital for stitches. Recently she remembered seeing someone burying her cousin."

"You found a body?"

"No. But the Reeds appear to be hiding something."

"I put that in my file, too." Fred scratched his head. "Poor Annie. She doesn't deserve that."

"I know," Mark said.

The old man grabbed ahold of the back of a chair as if his knees were giving. "You and Annie had a falling-out, didn't you?"

Mark debated answering, but... "You're right. I don't deserve her."

Fred pulled out the chair and sat down. Mark saw pain flash across his face.

"How long do you have?"

Fred frowned. "Three to twelve months. Depends if this last round of chemo slowed it down."

"I'm sorry," Mark said.

"I'm not. I'll be with Gertrude."

Mark wondered if he had any family, kids, anyone to help. "Do you need anything?"

"Nope."

Mark nodded. "If I need you to speak to a judge about the case, would you?"

"Hell yeah."

Mark dropped his hands into his pockets. "Be careful where you buy your smoke. It can come laced with things you don't want."

"I know. Things haven't changed that much since I worked the streets."

Mark nodded. "I'll see myself out." He started for the door.

"Do you care?" The old man's question had him turning around.

"Excuse me?"

"You care about Annie?"

Mark stared at his shoes. "More than I should."

"You could change. I did."

"Yeah." He got to the door. He reached the knob, then stopped. He didn't even turn around. "How?"

"You tell her everything. You forgive yourself and others. That bitterness, it can kill you. You accept that you can't make this world right. Even with that badge. But you can try to make it right for those you love. I had to park my ass on a shrink's sofa once a week for a year."

Mark stayed silent, but faced the old man.

Fred continued. "You work damn hard to live up to the man she thinks you are. To this day, I don't think I was as good as Gertrude believed me to be, but I was a better man for trying."

Mark swallowed. "That's a hell of a lot to ask of someone."

"Yeah. But here's two questions to consider. One: Is she worth it? Two: Are you happy the way you are?"

* * *

That night Annie made a trip to the grocery store. Pirate needed food. So did she. Her jeans were getting looser. She needed to start eating.

She drove to her parking spot at the apartment and moaned when she found it was taken. Visitors didn't know it was designated parking. Normally she didn't mind, but with groceries? She drove around until she found a spot in visitors' parking.

About to get out, she remembered Mark's warning to be careful. She looked around. It seemed extra dark. Then a car pulled into the lot. Another car one row over had its lights on. She wasn't alone.

She was safe. So why didn't she feel safe?

Telling herself she was overreacting, she got out and grabbed all her bags, determined not to have to come back.

Weighted down, she started walking. Feeling darkness again, she now noticed that the lights on two of the poles were out. Another kept hissing as if threatening to blow.

She got about twenty steps when she saw a figure stand up between a row of cars.

Then she saw the shadow lift its arm. A pop exploded in the darkness. She felt the pain in her arm and fell backward. Now the pain exploded in her head. Had she been...shot?

She lay there, air locked in her chest, fear scratching at her mind. She turned her head and saw a pool of her own blood.

* * *

Mark, holding his cell between his shoulder and ear, unlocked his front door while Bacon barked and whined behind it.

"Talk to a judge," Mark said.

"With her being mentally challenged, I'm not sure what she says will hold water," Connor said.

"We have to try." Mark walked into his house.

"The lawyer seemed adamant."

"Then get a warrant," Mark bit out. "Ruffin thinks she's the key to this and I agree."

"Okay, I'll contact a judge in the morning."

Five minutes later, making Bacon happy, Mark sat on the floor playing tug-of-war with his sock while his thoughts played tug-of-war in his mind.

Is she worth it? Are you happy the way you are?

Yes. And no.

But forgive himself? That seemed impossible. Forgive his piece-of-shit stepfather? Fucking impossible.

His gaze went to the saxophone sitting there like a trophy, a reminder of what he'd once loved. With vivid detail, he could remember how the instrument felt in his hands. How it felt to play it. How when he played, his world seemed so damn right. Even during the time when his life had kinda sucked.

His mom's marriage had gone downhill. His step-father had started drinking again, losing one job after another. The money Mark made playing in bands went to the bills. Mark didn't care. He loved making music.

With his size, everyone had wanted him to play ball. But he loved music. And as odd as it sounded, he'd felt music loved him back. It fed his soul. Made him feel...complete. Sort of like being with Annie did.

Odd was the fact that the only other thing that came

naturally to him was police work. And instead of feeding his soul, that took it away.

His phone rang. Thinking of Annie, he made a mad dash into the kitchen where he'd left it.

When her number flashed on the screen, his chest widened with something akin to hope. Damn, he needed her back in his life.

"Hey," he answered, emotion leaking out in that one word.

"Mark...?" The voice shook with emotion. His head spun. It wasn't Annie's voice. It wasn't Annie crying.

"This is Isabella. Annie's been shot!"

That huge space in his chest where hope had just existed became a vise grip and threatened not to just take another piece of his soul, but to kill it.

"What? Is she okay?"

"I don't know. When I got to the parking lot they had her in the ambulance. They drove off. Someone said they're taking her to the Regional Hospital."

* * *

Regional Hospital was thirty minutes away. Mark made it in twenty. Annie's apartment was only five minutes from the hospital, so she should already be getting treatment.

The ambulance was still parked in the circled drive.

He parked, hauled ass out of his car and ran into the emergency room. He slammed his badge against the glass separating him from the desk person. "Where's Annie Lakes?"

The clerk's eyes went to his badge. "Who?"

"The woman who just came in that ambulance," he spit out, no patience.

"She's being treated."

"What room?" He hit the glass with his badge again.

The clerk jumped. "Seven. But you can't—the doctors are working on her."

"How bad is it?"

She didn't answer, but the expression did.

Right then someone walked out and Mark flew through the door. His gaze shot left, right, scanning, looking, then finding room seven.

Two doctors walked out.

"Is she okay?"

They both looked at him with the same look as the desk clerk.

"Mark?" He turned around and saw Isabella walking down the hall. She'd been crying. A man had his arm around her.

"I can't accept this," Mark growled.

CHAPTER
THIRTY-ONE

Accept what?" Isabella asked, sounding scared.

Mark looked back at the doctors.

"Are you with the Lakes patient or the Campton patient?"

"Lakes," he said.

"She's fine," the doctor said.

Isabella moved in and away from the man. "They are stitching up her arm and her head."

His breath caught. "Head?"

The man with Isabella spoke up. "The bullet grazed her arm, but when she fell she cut her head."

Relief that Annie was okay made Mark's knees weak. He noticed the way the man with Isabella continued to look at him, and he suddenly remembered being drunk on his ass and knocking on Isabella's door.

"I'm sorry about the other night," he said, leaning against the wall.

"Yeah," the man said.

"Seriously, I'm sorry. I don't recall your name," Mark said.

"Jose Moreno." He held out his hand as if saying he didn't hold grudges.

"Mark Sutton." They shook hands.

"Isabella tells me you're a detective," he said.

"Yeah." Mark realized he needed to start acting like a detective. "Were there police at the apartment?"

"Yeah," Isabella answered.

"Did they catch the shooter?"

"Not when we left. They were telling everyone to get inside. They were thinking it was just a drive-by. I saw Annie's phone and purse on the ground. That's when I called you."

His gut clenched. "Were there witnesses?"

"Yeah," Isabella replied. "But I heard them tell the police they didn't see where the shooter went."

Jose put his arm around Isabella. "Someone else said they saw a car leaving the parking lot right after that. I don't know if they got a license plate."

"Thanks." Mark stepped away, intending to call Connor, when he saw an officer walking toward him.

"You here for the Lakes shooting?" Mark said, flashing his badge.

"Yeah."

"What do you know?"

"Other than someone tried to kill her, not much."

* * *

Annie leaned back on the gurney in the emergency room. The whiteness of the walls reminded her of Mark's house. The smell crawled up her nose. Her head hurt. Her arm hurt. Then Mark walked in and a sharp pain sparked in her heart and settled into a deep emotional ache that hurt more than anything.

"Hey." His gaze swallowed her up. Her vision went watery.

"It's okay." He leaned down and pressed a soft kiss on her forehead.

Then he brushed a few tears off her cheeks. "I'm going to catch who did this."

"I did what you said." Her voice quavered. "I only parked there because another car had pulled up."

"I know." He slipped his hand in hers and squeezed, and glanced at her arm.

"It's barely anything." She swiped at her own tears, trying to be strong. "I don't know why I'm crying." But she did. Someone had used her for target practice.

"Getting shot does that to you." He half-smiled. "Can you tell what happened?"

The question reminded her that he was here as a cop, not her boyfriend.

"Did you recognize the shooter?"

"No."

"Man or a woman?"

She closed her eyes, but all she could see was her blood on the pavement. "I don't know."

"It's okay." He kept holding her hand, his thumb brushing across her wrist. Did he do this with all the witnesses?

"Someone else might have seen more than I did."

Mark nodded. "I need to leave to speak to the officers at the scene, but there's an officer outside your door. You're safe. The doctor said you'd be released tonight. APD is putting you up in a hotel."

"A hotel? But I work tomorrow."

"No." His expression turned serious. All cop-like. "Tonight changes everything. Someone tried to kill you. They may have killed your cousin. You're taking some time off."

His words, his tone made it even more real. She could have died tonight.

He squeezed her hand as if to say good-bye. She tightened her grip.

Then Annie remembered. "I got a call. Earlier tonight."

"From who? Why didn't—"

"I didn't recognize the number. There was static, but they said my name. I called back and no one answered. I'll show you." She sat up. "My phone...?"

"Isabella has it. I'll get your phone from her and check into the number. Until then, don't call your mom."

Her chin trembled. "She wouldn't—"

"I know you don't want to think she's involved in this. And for your sake I hope you're right, but at the very least, she's with people I think are behind this."

The lump in her throat doubled. "Fine." But it wasn't. Nothing was fine.

He exhaled. "I'm sorry. I hate to leave, but I need to get to the scene."

His hand was still in hers and it felt so right. She

wanted to ask when he'd be back, but was afraid he wouldn't. "Be careful. If they'll shoot me, they'll shoot you."

His palm tightened against hers. "Your halo's showing again."

She glanced up into his blue eyes. "So is yours."

She remembered him talking about the guilt he felt about his sister and yet, he still worked cases that brought it all back. Maybe he did it to punish himself, but she knew he cared.

"I don't have a halo."

"Yes, you do. I see it."

A flash of emotion crossed his expression. He looked as if he was going to say something, something meaningful, something she could hold on to. Instead he pulled his warm hand from hers and left.

A cop. Not a boyfriend.

* * *

It was after eleven before the doctor gave Annie her walking papers. Because she was leaving for the hotel, she hugged Isabella good-bye. When the hug ended, Annie asked, "Did you talk to Jose?"

"Yeah." Isabella sighed. "He was upset that I didn't tell him. But he says it wasn't my fault, and he never would've left me for it."

"He loves you." Annie smiled.

"Yeah. What about you and the hot detective?"

"I don't think..." Annie let her words drop off and her heart and hope dropped with it.

"Don't give up. If you could've only seen how scared he was when he got here."

Annie nodded, but she couldn't believe it. Plus, Mark might've been drunk when he talked about the white picket fence, but he was right. She wanted marriage and family.

* * *

Annie had a police escort to the hotel. He even walked her to her room. Before he left he assured her that he or another officer would be parked outside. Shutting the door, she sat on the hotel bed, stared at the other empty bed, and felt lonelier than ever.

And scared.

What if the person who'd tried to kill her came here? What if they got past the officer?

She got up to make sure she'd locked the door. She had.

With no toothbrush, no pajamas, no one to lean on, she rinsed her mouth out, pulled her bra off, and crawled into one of the beds. She'd slept some in the emergency room, but now sleep evaded her. She was still staring at the ceiling, worrying about her mom, about Fran, when someone knocked on the door.

She shot up, her heart pounding.

"Annie. It's Mark." The voice whispered through the door and went right to her heart.

She let him in. He had one of her suitcases. "Isabella packed it for you."

"Thanks."

He shut the door. "You okay?"

No. "Barely hurts."

"Wait till tomorrow."

"Something to look forward to," she said with a slight laugh. "The scar on your leg is a bullet wound?"

"Yeah."

"Who shot you?"

He grinned. "The devil." When she rolled her eyes, he chuckled. "It was Halloween. They wore costumes to rob the jewelry stores."

He looked at the door, as if to leave. *Please don't go.* "Did you get anything?"

"The man who called the ambulance didn't see the guy. Another neighbor saw a small dark-colored car racing out of the parking lot. So nothing there either. But the number that called you belongs to a Jimmy Birch. Lives in Burnett, Texas. You know him?"

"No," she said.

"We got an address on him and had a patrol car go by there. No one was home. You sure the caller said your name?"

"Yes, and it was a woman."

"I'll look into it tomorrow. We did find a bullet. It's being tested."

He sat on the extra bed. He looked tired. His hair was a little mussed, as if he'd run his hands through it one too many times.

"You mind if I camp here for the night? To sleep."

Relieved, she smiled. "I've heard you tell me that before."

He smiled. She'd missed seeing it. Other than when

he was drunk, she hadn't seen that crooked grin in a while.

"That time wasn't on me. Besides, this is different. You can't have sex after you've been shot."

She grinned. "Doctor told you that, huh?"

"No." His smile widened. "It's in the official police handbook."

They laughed. When the laughter stopped, it got awkward again.

She rolled the suitcase into the bathroom and brushed her teeth. Isabella had packed her new two-piece pink pajama set. Annie decided to sleep in a pair of shorts and a T-shirt instead.

When she came out, Mark, fully clothed, was re-clined on the bed.

She crawled into her bed.

"Lights out?" she asked.

"Sure."

Lights went out. Dark silence followed. Five minutes passed. Ten. Fifteen.

She heard the slight rumble of the mattress shifting and glanced over.

Through the dark, she saw him on his side looking at her.

"I'm sorry about showing up drunk. I don't remem-ber everything, but what I remember I'm ashamed of."

"Other than being drunk, you didn't do anything to be ashamed of."

They stared at each other in the darkness. He ex-haled and asked, "Do you think anyone abused you when you were a kid?"

His question hurt. She understood why he'd think it. "No. I know you believe my mom is a monster, but she's not. She loved me and so did my dad."

"Good," he said. "I couldn't handle thinking someone hurt you."

The way he said it brushed across her heart. Why did he act like he cared when he was the one to push her away? In the distance, someone slammed a hotel room door.

He readjusted his pillow. "How did you know those kids were being abused?"

She lifted up on her elbow. "What do you mean?"

"Didn't I tell you?"

She sat up. "Tell me what?"

He sat up and turned on the lamp. Light flooded the room. It felt too harsh. "Three of the kids you reported to CPS have since been removed from their homes. You were right—they *were* being abused."

Annie fisted the sheet into her hands. Their faces flashed in her heart. Lucy. Jamie. Tommy. Brittani. She'd forced herself to stop thinking of them because it hurt too much, because it made her question herself.

A lump, too big for her throat, formed between her tonsils. Anger, resentment, fury boiled inside her. "How long did they suffer before someone helped them? And which one wasn't removed?"

"I don't know. But I'll find out if it's important to you."

She grabbed a pillow and punched it. "I wanted to be wrong."

He came and sat beside her. His arm came around

her shoulders. She leaned into him and cried. Not for herself, but those precious kids. The kids she'd tried to help and failed.

Why hadn't she kept insisting? Made someone believe her?

CHAPTER THIRTY-TWO

After a few minutes, she pulled herself together. "No one believed me."

"They do now." His hand stayed on her shoulder. "What made you suspect this?"

"Their eyes." She teared up again. "They were hurting and not just physically." A realization hit. "In the picture Fran had the same look. Wounded." She put her hand over her lips, and leaned against his arm again.

"I'm sorry they didn't believe you. I'm sorry I doubted you. Even if I doubted you only a few minutes."

She sat up. "How did you find out?"

"I went to see the cop who arrested you for breaking the restraining order. He told me that a caseworker on that case had called him looking for information. She told him they were having to remove the child."

"Lucy." As she said the girl's name, she remembered the sad look in her eyes, the emotional weight on her tiny shoulders.

"I went to see the caseworker."

She looked up. Their eyes met. And held.

He pulled his arm from around her. "You okay now?"

"Yeah."

He went back to his bed. "Lights out?" he asked.

"Yeah."

The sound of them both reclining filled the dark hotel room. Then came the silence. She could hear him breathe. Hear herself breathe.

"I don't remember my father," he said, almost a whisper. "I was a few months old when he left. It was just Mom and me. She worked two jobs. Waitressed during the day, and sang in a band at night. She'd wanted to be country western singer. I spent more time with a neighbor than her. She wasn't the greatest mom. Most of her days off, she'd date. But I knew she loved me."

Annie had no idea why he'd decided to tell her this, but she held on to his every word.

"When she didn't have a date, she'd play the guitar and sing to me. One Saturday morning she took me to a yard sale. I saw a saxophone. I begged her to buy it for me. She did. I loved playing that thing. She loved hearing me play, so I kept practicing. I wanted her to be proud of me." He paused. "When I was nine, I entered into a talent show and I won a two-hundred-dollar prize. We went to an amusement park. I still remember that day. The cotton candy. The hot dogs. Her laughing."

He stopped talking again. "Then Mom met Logan. I

was ten. At first, he treated me nice. She got pregnant. We moved in with him. It was a nice three-bedroom house, even had a picket fence. I got a baby sister." She heard the hurt in his voice.

"What was your sister's name?" Silence followed and she didn't think he was going to answer.

"Casey." Several seconds passed before he continued. "Mom quit work and stayed home with us. Shortly after that, Logan got hurt at work. He lost his job, started drinking more. He was a mean drunk. He'd come home from the bar and they'd fight. I'd get between them. He somehow knew not to hit me."

Mark inhaled and it sounded like pain. "Mom got a job, he kept drinking. I took care of Casey. My sister counted on me for things. When she'd wet the bed at night, she'd sneak into my room so Logan wouldn't get mad about her waking them up. The next morning I'd wash the sheets so no one would know."

She heard him swallow. "She was scared of her own dad. He'd never hit her—Mom took all that. But he'd yell and throw things, and she'd cry. I got into the school band and when my bandleader heard me play, he got me some gigs playing a song or two in various bands. Mom would take me and she'd get a babysitter for Casey. Mom was so proud of me. We shared the love of music. Logan hated that she spent so much time with me, but he sure didn't mind taking the money I made."

He drew in air that sounded raw.

"When I was fifteen, a friend of mine had a party. His parents were out of town. He had beer and girls staying there." Mark drew in a quick breath. "Casey asked me not to go. Asked who'd protect her from her daddy."

She sat up. "You were a teenager, Mark."

"Mom got called in to work. They were low on money. When she got home, he was high on something. He said Casey had gone out to play and hadn't come back." Mark draped an arm over his face. "They found her the next day. He'd dumped her body in one of those garbage bins. He finally talked. Said he told her to get him a beer, and she dropped it. He got mad, and the drugs and the alcohol made him lose it."

Annie fisted the sheet in her hand.

"He killed her because she dropped his beer. Then he threw her away." His voice shook. "Mom killed herself the next day. I was so angry at Logan, but I was angrier at Mom. She left me."

Annie gasped then got up and went to sit beside him. He kept his arm over his face.

"I'm sorry." He didn't move. She put her hand on his chest.

"I went to foster care for two years." His voice grew hoarse. "I learned to depend on myself. Got passed around a lot. At eighteen I left. Renting a room in someone's house. I worked two jobs and went to college. I became a cop to stop the Logans of the world. I do okay. Some days I do great. Until it's a kid and then...it all comes back. The anger. The guilt. If I get drunk enough, I can forget."

Annie stood and went around to the other side and crawled in bed with him. He kept one arm over his eyes, she put her head on his shoulder and listened to his heart beat, felt his chest shift up, then down.

"I lived in that house with a white picket fence and two kids. A mom and a so-called dad. And it wasn't pretty. So there it is. I've told you everything. But I don't think I can forgive. Not them, or myself."

"Listen to me. You didn't do anything to be forgiven," she said.

"I already hurt you, Annie. I don't want to hurt you anymore."

He pulled her closer. They lay there, neither of them said another word. It was just them. In the dark. The pain of the past. And an unknown future.

When Annie woke up the next morning, Mark was gone.

* * *

Mark held the phone close to his ear. "Ms. Birch, I'm Detective Sutton with the Anniston Police Department. Your husband's number came up in an investigation. Can you tell me where he is?"

"Did you say Anniston?" Ms. Birch sounded half asleep.

"Yes ma'am."

Mark had arrived at the office at six. He'd left Annie sleeping, looking like an angel. He'd waited until eight o'clock to call Ms. Birch. The fact that he'd slept at all the previous night had been a miracle. Or maybe not. Baring his darkest secrets to Annie had left him exhausted and somehow liberated. He'd actually slept for five straight hours. He hadn't done that in forever. Not when he went to bed sober.

Call it a hunch, but his gut said the call Annie had gotten from Mr. Birch's number could lead them somewhere.

"What has he done now?" Ms. Birch asked.

"Like I said, his number came up."

"I haven't seen or spoken to him in a month. We separated. You might want to look for him in jail. I heard he got another DWI."

Connor walked in.

Mark held up a finger. "Do you know where he's living?"

Mark had learned the call had bounced off a tower in a town halfway between here and Austin.

"I heard he was with his sister who lives in Burnet. But I think he was arrested."

The line beeped with another call. Glancing down he saw it was from the front desk. Mildred probably wanting coffee. "Can you give me his sister's number?"

After jotting it down, he thanked her and hung up. "Hey," he said to Connor.

"I got a meeting at eleven with a judge today in Jordan County about getting a warrant to talk to Sarah Reed. I suspect he'll only do it if a psychologist speaks to her. So it won't happen quickly. I'm also going to take another ride up to Pearlsville and see who doesn't have an alibi for the time of the shooting."

"Good," Mark said. "That was the wife of the Jimmy Birch whose phone called Annie yesterday. The wife suggested he might be in jail."

A clearing of a throat had Mark looking at the door.

Mildred, with an I-come-bearing-gifts smile, stood there. At her side was a petite blonde. A blonde who looked familiar.

"He's not in jail," the woman said.

"What?" Mark asked.

"Jimmy's in rehab."

Realizing why the woman looked familiar, he stood up. She appeared older, and somehow harsher, but she could be Annie's sister. "Fran Roberts?"

She nodded. "I hear you've been looking for me."

"We have. Come on in."

Mildred walked out. Ms. Roberts walked in. "Do you know where Annie is?"

"We might." Mark sat on the edge of his desk.

She tightened her eyes, showing a hint of annoyance. "Someone at her apartment told me she'd been shot. Is that true?"

"Yes."

Her eyes rounded. "Is she okay?"

"Yeah." He stood up. "Why don't we move to the conference room? It's more comfortable." He stopped at the door.

She didn't move. "Do you know who shot her?"

"Not yet," Mark said. "Do you?"

She shook her head. "You think I . . . I've been in rehab."

"All this time?" Connor asked.

"Yes. Call them."

"We will," Connor said.

She frowned at his partner.

"This way." Mark led the way. The woman's heels tapped against the tile floor. Mark didn't walk fast; he needed a few seconds to figure out his approach.

When they were all seated, he looked up. "Why were you trying to call Annie Lakes?"

"I heard a detective from Anniston was looking for me, I assumed it had to do with her."

"Why would you assume that?"

"She lives here." Was she purposely being vague?

"And if you had to guess what this was all about, what would you say?"

She hesitated before answering. "That Annie finally did something that I wish I had the courage to do a long time ago."

"What's that?"

She tilted up her chin. "Report the murder of Jenny Reed."

Mark leaned forward. "Who killed her?"

"I don't know. Do you think that's why Annie got shot?"

Mark debated his answer and went with the truth. "I do. Do you think someone in your family would've done that?"

She sat there as if contemplating. "I don't know. I haven't been as close to them. I saw my mom some, but not much."

"Your ex said you told him someone in your family was trying to shut you up. Did someone threaten you?"

"Sort of. I was drunk at the funeral. Annie and I...talked about Jenny. Someone heard us."

"Who?" Mark asked.

"I don't know, but my uncle George drove me home. He screamed at me that I needed to forget about the past. That it'd cause all kinds of hell if it got out."

"Did it feel like a threat?"

She hesitated. "He was angry. But he's always angry." She looked down at her locked hands.

Mark continued. "That night at the park. Do you know who was burying Jenny?"

She lifted her gaze, and again Mark got the feeling she'd seen too much ugly in the world. "Didn't Annie tell you?"

Mark settled back in his chair. "Ms. Lake's memory is spotty."

Fran inhaled. Exhaled. Her hands shook. "It was Patrick Reed. My uncle."

"He killed her?" Connor asked.

"He said he didn't do it. He said it over and over again. He was acting weird."

Mark studied her. "If he didn't kill her, who did?"

"I don't know."

It was the first time he heard a bit of lie in her tone. His frustration rose. "Who tried to kill Annie?"

"I don't know!" Tears filled her eyes.

"Then why didn't you tell the police that morning?" Mark asked.

"Mama said I hadn't seen what I thought. That Annie and I were making things up, and if I told the police, she'd take a belt to me."

Tension filled the air. "You think your mom did it?"

She flinched and Mark saw how difficult it was. "I don't want to believe it. But she's the one who told me to lie. Said to tell them that I had seen Jenny go under the water."

Mark recalled Annie's memory of that. "Was she playing in the water?"

"The day before. She got in over her head. I grabbed her. She'd swallowed so much water she puked."

Connor shifted in his seat. The scrape of the chair legs cracked the silence. "You're saying no one in the family said anything else about what happened to Jenny? Not even after all those years? As if she didn't exist?"

She closed her eyes as if remembering. "I found...a picture of Jenny once in my aunt Sarah's room. I told my mom and she went ballistic. She charged into Sarah's room, yelling at her. She slapped Sarah, and Sarah cried for days. I felt terrible."

Fran became silent and looked away at the wall. "When my mom got drunk, she got mean like the rest of them."

"Was she drinking at the park?"

"Everyone was." Fran paused. "Well, not Annie's mom. She never drank. The only one who escaped the ugliness of this family was Annie. Her dad was different, too. Even when they lived in town, we only saw them on big holidays. I heard her mom say her husband was mad about her coming on the camping trip. After that night, they moved away. I never saw Annie again until the funeral."

Mark took it all in. It was exactly as Annie had remembered.

"And you never asked your mom what happened to Jenny?" Disbelief rang in Connor's tone.

Fran frowned. "Yeah, and I got my mama's handprint on my face for asking. The Reeds followed the rule that kids were to be seen, not heard. Unfortunately, I had a big mouth and wore my mama's handprint way too often. I left when I was seventeen."

Mark spoke up. "It's not that we don't believe you. We just want to understand."

"Understand?" she said in a numb voice. "I'm thirty years old and I've been trying to understand all my life. Why they are the way they are. Why I'm like them!" Tears filled her eyes. "I had to leave my daughter because I was afraid I'd end up like Mom."

Mark reached behind him where they kept tissues and passed them to her. She dried her eyes. "I love my daughter. That's why I went into rehab. My ex said I couldn't see her until I got sober." She stared at the tissue. "He threatened that before, but this time a switch just turned inside me. I didn't want to be who I was. I want to be a family. My daughter and husband." She wiped her eyes and then laughed. "Why am I telling you this?"

Mark remembered last night. "Sometimes unloading one secret leads to another." He paused. "How well did you know Patrick Reed?"

"Enough to know you stayed away from him when he got drunk. Of all my uncles, he was the meanest."

"Did he ever assault you?" Connor asked.

"He slapped me once when I mouthed off to Mom."

Mark hated to ask, but... "Was there sexual abuse?"

She made a sound from the back of her throat. "They weren't perverts, just mean drunks."

"Can you tell me about that night at the park?" Mark asked.

She took a deep breath, then released it as if it were too big. With pain in her voice, she told the same story that Annie had. When she finished, she asked, "If someone shot Annie, are they going to come after me now?"

"Not if we catch them," Connor said.

Mark asked, "Do you know where it was you saw him burying her in the park?"

"Yeah. I went back there when I ran away. I thought if I faced it, I could deal with it."

"Could you show us?" Mark asked.

"Yeah. But it won't help."

Mark's shoulders tightened. "Why not?"

"I don't think her body's there anymore."

"Why would you think that?" Connor asked.

"Because...Sarah used to take flowers to the old barn, the one way in the back of George's house. I asked why she did it. She said flowers belonged on graves. One time my uncle George caught her doing it. He smacked her."

CHAPTER THIRTY-THREE

Mark's phone dinged with a text. Annie's name flashed. He glanced at Fran. "I'm going to grab a drink. Do you want something?"

"I want a Jack and coke," she said with a wry smile. "But coffee would be nice."

He nodded. When Mark got up, so did Connor.

The moment the door closed, Connor looked at him. "You believe her?"

"Yes, but it doesn't help. Why's someone trying to kill Annie if the murderer is dead?"

"Because he's not the killer," Connor said. "I'm heading out to see the judge. I'm asking permission to dig up the old barn."

"Get the sheriff to go with you. He probably knows the judge," Mark said. "In fact, let me call him. I haven't told him about the shooting."

Connor motioned to the door. "What are you doing with her?"

"I don't know yet," Mark said.

Connor walked off, Mark read Annie's text.

Hi. You said call, but I thought I'd text.

He leaned against the wall and started typing. Hey. Sorry about last night.

He deleted it. And typed, Thanks for last night.

He deleted it. And typed, I think I love you.

Shit. He deleted it. And typed, Fran's here. She's fine. Been in rehab.

* * *

"Shot? When?" Adam asked.

Mark explained.

"Is she okay?"

"Yeah." Mark leaned back in his desk chair. Fran Roberts had wanted to call and speak to her ex before they went to see Annie. So Mark took that time to call the sheriff. "We also got ballistics back on the bullet. It was a nine-millimeter, a wad-cutter bullet. We're thinking someone used it more for target practice than a weapon. I've got someone checking to see which Reeds have guns."

"I've already checked. They don't have any registered."

"None?" Mark asked.

"Nope. I checked that after I was held at gunpoint with that BB gun. As eager as she was to shoot me, I decided I'd better be safe than sorry."

Mark continued to explain Fran Roberts showing up. How she thought they'd moved the body and buried it under the dirt floor of the barn. How she suspected her mother.

Mark asked Adam to go with Connor to request the warrant.

"Sure. I know Judge Benton. Have you told JoAnne Lakes about her daughter being shot?"

"No."

"Would you mind if I called her?" Adam asked. "I think if she knew her daughter's life was in jeopardy, she'd open up. She almost told me something at the interview."

"If you think she'll talk to you, go for it. But she's not seeing Annie until this is solved."

* * *

Annie changed her clothes and combed her hair, wishing she had makeup. She didn't know why she felt like she should dress up for Fran. Maybe just nerves. The last time she'd seen her, it hadn't gone so well.

Her phone rang. Annie checked the screen. Her mom again. She'd called twice. Each time, Annie wanted to answer. The little girl in her still wanted her mother. But Mark... She turned the phone off. She could handle only so much. Her mom issues would have to wait. So would the Mark issues.

Looking around the hotel room, she collected the paper plate that the officer had brought up to her for breakfast and tossed it in the bathroom's garbage. When she looked up, she stared at her scared reflection.

She'd actually slept through the night, using Mark's shoulder as a pillow. The dark circles were still there, but she guessed she looked good for someone who'd been shot. She touched her head where she had stitches.

Mark had texted her then called. Her cousin wanted to see her. Annie wanted to see Fran. Though she didn't know exactly what she wanted to say.

Except, *Thank you for coming back for me that night.*

She still didn't remember what happened afterward. But Fran's voice kept echoing in her head. *Let her go! Let her go right now!*

A knock sounded at the door. She came out of the bathroom.

Mark walked in first. The second his gaze landed on her she got nervous for another reason. Him and her. Her and him. Them. Was there still a them?

He'd said a lot last night, but her gut said there was still something left to say. Or maybe it was her who needed to say something. Did she tell him it didn't matter? That she wanted him in her life even knowing that they wanted different things?

Was she selling herself short?

She saw Fran and her thoughts switched course.

"I'll let you two talk," Mark said. He walked out. Annie sat down on the edge of one of the beds. "Sit down," she said and motioned to the bed beside her.

"Yeah." Fran moved in. Their knees almost touched.

"You look good for someone who just got shot," Fran said.

"Mark told you?" she asked.

"I went to your apartment. Your neighbor told me. I went to the police department. A friend of mine called and said a cop from Anniston was looking for me. I figured you were behind it."

"I was afraid...something terrible had happened."

She smiled. "It did. I went into rehab."

Annie didn't know what to say to that. So she didn't.

"I'm joking. Sort of. It was awful, still is, but I needed to be there." She drummed her hands on her jean-covered thighs. "I'm sorry I was a bitch at the funeral."

"You weren't a bitch. I—"

"Yeah, I was. I was angry. Or maybe 'jealous' is the right word."

"Of what?"

"You got away from all that shit."

"I'm sorry."

"Don't be. It's not your fault."

"I know, but I'm sorry you didn't get away. I don't remember a lot. The day at the funeral, I didn't remember...Jenny. But then parts of it started coming back."

"Detective Sutton told me. Said you had nightmares."

Annie nodded. "Then I remembered you came back for me. That night at the park." Her throat tightened. "I was terrified, but when you came back I was able to breathe. Thank you."

"It wasn't a big deal."

"Yes, it was." Annie inhaled. "Mark told me that you said Uncle Patrick was burying Jenny?"

Fran nodded.

"But you don't know if he killed her?"

"He kept saying he didn't do it. He could've been lying. They're one messed-up bunch of folks."

Annie nodded.

"Which is why I've stopped drinking."

"I hear you have a daughter."

"Yeah, Lily. She's beautiful. Looks like her dad. Not that that's a bad thing. He's nice to look at. He's nice. I spoke with him earlier. His parents own a lake house, and he said I could go stay there until this is over. If you need a place, you could come, too. Don wouldn't mind. You could meet my daughter."

"I'd love to meet her, but I have to go back to work soon."

"Yeah." She looked disappointed. "So you and the detective are a thing?"

Annie didn't think Mark had told her. "How…?"

Fran grinned. "You called him Mark, and I saw the way you two looked at each other."

"Yeah. I don't know if…it'll go anywhere." Not wanting to talk about that she asked, "How old is your daughter?"

"Four." Fran pulled out her phone to show a picture.

"She's precious," Annie said.

"Yeah. Here's one when she was two, and one when she was a year and a half."

Annie studied the pictures then glanced up. "She looks like you a little. I see it in the nose."

Annie handed back the phone. "She's why I'm going to do this. Stay sober."

"She'll be worth it," Annie said with meaning.

"I know." Fran stood up. "It'd be nice if you'd meet

her. She thinks I don't have a family. My mom's only seen her once." She bit down on her lip. "How sad is it that I'm scared to let her see her granddaughter?"

"Pretty sad," Annie said. "But...there was a body found and they thought it was yours. She was really upset."

"So when I die, she'll love me?" Fran snapped.

"Sorry. I—"

"No, I'm sorry. It's just not enough. I haven't been enough of a mother for Lily, either. But it stops now."

Annie nodded. "We'll for sure get together."

Fran walked to the window, pulled the curtain back, and stared out. "Your mom ever hit you?"

"No."

"She never drank?" Fran kept her gaze out the window.

"Never." The question gave Annie pause.

"Was she a good mother?"

Annie inhaled. "If you'd asked me that two months ago, I'd have said yes. Truth is she...she was distant. My dad was closer to me. And now..."

Fran turned. "Now what?"

"Now, I can't understand why she lied to me all those years. Why she's still lying. It feels like she chose them over me."

Fran's eyes rounded. "They don't think she's the one who shot you?"

"No, but she's hiding something. I don't know what kind of a relationship we'll have when this is over."

"I'm sorry," Fran offered.

Annie nodded and her heart hurt.

"When I heard your father died, I wished I'd found out sooner so I could have gone to the funeral. He was like a television dad. You know, good. I liked him."

"Me too," Annie said.

Fran crossed her arms. "Family's important. I want to give my daughter a family. A normal one. A place where she feels safe."

"I think that's what we all want," Annie said, and they stood in silence. Both lost in the hurt of the past. "What made them this way? The Reeds?" Annie asked.

Fran shrugged. "Alcohol, maybe."

"Did you know our grandmother?"

Fran nodded. "She was as crazy as the rest of them. She died when I was like thirteen."

"And our grandfather?" Annie asked.

"Never knew him. I asked Grandma one day. She told me he'd met his maker and was paying for his sins." Fran rubbed her shoulder. "Did your mom ever talk about her childhood?"

"No," Annie said. "I asked, but she wouldn't talk about it."

Fran hugged herself. "Mom would tell me I didn't know how lucky I had it. Usually after she'd slapped the shit out of me."

* * *

A little after noon, Mark, waiting for Connor to call to say if they'd gotten the warrant, combed through Juan's file of everything Reed. Nothing jumped out except a whole hell of a lot of dysfunction. And coming from dysfunction, he knew it when he saw it.

Juan's tapping on the computer keys echoed in the tiny room. He stopped. "You know when this is over, the three of us should do something fun. Like go fishing. Spend all day sitting by the water and trying to forget about this shit."

"I don't know. I have a lot of shit to forget," Mark said. "But yeah, let's do it." Dropping the file, Mark recalled spilling his guts to Annie and wished he hadn't. She had enough crap on her plate.

He and Annie had barely spoken today when he showed up with her cousin and returned to pick her up.

He could tell that seeing Fran hadn't been easy on Annie, and he wanted to pull her against him and hold her, but with Fran there he'd refrained. But at least they were making headway on the case.

His phone finally rang. "Connor," he said, and put it on speaker. "And?"

"We got it. Got everything," Connor said. "The warrant to speak to Sarah, but a psychologist needs to be present. And a warrant to dig up the barn. Sheriff Harper already has a dig team from the county morgue heading to the old barn."

"That fast?" Mark asked.

"Harper said that's the way it works in the country." Connor chuckled. "Before I hit the judge's office I stopped off and spoke with Doris Roberts and Sam and George Reed about where they were last night. Doris Roberts has an alibi. Harper's deputy checked it out while we were talking to the judge, and the bartender accounted for her drunken presence. Sam and George say they were both home alone. Both their wives had gone for the weekend. So it could have been either of George or Sam, or both."

"Shit." Mark supposed it was best Connor had done the questioning. He'd have ended up beating the shit out of someone for hurting Annie. And he wouldn't have felt guilty about it, either.

Connor continued, "I'll call you when we find something from the dig."

"No, you won't." Mark reached in his gun drawer. "I'm coming."

* * *

A little over an hour later, Mark pulled up to George Reed's place. Yeah, he'd driven like a demon and he'd been too damn antsy to wait for Connor's call. He spotted a patrol car pulled in the back of the house beside a falling-down building. Walking through the knee-high weeds, he stepped inside the dilapidated barn. Slices of sun leaked in through the rotted wood. There was already a huge-ass hole in the center of the barn. At least three officers wearing San Antonio uniforms, and one dog, crowded around the hole. Two more men were in the hole. Connor and Sheriff Harper spotted him and waved him over.

"Anything yet?" Mark asked.

"Not yet," Connor answered. "But the dog marked the spot. Let's hope it's not a turtle this time."

Harper introduced Mark around. "How did the Reeds take this?" Mark asked Harper.

"Pissed. Really pissed. They called their lawyer and he came and swooped them away."

Mark wasn't there an hour—but long enough that his shirt was soaked with sweat—when one of the men digging spoke up. "I got something."

Everyone crowded around. Everyone but Mark. He didn't have to see it to believe it. He just wanted this case closed. Maybe then he and Annie could find their place again. If they had a place.

"Is it a body?" Harper asked.

"Yeah." The man answered. "But it's not what you're looking for."

"What?" Mark moved in. He looked down and saw parts of skeleton remains still half covered with dirt.

"This ain't no kid. Whoever we just uncovered is over six feet tall."

*　*　*

When the Reeds' lawyer wouldn't agree to allow his clients to be interviewed until the next day, Mark headed back. By four he walked back into the precinct. On the drive, he'd tried to make sense of the new body but nothing made sense. Harper was supposed to send a list of all the Missing Persons cases for the past twenty-five years, but he said it could be a few days.

Mark wanted this thing solved. Now. He wanted to call Annie with good news.

His phone rang. Annie's number appeared on the screen. "Hey." He tried to decide how to tell her about the body.

"Hi, uh, I spoke with my mom."

Mark's frown curled in his gut. "You didn't tell her where you are, did you?"

"No, but I'm meeting her at the coffee shop."

"Annie, I—"

"She's my mom." Her voice quavered. "Right now I'm pissed at her. I don't understand why she's doing this. But after speaking with Fran, I realize she hasn't been a terrible mother. She heard I was shot and she's been worried sick. I love her."

He exhaled. "What time are you meeting her?"

"I'm in a taxi heading there now."

"Okay." What else could he say? "Call me when you're finished and I'll pick you up." He'd tell her about the body then.

"Yeah."

* * *

After the body had been carted off, Adam drove back to his office. His mind was racing over the new body. This case was his. He needed a plan. When he walked into the office it was unmanned.

Then Jennifer walked out of the ladies' room, phone in her hand. Her face was puffy as if she'd been crying.

"You okay?" he asked.

"Allergies."

She moved to her desk and sat down. Questions about her father, about any missing family members, danced on his tongue—but without more information, he didn't know what to ask. He started back to his office when something tacked to the wall behind her desk caught his attention. A paper target.

And then he remembered she went to the gun range.

She was a Reed. She had a gun.

He walked back to her desk.

She looked up.

"What kind of gun do you have?"

Her head slumped forward. Adam knew guilt when he saw it.

"What kind?" he demanded.

When she didn't answer, he raised his voice. "Answer me!"

"A Ruger nine-millimeter."

"Where is it?"

"I don't know." Her voice cracked.

Adam leaned down and pressed his hands on her desk. "Jennifer, where is your gun?"

Tears filled her eyes. "Mama took it. She's been obsessed about this whole thing. I don't know why. She made me tell her things about the case."

Adam clenched his jaw. "Where is your mom?"

"I don't know."

Adam snatched up the phone and handed it to Jennifer. "Call her. Ask her where she's at. Tell her she needs to come home. Now!"

* * *

Mark's phone rang. He recognized Harper's number.

"You were right," the sheriff said.

"About?"

"I didn't check all the Reeds for guns."

"Who has one?"

"Jenny Reed."

"Your desk clerk? You think she—"

"No. Her mother, Patrick Reed's wife. She took Jennifer's gun. Jennifer admitted that her mom's been obsessing over the case. Jennifer called her and asked her where she was. The mom said she was in Anniston with her aunt JoAnne. When Jennifer told her she needed to come home, she hung up."

"Fuck!" Mark said. "Annie's meeting her mom now."

Mark slammed the phone down and called Annie. It rang. And rang. Then went to voice mail.

* * *

Annie walked into the coffee shop. It was empty except for Fred. He waved and smiled. Annie smiled back. She ordered coffee and sat fretting about what to say.

When her mom walked into the coffee shop Annie gasped. She looked as if she'd aged ten years. Her clothes were wrinkled. Her makeup smeared.

Annie didn't take all the blame for not seeing her, but she still felt guilty. She'd promised her father she'd take care of her.

Her mom's eyes filled with tears when she saw Annie. Annie's eyes did the same. She stood up.

"Oh, baby." She ran and hugged Annie tighter than she ever had. And longer. Annie soaked in the feeling of being loved. When her mom pulled away, she said, "I'm sorry. Sorry for everything." She looked her up and down. "I thought you were shot."

"I was." Annie pulled up her sleeve to show her mom the bandage. "But I'm fine."

Her mom's lips trembled. "George and Sam swear they didn't do it. But it doesn't matter. It has to end." She dropped down in a chair.

"What has to end?" Annie's chest tightened. The sound of coffee beans being ground echoed around her, but her attention lay completely on her mom.

"The secrets. The lies. It was so ugly, it was best it stay buried. Nobody needed to know. But more lies are piling on top of lies. It has to stop."

"You swore you'd never tell!" an angry voice said.

Annie looked up. The gray-haired woman standing there. She looked vaguely familiar. Then Annie recalled seeing her at the funeral. Aunt Karen, her uncle Patrick's wife.

"What are you doing here?" Mom asked.

"I'm protecting your brother's name. You, both of you, need to shut up. They'll blame Patrick. He always got the blame. On his deathbed, he made me promise to never let his daughter find out. He lived with that shame and guilt."

"He wasn't any more at fault than any of us," her mom said. "It needs to come out."

"I won't let you do this." She pulled a gun out of her purse.

Panic spiraled in Annie's chest. But somehow a shot of adrenaline had her jumping up and putting herself between her mom and the gun. "Put that away. We won't say a word."

Her mom tried to push in front of Annie, but Annie pushed her back. She'd die for her mom.

"Gun!" yelled Mary the barista.

The woman turned. That's when Fred grabbed the crazed woman's arm. The gun clattered on the tile. While those two wrestled, Annie dove for the weapon.

The moment she had it, the door slammed open. She saw the gun before she saw Mark. Fury made his eyes bright.

Fred had the woman pinned to the floor. "I got her," he yelled up to Mark. "You read her her rights."

* * *

Thirty minutes later, Annie and her mom sat in a small room with a big table at the police station. Her mom's eyes were still teary. Annie took her hand.

Mark sat down. "Ms. Lakes, I'm going to need you to be honest with me."

She nodded, but didn't speak.

"Patrick killed Jenny, didn't he?"

Her mom looked up. "No."

"Mom, please, just tell him everything."

Frustration filled Mark's expression. "Whose body did we just dig up in your brother's barn?"

"What body?" Annie asked.

CHAPTER
THIRTY-FOUR

W e should have told a long time ago," Annie's mom said, and her expression, her tone, reminded Annie of how Mark had sounded and looked last night.

"I was pregnant with you. We lived on the other side of town, Doris called and said I needed to get there. Our daddy was having one of his fits." Her mom swallowed. "Your father, he worked the third shift. He didn't like it when I went to see them, but they were my family."

Annie tightened her hold on her mom's hand as she continued. "For some reason, my daddy would listen to me. Don't know why, he beat me like he did everybody else. But when he got the meanest, I could talk him down."

New tears formed in her mother's eyes. "When I got there, Daddy had everyone against the wall and he had his gun on them. He asked me which one he should kill 'cause he was tired of feeding them all."

Her mother's voice became slower, her eyes blank, as if she saw it. "Mama and Patrick were beaten. They'd tried to fight him off, but Daddy was a big man. And when he had whiskey in him, he was so mean."

She inhaled. Her gaze locked on the wall. "I begged him to hand me the gun. He told me that Sarah was the devil and made him do things he shouldn't. I finally got the gun from him. But Sarah grabbed it. She shot him. Blood was everywhere. He died. Mama made us take him to the barn. The boys buried him. She said they'd put us all in jail. That they'd lock Sarah away forever. She made us swear on the Bible that we'd never tell. It had been our secret that he'd beaten us all those years. Now our secret was that Sarah had killed him."

Annie covered her mouth to keep from crying aloud.

"Eight months later, Sarah gave birth to Jenny."

Her mom's lips trembled. Annie's heart quietly broke. Broke for her younger mom. For the pain she'd endured.

Mark spoke up. "So what happened to Jenny?"

"We were camping. Sarah, Doris, and I were sharing a tent. Jenny came in and needed to go potty again. I offered to take her in the woods to pee. But Sarah said she'd do it. She loved Jenny. She really did."

Her mother dropped her face into her hands and sobbed. Mark didn't push her to continue. The sound of her crying filled the room. Annie hugged her. She finally lifted her face. "They were gone a while and when Sarah came back she was crazy. Not making sense. She said it had happened again. She had blood all over her."

"We found Jenny, she was dead. Mama said we had to bury her 'cause Sarah would tell everything. I pleaded for them not to do it. But the boys said Mama was right. Sarah just sat on the ground, hugging herself, saying she hadn't shot her."

Her mom looked at Annie. "My brothers found a place to bury her at the park. You and Fran woke up and went into the woods. When you came out, your knee was cut. I grabbed you away from Patrick and took you to the hospital. You'd told me you'd seen Jenny with dirt all over her. I told you it was a dream. I know I lied, but I didn't know what else to do. When I called your father and told him, he got furious. He said the only reason he didn't tell the police when Daddy died was because he was afraid I'd go to jail. He said they were all becoming like my daddy."

Her mom stared at the wall again, but Annie could swear she saw things. Ugly things. She finally started talking again. "I'm told that later when Sarah came to her senses, she told everyone that Jenny had fallen by the creek and hit her head. She said Jenny went to sleep. She held her for a long time then realized she was dead, like Daddy. They'd already called the police and told them Jenny was missing. It was too late to change the story." Her mom's gaze cut to Annie again. "Your father packed us up that night and we moved to Houston. He told me you were never going to be with my family again."

She pulled in a deep breath. "I knew he was right. They all drank like Daddy did, but they were my family. Living with Daddy was war, and the rest of us counted on each other. We protected each other. They understood what was wrong inside of me."

Her mom folded her hands together. "When your

dad died, I was so alone. He was my north star. As long as I had him I was good. But without him I felt lost. I needed someone. I didn't want to be a burden on you. So I turned to them."

She sat up straighter. "No one knew Karen was doing this. We only saw her twice these last two weeks. I would have never let anyone hurt you."

Annie held her mother and they both cried. The painful sound echoed in Annie's heart.

Mark stood up. "I'll give you some time."

Annie and her mom stayed in that room for almost half an hour. Annie felt emotionally drained. She could only imagine how her mom felt. When she finally walked out, Mark was standing at the end of the hall with his two partners. He saw her and rushed over.

She wanted him to fold her into his arms, to hold her against his strength. She'd had to be the strong one for her mom, but now she felt depleted. He didn't even touch her, but the softness, the caring, and concern in his gaze was almost an embrace.

"What now?" she asked.

"We're bringing in the other family members. And we'll collect the bodies."

"Any charges?" She held her breath.

"For shooting you. Yes. For the murders, they'll have to look at the evidence. But if it went down like your mother said, I doubt it."

Tears watered down her vision and she remembered his own story of pain, regret, and guilt for something that wasn't his fault. "And you thought *you* had a messed-up family."

He half-grinned. "You know it wasn't a competition."

She nodded. "Can I take her to my house?"

"Let me make sure the DA doesn't want to question her now, and if not, I'll drive you."

* * *

That night, Annie's mom had been asleep for about an hour when a knock sounded on her door. She opened it and was instantly caught in Mark's gaze.

"Your mom?" he asked.

"Asleep," she said. He pulled her against his warmth. His scent filled the air and smelled like comfort, like peace. But his touch hurt like fire. An emotional burn. He released her, and they stared at each other.

So much needed to be said, but Annie didn't have the energy now. Or was it that she didn't know what to say? He had made it clear. *I lived in that house with a white picket fence and two kids. A mom and a so-called dad. And it wasn't pretty.* She wanted all the things he couldn't offer her.

Thankfully, she was going to have some time to figure it out.

"You want something to drink?"

"I'm fine. I wanted to bring you this." He had her suitcase that she'd left at the hotel.

"Thanks." She moved to the sofa and he followed. When he sank down into the cushions, her shoulder came against his. The physical contact sent another spark of pain.

"You going to be okay?" Gentleness sounded in his words.

"I feel raw right now," she admitted. "And a little guilty for not being there more for Mom after my dad's death. I didn't realize how much she was hurting."

"You didn't know all this." He brushed a strand of hair from her cheek.

"I know." She lifted her eyes to his. "Neither did you." Meaning that night years ago, when he'd gone to a party.

From the look in his eyes, he understood what she meant. "True."

A crazy thought hit. She'd gone to him to help her find the truth. Because she believed knowing it would fix things. He hid from the truth, because he didn't think they could be fixed. She wanted to show him they could, but her gut said he needed to figure that out for himself.

She ached to take his hand in hers, but she refrained. "I called and talked to my boss. They're giving me some time off. Mom said she's been thinking about moving into a retirement community, and I thought I'd help her look."

He ran a hand over his brow. "For how long?"

"Two weeks or so."

Her words hung in the silence. Finally, he spoke up. "If you're moving her, I could help."

His offer said a lot. Said he hadn't given up on them. But what kind of *them* would they be? Her heart wanted to hope, to believe they could be each other's north stars, but could someone who ran from commitment be her north star?

"I don't think she'll move yet. She'll want to sell her house first."

"When are you leaving?" he asked.

"Tomorrow, right after she speaks to the DA."

"Two weeks is a long time," he said. He took in a deep breath. "I'm going to miss you."

Her heart dropped. "I'm going to miss you, too."

He kissed her. A sweet good-bye kiss that brought tears to her eyes. *Please let me be your north star.* He stood up. She walked him to the door.

He touched her cheek. "When you get back, we should...talk." He turned to leave.

She nodded. "Can you do me a favor?" she said, right before he walked out.

"What's that?"

"Take that saxophone off the stand in your game room. And play it. You deserve to be happy. You do deserve music."

He ran his thumb over her lip. "You don't ask for small favors, do you?" He leaned in and kissed her again, then walked away.

She walked back to the sofa, dropped down on it, and cried.

* * *

Annie spent the first few days helping her mom clean out her father's items. They both cried a little. She realized she and her mother had never really mourned together. It felt right.

At night, Annie missed Mark so much her toenails

ached. Every night, she almost called him but decided the space might be what they needed.

Four days in, she and her mom were having breakfast at a diner. Her mom asked her, "Do you want to get married? Have kids?"

Annie set her coffee down.

"You don't have to answer. And I'm not going to be upset if you say no. I'm just curious."

"It's okay," Annie said. "Yeah, I want it. I just haven't...found the right man yet."

"Detective Sutton isn't the right man?"

That was the first time her mom had brought up their relationship. The question sent all kinds of raw pain circling her heart. "I don't know."

Her mom stared down at her teacup. "Would you be upset if I dated?"

Annie's mouth fell open. "No. Who is it?"

"I'm just talking what-ifs." She looked away too quickly.

"No, you're not." Annie put her hand over her mom's. "You deserve to be happy."

She nodded and turned her cup. "The sheriff from Pearlsville. Every time I was around him, I found myself wanting to play with my hair." She took a deep breath. "He called me last night and said he finds himself in Houston a lot and wanted to know if he could...call me."

Annie's smile widened. She'd been so afraid her mom would become a lonely recluse. "That's great." She squeezed her mom's hand.

In such a short time, she and her mom had found this

new place in a relationship. It wasn't quite what she'd shared with her dad, but it was comfortable and good.

Fran called that afternoon and asked if they would come for a visit. The next morning, they drove up. Lily, Fran's daughter, was precious. Annie and Lily drew and colored while Fran and her mom sat on the front porch talking. It was good for both of them.

The little girl stopped coloring and looked at her. "You look like my mom."

"I know," Annie said.

"I think she's pretty," she said.

"She is," Annie said and touched the girl's cheek.

"You're pretty, too." She smiled up with innocence.

"Thank you. I think you're absolutely beautiful."

Lily grinned. "I know you're my cousin, and your mother is my aunt, but you're older than me. Can I call you my aunt, too?"

Annie grinned. "I'd be honored to be called your aunt."

"Will you come and see us again?"

"Of course."

"Promise?" Lily gazed up at her. "I don't get to see Mom's family much. She says they aren't fond of kids."

"Well, I'm very fond of you. I'll come to see you. Promise."

She grinned. "Mom used to break promises, but she says she won't anymore."

Annie felt her heartstrings tug. "That's good."

Later, Don, Lily's daddy, came over and they cooked dinner together. Annie could tell he and Fran still loved each other. Fran had whispered earlier that they were going to give their marriage another try. It validated Annie's lifelong plan to someday have that. A family and all the trimmings that went with it.

And to have that she might need to walk away from Mark.

* * *

Mark sat at his desk, filling out the report that would close the Reed case. They'd found both bodies. All the Reeds had been interviewed, even Sarah Reed. The DA was still looking at the case, but they'd pretty much said they'd decided not to prosecute.

"I think I found a case we should take on next," Juan said.

"What?"

"Seven years ago, a couple went missing. It was looked at as a possible homicide, but with no bodies no one was arrested."

"Did they have suspects?"

"Yeah, they thought it was connected to a deceased drug dealer. But they suspect this hit came from his boss."

Mark looked up and his right eyebrow rose. "Guzman?"

He just happened to be the drug lord who'd blown up Juan's house, killed his wife and unborn child, and nearly killed Juan. He spent weeks in the hospital and was outraged when he returned to work and wasn't allowed to work the case. Juan worked it anyway. It didn't look good when Juan found Guzman and the son of a bitch pulled a weapon. Thankfully, there had been a witness, and it was ruled a good shoot. And because it took place in a public place, Juan denied he'd been working on the case. Juan got off for that, but it still got him demoted to the Cold Case Unit.

Mark didn't blame Juan, but right now he didn't need Juan going rogue, either.

"Don't worry," Juan said. "I'd love to catch the bastard, just because of his ties to Guzman, but the guy who killed my wife and kid is dead."

Mark nodded, realizing this was the first time Juan had spoken about it.

Silence followed. When it got awkward, Connor and Juan started chatting about the case. Mark was struck by how much it must hurt to lose a wife and child to some lowlife gangbanger. He remembered how scared he'd been when he rushed to the coffee shop knowing Annie had been in danger. He stared at the coffee on his desk. He'd picked it up from the coffee shop an hour ago, but hadn't drunk it.

Nothing tasted right. Nothing felt right. His chest felt empty. His life felt empty. Annie had been gone four days and it felt like fifty.

He leaned back, stared at the ceiling, and thought about Fred. He'd been high on weed at the time, but his advice had a ring of truth to it. And those questions he'd told Mark to consider.

Is she worth it? Are you happy the way you are?

Damn it! Annie was worth it. And hell no, he wasn't happy.

"Mark? What do you think?" Juan's words finally got through.

"I think . . . I think I have to change."

"What?" Connor asked.

Mark shot up from his chair.

"Where are you going?" Juan asked.

He didn't answer. If he stopped, he might chicken out.

He took the stairs two at a time. He walked in the door with Dr. Murdock's name printed on it.

The secretary looked up.

"Is he in?" Mark asked.

"Yes."

"He alone?"

"Yes." She reached for the phone.

Mark walked in.

Murdock sat at his desk, reading. He looked up. "Can I help you?"

Mark dropped on his sofa. "Did you bring your coat?"

The man looked puzzled.

"Remember I told you it'd be a cold day in hell when I came to see you on my own?"

"Yeah."

"Well, I think hell just got its first frost."

CHAPTER
THIRTY-FIVE

Ten days into the trip, Annie had gone to bed early to read. It felt odd being in her old room. But it also felt sort of comforting. Like reconnecting with her younger self. She even found some of her old books and was rereading one when her phone rang. Mark's number flashed on the screen. And emotion flashed in her heart.

"Hi," she answered, her chest opening with hope and fear.

"Hi," he said. "Hasn't it been two weeks yet?"

She laughed. "Not quite." She sat up and put her book down.

"Can you talk?" he asked.

"Yeah, I was just in my old room reading."

"Do you have pictures of old boyfriends around or posters of hot guys?"

"No."

"What does it look like?" he asked.

"It's pink and girly. And filled with books."

"I should have guessed." He paused. "How's your mom doing?"

"Better than I thought she'd be. We're going to look at some more retirement homes tomorrow. Did you know Sheriff Harper has asked my mom out?"

"No." Mark said, sounding shocked. "Then again, the sheriff was always saying she was innocent."

Their conversation went quiet and Annie heard Latin music on the line. "Where are you?"

"In San Antonio."

"What are you doing there?"

"Fred has a cousin who lives here. He wanted to see him, so I offered to drive him up."

"Fred? My Fred? The coffee shop Fred?"

Mark laughed. "I go to the coffee shop, too. Why is he your Fred?"

"No, I'm just surprised. I sent him a birthday card to the coffee shop yesterday. His birthday is in three days."

"Yeah." Mark inhaled. "Uh, I forgot to tell you something."

"What?" She leaned back in her bed.

"Remember the cop that I was looking for? The one who worked Jenny's case years ago?"

"Yeah."

"Well, that's him."

"You're kidding me."

"No. And something else, too." His tone got lower. "Don't tell him I told you this, but he's got cancer. The doctor gives him three to six more months."

"Oh, Mark. That poor man. Is he in pain?"

"If he gets to hurting, he just smokes a little pot."

"What?" Annie asked.

"You heard me." He chuckled.

Annie laughed. "And you're not duty bound to arrest him?"

"When have you known me to be a stickler for the rules?"

"Oh, yeah. I forgot. Speaking of which, did you take the day off work to go up there?"

"Actually, I have six weeks of vacation time I need to use up. So, I've been hanging out with Fred a lot at the coffee shop."

"Be careful," she said. "Your halo is showing."

He laughed. "Damn thing gets in the way sometimes."

Annie realized it was the first time he didn't deny he had one. She wondered what that meant.

"When are you coming back?" he asked.

"Early Friday."

"Can we see each other Friday night?"

Her heart twisted. Was she going to continue to see him? Even knowing they wanted different things. "Sure," she answered before she'd thought it through.

"Good. I can't wait."

* * *

Annie got home Friday morning. First she went to collect Pirate at Isabella's apartment. After spending some quality time with her cat, she went to school to let the dean know she was back and ready to work. Afterward, she picked up salads for herself and Isabella.

"I've got some bad news for you," her friend said.

Annie's stomach dropped, afraid things had gone wrong between her and Jose. "What?"

"I'm moving back in with Jose. I'm going to miss being neighbors. Drinking wine. Dinners."

Annie stuck out her bottom lip. "I'll miss you, too. But let's face it, I can't give you the hot sex he does."

Isabella laughed. "Oh, so true."

"But don't tell me you're quitting work."

"No. It's only a twenty-five-minute drive from our place."

Annie heard the *our* in the sentence and her heart warmed. Her friend was going home to the man she loved.

"What about you and Mark?" Isabella asked. "Has he called you yet?"

Annie and Isabella had spoken several times while she'd been away. Annie shared all her Mark woes. "No. I'm assuming we're still on for tonight."

"He'll call," Isabella said.

"I hope so." And she did hope.

Isabella started bagging their lunch mess. "Have you made up your mind about continuing to see him?"

"Is it wrong to say I plan to play it by ear?" Annie sighed. "I missed him so much. And if this isn't love, it's damn near close. If he really doesn't want a serious relationship, I might be wasting my time, but that's not what my heart says."

"Then listen to your heart," Isabella said. "If I'd listened to mine, I wouldn't have left Jose."

* * *

It was three o'clock, and she'd just gotten back to her apartment when Mark called.

"Tell me you're home," he said in lieu of hello.

"I'm home."

"Will you meet me somewhere tonight?" he asked.

"Meet you?"

"Yeah."

Her heart cramped a little. "You can't pick me up?"

"It'd be better if you met me."

"Okay," she said, wondering if he was officially breaking up with her. Again.

"I'll text you the address in a bit. Say at six?"

"Sure."

She spent the next hour preparing herself for whatever happened. If Mark ended it, it was meant to be. She had to accept that. She would accept that. Just as soon as her broken heart healed. She looked at her reflection in the mirror. "Accept it." She bit down on her lip. *But it doesn't mean I can't look damn hot to remind him of what he's missing.* She headed to the bedroom to find the sexiest pink outfit she owned.

* * *

He texted her the address. It wasn't until she parked that she realized it was Buck's Place, the restaurant where they'd had their first date.

As they walked in the door, the smell of smoked meat and Cajun spices filled her nose. The hostess was seating someone, so Annie continued inside. As her eyes adjusted to the dark atmosphere, she realized she was hungrier to get her hands on Mark than on any food.

"Annie." Someone called her name. Fred?

She looked over. Fred sat at a table with several other people. But Mark wasn't one of them.

Fred walked over. Annie met him, her heart aching as she remembered her coffee buddy was dying. She hugged him. And held on a little too long.

He frowned. "I told him not to tell you."

"I needed to know. And you need to know I'm here for you."

"I know. I haven't been able to get rid of your boyfriend."

Boyfriend?

"He's a keeper, by the way. We saved you a seat." They moved to the table.

"Hey," Connor Pierce and Juan Acosta said. Annie also recognized Mildred, the front desk clerk at the police station. These were all Mark's friends.

"Albert Stone," the man said next to him. "We met...before." Annie recognized him from the morgue.

"Sit down," Mildred said.

"Sure," Annie said, still confused. She was about to ask where Mark was when a voice came on the loudspeaker.

"Hey everyone."

Annie looked at the stage, air caught in her chest.

Four men stood on the stage. At center stage, holding the mic, was Mark, and he held a saxophone. His gaze was on her. Only on her.

"It's been a long time since I played on a stage. Actually, until a couple of weeks ago, I hadn't played in years. I gave up music because I lost someone special to me. But recently I've found someone else who's very special to me. She wanted me to play for her. So if I make a fool out of myself tonight, you can blame Annie."

Tears filled Annie's eyes. Fred leaned over to her and said, "I've had to listen to him play all week. He's been practicing for you. You look beautiful, by the way."

Annie grinned as tears formed in her eyes. The band started playing. She didn't know jazz well enough to know if Mark missed a note or if his playing was up to par, but it was music to her ears. Music to her heart.

When the band finished the song, Mark spoke again into the mic. "I'm going to turn it back to these guys."

He walked off the stage. Walked right to her. He held out his hand. "Come with me a minute."

She placed her hand in his, and emotional sparks traveled up her arm. Blinking away tears, she followed him. And just like that, she knew she'd follow him anywhere. She'd take him, commitment or not. He walked her out to the side of the restaurant, where there were patio tables but no people. He pulled her against him. "I missed you like the devil, Annie Lakes."

He kissed her, tasting like coffee and a flavor that was simply Mark. His lips were moist and slid softly across hers. His hands held her by her waist and brought her closer, they fit, felt so right, yet she ached to be closer.

"I missed you," she said, when he stopped kissing her.

"I used to think nothing made me happier than playing that damn instrument, but that was before I met you. You are music to my soul. And if you'll hang in there with me, I promise I'll do my damnedest to turn into the man you deserve."

She smiled through more tears. "I think I've changed my mind."

"About?" Concern sounded in his voice.

"Jazz music. I didn't know saxophone players were so sexy."

He laughed and pulled her against him again. "We have to go in there and have dinner with those guys, but afterward, I'm going to take you home and I'm going to show you just how sexy a saxophone player can be."

He brushed a finger over her lips. "I think I love you, Annie Lakes."

She rose on her tiptoes and touched his cheek. "I think I love you, too."

When Juan Acosta meets his gorgeous neighbor, he knows she's hiding something. As he gets closer to the mysterious woman and her daughter, his investigation uncovers dark secrets that will put them all in danger.

Please turn the page for an excerpt from *DON'T BREATHE A WORD*.

PROLOGUE

Three years ago

Juan held the camera and filmed his wife as she spoke. Angie had come up with this idea of making videos for their unborn daughter, so that when she grew up she would know how wanted and loved she was.

No doubt the idea stemmed from his wife's childhood insecurities. Being adopted had left a mark on her. Probably similar to the mark left on him when he lost his parents at fifteen.

"I love you, baby girl, and I love your daddy," Angie said to the camera. "This is me, and you before you were born. See." She pulled up her shirt and showed the basketball-sized bump from her seven-month pregnancy. She grinned up at him. "We're so happy to be having you."

Juan stared at his wife of two years, love in her blue eyes and a smile of pure happiness added a glow to her expressions. Her love for their baby was so bright that sometimes it hurt him to look at her. The halo of blond hair rested on her shoulders. But she was indeed an angel. His angel.

He wasn't sure that he deserved her, but if Fate ever realized it had screwed up and tried to change it, he was prepared to fight. And fight dirty. He was keeping her. She made the bad things in his past feel small. She made the bad things he saw in the world every day feel less so.

She waved him forward. "Now put the camera on the stand and come be in the video."

"I'll ruin the video."

She made her cute face and beckoned him to her. "Don't be shy."

He did as she said, because telling her no was impossible. Which was why next week was his last week working undercover for the gang squad. After that he'd start working homicide.

She wrapped her arm around his waist. "This is your daddy. Say something to your daughter." She playfully bumped him with her hip.

"I'm camera shy," he said, explaining his awkwardness, but it was a lie. Even though he was excited about the idea of having a child, somehow it just didn't feel real. Sure, he'd placed his hand on his wife's middle and felt the baby move, and he'd seen the fuzzy sonogram video that dubbed the child a girl, but it still didn't feel...true.

And that worried the hell out of him. He saw what Angie felt for the unborn child. As hard as he tried, though, he couldn't tap into those emotions.

His older brother, a father of two, assured him it

would change when they placed that child in his arms. He hoped like hell Ricky was right. He hoped losing his parents hadn't somehow damaged him and prevented him from being the kind of dad a kid deserved.

"Juan." She touched his arm. "Say something."

"Okay." Pause. "I think you are going to be the luckiest little girl in the world, because when your mama loves someone, that person has everything they'll ever need. Look at her, she's smart and beautiful."

"Right," Angie said. "Like you aren't easy on the eyes." Angie looked into the camera. "Your dad's friends call him Pretty Boy. He even did a few TV commercials."

"Don't tell her that." He'd done it only to pay for school.

Angie laughed. "But I don't love him just because he's a hottie. The day I met him he was getting a kitten off the roof of my apartment building for an elderly neighbor. He was kind to the kitten. And he was kind to the neighbor who was being a pain in the butt. I fell in love with him right then."

Juan leaned down and kissed her.

The kiss lingered. "Okay." Angie pulled back. "Let's cut off the video."

"And then what?" he whispered and wiggled his brows.

She cut off the camera, pushed a few buttons to send the video to the cloud, then shot him a sexy smile. "If you go get the tools to put the crib together you might get lucky."

"You want to tape that, too?" he teased.

She swatted him on his ass.

He laughed and went to the garage to get his tools. As he made the door, his wife's dog, Sweetie, followed him out.

He'd found the wrench and the screwdriver when his phone rang. Although he didn't recognize the number, he still picked up. "Yeah?"

"You didn't think you'd get away with it, did you?"

The voice yanked his good mood right out of his chest. Then the blast sounded. The wall of the garage imploded and he was thrown to the other side. Disoriented but conscious, he managed to push his way out of the collapsing garage. Pieces of his roof were scattered all over the lawn. Fire was claiming what was left of his house, but it didn't stop him.

"Angie!" he screamed and ran inside.

About the Author

Christie Craig is the *New York Times* bestselling author of thirty-nine books. She is an Alabama native, a motivational speaker, and a writing teacher who currently hangs her hat in Texas. When she's not writing romance, she's traveling, sipping wine, or penning bestselling young adult novels as C. C. Hunter.

You can learn more at:

Christie-Craig.com
Twitter @Christie_Craig
Facebook.com/ChristieCraigBooks

Fall in Love with Forever Romance

USA TODAY BESTSELLING AUTHOR

DEBBIE MASON

Sandpiper Shore

"Heartfelt and delightful!" —RAEANNE THAYNE,
New York Times bestselling author, on *Mistletoe Cottage*

SANDPIPER SHORE
By Debbie Mason

USA Today bestselling author Debbie Mason's latest novel in the
feel-good and charming Harmony Harbor series. Jenna Bell loves
her job as a wedding planner...until she meets with her newest
clients and discovers that the groom is the man she's loved for
years. For Secret Service Agent Logan Gallagher, seeing Jenna
after all these years brings back feelings that he's fought hard to
forget...and makes him wonder if getting married to someone
else would be the biggest mistake of his life.

IT TAKES TWO
By Jenny Holiday

In this hilarious romantic comedy, *USA Today* bestselling author Jenny Holiday proves that what happens in Vegas *doesn't* always stay in Vegas. Wendy Liu *should* be delighted to be her best friend's maid of honor. But it means spending time with the bride's brother, aka the boy who once broke her heart. Noah Denning is always up for a challenge. So when Wendy proposes that they compete to see who can throw the best bachelor or bachelorette party in Sin City, Noah takes the bait—and ups the stakes. Because this time around, he wants Wendy for keeps.

Fall in Love with Forever Romance

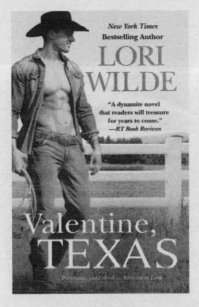

VALENTINE, TEXAS
By Lori Wilde

From *New York Times* bestselling author Lori Wilde comes a heart-warming story about love, second chances, and cowboys...Rachael Henderson has sworn off love, but when she finds herself hauled up against the taut, rippling body of her first cowboy crush, she wonders if taking a chance on love is worth the risk. Can a girl have her cake and her cowboy, too?

* Formerly published as *Addicted to Love*.